PENGUIN BOOKS

THE CHIP-CHIP GATHERERS

Shiva Naipaul was born in 1945 in Port of Spain, Trinidad. He was educated at Queen's Royal College and St. Mary's College in Trinidad and at University College, Oxford, where he read Chinese. The recipient of a number of literary awards for his work, Mr. Naipaul is the author of another novel, *Fireflies,* and two books of nonfiction, *North of South: An African Journey* and *Journey to Nowhere: A New World Tragedy*. They are all published by Penguin Books.

Shiva Naipaul

The Chip-Chip Gatherers

Penguin Books

Penguin Books Ltd, Harmondsworth,
Middlesex, England
Penguin Books, 40 West 23rd Street,
New York, New York 10010, U.S.A.
Penguin Books Australia Ltd, Ringwood,
Victoria, Australia
Penguin Books Canada Limited, 2801 John Street,
Markham, Ontario, Canada L3R 1B4
Penguin Books (N.Z.) Ltd, 182–190 Wairau Road,
Auckland 10, New Zealand

First published in Great Britain by
André Deutsch 1973
First published in the United States of America by
Alfred A. Knopf, Inc., 1973
Published in Penguin Books in Great Britain 1976
Published in Penguin Books in the United States of America 1983

LIBRARY OF CONGRESS CATALOGING IN PUBLICATION DATA
Naipaul, Shiva, 1945–
   The chip-chip gatherers.
   I. Title.
PR9272.9.N3C48 1983   823   83-4255
ISBN 0 14 00.3956 2

Printed in the United States of America by
R. R. Donnelley & Sons Company, Harrisonburg, Virginia
Set in Intertype Times

For Jenny

Chapter One

1

Egbert Ramsaran kept cows. In itself, there was nothing strange about this: most of the people who lived in the neighbourhood reared a few domestic animals. What was strange, however, was that Egbert Ramsaran had no real need of his cows. In keeping them, he disobeyed an unwritten though very powerful law: that the rich man, outgrowing his peasant status, bought his milk from others. It was a symbol of progress, practical, moral and aesthetic. His son was accosted on the street by the neighbours. 'But Mister Wilbert, tell me why your father does keep he own cow for? Why he so stubborn and hard-hearted for? Like it have something wrong with other people cow? You want to tell me that with all that money he have, he still too stingy to buy milk from we?'

The young boy had no ready answer and, instead – for no reason they could quite fathom – he gave them money. These acts of charity pleased Wilbert. The mingled feelings of guilt and power which accompanied them were not wholly unwelcome. As for the recipients, they never refused these unsolicited handouts. 'I glad to see you not the same man as your father,' they said pocketing the paltry gift. 'You have a heart. You have a conscience.' He was too young to understand that what they were in fact saying was: 'At bottom you is the same sonofabitch as your father. Only more foolish to be giving away good money like that.'

It was a common occurrence for the animals in the neighbourhood to bring traffic to a halt on their way to and from the field where they were allowed to pasture – particularly late in the afternoon on their return journey home. They maundered with uncanny preference down the middle of the road, trailing broken bits of rope looped loosely round their necks and looking about them with indifferent vacuity, staring with their rounded, bulbous eyes. Occasionally, their steps would falter and they wandered across to the sides of the road – momentarily freeing the blocked stream of traffic – and nibbled idly at the weeds growing on the verge before returning to their more customary path.

There were other animals as well which marched along the road in stately procession: a flock of goats and three old, yellow-fleeced sheep. The owner of the sheep – if there were such a person – never declared himself. This irritated Egbert Ramsaran. By not declaring himself, their putative owner opened himself to the charge of highhandedness and this could not be tolerated. 'If I ever lay my hands on the sonofabitch who own those blasted sheep...' The sentence ended in a stream of imprecation and the threat remained tantalizingly undisclosed. He made numerous enquiries but to no avail; with the consequent worsening of his temper and multiplication of invective.

If by chance his front gate had been left open (a rare oversight), the animals would come strolling into what he euphemistically described as 'the garden', in reality an extension of the verge: succulent grasses and weeds of all varieties flourished there. This drove him wild and he would hurl whatever came to hand – stones, bottles, tins – at the intruders, and this too would be accompanied by a chorus of piping invective. For his own cows, let it be known, were kept distinct and separate from these others. They were the aristocrats among the animals in the neighbourhood; they were not markedly different to look at from their hated colleagues who trod in single file down the middle of the road. They were as unkempt and as emaciated as the latter. But, they were Egbert Ramsaran's cows and, as such, they possessed certain very special privileges.

They had their own pasture. Egbert Ramsaran owned a sizable field adjacent to his house. It was as big as a football pitch and fenced in from the road by tall, rusted sheets of galvanized iron. Access to it lay through a gate opening into the yard behind the house. His cows, therefore, never used the public highway and they became, like the field which was exclusively theirs, objects of mystery. The field was bordered at the back by the Victoria river, at this point no more than a narrow, boulder-strewn water course edged with trees and polluted by the cows and the refuse dumped into it. It was possible to circumvent the fence and approach the field by following the course of the stream which, in the dry season, was barely a foot deep. To discourage curiosity, Egbert Ramsaran had erected a notice-board warning trespassers of the dire penalties they would incur if they were foolhardy enough to venture on to his property. The river itself was public property and he could not legally prevent people going to and fro as they pleased. Egbert Ramsaran had little time to squander on legal niceties. Not averse to exceeding his rights, it was one of his favourite pastimes to install himself at the kitchen window with a rifle and fire above the heads of those who were rash enough to stop and stare. Few things caused him greater amusement than the ensuing panic.

There were other reasons why this field exercised so powerful a fascination on the minds of his neighbours. For a start, there was the bull which roamed there. Originally, it might have been acquired for purposes of procreation but, if this had once been the case, it had long since ceased to be of primary importance. No calf had ever been born of it. Partly through its mere association with its owner and partly through assiduous propaganda, it had come to be credited with great ferocity and malevolence. The bull held its neighbours in thrall. It was a more secure barrier against their depredations than any fence or barrage of rifle-shot could be.

The field had a further use beyond that of pasturage. It was the graveyard for the trucks of the Ramsaran Transport Company (the sole enterprise of any stature in the area) which had come to the end of their useful lives. It was one of Egbert Ramsaran's inexplicable quirks that he refused to sell them to the scrap merchants. Salvage of any sort was strictly forbidden. Once they had been brought to the field, they were allowed to rust and fall to pieces slowly – ritually one might say – in the sun and rain. Their disintegrating skeletons scattered at random over its surface, resembled the dried, washed-out bones of a colony of prehistoric monsters.

The field was a fertile source of nightmare for his young son. During the day, while his father was away at work (at a time when Wilbert was not yet old enough to be sent to school) he would sometimes draw a chair up to the kitchen window which gave a conveniently panoramic view of the field. From it he could see the raggle-taggle herd lazing hunched together in a group among the rusting, decaying hulks and flicking their dirty tails at the swarms of flies and other insects. The bull would not usually be immediately visible. As if under instructions from his father, it held itself rigidly aloof from the lesser creatures with whom it found itself forced to live, preferring to lurk in the shadow of the fence and moving with the sun. Indeed, the animal's nervelessness was perhaps its most striking characteristic. It never broke into a trot or, come to that, betrayed any urge to activity that went beyond the strictly utilitarian. 'Don't let that fool you,' his father was in the habit of saying to him, 'the day he look you straight in the eye is the day he will eat you up. So you better watch out!'

Thus, to the young boy, the bull's very nervelessness seemed a threat; a premonition of the vengeance it had stored up within its breast for the unfortunate one who should catch its eye. Ultimately, it monopolized his childish nightmares. There was a recurring one. He would be standing alone, in the pitch dark, near the gate leading into the field, tempting the bull to see him. Every succeeding moment found him more sensible of the needless danger in which he had placed himself but, even so, unwilling and unable to withdraw to safety. He would wake with a loud cry which invariably brought his mother rushing into the room. Frequently, she would stay there cradling him ineffectually for what remained of the night, falling asleep herself, her head resting on his shoulder.

In the evening, the herd returned through the gate, leaving the bull to his solitary meditations. The row of cowsheds had been built not many yards from the house and the rich, sweet odour of the cows spread lushly over all its rooms. And there were the flies. They were everywhere. It was one of the marvels of the place no visitor would fail to remark on. Their chief place of repose was the dining table. Poised delicately on his chair, the dishes of food arranged neatly about him (he took his meals alone), Egbert Ramsaran would gaze solemnly at the assembled hordes as if he were gathering his energies in order to deliver a stirring oration to the mutlitudes come to hear him. Picking up a spoon, he would bang it with sudden vehemence on his plate – he broke many in this fashion. The flies rose in a black, obedient cloud to the ceiling and circled balletically round the naked electric lightbulb before descending to carpet the surface of the table once again. Having expressed his disapproval, he ignored them. The flies in his house were as natural a part of the scenery as the furniture.

By the time he was thirty, Egbert Ramsaran was already considered a rich man. The gaunt, fortress-like building in Victoria which housed the offices and workshops of the Ramsaran Transport Company was a monument to his achievement in the space of a few short years. He was spoken of with wonder and respect – if not affection. It was impossible not to wonder at and have respect for a man who had risen to such tangible prominence in the business world out of what seemed to be absolutely nothing.

He had been born in the Settlement, which was not deemed worthy of mention on even the larger maps of the island. The mapmakers did not acknowledge its existence and it can hardly have existed in the minds of its unfortunate inhabitants. The eye shied away from focusing on the mean huts and houses clinging despairingly to the curves of the narrow main road which wound its way to distant places like Port-of-Spain and San Fernando. No hill broke the monotony of that flat landscape divided into neat rectangles of sugarcane stretching unbroken to the horizon. Where there was no sugarcane it meant normally that the land was swampy and good for nothing. Nothing grew there but a reddish-green grass with long blades. In the wet season when hardly a day went by without its heavy, thundery showers of rain and the big, grey clouds came rolling in at noonday over the acres of sugarcane, the uncultivated land around the village became an extension of the swamp and the yards were lakes of squelching, yellow mud. In the dry season, the earth was caked hard and scorched by the sun and the swamp grass stunned into a brown and withered dormancy. The sugarcane alone flourished in that intractable environment: a bright, burning green offensive to the eye seeking escape from its limiting and limitless horizons.

Yet it was from precisely this unpromising background that Egbert Ramsaran had emerged; much like the first adventurous sea-creature who had crawled out of the primeval waters and taken to the land. He was a different species from those around him; a mutant in whom implacable urges had been implanted. The Settlement watched with astonishment as he painstakingly taught himself to read and write and perform elementary arithmetical calculations, labouring over the appropriate primers until late in the night. Eventually astonishment turned to amusement and he was treated as a 'character'. They dubbed him 'the Professor'. 'Professor!' they would call after him, 'what are you going to do with all that book-learning? You going to water the sugarcane with it?' They roared with laughter. 'Laugh,' he retorted furiously, 'that don't bother me. But the day going to come when I'll show you who's boss.' 'We waiting, Professor,' they replied, 'we waiting.' He refused to share in the work of the fields. 'That is for slaves,' he said, 'and I is no slave.'

Egbert Ramsaran had virtually no friends in the village. He had two brothers but they were considerably younger than he was. His closest acquaintance was Vishnu Bholai, a boy of roughly his own age, who was his admiring disciple, though he could hardly compete with Egbert Ramsaran whose single-minded determination and harshness both impressed and unnerved him. Vishnu nurtured hopes of being a lawyer, an ambition he dared disclose only to his friend, 'It have more money in business,' Egbert said. 'The money don't bother me all that much,' Vishnu replied. 'I like the law for its own sake.

Once I have enough clothes to wear and food to eat – and a wife and family – I will be the happiest man on this earth.' Egbert was scornful. 'Food to eat and clothes to wear! I want more than food to eat and clothes to wear, believe me! I want money. I want to be rich. To be powerful. Not to take orders from any sonofabitch. That is what I want. I going to show all of them who does laugh at me what a real boss is. I going to make them bleed before I finish with them.' He stared with a shudder of disgust at the canefields and the mean huts. 'Money don't always make you happy,' Vishnu Bholai objected mildly. 'Happiness!' Egbert Ramsaran was almost shouting. 'Is not happiness I'm after. I don't give a damn for it. What the hell is happiness? Anybody could be happy. Ask any of these slaves who does live here and they will tell you how happy they is. They will say they is the happiest people on the face of this earth. Happy to be slaves! Happy to be living at the bottom of a dungheap! Well, let me tell you once and for all, I not interested in happiness. I don't want to be happy at the bottom of a dungheap. I would kill myself first.' Vishnu Bholai was penitent. 'Listen,' Egbert Ramsaran said, gripping him firmly by the shoulder, 'if you want to get anywhere, you have to forget about this happiness nonsense. You have to forget about having a nice wife and family. You have to be hard like steel to succeed. You understand that? You have to be prepared to do anything to get what you want.' 'Anything?' 'Anything,' Egbert Ramsaran repeated. 'You would even murder?' Egbert Ramsaran smiled. 'If is necessary – yes. If you was to stand in my way, I wouldn't hesitate to murder you.' Vishnu Bholai did not doubt him. 'Keep away from the Professor,' Vishnu was warned. 'He going to hang from the end of a rope one of these days.' Vishnu suspected they were not far from the truth; but he was the victim of a potent spell not easy to shake off.

Egbert Ramsaran's parents soon came to regard their eldest son as a burden on their slender resources; and, even worse – a dangerous liability. It was like living with an unexploded time-bomb. His father summoned up the courage to deliver an ultimatum. 'You don't do a stroke of work,' he complained. 'But the man who don't work shouldn't want to eat either. You is just an extra hungry mouth. The devil does always manage to find work for people like you in the end. I think the time come for we to marry you off. A wife and children might knock some sense into that head of yours. Either that or you must leave here and find out how to butter your own bread.' Egbert Ramsaran exercised his choice. 'I will learn how to butter my own bread,' he said. 'And not only that,' he added. He went to see Vishnu Bholai the same night. 'They throwing me out,' he announced. 'Pack what clothes you have and come with me. Or better still, come exactly as you is and don't take anything. We'll show these slaves what's what.' Vishnu baulked. 'Why you in such a hurry? Let we talk it over in the morning.' 'I have nothing to talk over,' Egbert Ramsaran replied, 'you will never get to be a lawyer if you stay here.' 'Let we wait until the morning come,' Vishnu urged, 'then we will decide.' 'Until the morning come!' Egbert laughed hollowly. 'The morning will never come if ... you have to decide now if you coming with me.' He squinted at Vishnu. 'You prefer to stay here and go on being a slave like the rest of them?'

Vishnu Bholai shuffled nervously, avoiding his friend's insistent stare. 'What will we do in Port-of-Spain?' he asked. 'Where will we go? Where will we sleep? I don't know anybody there. I couldn't leave home just like that ...' Vishnu kicked at the stones underfoot. 'Talk!' Egbert Ramsaran said, 'that's all it ever was with you. Talk and nothing more. You don't want to be a lawyer.' 'I do want to be a lawyer,' Vishnu pleaded. 'I do. I do. But I can't leave home just like that in the middle of the night. I can't.' 'You lying!' Egbert Ramsaran shouted. 'This is your last chance. If you don't come with me now is the end between me and you.' The wind rustled over the canefields, a bending, ruffling presence in the thick darkness. 'Don't take on so.' Vishnu clutched at his sleeve. 'It could wait for the morning. Is no hurry. You don't have to take on so.' Egbert Ramsaran shoved him aside roughly. 'You lying! You was lying to me all the time. Deep down you is a born slave just like the rest of them. You prefer to stay here and rot.' Vishnu cowered, shielding his face with his hands. 'I never say I would run away with you,' he murmured. Egbert Ramsaran slapped him hard across the mouth. 'Liar!' he hissed. Vishnu whimpered. He was trembling. 'Don't hit me again. I begging you not to hit me again. I never lied to you. Never.' His helplessness enraged Egbert. He slapped him again; and again. 'How you ever going to get to be a lawyer, eh? How? You think God will come down from heaven one day and tap you on the head? Well, let me tell you, God don't know about the Settlement. Nobody ever tell him about it.' He grasped Vishnu's shirt collar and rocked him back and forth with a violence bordering on ecstasy. 'God never hear about us,' he hissed. 'Nobody ever bother to tell him. You will end up cutting cane. You will end up a slave if you stay here and don't come with me.' Vishnu's tears flowed unhindered down his cheeks. 'I sorry. I truly sorry that I can't come with you.' At last Egbert let him go. Vishnu dried his wet cheeks and watched him walk away. He ran after him. 'In the morning ... in the morning ...' Egbert Ramsaran walked steadily on, not deigning to pay him the slightest attention.

It was in Port-of-Spain that he became a convert to Presbyterianism and sloughed off the name of Ashok which his parents had given him and adopted Egbert in its stead. Religious enlightenment had not determined the change: it was an integral part of his campaign and the motives behind it were severely practical. 'Egbert is a name nobody could laugh at and is easier for people to pronounce. That is all that concern me.' He became very angry if anyone called him Ashok. What he did in Port-of-Spain no one was certain. From time to time, dutiful son that he was, he returned to the Settlement bringing with him gifts of cigarettes and whisky and brandy which he gave to his parents. They were sensible enough to accept whatever was offered; and discreet enough not to press him too closely as to the source of these things. The vast majority of the Settlement, not benefiting from his largesse,

15

was inclined to be less than tolerant. 'Smuggling from Venezuela,' they told his parents mournfully. 'That's what the Professor is. A smuggler. If we was you we wouldn't take none
of them whisky and cigarettes he does bring. No matter how
innocent you say you is, that kind of thing could land you in
big, big trouble.' The Ramsarans were not unduly perturbed
by these dire forebodings: they were secretly proud of their
son's apparent success. 'If he was a smuggler,' they replied,
'the police would have catch up with him a long time ago.
Ashok – I mean Egbert – does work very hard.' 'You
shouldn't let that fool you,' was the answer. 'Them police and
them a lot smarter than you think. They collecting evidence.
And one day bright and early they going to come and cart
him away in one of them vans with iron bars. He will be
swinging from the end of a rope before you could blink.'
Vishnu Bholai contributed his portion of the lament. 'Receiving stolen goods is one of the worst crimes you could commit,' he intoned. 'The law takes a very serious view of that.'

The police did nothing and Egbert Ramsaran continued to
flourish. When his father died, he gave him a decent burial,
paying all the expenses of the funeral. It was also at about this
time that the flow of whisky and cigarettes stopped and his
career entered its final phase. The Settlement gawked the day
he drove a brand new lorry into the village. On its red and
black doors there appeared for the first time in neat white
lettering, 'Ramsaran Transport Company'. Egbert Ramsaran, propped negligently against the bonnet, gazed disdain-
fully at them. 'This is only a beginning,' he said. Over the
following months he acquired a second; and a third. One truck
seemed to spawn another. It was a startling progress and soon
the Ramsaran Transport Company could lay claim to at least
a dozen trucks and the Settlement abandoned its hostility to
lavish a fearful respect on the man who had flouted their
prophecies of doom. He replaced his mother's mud hut with
a modest brick dwelling and when she died he gave her too a
decent burial, paying all the expenses of the funeral. 'Now
it have no more reason for me to come here,' he said as a
funeral oration. 'I spend the first seventeen years of my life

here and, believe me, that was more than sufficient. If I come here again, it will only be to do one thing.' He scrutinized his mute audience. 'That will be to burn it down to the ground. From now on all you have to come to me.'

It was in Victoria he elected to establish the seat of his empire and raised the gaunt fortress of a building which together with the red and black trucks were the irrefutable and concrete expression of his achievement. The headquarters of the Ramsaran Transport Company bestrode the Eastern Main Road out of Port-of-Spain as it unravelled itself through the small town. It was the chief building of the place and its most common point of reference. Everything revolved around the 'depot' – as it was designated, since everything could be located as being to the right or left of the 'depot'; or to the back or front of the 'depot'. Around and about it, Victoria had anchored itself. Ultimately, the 'depot' became a virtual abstraction, like the lines of longitude and latitude on a map. Here in Victoria, Egbert Ramsaran reigned supreme and unquestioned.

He did not associate with the rich. There were no parties or extravagant entertainments. Neither did he go to other people's parties or extravagant entertainments: he shunned all contact that went beyond the normal course of business. 'A waste of time,' he said. 'Small talk is not for me. If I had spend all my time in small talk I would never have reach where I is today.' If a colleague wished to do business with him, he was invited to the depot: he was never invited to his home. He very rarely travelled outside Victoria once he had settled there permanently. His life moved along narrow rails and he swerved for nothing.

He was a small, wiry man. His hair had turned grey relatively early on and there was a smooth, glistening bald patch on the crown of his head. This combined with a sharp, prominent nose and a pair of penetrating, deepset eyes lent him an air of ferocious distinction. In later years he sprouted a moustache – looked after with fanatical care – which suited him. His lips were pinched and thin and his voice escaped through them like steam through the apertures of a whistling kettle. The analogy held in more ways than one. His voice was high and piping and querulous and the longer he talked (it made little difference whether the conversation excited him or not), the more high and piping and querulous did it become. He walked with a jaunty, hopping stride.

He had a shameless pride in his physical strength; a pride reinforced by the smallness of his build. 'Don't let my shortness fool you,' he was in the habit of saying. 'Some of the greatest men in the world was short.' He was addicted to showing off his muscles in public. On the slightest pretext he would roll up his shirtsleeves and flex his biceps for the benefit of some startled visitor to the house, challenging him to do better. Few of them ever could. The satisfaction these displays afforded him never diminished. And, after the display, there was the homily. 'The most important duty a man have in this world is to keep himself strong and healthy and in trim. How you think I manage to get where I is today?'

His day began and ended with exercises. He kept in his bedroom an impressive array of muscle-building apparatus which he allowed no one to touch but himself. In his passion for exercising was revealed another of his quirks of character. Despite his much vaunted enthusiasm for the well-being of the body, he never actively encouraged other people to follow his example. The well-being of the body which he lauded was the well-being of his own body. While eager to demonstrate the results of his exertions, the exertions themselves he surrounded in secrecy. He considered it an invasion of privacy to set eyes on him during the periods he set aside for his exercise and it was a prohibition strictly enforced. When he was asked – much of the time out of politeness, but he did not recognize this – about the techniques he employed, he betrayed a reticence the true import of which none could fail to understand: his preoccupation with health, universal as it pretended to be, began and ended with himself. Not only was he not interested in the health of his fellows: he was positively displeased if they decided to tread too zealously in his footsteps.

There was a further contradiction in his behaviour when it came to the 'health and strength' obsession. He hated doctors and the medical profession in general; part of a larger hatred of all professional people. To his son he said: 'I don't want you to get any funny ideas in your head about going away to study this or that. Your job is to look after the business when I die and to do that all you have to know is how to add and subtract. Don't try any of this doctor and lawyer funny business on me. If you come with any of that stupidness to me, I'll cut you off without a penny. Bear that in mind.'

If his wife, Rani, had the temerity to suggest that – perhaps – it would not be such a bad idea if he had a 'check-up', he would turn on her in a fury. 'When I want your advice, woman, and God forbid that I should ever need it, I'll ask you for it. What's all this damn foolishness I hear about me going for a check-up, eh? You think I'm stupid enough to go and throw myself in the hands of some swindling quack of a doctor? I would never have get where I is today if I was such a big fool. Take a good look at this, woman, and hold your tongue.' He would roll up his shirtsleeves and flex his muscles. 'Yes, Bap,' she would reply. 'Everybody know how big and strong your muscles is. But it have other things apart from muscles inside your body. You should look after those too.' This roused him to an even greater pitch of fury and, having no suitable arguments to combat the observation, he would most probably end the matter by striking her. It came to the point where the mere mention of the word 'check-up' was sufficient to send him into a towering rage. Finally, its use was banned altogether.

His contempt for doctors ended by throwing him into the clutches of the manufacturers of patent medicines. He had, to his disgust, an abnormally delicate digestion. Few foods were bland enough for it and he suffered interminable agonies. He had a medicine cupboard installed above the head of his bed. This he crammed with different brands of what were essentially the same medicines. There were blue bottles, brown bottles, green bottles, little square tins, little round tins, pills wrapped in shining silver paper, pills wrapped in cellophane. The strong, musty odour emanating from it competed with the odour of the cowsheds. Naturally, his wife and son had to act as if neither his indigestion nor the medicine cupboard existed. He had banished the word illness from his vocabulary – if not from his life.

He liked reading popular accounts of the Second World War. He had filled several scrapbooks with newspaper cuttings about it and, in his rare tender moods, he would show them to his son, praising his own industry in having collected them. 'That was a time,' he mused, fingering the fragile, yellowing newsprint. 'Men was men then. It have nothing like war to make a man out of a boy. Even from a stupid place like Trinidad you had people going out to fight. If I had had the chance I too ...' He clucked his tongue. His only other reading was detective stories. He bought one of these every week. A slow, plodding reader, he lingered days over even the quite short ones, always on the lookout for inconsistencies in the plot. He never discovered any and this annoyed him. It spoiled his pleasure. He read in bed, a thin cotton sheet drawn up to his neck, and, when he finished a book, he would toss it scathingly under the bed to join the scores of its rejected companions gathering dust.

If by friendship is understood a capacity for affection, intimacy and respect, then it becomes obvious that Egbert Ramsaran was incapable of friendship. His relationship with Vishnu Bholai had been the nearest he had approached to anything like it. He had never fully forgiven Vishnu for his desertion and the lapse of years had not done much to soften his scorn and rancour. He had relented to the extent of allowing Vishnu Bholai access to his house, but these visits parodied everything friendship ought to have been. Vishnu Bholai had fallen too far behind in the race for them to be comfortable in each other's company. The proprietor of the Settlement's only grocery had to bow to the proprietor of the Ramsaran Transport Company. Their meetings were sad, formal affairs wracked by guilt and inferiority on the one side and arrogance and conceit on the other. To compensate, Vishnu Bholai talked volubly of his wife and how rich her family was;

and of his son Julian and the worldly success that was assuredly to be his. Egbert Ramsaran gave an exhibition of his physical prowess. 'You must come and visit me,' Vishnu Bholai said when he got up to leave, 'the wife always saying how she dying to meet you.' Egbert Ramsaran was adamant in his refusals. 'You know I does hardly stir from this place,' he replied equably, 'and you know how I feel about the Settlement. If your wife want to meet me, bring she here with you the next time you come.' Vishnu Bholai smiled. 'Even if you don't come to visit we,' he countered, 'you could let Wilbert come. Julian is about his age and the two of them could play together.' Egbert Ramsaran would have none of that either. 'If you want Julian and Wilbert to play together, let Julian come here. I have nothing against that.' Each of their encounters floundered to this impasse and the matter remained unresolved.

Another very infrequent visitor to the house was Egbert Ramsaran's youngest brother, who was generally known as 'Chinese' because he had deserted the good Indian wife bestowed on him and taken a Chinese woman as mistress. Egbert, fulfilling his family duties, had settled a fairly sizeable sum of money on him which he had promptly squandered – much to the disgust of his brother who had thereafter stubbornly refused later requests for assistance. Chinese was spendthrift and irresponsible. He was inseparable from the odour of rum and tobacco and even when sober he tended – perhaps out of habit – to sway unsteadily on his feet. In all things he was the opposite of his brother. He was feckless to the point of stupidity and bereft of any kind of sustained resolution.

It was amazing how he had ever managed to do anything so positive as desert his wife. That one act of rebellion had apparently used up his limited supply of energy and it was inertia alone which kept him faithful to his mistress. He had a childish charm capable of disarming most of the people with whom he came into contact – his brother being the notable exception. 'That,' Egbert Ramsaran solemnly informed his son, 'is how I could have been if I hadn't set my mind early on. And that is what you could turn out to be if you don't set *your* mind.' When Chinese contracted a mild form of diabetes, Egbert Ramsaran could scarcely conceal his satisfaction. 'If you had listened to me and taken care of your health, none of this would have gone and happen. At your age it's a disgrace. I can't say I feel sorry for you.' Chinese was not in the least downcast. He merely shrugged and laughed.

Nevertheless, the rare visits of Chinese were a refreshing change from the stern realities which dominated the Ramsaran household. He fascinated Wilbert if only because he was the one person he was acquainted with who could be irreverent about his father. Whenever Chinese came, they went on long walks together with Wilbert perched on his shoulders. He chattered constantly. 'What's your father doing with all that money he have, eh? (Chinese rounded off nearly every sentence with 'eh') ... what's the good of money if you don't spend it, eh? I would know how to spend it, eh!' Chinese winked at him and roared with laughter. 'I bet you'll know how to spend it, eh! I'll teach you how. We'll paint the town red, me and you, eh!' And all the while he giggled and swayed unsteadily, smelling of rum and tobacco.

As for Egbert's remaining brother (on whom a fairly sizeable sum had also been settled), he had been no less a disappointment. An inveterate gambler, he had for many years past, after a chequered career in the gambling dens of Port-of-Spain, been living in Venezuela. All contact with him had long since been lost. He was always referred to as Mr Poker. From Egbert's point of view, he might as well have been dead for he never mentioned him.

Egbert Ramsaran had clients; not friends. Fortunately for him, as if to make up for the lack of friends, the clients were numerous. He had two days in the week set aside for seeing them: Saturday and Sunday. These clients were divided into two categories: there were those who had genuine business to transact with him; and there were his admirers from the Settlement. He saw the former on Saturday and the latter on Sunday.

Many of those who came to the house on Saturday mornings were people deeply in debt to him for Egbert Ramsaran was, among other things, a money lender at exorbitant rates of interest. Until Wilbert was old enough, he was not permitted to be present during these interviews. But from the kitchen he could hear what was happening in the sitting-room. The women especially would break down and Egbert Ramsaran was harshest with them. Sometimes they wailed loudly and Rani would put her hands to her ears. 'Is a terrible, terrible thing to do,' she murmured. Her son could never understand why it should affect her so.

Later, when he was deemed to have reached the age of reason, he was summoned into the sitting-room to observe and, if possible, to imbibe the techniques he saw practised there, stationing himself, silent and impassive, behind the magisterial chair. The clients were received en masse. Those dismissed with a rough reprimand considered themselves lucky and beat a hasty, thankful retreat. No doubt with the intention of adding zest to the audience, Egbert Ramsaran occasionally brought with him a darkly varnished box from which, with calculated unconcern, he would extract a pair of dull black revolvers. The squeaking voice pleading its cause would fall to a tremulous whisper and the tremulous whisper die into silence as all those eyes gazed with fixity at the rigorously veined pair of hands fiddling with the catches, toying with the trigger, counting the bullets and taking mocking aim at the heads of the assembled company. Simulating surprise, he would suddenly lift his balding, glistening head, laughing drily at the base of his throat. 'What happen to your tongues all of a sudden, eh? What stop them wagging? Like you never see a gun before?' He took aim again, squinting along the barrel. The cowering heads darted crazily, seeking shelter behind one another. He would laugh with greater gaiety. 'I thought you come here to talk and beg. Eh? Eh? Isn't that why you come? What you say, Wilbert?' He glanced at his son. 'Is to talk and to beg' (spoken with increased vehemence) 'they come, not so? That is what God give them tongues for – so they could beg.' Wilbert's set expression did not alter. 'If you don't start to talk again, I might put all joking aside and really shoot one of you. Like this.' The trigger clicked emptily. Arms raised in supplication, they fell back towards the door, bodies bundling. Standing there, they watched him. What was most striking was the total absence of hatred on those faces. There was terror. There was dumb incomprehension. But there was no hatred. On the contrary. There was a fatalistic acceptance of the situation in which they found themselves; as if they were confronted by a natural disaster, a mindless Act of God from which there could be no escape and over which they had no control. At length, tiring of his game, Egbert Ramsaran would return the revolvers to their box and, one by one, they would creep cautiously back into the room.

From about ten o'clock on Sunday mornings the petitioners from the Settlement began to arrive. They were made to wait a long time in the verandah at the front of the house; on occasions as much as two hours. It was a source of tremendous satisfaction to Egbert Ramsaran to listen to the low murmur of their self-effacing conversation and the embarrassed, apologetic shuffling of feet on the red concrete floor. If Wilbert went out to the verandah – and this he liked to do – they would crowd round him, the men and women alike showering him with kisses and cries of unbridled affection. 'But look at how big and strong he getting,' they exclaimed. 'He growing up to be just like his father.' 'Yes,' a second would chime in, 'he have all he father features. From head to toe. Father and son is as like as two peas.' They fawned, fondled and massaged him and smothered him with their embraces.

It was highly gratifying to be fussed over and compared to his father. They behaved as if Rani were no more than the indispensable physical vehicle necessary for bringing him into the world; to be discarded from consideration on fulfilment of contract. It would, they divined, have been insolence to suggest he had any other's but his father's features and their adulatory exclamations were pitched at a sufficiently high level to ensure penetration to the ears of Egbert Ramsaran who was locked in his bedroom reading. To enhance his prestige and as a mark of gratitude. Wilbert took them little offerings from the kitchen: overripe mangoes, bananas and oranges.

They accepted his offerings with renewed cries of gratitude and affection. 'You might still only be a boy. But you have a big, big heart all the same. Just like your father.' One or two of them would make a brave show of eating these fruit. Then, one day, he discovered some of the mangoes and bananas he had given them abandoned unceremoniously in the gutter a few houses away. He was genuinely shocked and hurt. His heart hardened and, inwardly, he accused them of ingratitude. He informed his father of his discovery, urged on by a dimly perceived desire for sympathy and revenge. 'Why you give them anything for in the first place?' Egbert Ramsaran asked. 'It will only help to encourage them in their bad habits. Anyway, that not going to make them love you, you know.' 'I not trying to make them love me,' Wilbert replied, somewhat put out by his reception. Egbert Ramsaran laughed. 'What you was trying to do then? You got to learn how to handle these people, boy. If you go on like that you going to end up by wasting all my hard-earned money.' He rested a hand on his son's shoulder. 'Listen to me and listen to me good. If they feel you have a soft heart, they will milk you dry. Is not mangoes and oranges they want from you – you yourself see what they do with them and you should let that be a lesson to you in the future. You have to make them learn to respect you. Frighten them a little! Horsewhip them! For once you take away the whip and start being softhearted they going to be crawling all over you like ants over sugar. I know what I talking about. I grow up with them. They all want what you have and it will be up to you and you alone to see that they don't get it. I won't always be here. Never feel sorry for the poor because they not going to feel sorry for you. You understand me? Is the way of the world.' It was a simple and appalling picture of the world he drew for his son – and drew with relish. Till then, the poor had seemed a harmless and immutable species. He had been shown his error and the evidence of those fruit in the gutter was adequate proof. Feeling beleaguered and hemmed in, he cast a more fearful gaze on the clients who crowded the verandah and sitting-room; and their self-effacing shuffle of feet and buzz of conversation became as pregnant with threat as the nervelessness of the bull. Wilbert stopped his weekly donations of rotting fruit. They did not mention the omission; though, needless to say, their cries of affection continued unabated.

When Egbert Ramsaran decided they had waited a sufficiently long time, he would push his head through the front door and call them into the sitting-room. They filed in, casting anxious glances around them. 'Sit! Sit!' he piped ill-humouredly at them. 'I can't stand here all day waiting for you.' They inched nearer the chairs but were still reluctant to do as he bid, as if fearing the floor would suddenly open under their feet and they would be plunged into a bottomless pit. 'Sit! Sit!' he screeched at them again, gesticulating angrily and, choosing the unfortunate nearest to him, shoved him forcibly into an armchair. Only when this had happened would the rest take courage and slump into their chairs. Giving the impression of having sunk into some deep and fathomless ocean, they stared, unseeing, around them. All being arranged to his satisfaction, Egbert Ramsaran went with heavy deliberation to the kitchen and brought one of the hard, straight-backed wooden chairs from there. Placing it squarely in the centre of the room and resting his palms flat on his lap, knees drawn tightly together like a shy schoolgirl, he glowered soundlessly at them, his bald head glistening. The audience had begun.

His moneylending activities, curiously enough, did not extend to this group. Scruple was not involved; or, if it were, only to the most minimal degree. They would have been eager and perfectly content to wallow in indebtedness to him but he had different ideas. If the interviews on Saturday mornings could be roughly described as business, then those on Sundays, with roughly the same accuracy, could be described as pleasure. Indeed, money played a relatively insignificant role in these Sunday morning proceedings. And, to do his visitors justice, they did not come to the house primarily for the money they might get. Admittedly, there were handouts; but they were irregular, unpredictable and tiny. Worse, they were accompanied by an avalanche of insult and abuse.

Their chief reason for coming was to reassure themselves that this man, who had sprung from the same environment as they had, really did exist; that it was not a dream or an illusion; that after all, no matter how unpromising everything seemed, it was possible to break out of the vicious downward-spinning spiral in which they were trapped; that there was hope for them yet. He was the greatest asset they had. It was easy to sense their desperate devotion by the way they looked at him. Their eyes caressed him, bore into him, dwelling with care on every distortion of his facial muscles, taking due note of every inconsequential movement of the hand and flick of the wrist, every tremor of the legs hidden beneath the well-seamed trousers.

While these sessions lasted, they did not dare open their mouths except to express enthusiastic agreement with whatever was being said. It did not matter that they were being called slavish, starving, peasant good-for-nothings. 'You right. You right,' they chorused, nodding their heads. It was doubtful whether they even heard what he was saying most of the time, so engrossed were they by his sheer physical presence. They engaged in an orgy of self-incrimination and self-denigration. Wilbert studied the performance from a distance.

The wealth symbolized by the red and black trucks and the gaunt fortress bestriding the Eastern Main Road was an abstraction and there can be no doubt that, in the fulsome warmth of their imaginations, the clients must have exaggerated its proportions to fabulous dimensions. Egbert Ramsaran lived no differently from hundreds of other people who were a great deal poorer than he was. Many of them ate better food – the rigours imposed by Egbert Ramsaran's delicate digestion were not confined to himself – and kept better houses. This, though, far from decreasing the respect and awe in which he was held, actually served to augment it: the dilapidation of his house added another element of mystery to his person.

The sole concession he had made to luxury was a refrigerator used chiefly to store what milk was obtained from the cows. Milk was the food best suited to his frail stomach. Even his own bedroom, where he spent most of his leisure time, he had let go to pieces. It was a bare, cheerless room. The walls were dull, sun-bleached pink and were festooned with cracks. There were no pictures. The single item of decoration was a large almanac printed in bold, black type giving the phases of the moon and a smattering of information directed to horticulturists. It was attached to a bit of brown string suspended from a nail which had been carelessly hammered into the wall. The nail was crooked and the almanac habitually awry. Thin strips of yellowing lace curtain fell drooping across the windows. The ceiling bulged in places and was stained with circular patches where the rain had leaked through.

He resisted every suggestion of renovation. 'I don't want to live in Buckingham Palace,' he used to say. 'I prefer to leave all that kind of fancy living to people like Vishnu Bholai. A roof over my head is all I need.' Yet, he was not a miser in the commonly accepted sense of the term. His wealth enabled him to indulge to the full a capricious streak in his nature: his despotism was not limited to the clients. Once, he had descended out of the blue on the local elementary school and offered to build them a lavatory. As it turned out (and as he probably knew) the school was already well provided for in that direction. The headmaster, risking his wrath, came to the house to see him and tried to persuade him to donate some books instead. Egbert Ramsaran was firm. 'I not donating no books to nobody,' he declared flatly. 'If it was books I wanted to give, it was books I would have give.' The headmaster pleaded. 'Come to the school and see for yourself, Mr Ramsaran. Half of the children don't have the books they need. Is not lavatories we need.' Egbert Ramsaran was not to be moved. 'Is a lavatory or nothing, Headmaster. Take your pick.' Rather than see the money disappear altogether, the school graciously accepted the lavatory. Needless to say, the lavatories in his own house were in a state of utter disrepair.

Somewhere along the line a vital spark had been extinguished in Egbert Ramsaran. He had performed his filial duties punctiliously but it was a punctiliousness devoid of genuine feeling. At bottom, he was tied to nothing. For instance, it caused him not a moment's real pain that Chinese lived in direst poverty: to him it was no more than a convenient parable; a counterpoint to his own achievement. Neither did he mourn the loss, amounting to death, of Poker. His parents might never have existed. He had expunged such foolish, unprofitable sentiment from his life. Sentiment got in the way of the particular brand of clarity he had come to value so highly. 'You must try and learn to see things clearly,' he tirelessly advised his son. 'Never listen to excuses. If a man let you down once, finish with him. Kick him through the door! If you don't do that, people will think you have water in your veins. Depend only on yourself. Think clearly! And always call a spade a spade. Remember that!' His cold-bloodedness was as tangible a trait as his well-developed muscles. He had the unshakeable conviction that he had mastered the ways of the world; a conviction bordering on fanaticism. Possessed by a completely amoral and neutral sense of righteousness, he tyrannized both others and himself. He pictured himself as an isolated individual pitted in a struggle to the death against other isolated individuals. All men were equally strangers to him.

It was this more than anything else which marked him off from his contemporaries. They, honestly or dishonestly, and with varying degrees of ruthlessness, were busy laying the foundations of empires expected to live on in their children and grandchildren. Egbert Ramsaran was animated by no idea larger than himself. He was incapable of the self-sacrifice it demanded. If he could have taken his money with him into the grave, he might have done so. He regarded it as an entity as inseparable from himself as were his arms and legs and it required an effort of concentration for him to appreciate that one day he would die and his wealth would pass to Wilbert who would be able to do with it as he pleased. A species of panic used to seize him whenever he recalled this. Therefore he did his best to see that Wilbert, from the tenderest age, received the distillation of a distorted life's experience.

He used his money to torment and humiliate. Beyond that it was of no intrinsic value to him. Success had effectively slaughtered his sensibilities. Years of struggle when, escaping from a fate that filled him with terror, he had cast all scruple aside and driven himself to the brink of nervous collapse, had gradually obscured the original purpose of that struggle. Years during which, for the sake of self-preservation, he had had to regard other men as things to be manipulated or jettisoned had, ultimately, clouded his vision and crippled his freedom of action. He was swept along by the momentum generated by an original act of will, as much its victim as those who had been crushed by it. Always within reach, forcing their attentions upon him like ghosts which refused to be laid, were the living representatives of the fate he had so narrowly avoided. He grew to depend on them much as he might have done on a pernicious drug, since he too had constantly to convince himself that his escape was neither dream nor illusion. Those closest to him were the worst affected and the first person on whom he was to unleash his true capacity for destruction was his wife.

2

Whenever Wilbert thought of his mother, he thought of her fingers: long and slender, though marred by swollen joints; the skin taut and yellow; the fingernails like little pink shells such as one finds by the seaside. She had married Egbert Ramsaran when she was thirty. In marrying her, he had broken his vow of never returning to the Settlement: it was there, when he felt the time was ripe, he had gone to find his bride. By the standards of her family, Rani was already an old maid and they had long given up all hope for her. Precedent dictated that she be banished to the kitchen and the back of the house – or rather, hut.

Circumstances made it relatively easy for her to endure her exile. Her physical unattractiveness had put her beyond the reach of temptation. The evidence was there in the photographs taken on her wedding day. She was a tall, gangling and sallow-complexioned woman. Her eyes were large and expressionless and her arms fell awkwardly on the sari she was wearing. It was as if the various parts of her body had been joined together artificially, like a puppet's. The impression conveyed in those photographs was that of a bloodless, boneless creature on whom the sun had never shone.

Egbert Ramsaran's marriage obeyed the logic of his own capriciousness. Nothing positive or altruistic could have driven him to embark on it. He was twelve years older than Rani and famous in his youth for having a taste for robust women. It was common knowledge too that he had an illegitimate son, Singh (the product of one of his fleeting liaisons in Port-of-Spain during the early days), about whom little was known for certain except that he was of mixed blood and lived by himself on an estate Egbert Ramsaran had bought in Central Trinidad – some said for the sole purpose of getting rid of Singh. From all angles, it was an unlikely match; especially for such a man. But these doubts were quickly stifled. It was the pride of Rani's family to see one of the red and black trucks of the Ramsaran Transport Company (he did not have a car) parked in front of their hut on a Sunday morning. Rani's mother, Basdai, was delirious with joy. 'Imagine,' she exclaimed, 'a man like Egbert Ramsaran for a son-in-law. I can't believe it. Is a miracle.' She was right. It did verge on the miraculous. His wealth, even if it had not opened every door to him, must have opened a sufficient number to make it seem inevitable that he would marry into one of the richer, less finicky Port-of-Spain or San Fernando Indian families. There would always be a ready supply of parents quite willing to sell their surplus daughters into marriage and who would have been as delighted as Rani's family to see a truck of the Ramsaran Transport Company parked in their paved driveways on a Sunday morning.

What a disappointment he must have proved to these last! He used to chuckle when he described how he turned down all their invitations to Sunday lunch. His having taken instead a poor and ill-featured girl, getting on in years, from the village of his birth lent itself to a fine interpretation of his

31

motives. Basdai – if one were to judge by her vociferous assertions – was among the firmest believers in his fine intentions. Egbert Ramsaran saw Rani only once before he proposed to her parents. They did not hesitate to accept on their bewildered daughter's behalf. Four successive Sundays he courted between the hours of ten and twelve in the morning. On the fifth, he was married. 'Once that man make up his mind to do something,' it was said, 'nothing in the world could stop him.' As if in punishment for what he had done to his daughter, Rani's father collapsed suddenly in the canefields and died a week after the marriage.

From the beginning they had slept in separate bedrooms except on Friday evenings when they shared the same bed. Basdai was pleasantly surprised and tremendously relieved when her daughter became pregnant: she was nervous about Rani's performance, sexual and otherwise. Unhappily, Wilbert's birth had done little to allay her fears. The delivery had been prolonged and complications had set in. Rani had been left considerably weakened by it. For several weeks afterwards she was ill and unable to nurse the baby and her sisters, despairing, took the child, as it were, to their bosoms: they, unhampered by their sister's inabilities, had been blessed with a prodigious fertility and had been called to the rescue by Basdai. Plump and healthy, they nursed the baby through the first tenuous weeks of its life. They never allowed Rani to forget her grave misdemeanour and the credit she had accrued during the months of her pregnancy was swiftly dissipated. Long afterwards, when Wilbert had grown up, his aunts seized every opportunity to remind him of the service they had performed on his behalf.

There were anxious sighs – but not out of concern for Rani's health – when she became pregnant a second time; and there were groans when she miscarried. Basdai descended on the house wailing. 'What she feel she have a belly for?' she grieved inconsolably. 'Is just plain stubbornness, if you ask me. She was always stubborn – even as a child. Never liked doing what anybody tell she. She was too great and own-way for that. What so hard about making a baby? It have women making baby all the time all over the world. Look at me. Look at my two other daughters. They don't stop making baby – is why God give them bellies. What wrong with she that she have to be different from them?' Rani was never forgiven for this betrayal. There were bosoms pining for further service to Egbert Ramsaran; service they were denied by one woman's malicious obstinacy.

After this failure, Rani was no longer summoned to the bedroom on Friday evenings and the marriage ceased, all but formally, to exist. Still, she did not surrender without a struggle. She continued to bathe and prepare herself specially on Friday afternoons, making herself presentable and sweet-smelling. At the hour enshrined by custom, she approached her husband's resolutely locked door. She would knock timidly, again and again. 'Bap, Bap,' she called, 'I come to see you now. Don't hide from me like that. Open the door and let me in. I come to see you now.' The knocking persisted, timid but determined. 'Bap, Bap, is me. Rani. Don't hide from me like that. I come to see you now. Open the door and let me in.' Knock. Knock. Knock. The sound drifted bleakly through the otherwise silent house. 'Bap? What you playing you not hearing me for? Why you playing like that for? I come to see you now. Let me in.' Unanswered, that voice rose and fell and rose again.

The silence would be abruptly shattered by a high-pitched, screamed imprecation. 'Why the hell you calling me Bap? I is not your father. Get out of here and leave me in peace, you no-good, childless slut of a woman. Get out! Get out!' His piping voice, like a kettle on the boil neglected for too long, swept through the darkness; and, to complete the harmony, there was that other rolling beneath it and complementing it. 'Bap, Bap, I make myself all nice and fresh for you. Just as you like. Let me in and you will see how nice and fresh I make myself. Just for you. Just for you.' The melancholy tones faded away, absorbed into the silence and the darkness. There would be a clatter as of someone stumbling and falling. The door had opened and he was hitting her and Rani's voice petered out into barely audible, controlled yelps of pain. Then the yelps disintegrated into unsteady, jerking whimpers and the door slammed shut, cutting off the torrent of her husband's obscenities.

For what appeared to be an eternity, she would remain crumpled against the locked door, her fingernails clawing the unresponsive wood, crying softly, though she no longer begged to be let in. Months passed in this fashion: the Friday baths, the perfumes, the journey through the dark and silent house, the vain knockings on the door, the voice rising, falling and rising again, Egbert Ramsaran's hoarse, piping imprecations, the slaps and subdued yelps of pain. Taken together, they seemed to form the indispensable elements of some hideous and ineluctable rite that had to be performed weekly. Came one Friday and Rani did not bathe and perfume herself. She had given up.

It was to silence she surrendered. She went as before to her son's room on those nights when his sleep was disturbed by his nightmares about the bull. But there was a strange and unfathomable vacancy in her eyes and her caresses and words of comfort were stilted and mechanical. 'Is nothing,' she would murmur. 'Is nothing at all. Only a bad dream. You shouldn't let a dream frighten you. What would your father say if he was to hear some foolish dream frighten you? Eh?' Her fingers explored his cheeks, kneading them. 'Is nothing. Nothing at all. Only a bad dream.' Dressed in a loose white cotton nightdress with an absurdly feminine ribbon of pink velvet drawn through loops in the collar and tied in a quaint bow at the front, her drawn, sallow face indistinct in the greyish twilight, she bent low over him, stroking his hair and forehead with those slightly swollen fingers. Her breath was warm and dry on his cheeks. Yet, her eyes never sought his, shying away from any direct contact, and there was something inescapably impersonal and remote in these attempts to solace someone other than herself whose need was so much greater.

No one could fail to notice the silence that gripped her. It was a sheath covering her. She glided noiselessly about the house, her gaze fixed on the ground. She stood interminably in front of the stove, cooking and looking out of the big kitchen window at the field where the dead, decaying bones of the Ramsaran Transport Company lay bleached in the unrelenting sun; and the cows grazed idly, flicking their tails at the hordes of flies; and the bull skulked nervelessly in the shadow of the fence. She boiled – endlessly boiled – pots of milk. She took up her station there in the hot kitchen with green and yellow tiles, her hair plaited in one thick plait, her back straight and immobile, watching the milk bubble and froth in the big enamel pots and stirring it with a bent metal spoon that burnt her fingers. Together with the milk, her life, little by little and day by day, boiled away inside that steaming kitchen.

After her fall from favour – if she ever had been in favour – Rani did not use the sitting-room. She appeared there to clean and to serve tea to whoever might require it; neither more nor less. The house, in which Egbert Ramsaran was only minimally interested in any case, reflected the aridity of her life. In the mornings she polished and shone in the sitting-room; in the afternoons, she scoured and scrubbed the bare floorboards in the rest of the house; in the evening, after she had prepared the food and waited on her husband at the table, she did what washing there was to be done. She went to bed punctually at ten and was up at five. To impress her servant's status upon her, she was given one free day every week. Egbert Ramsaran had perversely insisted on this. 'I don't want your family to think I overworking you,' he said. She put up a mild resistance. 'But I is your wife, Bap. You don't have to give me days off.' 'You! My wife! You might be that boy's mother' (pointing at Wilbert) 'but as for being my wife ... I thought you would have get that idea out of your head by now.' Thus it came about that Rani had every Sunday to herself.

To the public gaze, her most outstanding characteristic must have been her characterlessness. Even when she was physically present, there was an air of invisibility surrounding her. She was dry and impersonal, part of the lustreless texture

35

of the house. Her skin – so pale! – had a kind of unhealthy transparency, like cloudy plastic; or wax. But, on Sunday afternoons, Rani blossomed in the privacy of her bedroom at the back of the house. Then, she indulged her passion for collecting stamps. She had started her collection in the early days of her spinsterhood when she had been banished out of sight by her family. Having sprung out of hopelessness and despair, it had come to be intimately associated with them and it was natural that it should be revived now.

She had three albums with differently coloured covers: red, black and brown. These she kept wrapped in cellophane at the top of her wardrobe. It was only in connection with them she exerted anything akin to authority, permitting no one to touch the albums but herself. Whenever letters arrived for her husband, she would scrutinize each stamp very carefully. Anything from Europe excited her. But her excitement was firmly controlled. She would simply raise and lower her eyebrows in quick succession and, resting the letters on a saucer, carry them to her husband's room. Egbert Ramsaran read his letters with the same slow, cautious deliberation he brought to his detective novels. Her greatest fear was that he might tear the stamps. Torn stamps, as she informed Wilbert in a burst of confidence, had absolutely no value. 'And who is to say that the stamp he tear mightn't be very valuable. Worth hundreds of dollars!' She opened her eyes wide. 'Just think of that.'

Despite this, she was not a discriminating collector. Every stamp, no matter how common and no matter how many of them she already had, was grist to her mill. She retained scores of Trinidad one-cent stamps and was terribly upset if one of them got torn or misplaced, treating each with the same care she devoted to her rarer specimens. Sunday afternoons were her time for sticking them into the albums. She sat on the edge of the bed, gingerly balancing on her lap a chipped white saucer filled with water in which the scraps of envelope with stamp attached floated. Beside her on the bed were the three albums and, scattered round her feet, piles of envelopes waiting to be plucked of their treasures. She worked with studied concentration for two or three hours, worriedly attentive to any sign of her husband's encroaching presence: she did not want him to find out what she did with her 'free time' in case it should occur to him to disapprove. Although she never explicitly asked Wilbert to keep silent about it, they did have a tacit agreement and avoided talking about her hobby when he was around.

Her bedroom, unlike the rest of the house, bore the stamp – so to speak – of her personality. There was the pleasant smell of old but scrupulously clean clothes; the tiny clay and brass ornaments cluttering the dresser; the coloured prints of Hindu deities pinned to the wall; the photograph, in awkward juxtaposition to them, of skiers racing down the slopes of a Swiss mountain, which she had cut from a magazine; the worn rug with the fold across the centre which she tried never to step on. It was a curious collection of odds and ends, for the most part relics of childhood, and it was never added to. Neither did she throw anything away. If one of the clay ornaments got broken, she simply kept the pieces. Her room and its furnishings were a final and complete expression of the nonsense her life had been.

Chapter Two

1

Singh came to the house in Victoria about once a month, bringing with him sacks filled with fruit from the estate which Egbert Ramsaran owned in Central Trinidad. He would dump the sacks carelessly on the kitchen floor. 'Oranges,' he said. Or: 'Mangoes.' Rani would immediately tear open the sacks and proceed to sort the fruit. Singh, propped up against the sill of the big kitchen window and drying the shining beads of sweat on his forehead, watched her. He smiled with a wry and gentle contempt. His conversation with her followed a set pattern.

'And how is the master these days?'

'He been very well, thank God.'

'He still doing his exercises?'

'Yes.'

'Good. And you. How have you been?' He looked searchingly into her tired face.

'I been very well too, Singh. Thank God.'

He grinned at her, his gold teeth flashing. 'I bring some more stamps for you to put in your album.' Unbuttoning the flap of his shirt pocket, he flourished before her some Trinidad one-cent stamps.

'Thank you, Singh. It was very kind of you to remember me. God will bless you.'

Singh half-laughed and half-grimaced. 'I hope so.' He turned to Wilbert next. 'And how has the little master been doing this month?' He did not usually wait for an answer, but delving – this time into one of his trouser pockets – would bring forth some crudely carved wooden toy he had made with his penknife. His favourite was a human face, elongated out of all proportion, with thick Negroid lips and round, black holes for eyes. Executed without charm, it was, in its odd way, rather frightening. 'I carve this specially for you,' he would say, thrusting it close to Wilbert's face. 'You like it? Specially for you I make it. It wasn't easy – take me days.' A peculiar intensity invaded his expression. If Wilbert tried to take hold of it, he would tighten his grip. Then, abruptly, he would erupt into a bout of high pitched laughter and, loosening his grip, allow Wilbert to have it.

Singh was in his middle twenties. He was very dark and stockily built and his face had not rid itself of the ravages of adolescence. It was scarred and pitted with craters. When he laughed his gums were exposed and one saw his crooked, yellowing teeth, like those of an old man. Singh laughed a great deal but there was something mocking and furtive in his laughter. It did not inspire trust. His laughter was just that shade too loud, too ringing and too ready; and it was interspersed with those briefly glimpsed flashes of ferocity – instantly suppressed and converted into brittle merriment – when the blood darkened his rough face and he bit hard on his twitching lower lip.

From early on, Wilbert had recognized that Singh occupied a significant place in their lives. It would never have occurred to him to give Singh the half-rotten fruit he used to dole out among the clients. He exuded an authority of his own. Singh did not cringe in front of his father. He could be sullen and mildly defiant. On the other hand, it was possible to detect in Egbert Ramsaran a desire to placate him; not to contradict him; not to lose his temper.

After the fruit had been sorted, Rani prepared him a cup of tea.

'Go and tell your father Singh come,' she said to Wilbert.

When Egbert Ramsaran came into the kitchen he glanced briefly at Singh. There would be an embarrassing silence. Singh was never the first to break it.

'How is everything on the estate?' He did not look directly at Singh.

'The same.'

'You have everything you need down there?'

Singh nodded. 'Everything.'

Egbert Ramsaran handed him the twenty-dollar bill he had been holding in his clenched fist: Singh's monthly allowance. Singh folded it carefully and put it in his pocket. He did not thank him. There was another embarrassing silence. Egbert Ramsaran stared at the fruit Rani had sorted into neat heaps.

'What you bring for we this week?'

'Mangoes.'

Silence.

'If you ever want anything extra . . .'

'I'll ask,' Singh said.

'Well . . . that's it for now . . . when you going back?'

'When I finish my cup of tea.'

Egbert Ramsaran stared vaguely at him and returned to his bedroom. He would be in a bad mood for the rest of the day. Perhaps it was because of a strong mutual repulsion that the two men seemed to generate a sort of electricity between them.

It was Singh who first suggested Wilbert should come to the estate and spend some days with him. Wilbert was hesitant; reluctant to commit himself to such an adventure. His father never went there and, apart from the fruit it yielded and Singh's monthly visitations, it did not impinge on their lives. To Wilbert, as a result, 'the estate' was something remote and unreal. It was only its association with Singh that kept it alive – undesirably alive – in his mind. He had no wish to go there. Singh had understood at once. He laughed loudly.

'Imagine not wanting to see a property that going to be your own one day. Like you frighten of me?' He turned to Rani. 'Why this boy so frighten of me? He does behave as if I going to eat him every time he sees me. I is no cannibal.'

'I sure he don't think that of you,' Rani said soothingly. 'Is just a little shyness he have. That's all.'

'What he have to be shy with me for? After all we is . . .' Singh, biting on his lower lip, gazed fiercely at him. However, he recovered himself quickly and laughed resoundingly. 'So, is shy you shy. Well! Well! You coming with me? You will

40

soon learn not to be shy.' His mouth distended in a wide, scornful grin. 'It have a lot of things a boy your age could do out in the country. I have a gun out there. We could go out and shoot birds. It have a river out there – a real river. Not like the little canal you have behind here. A real river with fish in it. We could go out and swim and catch fish. What you know about shooting birds and catching fish?' He gazed scathingly at him. No one else would have dared to talk thus to the son and heir of Egbert Ramsaran. He turned again to Rani. 'What you say? I sure you agree with me that is high time the young master learn about these things.'

'I have no objection to him going with you, Singh. But is not up to me. Is his father permission you have to get.'

'I will get that today self.'

When Egbert Ramsaran appeared, they performed the motions of their ritual, halting exchange while Singh sipped his tea.

Egbert Ramsaran got ready to depart. 'If you ever want anything . . .'

'Yes,' Singh said, 'it have something . . .'

Egbert Ramsaran, already in the doorway, stopped in surprise. 'Oh? What is that?' He cast a questioning, quizzical glance at Singh, touched with the faintest hint of irony.

'This boy,' Singh said, indicating Wilbert.

'What about him?'

'I was thinking what a nice thing it would be if he could come and spend some time with me on the estate.'

Egbert Ramsaran said nothing.

'I could teach him a lot of things. Show him how to fish and shoot and catch birds. Show him another kind of life.' Singh giggled. 'But he frighten of me. He think I will eat him up.'

'Is that so?' Egbert Ramsaran looked at his son. 'You frighten of Singh, child?'

'Is 'fraid he 'fraid,' Singh jeered.

'When you was planning to take him with you?'

'Today self – if you don't mind. I have the jeep with me.'

'A good idea, Singh. No point in postponing it. You take him back with you in the jeep today.' Egbert Ramsaran studied Wilbert critically. 'It will toughen him up a bit. Yes. Take him with you and toughen him up for me. Is exactly what he need. I glad you thought of it.'

So, it was decided. Settled. Singh leered triumphantly, showing his crooked, yellow teeth.

Egbert Ramsaran's estate was by no means vast. Its meagre seventy-five acres were barely capable of comparison with the two and three hundred acre giants surrounding it. But it was not its limited acreage alone which distinguished it and put it in a different class altogether from its neighbours. What was inexplicable to Egbert Ramsaran's fellow landowners was that he made no proper use of it at all. Their ordered and minutely tended cocoa and orange groves contrasted queerly with the disordered, untended wasteland wallowing in their midst. It was a blot on conscience. Over the years, several of them had offered to buy it at prices undeniably generous. 'It's a sin, Mr Ramsaran, to let good land like that go to waste. You could grow a hundred different crops on it if you really try. If you don't want to sell it at least take some advice – free of charge.' He rejected their offers out of hand. 'You could keep your money and your advice,' he told them bluntly. 'Why you buy it for in the first place?' they persisted in bewilderment. 'That is nobody business but mine,' he replied. 'Is my land and I'll do what the hell I want with it.' 'Shame on you, Mr Ramsaran,' they said. 'Shame on you to be like that.'

As was to be expected, their disapproval only had the effect of further strengthening his resolve. If such a thing was possible, he intensified his neglect of the estate and without Singh's efforts it would have stopped producing even the few mangoes and oranges that it did. It was a shock after driving along rough country roads bordered on either side by industriously cultivated tracts to come suddenly upon this enclave given over to abandonment and decay, deadened in the heat of mid afternoon. Singh, who had driven all the way in uncompromising silence, spoke for the first time.

'Well, young master, what you think?' He lifted his hands off the steering wheel and embraced in expansive gesture the wilderness of grass and bush and tree confronting them. 'That is what I does call home.' He laughed. 'Is no mansion but I hope a little bush not going to frighten you.' He grinned pleasantly at Wilbert. They got out of the jeep and stood for a while in the burning sun, the heels of their shoes sinking into the road's softened tar surface. Insects hummed, darting among the wild flowers, their wings lit up by the sun. Singh whistled long and piercingly. Two dogs rushed bounding through the grass, barking excitedly. He bent down to stroke the dogs who were nuzzling at his trousers. 'You missed me?' He pummelled them friendlily. 'You missed your Singh?' It was very still at that time of day and his voice, piercing the heat and stillness, was loud and startlingly sharp. The dogs whined. 'Is food they after,' he said. 'Is only when they hungry that they like me. If another man was to feed them, they would forget about me straight away.' He pushed them away and stood up. 'Ungrateful bitches!'

Wilbert's throat was parched after the long drive. He asked if there was any water.

'Water!' Singh grinned. 'We have lots of that here. Come. I'll show you water.' He led him, running and stumbling, up a rutted dirt track, meandering through waist-high grass. The land climbed fairly steeply to the brow of a hill. This, commanding a fine view of much of the estate, had been cleared of all vegetation; an arena of beaten yellow earth on which had been built a small, wooden hut on stilts about ten feet off the ground. With its precipitously ridged, corrugated iron roof and the square holes covered with strips of canvas that passed for windows, it resembled a watchtower. To complete the resemblance, there was a ladder leading to the entrance which was also screened by a strip of canvas.

Holding his arm, Singh led Wilbert under the hut and pointed at three red oil drums balanced on bricks and standing side by side. Their tops were protected by sheets of corrugated iron. The ground around them was sodden and mossy. Singh removed one of the protective sheets. The drum was filled to the brim with greyish water. Insects hummed and darted over the surface. 'Not to your liking?' Singh asked. He removed the lids from the other two drums. In both of them drowned insects floated on the surface. Leaning carelessly against one of the pillars of the hut Singh watched him. 'Well,' he said quietly, 'what you waiting for? Drink.' Singh idly flicked open and shut the blades of his penknife. 'What other water you suppose it have in a place like this? Eh?' His voice grated. 'We don't have no clear spring water here, you know. Is why your father send you – to toughen you up. This is the water I does have to drink week in, week out.' Wilbert moved away from the drums, his back to Singh. The blades of the penknife clicked. Open. Shut. Open. Shut. Walking out from under the hut, Wilbert stood in the sunlight, his shadow a black dwarf in front of him. A few feet ahead, the narrow track up which they had recently climbed resumed its twisting, indecisive course through the grass, dropping swiftly to a muddy pond beyond which the land rose again, though not to as great a height. All around the trunks of tall trees rose like poles into the sky. He listened for the river which Singh had mentioned but could hear nothing except the indolent whirr of insects in the undergrowth. Singh relented. He came up behind him and rested a hand on his shoulder. 'Lower down near the road it have some orange trees. I'll pick some for you to suck.' The harshness in his voice was muted. He seemed subdued.

They returned down the path to the road, the dogs trailing behind them and sniffing their footsteps. Singh plunged heedlessly into the tall grass, disappearing from view almost immediately. Wilbert followed, the grass closing over his head, irritating his bare arms and tickling his cheeks and nose. Somewhere in front of him and invisible, he could hear Singh crashing through the undergrowth. Unable to see where he was going, Wilbert moved more circumspectly. The noises ahead of him ceased. Wilbert stopped too. The latticework of blades was featureless, a uniform crackling green. 'Singh!' There was no answer. He panicked, thrashing uselessly as if he were drowning. 'Singh! You there?' This time Singh did reply but it was impossible to tell from which direction his muffled voice came. The dogs were barking distantly. 'I can't

see where you is,' Wilbert shouted back blindly into the crackling latticework. Singh cursed. The crashing noises recom-
menced, coming nearer, and soon Singh's dark, unsmiling
face was hovering above him.

'You should have waited for me out on the road like I had
tell you to.'

'You didn't tell me nothing.'

'You should have use your common sense and stay there.
This is no place for a child. Is bad enough for me without
having you to bother about.'

Wilbert did not say anything. His arms and face itched and
he started to scratch them.

'And all you could do is stand there and scratch!' The
blood flooded his face and his teeth pressed hard on his lower
lip. He grew calmer. 'Come.' He grasped his hand roughly.
'Next time make sure to listen to what I tell you. And if I
don't tell you anything, then use your common sense. Use
what you have up there.' He screwed his index finger into the
side of his head.

They resumed their journey through the grass, Singh
marching ahead with giant strides. 'Just there,' he said. The
group of orange trees was nearly suffocated by the profusion
of growth pressing in on them from all sides. Surprisingly,
they were laden with pendulously drooping fruit which
looked as if they had been artificially attached. Singh skirted
the fringes of the group of trees, gazing up warily into the
branches. 'Watch out for the jackspaniards. They could sting
you real bad if you not careful.' Wilbert waited while he completed his examination. 'Okay,' Singh announced, 'I don't
see any so we could start to pick oranges now.' He smiled
goldenly at Wilbert, becoming more expansive. 'You see,
young master, everything is a art. Everything! Take picking
oranges, for instance.' His head disappeared among the branches as he reached up on tiptoe leaning into the tree. He re-
emerged with a grunt. 'Is not just a simple matter of pulling
them from the tree. You have to know about jackspaniards,
then you got to know which is the right time to pick, then you
got to know which will be the best and most juicy ones.' He

45

paused, staring intently at Wilbert. 'Yes, young master, even the simplest thing like picking oranges is a art. Is very important for you of all peope to realize that. You will have to be worrying your head about all kinds of things which I will never have to worry about, so now is the best time for you to start learning.' He laughed. 'Because when you stop being the young master and become the real master ... well, that is the biggest art of all, not so? You couldn't afford to lose yourself in the grass then.' Wilbert turned away from him. Singh giggled, but already his mood was changing; the expansiveness dying away. 'Yes,' he said morosely, staring at the fruit strewn on the ground, 'I expect you will discover that for yourself in time. I think we have more than enough oranges now – even for a thirsty man like you.'

He gathered the fruit and bundling them in a pile next to his chest he retraced his path gloomily through the grass, muttering under his breath. They returned to the hut where, one by one, Singh peeled the oranges with his penknife and passed them on to his guest. When he had finished, he washed his hands in one of the drums and, from another, drank some water which he scooped up in his cupped palms.

'It don't kill me to do that,' he said, scrubbing his lips and hands dry on the front of his shirt.

They slept in the hut that night, Singh drawing up the ladder after him. In one corner of the room there was a rusting, two-burner kerosene stove and, on a smoke-blackened shelf above it, pots and spoons and enamel plates. Ranged along the wall opposite the stove was a low, extremely narrow camp bed covered with a thin cotton bedspread. It looked uninviting and uncomfortable. There was a solitary chair in the room which Singh offered to Wilbert.

'It don't have much to do here after dark,' he said, loosening the canvas flaps over the windows and rolling them up. 'No radio. No newspaper. Out here in the country you does have to go to sleep with the chickens and get up with the chickens. Not like Victoria, eh?' He uttered a choked but not unfriendly laugh. 'Mind you, I don't care for newspaper and electric light and that kind of thing. I'm a simple man with simple tastes. I like the country life. It have too many crooks in the city. A few hours in Port-of-Spain is enough for me.' Lowering his head, he peered closely at Wilbert. 'Like you sorry you come?'

Wilbert stared unblinkingly at him. He did not answer.

'Ah! That's good. That's very good. Toughen you up. That's what we have to do.' Singh nodded vigorously. He bit round the edges of his thumbnail. 'Who is your best friend, young master?'

'I don't have a best friend.'

'But you must have a best friend. Everybody have to have a best friend.'

Wilbert was unblinking.

Singh chewed on the slivers of fingernail. 'What about Julian Bholai?' he queried. 'They say he is a very bright boy. Going to be a doctor one day. You want to be a doctor too?'

'I don't know. Pa don't like doctors.'

'What you want to be then? A lawyer? A engineer?'

'I don't know.'

'You don't know!' Singh pretended to be amazed. 'These is things you have to know, young master. Julian Bholai know he want to be a doctor.'

'The only thing doctors good for is to cheat people.' Wilbert was suddenly aggressive.

Singh laughed. 'Who tell you that? Your father?'

Wilbert scowled. He and Julian went to the same school in Port-of-Spain, a deliberate choice on the part of Vishnu Bholai who had hoped they would become the greatest of friends. He was disappointed. 'I going to be a doctor, Ramsaran,' Julian had declared at the outset. 'My father saving up for me to go to England. How about you?' 'I going to run my father business when he die,' Wilbert had replied. Julian could not conceal his contempt. 'That is all?' 'My father don't like doctors,' Wilbert said, 'he say they only good for cheating people.' Julian guffawed. 'Your father must be a funny kind of man. He don't know what he talking about.' Wilbert squared, ready to settle for blows. 'What about your father? Tell me what *he* does do.' Julian backed down. 'I don't want to pick no fight with you, Ramsaran.' A quiet, unspoken hostility developed between the two boys after this incident and they avoided each other's company. For Wilbert, the memory was fresh and painful; an open wound which any discussion of the subject was likely to irritate. It did so now.

"A profession is what is important nowadays,' Singh was saying. 'Money alone is not enough. You need a education to really get on in this world. Take me. You suppose if I had a little education I would have been shut up on this estate like some animal?' He stopped speaking suddenly.

Wilbert was tired and sleepy. The day was dying fast. A blinding red sun was sinking beyond the most distant line of trees and the dust particles had turned golden. It was cooler too. After the brightness he had been gazing on, it was black in the room. Amoebic globules of colour floated before his eyes. He closed them, concentrating with drowsy stupor on the restless play of colour and shadow on his eyelids. Singh prodded him into wakefulness, his face melting and immaterial.

'Education is the important thing, young master.' His voice floated dreamily, wrapping itself around Wilbert and insinuating itself into the darkness. 'You ever ask yourself why it is I does have to make do with that dirty rainwater which even a dog shouldn't have to drink? You think is because I have a different kind of stomach from other people?' His head swivelled slowly around the room. 'You think is my fault I have nigger blood running in my veins? You think is I who put it there? You believe was me who was responsible for that?' He spoke with mounting, importunate excitement; with a sense of relief. 'Whatever happen to my nigger mother? I never see she face. I would like to see she face. Just once. I would like to see the face of my nigger mother.' The ugly head leered at Wilbert, thick-lipped, with eyes like holes. Singh sank to his knees, head drooping. 'Poor young master. No pity for Singh at all who never see his nigger mother. And if is anybody should have pity is you.'

It happened before he was aware of it. He had reached forward and slapped Singh hard across the mouth. Singh covered his lips with the back of his hand. Wilbert drew back, looking round him wildly. But Singh did not move. He remained as he was, kneeling on the dusty floor and rubbing his hands back and forth in a measured rhythm across his bruised lips.

The mosquitoes had invaded the room, their humming louder in Wilbert's ears than the croaking of the frogs outside. He sat there in the darkness, numbed, hungry and afraid of what he had done, warding off the attacking mosquitoes feeding greedily on his arms and face while Singh brooded exhaustedly at his feet. At length, Singh roused himself and stood up. Wilbert listened to him blundering about the room and cursing as he groped among the pots and pans on the shelf above the stove. A match scraped and he was bathed momentarily in a flickering, yellow glow that cast mountainous shadows on the walls and ceiling. The match went out. Singh swore softly and lit a second which he held aloft while he searched in the cupboard near the stove and brought forth a sooted oil-lamp. The lamp flamed into life. Singh bent low over it. Having adjusted the height of the wick, he set it on the floor. Singh rolled down the strips of canvas but not before a bevy of insects had swarmed into the room, orbiting round the glass funnel and a large black moth with red markings on its wings had settled on the ceiling.

He cooked a simple meal of vegetables, most of which he had grown himself, and rice. He apologized with sarcastic humility for the simplicity of the food as he doled it out on to their plates. 'Is what I myself does have to eat every day of the week.' After they had eaten, he brought some sacking and spread it on the floor. 'The bed is for you,' he said. Wilbert demurred. Singh lost his temper. 'Is not manners what make me offer it to you,' he shouted. 'I have no manners. I don't know what manners is – nobody ever take the trouble to teach me. Out here in the country a man doesn't have time to waste on things like that. You think if I really wanted to sleep on the bed I would offer it to you or anyone else?' He must have startled even himself by this unexpected outburst

for he finished by saying in a more subdued, placatory tone:
'Is because I not accustom to sleeping on beds. That's why.
I prefer the floor.'

He dimmed the oil-lamp and lay down on the sacking in the
same clothes he had worn all day. He yawned. 'I hope you
rest well tonight, young master. Tomorrow it have somebody
coming here who want to meet you. Is a person who been
asking to meet you a long time.'

'What person?' Wilbert asked mechanically, too weary to
be curious.

Singh, propped on his elbow, was looking intently at him.
'You'll find out soon enough in the morning. Now stop asking
so much question and go to sleep. We have a long day ahead
of we tomorrow.'

The bed was hard and uncomfortable and the fibre protruded from the mattress, grating against his skin. Wilbert
drew the thin blanket provided up to his neck – in the manner
of his father. Singh had not been telling the whole truth. The
bed and the blanket had the smell of nightly use. Tired as he
was, he could not fall asleep and tossed from side to side.
Wilbert stared at Singh. He had drawn his knees up to the pit
of his stomach and his big, clumsy hands pillowed his head.
Watching him sprawled thus across the sacking, his fears lessened. Asleep, Singh seemed trusting; vulnerable; even innocent. He had thrown his head back – like a creature crucified –
and he breathed laboriously through his wide open mouth.
The lamp burned dimly, casting its mountainous shadows on
the walls and ceiling; and outside, the unexplained noises of
the night. Wilbert closed his eyes and waged ineffectual battle
on the invisibly whirring mosquitoes.

Well before daybreak Singh had risen and gone off with
the gun and the two dogs. It was the report of the gun and the
dogs' frenzied barking that awoke Wilbert. At first, he did
not remember where he was. Then he saw the oil-lamp and
the dishevelled sacking and he remembered. The mosquitoes
had vanished with the coming of the day and the moth too
had departed its ceiling roost. Sunlight streamed into the

50

room and the strips of canvas flapped in the breeze. It was still pleasantly cool. This, together with the absence of the mosquitoes and the brightness of the morning, cheered him up considerably. However, the sound of Singh's rasping voice calling to him from just beneath the window did much to dispel his cheerfulness.

'Time to get up, young master. Remember what I was telling you. Out here in the country we does get up with the chickens. I have a little present for you.'

Wilbert kicked off the blanket and, rubbing the sleep out of his eyes, went to the window and looked out. Singh held up a dead blackbird for him to see, its bedraggled feathers stained with clotted blood. It swung from the tips of his fingers. The dogs were leaping around it. Singh dangled it tantalizingly close to their gaping, snapping mouths. He laughed.

'I shoot three of them this morning,' he said. 'I thought I would bring this one to show you. Not very pretty, what you say? But you mustn't feel sorry for it. If I didn't shoot them, I wouldn't have a single vegetable left. I does shoot them and give them to the dogs. So!' The bird plummeted from his fingers and the dogs, barking furiously, fell upon it. 'They have a feast,' he said, smiling up at Wilbert. 'Go and get dressed now. Don't forget we having a visitor this morning.' The dogs scrambled and fought over the dead bird, growling and snarling at each other.

Wilbert's curiosity was stronger now. 'What visitor?'

'You'll find out soon enough. Go and make yourself ready.'

Wilbert left the window and picked up his clothes draped on the back of the chair. Singh's dark face appeared at the top of the ladder, the gun slung across his shoulders. He hauled himself grunting through the door. Beads of sweat watered the tip of his nose and his forehead and he breathed in sharp, irregular spasms. His knee-high boots were coated with mud. He eased the gun off his shoulder and rested it on the floor. Downstairs, the dogs growled.

'Go downstairs if you want to wash,' he said.

The ladder leaned at a steep, precarious angle and it swayed alarmingly as Wilbert inched his way down the rungs. Singh's boots resounded overhead: he was pacing and muttering to himself. The two mongrels, having finished their feasting, came running up to him, nuzzling his legs and whining. There was a mess of scattered feathers on the ground. One of the dogs rolled over on its back, exhibiting its spotted pink underside. It was pregnant and the sight of its distended teats filled him with sudden revulsion, and, following Singh's example, he kicked it away. With its tail tucked between its legs, it shrank away from him. His attention was caught by something else. To his astonishment, there was, next to the oil-drums – the prospect of which he had been dreading – a bucket freshly filled with water, a new bar of soap and a towel. He gazed up wonderingly at the resounding floorboards and proceeded to wash.

He thanked Singh on his return. Singh scowled and rejected his thanks gruffly. 'Drink your tea,' he replied, handing him a steaming mug, on top of which was balanced a slice of buttered bread. 'Drink your tea and forget your thanks.'

They had their breakfast in silence. When they had done, Singh, refusing Wilbert's offer of help, washed the mugs, tidied up the bed and swept the room. The shrill voice of a woman called out to him.

'That you, Myra?' Singh shouted back.

'No. Is King George.'

'Bitch,' Singh muttered. 'Well,' he shouted, 'come up then. What you standing there for? You expect me to lift you up here?'

'Don't be stupid, man. I have the child with me. How you expect me to climb the ladder with she?'

'You could manage.'

There were rebellious murmurs but Myra did manage to ascend the ladder with the child clinging to her waist.

'You see,' Singh said, 'you could do it without my help. Safe and sound.'

'No thanks to you,' Myra puffed. 'If I had fall and break both mine and the child neck ...'

She was a plump, dark-skinned woman of uncertain race –

probably Indian and Negro. Her hair cascaded in untidy coils over a crude, heavy-jowled face. She wore a loose, pink dress and a pair of leather slippers. The baby, its thumb buried in its mouth, clung limpet-like to her hips. 'I don't know how you could be so inconsiderate as to make me climb the ladder with the child,' she continued, smiling. 'Sometimes I does feel you mad...' The smile evaporated when she saw Wilbert standing in a corner of the room. She stopped speaking, looking at him and Singh in turn.

'You guess right. That is him.' Singh indicated Wilbert with an unceremonious jerk of the thumb.

Myra glanced at Wilbert a second time as if to ascertain that he were really there and not a figment of the imagination. Her scrutiny, though unabashed, was neither friendly nor unfriendly. She hitched the straps of her dress further up her shoulders. Singh took the baby from her. 'This,' he said, 'is Indra and that woman who can't take she eyes off you is Indra mother. Indra is my daughter.' He gazed at Wilbert defiantly. The baby started to cry. Singh peered at its pinched features and rocked it in his arms; but without real affection. Myra had retreated to the corner near the stove, her eyes fixed alternately on Singh rocking the screaming baby and Wilbert.

'Like you didn't feed she?' Singh asked.

'You think I would let she starve?' Myra was offended. 'It must be gripe she have.'

'Gripe!' Suddenly, Singh thrust – almost threw – the child at Wilbert, and instinctively he held out his arms to catch it.

'Oh!' Myra exclaimed involuntarily, clapping her hands across her mouth. 'One day you going to kill the child with you foolishness. I never see a father behave like you in my born days.' Nevertheless, she remained in the corner, making no move to interfere.

'Shut up,' Singh commanded.

The baby screamed louder than before, squirming like a fish in Wilbert's grasp.

'Let me hold she,' Myra said. 'She not accustom to strangers.'

'Stay where you is.' Singh pushed her back rudely. 'Let him hold she. He is not a stranger.' He laughed.

'How long he going to stay with you?' Myra asked.

'A day or two,' Singh answered absently. 'I haven't decided yet. I been trying to learn him a few things.'

Myra looked at Wilbert. Her neutrality was weakening: she seemed marginally more well-disposed towards him. 'Be careful with him,' she said. 'You see how he does treat his own daughter. He half-mad.'

'Nobody interested in your opinions,' Singh replied angrily. 'You better leave now.'

Myra took the baby from Wilbert. 'Somebody got to help me down the ladder. Coming up is one thing but going down ...'

'I will help you.' Wilbert stepped forward.

'You is a gentleman,' Myra said. 'Not like some I could mention.'

Wilbert assisted her down the ladder. Myra departed.

'Well, young master, that is my little family. What you think? As you see, we doesn't even live together. A man can't bring up a family here.' Singh stared round the room. 'Look at my daughter. What she have to hope for except to be somebody servant one day? Is not a fair world at all.' He winked at him. 'You agree with me?' He picked up the gun from the floor. 'Your answer wouldn't make any difference anyway. Come.' He went to the ladder. 'Let we go for a little walk now. Show you the estate.'

The early morning coolness had already vanished. Singh strode on purposefully ahead of Wilbert, the gun slung negligently across his shoulders. He started to whistle, raucous and out of tune. The two dogs skipped playfully back and forth, darting into the thick bush on either side of the path. Singh stamped and yelled at them but they paid him no attention. The path led steeply down from the hut to the muddy pond which Wilbert had noticed the previous afternoon. Singh paused by the pond.

'It have a lot of cascadoo in there.'

The dogs chased each other round the circumference.

'You should see how big it does get in the rainy season. It does flood all over the place.' He extended his arms in a wide sweep. 'It does get deep too. A man could drown in it then if he didn't take care.' He spoke with relish and Wilbert could see for himself how much the pond had shrunk in the dry weather. It was surrounded by a broad band of caked, creamy-white mud, minutely veined and segmented by a mosaic of tiny cracks. Singh prodded at it with the butt of a gun. 'Just think,' he commented wonderingly, 'that in another few weeks or so, all where we standing now will be under deep, deep water.'

Not far away, but out of reach of the floodwaters from the pond, was the neatly fenced-in enclosure where Singh grew his vegetables. A lovingly detailed scarecrow had been pinioned on a wooden cross in the centre of the enclosure. Wilbert recognized Singh's handiwork in the face it had been given: it was a replica of those he carved for him except in this one, to increase the effect, its cheeks were streaked with red and green paint. Wilbert tried not to look at it. This was the only cultivated spot in the estate and Singh was clearly very proud of it. 'I does grow nearly everything I need here,' he said. 'Cabbages. Tomatoes. Peas. Beans. You name it.' The banked beds were well watered and weeded. Singh vaulted the fence and strolled along proprietorially between the arrow-straight rows of plants, examining the leaves. He scooped up a fistful of earth and let it run through his fingers. 'All my own work,' he said. 'From start to finish. Not a soul help me in doing this. It was high grass here, more than waist-high – just like it is down by the orange trees. I spend weeks clearing it and digging it, working with my bare hands in the sun and rain.' He meditated on his calloused palms. 'In sun and rain and with my own two hands I make this – so that I wouldn't starve to death. Not a soul help me.' The blood flooded his unattractive face and he pressed his teeth on his twitching lower lip. 'So you see, when the birds come and try to . . .' He laughed and, going across to the scarecrow, hugged it. 'But with the help of my friend here, I does get by.' He kissed the macabre countenance. 'He and me is very good friends,' he said. 'He mightn't be very pretty but he is my best friend.' He smiled. 'In that way, I luckier than you. I know who my best friend is.'

Away from the pond, the land rose again and the deeply rutted track disappeared in the high grass. The wall of the forest approached closer and the crowns of tall trees drooped somnolently overhead. Birds flew and twittered among the branches that seemed to brush the sky. Their feet crunched on fallen twigs and leaves. Singh moved with assurance, naming unfamiliar trees and flowers. There were a great many varieties of palm. The grey monumental pillars of the royal palm towered all about them; as did the less spectacular cabbage palm; and the gru-gru palm with its clusters of shining red nuts, the size and shape of marbles. There was another palm whose name Singh did not know, the trunk of which was nailed with hard, sharp thorns. There were clumps of bamboo whose polished stems curved upwards in gentle arcs with leaves like the brushed strokes of Chinese writing.

'It have something I want to show you,' Singh said.

They left the track and waded a few yards into the forest.

A damp hush enclosed them and the sky was lost from view. 'Look.' Singh pointed with his rifle at an avenue of stone pillars buried in the dim recesses of the bush.

'What is it, Singh?'

'That used to be a house, young master. A long time ago that used to be a house. Rich people used to live there.' He spoke with the same sense of awe and wonder as he had done when describing the desiccated pond's transformation in the rainy season. They could see the ruins of a porch and the broad flight of weed-choked steps leading up to it. They climbed the steps and looked in through the yawning gap that must once have been the main entrance, and entered with the trepidation of interlopers defying an invisible, guardian presence. There were scattered heaps of crumbling masonry everywhere. Trees had established themselves in the crevices of the brick pediment, marauders pillaging the ruins. Jagged

56

portions of the outside walls had survived the battering mira-
culously intact – though much overgrown with strangling net-
works of vines and creepers – and the vague outlines of rooms
were discernible; ghostly outlines traced in the rubble. What
had they been? Sitting-rooms? Bedrooms? Kitchens? There
were no clues left in this gutted shell. Their footsteps were
dogged by the invisible guardian presence that haunted the
place, intimating, by a chill of discomfort, its displeasure with
their unwarranted intrusion. They hurried between the aven-
ues of decapitated pillars, not speaking. Many of the pillars
had tumbled to the ground. Bits of glass glinted among the
rubble and foliage. At the back they found the ruins of outhouses: the stables and servants' quarters, dank, dark cells
with the subterranean atmosphere of caves and carpeted with
velvet moss. There was a flutter of wings inside and they
drew back. Beyond the outhouses were the skeletal remains
of a garden planted with fruit trees gone wild; an ornamental
pond, paved paths wandering through the grass, leading nowhere. They saw rusting water-tanks lying on their sides and
mud-filled drains and ditches. Further beyond, the collapsed
drying-house for cocoa and scattered rusting pieces of machinery, abandoned to the encroaching jungle. It was a compre-
hensive, abject surrender without terms.

'The people around here believe this is a haunted place.'
Singh laughed heavily. They had come to a clearing in the
trees. He slumped on a half-rotten log. 'They does never
come here. Only I brave enough to do that – I don't believe in
ghosts and all that stupidness.' He squinted slyly at Wilbert.
'You believe in ghosts, young master?'

Wilbert sidestepped the question. The chill of their recent
explorations was strong upon him. 'Who used to live here,
Singh?'

'Some Scotsman or the other. He used to own not only your
father estate but nearly all the land you see around here. But
that was a long time ago. Before even your father was born.
Or before even his father father. A long time ago.'

'Why he leave?'

'That, young master, is a mystery. Maybe he died and

didn't have any children. Maybe he thought he had made enough money out of it. Maybe he just get fed up and wanted to go back home – to Scotland. Who is to say what happen? Is a mystery. Nobody will ever know why.' Singh laid the gun across his knees. 'What this place must have been like! Is almost as if you could still hear them talking and laughing. You could almost smell the cocoa drying.' He appeared to listen. 'You hear the talking and laughing, young master? Listen carefully and you will hear it. Listen!' Singh cocked his head.

Wilbert shuddered. 'Let's go from here, Singh.' He looked around fearfully.

Singh roused himself from his reverie. 'You frighten young master? Like you too believe in ghosts?'

'Let's go from here.'

'In a minute, young master. I want to have a rest. Remember I been up from sunrise.'

The dogs settled at his feet panting, tongues drooping from their mouths. Imperceptively, the wind, which all morning had fanned through the grass, died away. The sun climbed higher; the day's heat coalesced. A faint roar of water was borne to them through the trees. The air was dank and acrid.

'You know what I would do if this place was mine? And if I had the money that is?' He screwed up his eyes, staring into the white, shimmering heat of the clearing. 'I would make this into a flower garden. I would plant all kinds of flowers and trees people never hear of before. Orchids especially. They is the prettiest kind of flower. And I would build a little house where the hut is now because that is the nicest spot for a house being so high up. Nothing too fancy, you understand. Something cool and shady where I could sit in the afternoon and look at my garden. I would never want to stir from here then.' Singh, laughing softly, waved his hands and brushed away the dream. 'That will never happen though. Not here. If you turn your back for one minute – well you yourself see what does happen. Maybe that was why the Scotsman leave. It was too much hard work. Maybe is easier in Scotland.'

His expression hardened. He drew a wavering circle in the dust with his finger, enclosing a long column of brown ants moving in steady procession past the log. Viciously, he ground his boots into the middle of the column and watched the survivors scurry in crazed disarray. Wilbert stared at the dead and dying ants.

'Ants is funny things,' Singh went on absently, stirring the dust with a twig he had picked up. 'These fellas you see here for instance, they have a nest right under this log. Sometimes when it get too hot – I don't like the heat – I does come and sit here for hours just watching them carry a tiny piece of leaf somewhere. They don't pay no attention to me. And yet, in a second, I could kill every last mother's son of them.' He bowed his head low to the ground, watching the ants. 'Is like that with anything anybody try to do. It always have something that bigger than you. Like what the jungle do to that place we just see. What it do there is just like what I do to the ants. No difference.' Singh smiled. 'As the master you will be able to do exactly the same to me one day. You could throw me out of here – do anything you want. But, it also have something bigger than you. Except we don't know what it is as yet. That is why you have to be careful. That is why you should try and get a profession. To protect yourself. Remember, young master, what Julian Bholai going to be. You should try and . . .'

'Don't call me young master, Singh. And don't talk about Julian Bholai.' Wilbert rose from the log.

Slapping his thighs, Singh erupted into a bout of prolonged, mocking laughter. 'Why you don't want to talk about Julian Bholai? The young master is a real little tiger when you get him angry. I better watch out.'

'Don't call me young master, Singh. I don't like it.'

'That is exactly what you is all the same. The young master. Next to you, I is like one of them ants. Like them all I could do is bite. But you . . .'

'Leave me alone, Singh.' Wilbert had raised his voice. 'I do nothing to you.' The fiery smell of the day burned in his nostrils.

'Be sensible young master. Face the facts. Who else but the young master would slap me? You should be proud . . .'

There was a muffled explosion somewhere deep inside Wilbert's head. The heat and fire seemed to be drawn out of the day and sucked into him. That scarecrow face, thick-lipped and with holes for eyes, leered at him. The world went black and fathomless. When he came to, Singh was crouched low over him and his head was pillowed on a bundle of grass and dried leaves.

'Is only the heat,' Singh murmured in his ear. 'Only the heat.' He fanned Wilbert with his shirt which he had taken off. The sarcasm and mockery had disappeared and in their stead had come something approximating to dread and concern. The sound of water filtering through the trees, though choked and distant, cooled the day. Wilbert closed his eyes and listened to it.

'How long I been like this Singh?'

'Five minutes. If that. Even I feeling the heat more than usual today.'

'Is that the river you was telling me about, Singh?' Wilbert tried to raise his head but Singh would not let him.

'Yes. That is the river I was telling you about. I going to take you there. But you must rest a little longer. I sure you wouldn't want the blood to rush like that to your head again.' He forced his head back gently on to the pillow of grass and leaves and fanned his face. For some minutes, they remained as they were. The sky was an unrelenting blue, flecked with whiffs of high, white cloud. There was not a breath of wind. Singh, squatting, rocked backward and forward on his heels fanning Wilbert with his shirt. The two dogs slept and the forest around them slept, the leaves of the trees limp and motionless. Leaning forward, Singh peered into Wilbert's face. 'How you feeling now?' He assisted him to his feet. 'You sure you feeling strong enough to walk?'

'Yes. Yes.' Wilbert pushed him away irritably.

Stepping back, Singh regarded him with a faint air of irony. His compassion was weakening again. He kicked the dogs awake and hoisted the gun on to his shoulders. Without another word, he stalked across the clearing and disappeared into the thick bush, heading towards the sound of the river. The dogs, fully restored to life, leapt on ahead of him through the crackling grass. There was not the slightest indication of a path but Singh moved with arrogant assurance, looking back at Wilbert from time to time. The sun, to begin with, had shone directly into their eyes but, as they descended, it gradually disappeared over the crowns of the trees.

They slid stumbling over jutting roots, through a green, subaqueous gloom of tangled undergrowth and slim grey trunks banded with creeper. The sound of the river, somewhere below them, grew louder and the air became cooler and moister. For the last few yards, they scrambled among some rocks and big boulders, holding to the festooned treetrunks for support. Apart from the water's distant applause, everything was hushed. Wilbert squirmed his way between the slippery boulders down to where Singh stood, head thrown back and arms akimbo. The dogs had disappeared.

'There,' Singh said quietly, extending an arm but not looking at Wilbert. 'This river is the boundary of the estate on this side.' The river, brown and slow-flowing in the sunlight, wound its way in a leisurely loop beneath them, uncoiling itself with a lank lethargy as if it too were affected by the heat of the day. It lay in a deep, steep-sided ravine about forty feet across, gouged out of the flaking rock. Elongated tongues of greyish sand and gravel were visible here and there. A profusion of fern flourished in the niches between the rock and lianas trailed in the water from the branches of overhanging trees. Lower down, there were clumps of bamboo. The balisier, like many-branched candelabra, flamed redly on the opposite slope. Singh and Wilbert slid down to the gravelly bank and followed the loop of the stream. They could hear the dogs barking now. Soon they came to an amphitheatre of rock fed by a stretch of low rapids over which the water foamed and spluttered. The dogs greeted them with happy barks. Singh cursed and they skulked away. Then he took off his clothes and advised Wilbert to follow suit. 'I'll teach you how to swim,' he said. 'Is nothing to it at all.'

After the heat, the water was icy to the touch and Singh, when he had swum, lay naked on the warm rock, face downwards. He appeared to have fallen asleep. Wilbert sought the sole shaded refuge and watched him. Again he thought of him as trusting, vulnerable and innocent; a creature crucified on the burning rock. Singh sat up and turned to look at him.

'I would like to travel far, far away from here,' he said. 'So far that even if I wanted to I could never come back.'

Wilbert was sufficiently astonished by this declaration to smile.

'And what about your flower garden?' he asked.

Singh gestured irritably. 'Forget the flower garden. As I said, it would never work here.'

'Where would you go?'

'Is all right for you to laugh,' Singh replied. He rested his chin on his knees. 'But you don't know how much I hate this place. I didn't choose to live here. I had no say in the matter.' Then he added slowly and deliberately, 'I think I hate it more than anything in the world. I hate it even more than I hate ...' He checked himself. 'Never mind.' He gazed with a shudder of revulsion at the yellow, sun-covered rock and the unrestrained masses of vegetation cascading down the slopes of the ravine. He had been set down in this place to run wild – like a pig. And, like a pig, he had run wild. The heat and the vegetation had washed in torrents over him and had drowned him. 'I would like to go somewhere cold,' he said. 'Somewhere very cold. Somewhere with ice and snow. Go to Greenland and live like the Eskimos and forget about all this.'

'You might get tired of all that snow and you mightn't like the cold at all.'

'How you know what I would like and wouldn't like?' The blood flooded his face and he bit on his lower lip. 'I would never get tired of it. Not me.' He juggled his head obstinately. 'I could sit for hours fishing through a hole in the ice – just like I does sit for hours watching them ants carry a little piece of leaf.'

'Where you learn all this, Singh?'

Singh darkened with sudden embarrassment. 'I see it in a picture,' he admitted sheepishly. 'A long time ago in Port-of-Spain. That's how the Eskimos does fish. Through a hole in the ice.' He gave way to a musing silence, his chin still resting on his knees. The shadows of the trees stretched out blackly across the water in which the orange clouds of the setting sun were reflected. 'Come,' he said suddenly, rising to his feet. 'Enough of this nonsense. Is getting dark and time for we to be getting back.'

They returned to the hut through the gathering gloom.

The visit lasted a week and the invitation was never repeated. Singh seemed anxious to forget it and turned aside every reference to it. He was more cold and aloof to Wilbert than he had ever been. As for Wilbert, the estate was no more a real place than it had ever been; and Singh himself no less a threat. The visit had merely provided him with a landscape: he became inseparable from images of intolerable heat, prolific vegetation and ruin. He remained one of the dark faces governing Wilbert's childhood. The innate fear and revulsion he had always felt did not lessen. It simply ceased to be arbitrary and gained shape and coherence. Some things are never expressly told one. There are bits and pieces of information which gradually seep into the consciousness. It was like that with Singh and his connection with him. No one ever told him Singh was also his father's child. Slowly, and without any deliberate effort on Wilbert's part, the realization took shape.

Chapter Three

1

All morning it had been raining steadily and the sky was
black with gust-driven cloud. It was Sunday and Rani was
sitting on the edge of the bed, an album opened on her lap
and the envelopes arranged in neat piles about her feet. The
rain sprayed against the misted windows. The sky flurried with
lightning and shortly after there was a tremendous crash of
thunder, rattling the ornaments on the dresser. She looked
up eagerly when Wilbert came into the room.

'You call me?' He seemed put out and annoyed.

She jerked her head quickly up and down. 'Why don't you
sit with me a little this afternoon? Eh? Like you used to do?'
Thick lines of rain slanted against the window-panes and the
wind tore through the trees. 'The rain,' she explained halting-
ly, staring at the stamps. Her swollen fingers rested lifelessly
on the album. 'Only till the rain stop.' She was coaxing. 'After
that you could go.' Lightning, blue and instant, flashed on the
ceiling and the thunder crashed swiftly in its wake. The room
shook and two of the clay ornaments fell off the dresser and
shattered. She collected the pieces and held them in her hand.
Wilbert went and pressed his face up against the cold glass of
the window. When the wind gusted especially hard, she would
turn and look at him, shivering a little as she did so. Wilbert
walked to the door and stood there with his hand on the
knob.

'I coming back soon,' he said. 'I just going out to the front
to have a look. I won't stay long.'

She did not try to stop him and he went out. When he had
gone, she gazed at the spot where his breath had condensed
on the window-pane.

The swollen Victoria river had burst its banks and brown tides of fast-flowing water had inundated the road at the front of the house. Branches, tins, bottles and pieces of wood bobbed and staggered on the surface. The field was a lake reflecting the black sky and the cows were huddled together in a group near the galvanized iron fence, miserable and wet. Wilbert saw the bull, drenched and haggard, flicking its tail across its haunches. It no longer frightened him. The water had invaded the front 'garden' and licked the bottom step of the verandah. Some boys were splashing in the flood. The rain sprayed stingingly into Wilbert's face as he listened to their shouts and laughter and to the wind ripping at the roof. He returned to his mother's room.

Rani did not hear him open the door and come in. Her chin propped on her hands, she was staring at the ceiling. The angle at which she held herself was unfamiliar to her son. There was an air of expectancy about it; of tension.

'I come back.'

'Oh! Is you!' She jumped up, startled.

She did not speak after this, resuming her examination of the album on her lap. Throughout the day the radio had been issuing hurricane warnings. But the weather grew no worse. The hurricane had veered, missing the island in its sweep northward. By nightfall, the wind had died away into weak and ephemeral gusts and there were many breaks in the driven cloud. The rain lessened. Rani shed her air of tense expectancy. She sat on the bed hunched over the stamp album, limp and flaccid – a punctured balloon. The rain became lighter; a gentle drizzle. Then it stopped altogether. The night was fresh and clear and the moon had a washed, watery brightness. Streaks of tattered cloud hung like rags in the sky.

'I could go now?'

Wilbert went to the door and opened it. She raised her head and looked at him. She had been crying. The world had not been destroyed after all. She had been deprived of the greatest excitement life would have given her.

'Yes,' she said. 'You could go now. It was very kind of you

to stay with me. You could go now and tell your father I'll have his food ready for him soon.'

Rani's death seemed little more than an empty formality; the final ratification of a condition long existing. Yet, in death, she acquired a substance and reality which she had lacked in life. It was her true fulfilment. For Wilbert, it was an immense relief. It was not that he had not pitied her (though he could not love her – she was too ghostly to provoke so positive an emotion) but pity was, in the end, swamped by the extremity of her suffering. Like everyone else, he had grown accustomed and inured to it. He could not help her. Pain was the very stuff of her existence and he was powerless before it. Remove it, and there might be nothing left. While she lived, she was a vacuum round which people skirted, afraid of being sucked in. So, like everyone else, he had rejected her thereby completing the injustice.

Inwardly he had begun to blame *her* for the awfulness of her life. He had become increasingly short and sharp with her, discouraging her displays of tenderness which, he succeeded in convincing himself, were designed to do no more than lure him into the vacuum. The Sunday afternoon of the abortive hurricane was the first time he had been in her room for many months. He had been doing his best to avoid entering it and Rani had not complained. She accepted his betrayal as she had accepted all those other betrayals of which her life had been compounded. It was as if those Sunday afternoons with her son had never existed.

During the last months of her life, Rani shrank further and further into some impregnable part of herself. She continued to boil the endless pots of milk, standing interminably in front of the stove and stirring the bubbling, frothing liquid with the bent metal spoon that burnt her fingers; she continued to sweep and scrub and polish; and she continued to serve her husband his food in silence, a daily witness to the ritual banging of the spoon on his plate and the cloud of flies ascending to circle balletically around the naked electric lightbulb. She was receptive to suffering in a way that most people are

66

not. Her dark eyes, deep-set in the recesses of a cadaverous face, gazed out blankly at the world and did not question the origin or purpose of that suffering. She had no standard of happiness against which to judge it.

In these last years, there was only one dramatic change: she took to wearing glasses. They were round and gold-rimmed, and, if not her most sentimentally precious, they were certainly her most expensive possession. She had saved up for them out of the monthly 'allowance' her husband had given her. 'Real twenty-two carat gold she gone and buy,' he exclaimed. 'Is why she family never get anywhere. All slaves is the same. Never-see-come-see – that's what they is.'

Egbert Ramsaran was disturbed by his wife's new acquisition: it reminded him of her presence. Her eyes, magnified to almost twice their normal size by the thick lenses, stared out from behind them and loomed at him, weak, wandering and jelly-like. He read into them accusation and resentment which she was not capable of intending. But he was not to know this, and he forbade her from wearing them in his presence. Basdai could scarcely contain herself when she learned of her daughter's doings. She believed pride and vanity alone could account for it: it was a piece of flagrant effrontery. 'Imagine doing a thing like that at she age! Treating money like it was water. Mind, I not saying she shouldn't have glasses if she really need them – though I must say I have my doubts about that. But, leaving that aside, you seriously want me to believe' (and here Basdai was so overwhelmed by the audacity Rani had displayed that she spluttered into guttural incredulity and had to cough and thump her chest) '... you seriously want *me* to believe that at she age she need *gold* glasses? She can't even make baby and she want *gold*' (another round of coughing and thumping) '... and she want *gold* glasses?' Then Rani lost most of her teeth. 'I suppose she going to fill up she mouth with gold teeth now,' Basdai said. She was disappointed. Rani contented herself with simple false teeth which she kept in a tumbler on her dressing-table.

Rani died in the week following the abortive hurricane, quietly and without fuss during the night. 'Cardiac seizure,' the doctor pronounced. 'If you had brought her to me for a regular check-up, this need never have happened.' Egbert Ramsaran did not take kindly to this rebuke. 'Next you going to be saying I murder she,' he replied heatedly. 'Nothing of the sort,' the doctor said calmly, 'all I said was that it need not have happened if she was having regular check-ups.' The use of the forbidden word enraged him. 'I know what you mean by check-ups,' he said. 'You just want people to come to you and waste they money. But I not going to make you rich.' 'I didn't come here to be insulted by you, Mr Ramsaran,' the doctor replied. 'But make no mistake. Your turn will come.' He departed, bristling with injured feeling.

The brown coffin lay in the house for one day. Singh arrived on the morning of the funeral. He did not stay long, behaving as if he had come merely to verify the truth of what he had heard and identify the body. Going up to the coffin, he took from his pocket an envelope and shook out into his palm some Trinidad one-cent stamps. Standing over the coffin, he tore them into bits and stuffed them back into the envelope. Such was his farewell to the woman who had frequently invoked the blessings of God on his behalf.

'What's that Singh was tearing up?' Egbert Ramsaran asked his son.

'Stamps.'

Egbert Ramsaran was puzzled. 'Stamps? But why would Singh want to be tearing up stamps for?'

Wilbert did not break the tacit agreement he had had with his mother. 'I don't know,' he said.

Egbert Ramsaran shrugged and dropped the subject. In the afternoon, a curious rather than grief-stricken procession followed the coffin to the hole that had been dug for it in the Victoria cemetery. Egbert Ramsaran, who had an eye for the niceties, resurrected the photograph taken on their wedding day and had it framed in gold-painted wood. It was hung in her bedroom. 'She couldn't have asked for any more,' Basdai remarked bitterly. 'She always had a liking for gold.'

Nevertheless, Rani's death was a tremendous loss to Basdai. She showered extravagant condolences on Egbert Ramsaran.

He received them for the most part in silence and with a pre-occupied air; lost, so it appeared, in remote speculations. It was a not unwelcome change from the abuse he normally directed against her and this distant cordiality added to her distress. Rani's inopportune death was conclusive proof – if conclusive proof were needed – of her inherent unreliability and worthlessness.

'You mustn't harass yourself,' Basdai advised her son-in-law – although he showed no signs of doing so. 'I going to work out something. I not going to leave you stranded. Don't think I ungrateful for everything you try to do for that worthless daughter of mine.'

Her concern amused him. 'What you going to do for me?' he asked. 'Which of your family you want to marry me off to this time?'

Basdai looked solemn when he said this. What the 'something' was remained a secret.

There was a subtle – at first almost imperceptible – change of mood and temper in Egbert Ramsaran following Rani's death. The distant cordiality with which he had treated Basdai was extended to the clients as a whole; and the air of being lost in remote speculations persisted. He became marginally more open and communicative. His odd gaiety surprised and somewhat disturbed Wilbert. The tiny hints of uncharacteristic indulgence he had begun to exhibit towards others was a reflection of the indulgence he had begun to exhibit towards himself. More than a burden had been lifted from him by her death. A lifetime's iron restraint was weakening. Egbert Ramsaran was losing the desire to cling to the rope he had spun across the abyss. He was running out of energy. He was tired. Freed of one burden, there arose the gnawing temptation to be freed of all burdens. Fortunately for him, he did not realize this.

He would neglect his exercises. Wilbert reminded him.

'Is only one day,' he said evasively. 'One day is neither here nor there.

'You never used to miss a day before.'

Egbert Ramsaran looked at his son. 'Whether I miss a day, a week or a month is none of your business. I not as young as I used to be. You should take that into consideration.'

'You not feeling too well?'

'Fit as a fiddle!' He laughed uneasily. 'Anyway, what is all this? Since when I have to explain what I doing to you? Since when you turning into a slave-driver, eh?'

Compared to what they had been, his audiences with the clients on Saturday and Sunday mornings were – relatively – mild affairs. To the women who broke down and wailed, he said: 'Go outside and do your crying. You giving me a headache with all that bawling and screaming.' If he aimed the pistols at their heads, it was clearer than it had ever been that the threat was not meant to be taken seriously. Externally, little had altered: a stranger might not have noted anything out of the ordinary; and have interpreted literally the threat implied with the gun aimed at his head. However, the clients were no strangers; they were skilled and avid students of the behaviour of their tormentor. Some intangible, unforeseen alchemy had been at work corroding the soul of Egbert Ramsaran and the clients had sniffed it out. The harsh school of necessity and fear had trained them to detect the minutest shifts in behaviour and attitude of their subject and their noses had seized on the scent immediately. A fissure had been created which they could attack. Thus, despite the fact that the same wooden chair was brought from the kitchen; despite the fact that they were confronted by the same glistening head; despite the fact that there was the same piping invective, the clients were no longer frightened out of their wits. They were still frightened – but not out of their wits. That, from their point of view, was progress. When the gun was directed at their heads, they cowered to a lesser degree; and did not retreat with their former haste towards the door. The props remained: the difference was that they were recognized by the clients for what they were: mere props. Their eyes and ears and noses had informed them with unerring accuracy of a shift of which Egbert Ramsaran himself was not aware.

There were other signs of a faltering strength of will. He

was anxious to justify and rationalize what he had done in the past. In a sense, he had always done this: Egbert Ramsaran liked to hold himself up as a shining example. But whereas the philosophy of life described in his boastful moods had been instinctive, springing from the depths of his own personality and experience, it now seemed that that instinct was dying. He was shoring himself up with shadows of vanishing glories. The smouldering fire, which had impressed and appalled Vishnu Bholai, was being slowly damped down and extinguished and his words were like ashes. And perhaps, in an unconscious effort to fan the flames of the dying fire, ashen words flowed compulsively from his lips. His descriptions of himself and his exploits were tinged with an unperceived (unperceived, that is, by Egbert Ramsaran) nostalgia which increased Wilbert's uneasiness about his father. He could not accommodate himself to the change and it was lasting too long to be dismissed as simply another example of his capriciousness. The reduction in scale was unacceptable to the designated heir of the Ramsaran Transport Company. He had grown accustomed to the cut-out cardboard figure of the man of iron will and these glimpses of ordinary human frailty upset him.

2

Basdai was an extraordinarily thin and spare woman with arms and legs like knotted sticks. Her narrow, bony face was lined and wrinkled to an astonishing degree and her cheeks had caved in on her nearly toothless mouth. Being one of those people who consider the mere accumulation of years as in itself worthy of admiration and devotion, she was proud of her appearance: it was only her bright and alert eyes which hinted at something other than decrepitude.

She smoked cigarettes stooping in a corner of the hut, refusing to sit on either chair or bench, though there were several of these scattered about. Burying the cigarette inside her cupped palms, she inhaled with a hissing, sucking wheeze. The cigarettes made her cough terribly, especially at night when she lay on her pallet gasping for breath. There was another luxury which she did not scruple to indulge on the slightest pretext: her taste for cheap white rum. She asserted strenuously it was 'good' for her cough and used to send her grandchildren to the local rumshop, the Palace of Heavenly Delights, to buy her 'nips'. 'Remember,' Basdai warned, 'if Farouk ask you what I want it for say is for my medicine. Medicine for my cough – you understand that? And don't let him cheat you. You should get so much (marking off the amount on her index finger) for six cents.'

The rum was kept in a bottle which had formerly contained cough mixture and Basdai always referred straightfacedly to her 'cough-mixture'. These sessions of hers were strictly private and she emerged from them still coughing but more garrulous and bright-eyed than ever. 'Ma been soothing she chest again' became an established saying. Gradually, the amount Basdai spent on her cough-mixture crept up from six to eight to ten cents; and eventually, she added a new instruction. 'Tell Farouk I is a little short of cash at the moment and I go pay him at the end of the week.' The debt accumulated. But Farouk – some felt a shade too obligingly – never hurried her.

The immediate effect of Rani's death on Basdai was to push up her consumption of her cough-mixture from ten cents' worth to twelve cents' worth; the amount, in fact, represented by the length of her index finger. Her daughter's death had assumed in her mind the proportions of a catastrophe: the prospect of losing her connection – however tenuous it had been – with Egbert Ramsaran was too terrible for her to contemplate. She had derived nothing from it to date and now it appeared more unlikely that she ever would. It was one of the principles round which she had organized her life and it was inconceivable that she should discard it. Therefore, her response to the situation was as automatic as a reflex action: the vacancy in the Ramsaran household had to be filled somehow and filled quickly before it was too late. She cast around desperately for a possible substitute to replace the prematurely worn-out part.

Happily, Basdai was one of the most acute students of Egbert Ramsaran and she had instantly sniffed out the subtly altered atmosphere. She did not know quite what construction to put on it and returned home from the funeral in an extremely thoughtful frame of mind. Could she have been mistaken? To guard against error, she went again to the house in Victoria. And again. No. She was not mistaken. Basdai returned to the Settlement from their third visit to Victoria, her imagination teeming with plots. It was obvious that a mere substitute for Rani was not what was required. Something more was needed; a new departure.

But what. Basdai secluded herself and pondered over glass after glass of white rum. She smiled. The thought had occurred to her that Rani's death might not be the calamitous misfortune she had assumed it to be at first glance. She inched her way step by step, gradually refining and honing down her crude assessment until she arrived at the triumphant conclusion that her daughter's death was a blessing in disguise, opening new spheres of influence to her. An irritating obstacle had been removed. Had Rani been other than a liability? An unadorned animal-cunning guided Basdai through this maze of speculation. She was enthralled by her cleverness. It was like a game played for no end beyond the pleasure and satisfaction it afforded. She studied the bottle of cough-mixture in front of her. The solution was clear, writ large across the heavens and she was thankful she had been able to diagnose the symptoms so accurately. With the hunter's skill and intuition, she had divined the weakness of her quarry and was ready to bait the trap. None but Sushila would do. The only problem was to secure her cooperation.

For reasons unspecified, Sushila had been left in the care of Basdai when still a young girl. It was generally assumed that she was a distant relation, but the connection – if there was one – had never been satisfactorily explained and remained wrapped in obscurity. Sushila had combined considerable beauty with independence of spirit. It was an inflammable mixture, transforming the charming, self-centred child into the wayward, reckless young woman who, by the

73

time she was sixteen had twice fled from the constraints of the Settlement to taste the freedom that lay beyond its borders. Abuse and beatings did not deter her. Sushila, sustained by her beauty and the dividends it brought her, persisted in her contrariness. She duly scandalized everyone by becoming pregnant. The man responsible was never caught. Suspicion settled on Farouk, bachelor at large and proprietor of the Settlement's sole house of entertainment, the Palace of Heavenly Delights (he was a humourist).

It was natural that suspicion should settle on Farouk. The village had long harboured resentment against him. They disliked the niggardly quantities of rum he doled out over the counter in his cramped, smelly establishment; they disliked him because he himself ostentatiously never drank – at least not in public; they disliked him because he excluded a shabby, good-humoured prosperity; they disliked him because he was the only Muslim in a predominantly Hindu village; they disliked him because there was no alternative to the Palace of Heavenly Delights for miles around; they disliked him because he had the reputation of being an unscrupulous womanizer – they observed the way he eyed the young girls when they went with their buckets to fetch water from the standpipe. 'Is a scandal for a big man like that to be getting on so,' it was said. These were the concrete grievances, but there were others less concrete and possibly even more damning as a result. Farouk was a genuinely puzzling case to his neighbours: an enigma. He had not been born in the Settlement. Claiming to have lived many years in Port-of-Spain and to know the city as well as he knew the palm of his hand ('if not better'), Farouk had transported with him the superior habits of a man of the world. He endeavoured to dress with a certain style and panache and tended to use words and turns of phrase which no one but himself could understand. To the Settlement, it was a subject of wonder and speculation that, of all the possible places open to him, he should have chosen to come among them. It was taken for granted that no one in his right mind would voluntarily do such a thing. The Settlement was the sort of place where you had the misfortune to

74

be born or to which you had the even greater misfortune to come as an unsuspecting bride. It was definitely not the sort of place to which you came voluntarily. Therefore, from the very beginning, Farouk's presence had been highly suspicious. 'He have murder on he conscience,' they said.

Farouk steadfastly disclaimed all responsibility for Sushila's pregnancy and Sushila herself obstinately refused to throw any light on the matter. However, the fury and indignation aroused by the affair was not so easily quelled and in a burst of spontaneous anger an attempt was made to set fire to the Palace of Heavenly Delights, but the blaze was quickly put out and the damage was minimal. Farouk laughed the incident off. 'I have insurance,' he said, 'so I'll be only too glad if somebody burn me down one day. The money will come in very handy. But if I was to go from here, what you think will happen? You think it have other people crazy enough like me to come to a place behind God back and start up a rumshop? I could set up in Port-of-Spain or San Fernando any day, you know.' He clicked his fingers. 'I doing you people a favour. After what happen I have a good mind to up and go.' But he never did; and there was no further attempt at insurrection.

Sanctions could not persuade Sushila to divulge the name of the child's father and Basdai drew the appropriate conclusion. 'I wouldn't be surprise if Sushila sheself don't know who the father is,' she said. 'I wouldn't put anything past she. That girl was born with wickedness inside of she.' It was an opinion shared by the rest of the Settlement. Consequently, the child's ancestry was no less wrapped in obscurity than the mother's.

If as a result of what happened, Basdai expected Sushila to have learned a 'lesson' and to be suitably contrite and submissive, she must have been profoundly disappointed. Sushila exhibited no remorse whatever, shamelessly flaunting herself and boldly continuing to associate with Farouk. Her journeys to the standpipe to collect water were not walks: they were leisurely parades. She gloried in her notoriety and evidently relished the stir she had created. Pregnancy, far from being a 'lesson', had been her emancipation: she was a full-fledged woman after it. Basdai might still abuse her but she could not beat or strike her any more. Abuse meant nothing to Sushila; and if anyone struck her she was prepared to repay the compliment in kind.

Despite Sita (the name she had bestowed on her child), there were men willing and ready to marry her; to make, as they said, a respectable woman of her. Sushila was not ready, even in the face of Basdai's dire threatenings to murder both her and Sita, to be made a respectable woman. 'Is not my respectability they want,' she laughed, 'is something else.' 'Think of Sita,' she was urged by the more rational spirits, 'what the future going to be like for her? Think of what it would mean to Sita if she have nobody she could call father.' The argument did not impress Sushila. 'I manage well enough without anybody to call father,' she answered. 'What make Sita so special?'

When Sita was old enough to walk, Sushila disappeared from the Settlement, abandoning her daughter to the mercies of Basdai. Where and how she lived was a mystery. Now people claimed to have seen her in Port-of-Spain, now in San Fernando. And, although she had no visible means of support, the invisible ones were clearly ample and she appeared to prosper. As Egbert Ramsaran had done before her, she returned to the Settlement at unpredictable intervals, always looking cheerful, healthy and unrepentant and bringing gifts with her: toys and dresses for Sita and half-bottles of white rum for Basdai – who made a great show of reluctance before accepting what was brought her.

'How I know where you get it from?' she would ask. 'For all I know it might be thief you thief it and then, before I might realize what happening, the police going to be swarming all over the place searching and questioning.' It was substantially the same warning given to the parents of Egbert Ramsaran years earlier but the memory had dimmed.

'You could take it or leave it,' Sushila replied carelessly. 'I not fussy one way or the other. Is not water off my back.'

Basdai grasped the bottle more tightly. 'I'll take it this

time,' she conceded. 'But remember, if the police come round here asking question, I not going to lie for you. I going to say straight out is thief you thief it.' Her conscience soothed, she would hurry away clutching the bottle close to her bosom.

The duration of Sushila's stay was as unpredictable as her arrival, varying from barely an hour to almost a week. It was never clear what obscure impulses prompted her descents on the place and her abrupt removals from it. Sushila was not in the habit of divulging her plans and, if questioned, she would merely smile mysteriously and with a shake of her head say: 'I can't tell you because I don't know myself. It depend on how I feel.' Her visits could be more correctly described as appearances and disappearances rather than arrivals and departures. Without a word or a change of expression, she might suddenly arise and stroll out into the yard casually, as if she were going for a drink of water; and when after ten minutes someone called out for her and received no answer, it was understood she had gone for at least another six weeks.

It was Sita who, living in constant subjection to the vagaries of an unsympathetic household, received the curses that ought, by right, to have been reserved for her mother. 'You going to turn out just like that wretch,' she was informed gleefully. 'Good blood does never come out of bad blood.' Happily for her, she was never actually beaten; but it was only fear of what Sushila might do that saved her from the brutalities regularly inflicted on Basdai's grandchildren. Sushila, perceiving her power, made use of it. The first question she would ask on meeting her daughter (accompanied by a lowering glance at those present) was whether any of them had been mistreating and 'taking advantage' of her during her absence. To which Sita invariably replied 'No'. 'That's good,' her mother replied. 'Is exactly what I want to hear. I hope it remain like that because the day any of these bitches so much as lay they little finger on you, the Devil go have to pay the price.' These threats were vague; unenforceable bravado. But Sushila inspired sufficient respect to make them seem real enough.

Her attentions, while she remained, were devoted chiefly

to Sita. It was as if she desired in those few hours or days to erase from her daughter's mind the memory of her desertion and to compensate for all the maternal laxities of the preceding weeks; to demonstrate by public exhibitions of affection the abiding love she cherished towards her. She was unwilling to let Sita out of her sight or retreat beyond her touch, perpetually kissing, stroking and caressing her. Sushila demanded to be shown what she had been doing at school (she paid the fees) and went into ecstasies that she should be so 'bright' and get such good reports. She spent many hours combing and searching through her hair for lice; bathed her; and dressed her, promising to bring her more new clothes from 'town' the next time she came. They went for long walks together, brazening the disgust of the Settlement, Sita decked in her city finery and with Sushila's arms draped in defiant possession about her shoulders. It was an orgy of affection while her visits lasted.

At the end of each visit, Sita cried. This embarrassed and irritated Sushila. 'What you crying for, foolish child?' she chided her with something less than her usual benevolence. 'Look at the nice dress I bring for you. I'll bring more from town for you the next time. Now stop your crying and be sensible. Is not as if I going away for good.' Once, when Sushila had made her apparently casual exit, Sita had run screaming after her to the main road. 'Don't leave me here,' she begged, clinging to her mother's skirt. 'Take me away with you. I want to come and live with you.' Sushila was flustered by this demonstration. 'What nonsense is all this, child? You can't come to live with me.' 'Why?' 'Because you can't. That's why. Now stop fussing and let go of me. You spoiling my clothes with all those tears. If you don't behave yourself I won't bring anything for you the next time I come.' Sushila's maternity had melted tracelessly. She flagged down a taxi. Sita was still clinging tenaciously to her skirt. Sushila extracted herself brusquely from her daughter's grasp and, climbing into the taxi, slammed the door shut. Then she smiled radiantly into Sita's tearstained face. 'Be a good girl and stop crying. And if any of them lay they little finger on you . . .' The taxi drove off in a cloud of dust and Sushila's words were swallowed in the roar of the engine as it gathered speed. This incident, witnessed by the Settlement at large, more than counterbalanced Sushila's maternal pretensions.

'If you love Sita so much,' Phulo, one of Basdai's daughters-in-law, caustically observed to her on a later occasion, 'why don't you take her to live with you? That is what I can't understand about this whole business. You say you love she and yet...'

Sushila was momentarily thrown off balance and did not answer immediately.

Phulo pursued her advantage. 'You should hear how the child does cry for you. She does keep me awake all night with the crying and bawling whenever you leave. I feel you don't love she at all. Is only mouth...' Phulo became goading: there was no love lost between Sushila and herself.

Sushila did not recover her composure but she recovered her voice. 'Who the hell is you to talk to me like that, eh? What business of yours is it what I do or don't do? Whatever happen between me and Sita is mine and Sita's business. Not yours. But don't think I going to leave she here for the rest of you to take advantage of she.' Sushila cradled Sita. 'You mustn't let these foolish people and they idle talk bother you. You hear that? Is just they jealous...'

'Jealous!' Phulo expostulated. 'Me jealous! What you have for me to be jealous of? At least my children have a man they could call father...'

Sushila ignored her. '...one day you and me going to live together. I had that plan a long time ago. But is not convenient for me to do that right now. But the time not far off. You is my daughter. Don't let none of them forget that. My daughter!' Phulo sniggered. 'I'll eat my hat the day that happen.'

'The trouble is,' Sushila said, 'you don't have no hat to eat. You don't have a damn thing to call your own. You just wait. Soon you will be laughing on the other side of your face.'

It seemed that Phulo was right. The years slipped by and the 'day' did not arrive. Sita had stopped crying and the project appeared to have been shelved. Shelved – but not entirely forgotten because, periodically, Phulo would surface with her uncomfortable reminders to which Sushila responded with the unchanged mixture of promises and insults.

Sushila was astounded at the suggestion Basdai put to her on her next visit to the Settlement.

'You must be joking,' she exclaimed. 'Either that' or you going out of your mind. Like I have to stop bringing you all that rum. It must be rotting your brains.'

Basdai shook her head. 'I was never so serious in my life,' she replied. 'The rum have nothing to do with it.'

Sushila retreated a step or two and clapping her hands on her hips, surveyed Basdai incredulously. 'You must be joking! You couldn't really be serious – if I hear you right the first time, that is.'

Basdai shook her head again. 'You hear me right the first time. Is no joke I making with you. I is being serious. How you feel about it? I don't expect you to make up your mind straight away but . . .'

'What you take me for?' Sushila exploded. 'A servant? A housemaid? If that is the case, you talking to the wrong person. Why pick on me? That is what I would like to know. If you so anxious to find somebody to take Rani place – and frankly I don't see why you so concerned about him – why don't you ask Phulo? Or one of your daughters? Why ask me? I sure somebody like Phulo would be only too glad to help out.' Sushila tittered.

'Phulo and my daughters is out of the question – as you well know. They is married women with husbands to look after. You on the other hand . . .' Basdai smiled equably.

'Although I have no husband I too have my own life to lead. Imagine you having the nerve to suggest that I take Rani place! I can't believe it.'

'You not going to be taking Rani place,' Basdai explained patiently.

'What else you would call it then? And with a man like that to boot! I hear enough about him. They does talk as if he is the devil himself.'

'He is no devil. Take my word.' Basdai was serene.

'Look at what he do to Rani. If you think . . .'

Basdai smiled. 'What happen to Rani won't happen to you. For a start, is not as if you going to be married to him. If you don't like it, you could leave. Anyway,' she added slyly, 'I thought you would know well enough how to handle a man like that. You frighten of him?'

Sushila's professional pride was offended by the suggestion. 'No man could frighten me,' she replied. 'That have nothing to do with it.'

'That is exactly what I thought,' Basdai intercepted smoothly. 'And if no man could frighten you, then you have nothing to worry about. As I was saying, if you don't like it there . . .' Basdai clasped her hands together. 'Egbert Ramsaran is no devil and you could be the one to prove it. Just think of what it could mean.'

'You mean . . .' Sushila's anger dissolved. She burst out laughing. 'If I understand you right, what you trying to tell me is . . .'

'Exactly,' Basdai said. 'Exactly.'

Sushila's laughter flooded the small hut. 'What a little schemer you is! So this is what you been planning behind my back. But I haven't gone crazy as yet – not so crazy anyway.' She circled round Basdai. 'I can't think why I wasting my time standing up here arguing with you. If is a woman Egbert Ramsaran want, let him find one for himself. For a man with so much money, it shouldn't be hard for him to find somebody to come and jiggle they backside in front of him.'

Basdai looked pained. 'You being very crude,' she said. 'I didn't say anything about him wanting another woman to come and . . .' Basdai was considering. 'Whatever happen is up to you. Just try it out for a bit. It won't kill you. Just a trial. You never know . . .'

Curiosity welled in Sushila. 'Why me though? Who tell you he will . . .?'

'Don't worry your head about that.' Basdai was contemplative. 'Nobody else would do but you.'

'Like you ask him already?' Sushila narrowed her eyes suspiciously.

'No, no,' Basdai assured her hastily. She smoothed her voice down to a confidential, entreating level. 'Just think what it could mean for you. Comfort. Security . . .'

'If it was comfort and security I wanted, I would have got married long before now.'

Basdai waved aside her objection. 'He have a whole house with only Wilbert in it and you always saying you want somewhere for you and Sita to live together. Well, here's your big chance if you act sensible and stop playing stubborn. If he like you, you could get Sita in there in no time at all.'

'You is a sly one,' Sushila said laughingly. 'I never would have thought it. You really surprising me.'

Basdai was modest. 'Is not slyness. Is common sense. Think about it. Take your time. But remember is a once in a lifetime chance for you and Sita. What you have to lose?'

Sushila knitted her brows. 'One thing still puzzling me though. Why you doing all this? You can't be doing it for my sake. Or for Sita sake. I find that hard to understand. After all the things you call me in your time, then to want me to go and butter up your precious son-in-law . . .'

Basdai radiated a diplomatic discretion. She batted her eyelids sleepily. 'He might be grateful to me for bringing you there. But I not asking for anything. Even you might be grateful to me for . . .'

Sushila smiled reflectively. 'Is an interesting idea. Give me time. I'll have to think about it.'

'Take all the time you want,' Basdai said in an access of generosity. She was well pleased with her progress.

Later that afternoon, when the sun had cooled and was floating fiery and low over the canefields, Sushila and Sita set off on one of their excursions through the Settlement, following the extended curve of the narrow main road that cut its way like a scythe through the Settlement. The field workers were returning home, pedalling slowly on their bicycles. Women were filling their buckets at the standpipe. Sushila and Sita walked past them in silence, arm in arm, chased forward by their hostile gaze. One of the women muttered something and the rest giggled. Whenever a car approached they stepped on to the verge and waited for it to go by, Sushila holding her head with an erect insolence. The houses threw cool shadows astride their path. Children were playing in the dusty yards among clucking hens. Sushila and Sita were twin objects of curiosity to their parents rocking in their rickety verandahs and fanning themselves with newspapers. In virtually every house they passed, the radio was on. Sushila smiled at each face shielding behind its newspaper and received no sign of recognition in return. Sita tried to walk faster. These expeditions were a torment to her and she could not understand what compulsion led her mother to submit them both to this blatantly unfriendly scrutiny. Things were bad enough as they were: there was no need to make them worse by throwing down a pointless challenge.

'What you hurrying for?' Sushila held her back. 'They can't eat us.'

Sita slowed her pace and fell in step again beside her mother. Now and again Sushila giggled to herself: she was considering Basdai's suggestion from all its angles, trying as best she could to weigh up the advantages and disadvantages. The idea, outlandish as it was (doubtless because of that), attracted her more and more. Egbert Ramsaran! The devil himself! Sushila giggled. It would be interesting; amusing even. She had, as Basdai had said, nothing to lose and, with luck, much to gain from the adventure if it were successful; it would infuriate all those watching them go past. They would scarcely be able to contain themselves. She laughed out loud.

'What you laughing at?' Sita asked.

'Nothing. Nothing. Keep your eyes on the road.'

They were approaching the ramshackle splendour of the Palace of Heavenly Delights with its multicoloured signs for various drinks glinting in the sun. It heightened Sushila's festive mood. A hum of drunken conversation drifted out through the swing doors of the greying, wooden building. Two old men, nursing glasses of rum on their knees, were sitting on boxes in the shade of the eaves playing draughts and talking softly. They left off their game to watch the two figures approach and leant forward to exchange whispers.

'Talk all you want,' Sushila muttered. 'It never kill anybody yet.'

The sugarcane fields were visible behind the Palace of Heavenly Delights, blades bending before the wind. Clouds of golden dust swirled in flowing patterns; a shimmering, hazy curtain. Farouk appeared behind the swing doors of his establishment, drying the nape of his neck with a handkerchief, his face oiled with sweat, his curling, jet-black moustache shining. He folded the handkerchief and stuffed it into his shirt pocket.

'How you doing, Mistress Sushila?' he shouted. 'How long you staying with we this time?' He smiled genially. His teeth were very white and well formed.

Sushila waved gaily and tilted her head. She stopped. Farouk lurched nonchalantly towards them.

'How's business?' Sushila asked.

'The same,' Farouk said. 'Always the same. These bitches around here don't buy any but the cheapest rum.' He scrutinized her interestedly, his eyes travelling slowly down the length of her body. 'And you is the same too. As beautiful as ever.'

Sushila giggled. 'Enough of that,' she said pleasantly.

Sita stared at the man who people said was her father and then at her mother who held her head erect and unashamed.

'Is a good thing you never get married,' Farouk said. 'You'd have been too much for the poor fella.'

Sushila acknowledged the compliment with a smile of voluptuous approval. 'You shouldn't be saying such things in front of my young daughter.'

Farouk looked at Sita. 'A budding beauty too.' He was jocular. 'Soon she going to be having all the men around here basodee about she – just like you used to have them.'

'Is a long time till that,' Sushila said with the merest hint of displeasure. 'You shouldn't be putting such ideas into her head.'

84

Farouk tickled Sita under the chin. She shrank back from him.

'I surprised to hear you of all people say that. You wasn't much older when . . .'

'I am me. Sita is Sita.' Sushila pressed her lips together petulantly. 'She more interested in getting a good education. Not so, Sita?'

'You frighten of the competition?' Farouk squinted at her jokingly.

'It going to be dark soon,' Sushila said. 'We'll talk about all that another time.'

They walked on. Ahead of them was the Bholai grocery, dour and businesslike, its solid red doors shut and bolted for the day. Mrs Bholai was rocking on the verandah above the shop, the top of her head visible above the newspaper she was reading. Julian leant over the iron railings, his hair hanging down in front of his face.

'There's the future Dr Julian Bholai,' Sushila said, pointing at him.

Sita looked up, catching his eye. Julian grinned sheepishly.

'He's a good-looking little boy, don't you think?' Sushila went on. 'You know him?'

'Who?' Sita's mind was on Farouk and the torments of the return journey.

'Julian, stupid. Who else? You know him?'

'No,' Sita said quickly. 'His mother don't like me.'

'You shouldn't let that old bitch bother you.'

'She don't bother me,' Sita said.

At that moment, Mrs Bholai's voice spoke sharply but indecipherably and Julian's face disappeared behind the verandah rail, as if he had been tugged violently. The newspaper followed their progress. It was then Sushila made her decision.

'How you would feel if I was to say I was going to take you away from here soon?'

Sita looked up at her mother, surprised. She did not answer.

Her silence irritated Sushila. Delicious images of revenge were swirling like dustclouds in her imagination. 'You want to go on living in the Settlement for the rest of your life?'

'No.' Sita stared at her mother's indistinct face. 'But . . .'

'But what?'

'If you're only doing it because of Phulo . . .'

'Phulo have nothing to do with it,' she rasped. 'All I want to know is whether you want to go on living in the Settlement for the rest of your life?'

'No,' Sita said.

'Good,' Sushila replied. 'I always say I would take you away from here and I going to keep my promise.'

A few yards beyond where they were, the main road straightened itself and ran unhindered through the high banks of sugarcane, disappearing from view over the crest of a gentle rise. On it rolled to San Fernando and places further afield; places Sita had never visited. Sushila had travelled up and down its length so many times, she had long since ceased to be affected by its promises – real and illusory. For Sita, however, it was still a magic carpet.

'No,' she repeated. 'I don't want to live here for the rest of my life.'

Sushila laughed.

'Where you taking me? San Fernando?'

'No. Not San Fernando.'

'Port-of-Spain?' Sita glanced in the opposite direction.

'Not Port-of-Spain either. I can't tell you yet. Is not definite. But one way or the other I taking you away from here. You have to be patient though. It will take time to work out.'

'I can wait,' Sita said. 'A few more months won't make any difference.'

The sun had sunk out of sight and the first lights had come on in the Settlement. Verandahs emptied. The night was cool.

'Is time we was getting back,' Sushila said.

A week later Basdai arrived at the house in Victoria with Sushila in tow. Brushing importantly past Wilbert, she hustled Sushila into the sitting-room. Sushila did not need the encouragement. Wilbert followed speechlessly.

'Don't overdo it,' Basdai whispered. 'Remember you have to make a good impression. Let me do the talking.'

Sushila slowed her pace and laughed, allowing her stride to fall into a lazier, more slatternly rhythm. She winked at Wilbert and, resting her hands on her hips, stared inquisitively round her. In what was a good imitation of her son-in-law, Basdai pushed her into one of the armchairs. 'Sit there and behave yourself,' she commanded. 'You will spoil everything if you not careful.' Her calm growing with each new assault from Basdai, Sushila arranged herself with careful deliberation in the chair and, crossing her knees, she awaited further instructions. 'You have to learn to behave yourself if you want to stay here.'

'Stay here!' Wilbert exclaimed involuntarily and with deepening astonishment as the spectacle unfolded. 'She going to stay here?'

Basdai smiled serenely. 'Go and tell your father we come,' she said in the same peremptory tone she had been using with her wilful charge. Then, recollecting herself, she added more politely: 'He expecting we.'

'He didn't tell me he was expecting anybody today.'

'You just go and tell him we come,' she urged, primly confident.

'He resting. You know he doesn't like . . .'

'Since when I have to be asking your lordship permission for who I see or don't see? Eh? Since when? I is still the master around here.' The door to the front bedroom had opened and Egbert Ramasaran stood there in his dressing-gown, staring coldly at his son. He turned to Basdai. 'This boy been behaving very peculiar of late. I don't know what is the matter with him.'

'I didn't know you was expecting . . .'

'Quiet!'

Wilbert stuttered into obedient silence. He bowed his head.

'Good.' Egbert Ramsaran, pulling the cord of his dressinggown tighter, directed a sardonic gaze towards his mother-inlaw. 'Now,' he said, 'tell me what it is bring you here to disturb my peace.'

'Well, you remember, ever since Rani died . . .'

'Yes, yes. I remember well enough. Get to the point.'

Basdai discarded the speech she had rehearsed. 'Well, to

cut a long story short, Sushila here say she willing to come and look after you and Wilbert. She is a strong, healthy...' Basdai proceeded to enumerate all the desirable qualities her own daughter had so patently lacked.

'Sushila!' Egbert Ramsaran transferred his sardonic gaze to her, giving the impression he had only just then become aware of her presence. Sushila returned his scrutiny unabashedly, a smile animated the edges of her lips.

'Stand up, girl, when your elders and betters speaking to you. And wipe that smile off your face.' Basdai fidgeted.

Not taking her eyes off Egbert Ramsaran, Sushila uncrossed her legs and raised herself languidly from the chair in one smooth, fluid movement. Egbert Ramsaran was visibly discomfited by this accomplished performance. The sardonic expression which he had borne down on her seeped away and in its place came something like interest and curiosity. His self-assurance flickered unstably. He turned away abruptly, frowning, and addressed himself to his son.

'You expect me to spend the whole morning standing up like this?'

Wilbert did not understand immediately.

'A chair, boy! A chair!' he ground out irritably between his teeth. 'Go to the kitchen and get me a chair.'

Wilbert hastened to the kitchen.

In his absence, no one spoke. Egbert Ramsaran, his hands buried deep in the voluminous pockets of his dressing-gown, assumed his by now familiar air of being lost in remote speculations. Sushila, who had resumed her seat, watched him expectantly as did Basdai who was trying to decipher and assess his reaction. Wilbert returned with the wooden chair and placed it in its usual position in the centre of the room. Egbert Ramsaran sat down. It seemed to restore some of his composure. He drew his knees together in his schoolgirlish fashion.

'What kind of relation Sushila is to you?' He gazed sternly at Basdai.

'Oh!' she answered, waving her arms in a vague flourish, 'Sushila come from somewhere on my husband side.' She did not elaborate.

'Where on you husband side? The right? The left?'

'To tell the truth, I not sure from where she come exactly. My husband never tell me.'

'She just drop down out of the sky, eh! Plop! Like that.' Egbert Ramsaran clapped his hands.

Basdai's resigned smile seemed to suggest that this was precisely what had occurred. She was thankful he did not pursue the point any further.

'She married?' He was behaving as if Sushila were not there.

'Well . . .' Basdai executed her vague flourish.

'Either she married or she not married. You must know that.' Egbert Ramsaran glowered at the hapless Basdai.

'To be frank with you, Sushila not married,' Basdai admitted helplessly.

'How come? That is a little funny for someone of she age, not so?' His forehead furrowed questioningly.

Basdai hesitated. 'It just never work out that way with Sushila. Is like that with some people. But it don't mean nothing bad. Sushila just never meet the right man. That's all.'

Egbert Ramsaran looked at her doubtfully. 'It never stop any of you before,' he said.

Basdai giggled. She had nothing else to say to him. Her cunning was letting her down.

'Though I never get married,' Sushila broke suddenly into the conversation, attempting to lure his attention to herself, 'I have a child – a daughter called Sita. She's about your son age in fact. Maybe a little younger.' She sat forward on the edge of her chair, craning her neck towards him; willing him to look at her.

'I tell you to let me do the talking, girl. When we want to hear you, we will ask. Sita have nothing to do with all this.'

'I have a tongue to do my own talking with.'

'You don't have to worry your head about Sita,' Basdai assured Egbert Ramsaran hastily. 'That is why I didn't mention she in the first place. Sita going to be staying with me. We arrange all that already. Anyway, she's a big enough girl to take care of sheself.'

'Sita is a very bright child,' Sushila explained. 'She very

interested in education and that kind of thing. When she grow up she want to be a B.A. Languages.'

Caught in the crossfire, Egbert Ramsaran seemed not to have heard a single word.

'Why you never get married?' At last he turned to look at Sushila.

'Marriage didn't agree with me,' Sushila replied readily, pleased she had captured the conversation. 'Is not for all of us. I don't like being tied down too much.'

Egbert Ramsaran, rubbing his chin, nodded sympathetically. 'It didn't agree with me either.'

'Women is no different from men in that respect. For some – like me – is as bad as it is for some men. Even worse because is always easier for a man to get away.'

'What about the child father? Where is he?' Egbert Ramsaran asked.

Basdai fidgeted.

Sushila, however, was in firm control. She parried neatly. 'He run like greased lightning when he find out I was making a baby for him. He might be dead for all I know – I never see him since.'

'So, he give you a baby and he run. You let him fool you.' Egbert Ramsaran spoke with satisfaction.

Sushila was affronted. 'He didn't fool me. I wouldn't let no man make a fool of me.'

'Still, he give you a baby . . .'

'The baby was an accident – that is the price you have to pay for being a woman.' She grimaced. 'Mind you,' she went on, as if justifying herself, 'he was very nice. Very handsome. I even used to think I was in love with him . . . for a while.'

'In love!' He stared balefully at her.

Sushila laughed. 'I was a young girl at the time and I used to fall in love with nearly every man I meet.' Tilting her head, she stared at him out of the corners of her eyes.

Egbert Ramsaran smiled in spite of himself. But it was a smile tinged with a vaguely formulated apprehension.

'I could never stand the Settlement,' Sushila continued,

90

guiding the conversation away from her pregnancy and into what she suspected would be a more fruitful channel. 'I had run away twice when I was a girl – before I ever get pregnant.'

Basdai fidgeted.

'Is that so?' Egbert Ramsaran elevated his eyebrows. He showed interest. 'Where did you used to go?'

'Anywhere. The further the better.'

'I was like that too,' he said reflectively, retreating momentarily into that air of distant cordiality. 'I had . . .' (he laughed) . . . 'I had very big ideas. I always wanted to get away. Everywhere you turned in that place was one thing and one thing only. Sugar . . .'

'. . . cane,' Sushila completed the word triumphantly. 'I know exactly what you mean. Everywhere you turn . . .'

'Even now to see sugarcane . . .' He wagged his head.

Her tactic had worked. Sushila glanced at Basdai. 'She used to beat me up for running away.'

Basdai was apologetic. 'What else I could have do?' Nevertheless, she was pleased with the way things were going: very pleased and therefore happy to accept the blame.

A thought occurred to Egbert Ramsaran. 'Why you want to come and work here?'

Sushila laughed. 'I hear so much about you in the Settlement and everywhere else. I remember how excited everybody was when you married Rani.'

'What you hear about me?'

'That you was worse than the devil himself!'

'Not true,' Basdai put in. 'Not true at all.'

They ignored her.

'Supposing,' Egbert Ramsaran said tentatively, 'you came here, how long you think you will stay?'

'That depends. If you is really the devil they say you is, a few minutes at the most.'

'And if I is not the devil they say I is?'

'Then it will depend on . . . on how I feel. I never like staying in one place for too long.'

Egbert Ramsaran scowled. 'I is not an easy man to get on

with. When I say I want a thing done just so, I mean I want it done just so.' He was endeavouring, but in vain, to marshal his ferocity.

'So they say.'

'You don't believe me?'

'I believe you,' she said simply, her eyes feeding on his face. 'It have just one other thing. If I come here, I must be free to come and go as I please.'

'Of course. You is not a prisoner.' Egbert Ramsaran got up.

'Sushila is a very hard worker,' Basdai put in. 'She won't give you no trouble.'

'We'll wait and see,' he said. 'I'll give it a try. We need a woman about the place . . .' He paused in confusion.

Basdai beamed. 'That is all we want. A trial. If you not satisfy . . .'

The rest of her words were wasted on him as the door to his bedroom closed.

After the interview, Wilbert listened to his father pacing about the bedroom. Late that evening, he was summoned with an irritable shout. Egbert Ramsaran had stopped his pacing and was lying in bed, the thin cotton sheet drawn up to his neck. All the windows in the room had been thrown wide open, the lace curtains drooping lifelessly in the still air. The detective novel of the moment lay unopened on his chest and the almanac was awry on its rusted nail. From the cupboard above the bed was wafted the musty odour of patent medicines. But there all similarity with previous encounters of the kind ended. An infantile truculence had taken hold of Egbert Ramsaran. The untidy bed told the tale of his restlessness. His cheeks were flushed and he seemed unable to keep his arms and legs motionless. He hauled himself upright when Wilbert entered the room.

'What you standing up there looking so stupid for?' His voice whistled. 'Look at that almanac. Never straight. Nothing is ever straight in this house. Do something about the almanac. Make yourself useful for a change.' He shook the rippling sheet.

Wilbert straightened the calendar as best he could and waited.

'Sit! Sit! I can't talk with you standing up there like a statue.' Waving his hands pettishly, he tapped the edge of the bed. Wilbert sat down. Egbert Ramsaran massaged his stomach and groaned. He flung back the sheet. 'Look at it. Tight as a drum tonight.' Reaching up, he unhooked the catch of the medicine cupboard and feeling his way among the multitudes of bottles and boxes and tins, extracted from it the blue Milk of Magnesia bottle. 'Is all the same rubbish. Nothing does do the trick any more. My indigestion get a lot worse since your mother die. Like she haunting me from the grave.' He studied the bottle, rolling it between his fingers. 'What's the use?' he muttered. He tossed it away from him. 'Haunting me from the grave. Tight as a drum. Feel it!' He grasped Wilbert's hand and pounded it on his stomach. The skin was smooth and leathery. 'Well,' he continued after a pause and with heightened irritation, 'what you have to say for yourself, eh?' His piping voice whistled piercingly into Wilbert's ear, 'Your tongue couldn't stop wagging when Basdai bring that woman here. What happen to it all of a sudden?' Egbert Ramsaran pummelled the pillows into shapeless lumps. 'Don't pretend with me. You know damn well what I talking about. Ever since your mother die you been ... what's the matter with you? What's wrong?'

'Nothing is the matter with me. I didn't know you was expecting them. You hadn't tell me.' Wilbert stared at the network of cracks on the walls.

'And since when I have to tell you all my business? Since when?' Egbert Ramsaran glowered at his son.

Wilbert said nothing.

'Be more careful next time.' Egbert Ramsaran picked up the Milk of Magnesia bottle. Averting his face from Wilbert, he chiselled with his fingernail at the label.

Wilbert got up, moving to the door.

'Where you think you going?' Egbert Ramsaran asked. 'I not finished with you yet. Sit back down. I will tell you when to go.'

93

Wilbert sat down.

For some minutes Egbert Ramsaran did not speak. He chiselled assiduously at the label on the bottle; lost in his remote speculations. Then, still not looking at Wilbert, he said suddenly: 'That woman your grandmother bring here this morning – I can't remember she name now.'

'Sushila.'

'Ah! Sushila! Yes. That was it. Sushila. I can't think why I couldn't remember it. Sushila! I not too sure that I like that name.' Nevertheless, he seemed to enjoy pronouncing it. 'Is this Sushila I want to talk about with you.' He hauled himself further up the bed. He was behaving as though – because Wilbert had been the first to mention her name – he was absolved of some of the responsibility for bringing up the subject. 'What you think of this Sushila?' he asked.

Wilbert shifted uncomfortably, staring at the cracks on the walls.

'Answer me straight. I ask you a straightforward question and I expect a straightforward answer. None of this beating around the bush with me.'

Wilbert could think of nothing to say. There was no specific objection he could put forward to her coming; and, even if there were, he would not have dared. 'She very good-looking.' He astonished himself: the words had emerged of their own accord.

'Eh! But what is all this I hearing! My ears must be fooling me. Repeat what you just say.'

'I say she was very good-looking.' The words slipped from his mouth in an unsteady rush.

Egbert Ramsaran looked at his son strangely. For an instant, he seemed on the verge of confiding something to him. He collected himself quickly. 'She getting on in age though. You notice that?' He spoke with satisfaction. 'Getting on. Already you could see the wrinkles starting to form.' He uttered a shrill squeak of what might have been delight. 'Yes, my boy, your Sushila who you find so good-looking is getting on. How old you would say she is? Thirty? She can't be much younger than that if she have a daughter old enough to be . . .'

He massaged his stomach, absorbed in his calculations. 'Thirty,' he announced. 'Thirty to thirty-two. For a woman like she that is ... everybody have to get old. The beautiful as well as the ugly. I wonder if your Sushila know that. We all have to get old and die and whether you ugly or beautiful, the worms still going to eat you up. They can't tell the difference.' Again he uttered his shrill squeak of what might have been delight. 'Still, it have a lot of life left in these old bones yet.' He tapped his arm. 'The worms will have to wait a long time for me.' He glanced slyly at his son. 'You feel your Sushila too good-looking to come and work here?'

'I didn't say that.'

'Your problem is,' Egbert Ramsaran said with sudden vehemence, 'that you feel every woman have to be like your mother was.'

'I didn't say that either.'

'It would make a change to have a woman with some life in she about the place. Let the worms wait a bit. Your Sushila still have some life left in she. Is not a museum we living in here. It was your mother who try to turn this house into a museum. She had no life inside of she that woman. Right from the beginning she was food for the worms.' He spoke with rising vehemence. 'To marry she was one of the biggest mistakes I make in my whole life. You know that? She was as dead as a doornail.' Agitated ripples swept over the bedsheets.

'Maybe she wasn't to blame for the way she was,' Wilbert ventured.

'I don't care who was to blame or not to blame. I used to think she was so because of the way the family used to treat she. But I was wrong. She was born dead. And what was worse, she try to drag me down into the grave with she. Wouldn't leave me alone. Come here knocking on my door, whining, begging...' He stopped speaking, gazing down at the bottle he had not ceased to hold. 'You think I could have treated she better, not so? But I had no choice. Is a funny thing that of all the women in the world I could have marry I had to marry she. Maybe if I was a younger man when I had get married it would have been different. I could have marry the

95

way my blood wanted me to marry. But a mature man – a man with money to his name – have to be very careful. You can't marry the way your blood want you to marry. I wanted a nice, quiet woman. Somebody who wouldn't get big ideas in they head. Somebody who would know they place. But because a woman nice and quiet, it don't mean she have to be dead. That is what happen to me. It was my luck to marry someone dead as a doornail. He picked up the detective novel and flicked idly through the pages. 'You understand what I saying?'

'Yes,' Wilbert said.

Egbert Ramsaran leaned back further into the pillows. 'Mind you, I would never have marry a Port-of-Spain girl. No city girl as a matter of fact. Not after what happen to me.' He laughed. 'There was this girl – I can't even remember she name now. Something like Amelia. A stupid name like that. She father set a big Alsatian dog on me one day. It bit my leg – I still have the scar from it. Is a kind of souvenir. That is what teach me my lesson with them Port-of-Spain girls. After that – finish!' He dusted his palms. 'It was easy. All I had to do was look at that scar and remember ... let me show you.' He pulled up the leg of his pyjamas and showed Wilbert the scar. 'Once bitten, twice shy as the saying goes.' He laughed. 'You better watch out for them Port-of-Spain girls yourself. If you was a gorilla and you had money they would be after you like a shot. Sunday lunch and what not! But if you poor – as I was then – well, is a different story altogether.'

Voices drifted in faintly from the road. The night remained hot and stifling. Egbert Ramsaran's agitation had abated. He gazed tranquilly at his son.

'What I really wanted to say,' he said after a short while, 'was that it would be nice to have a woman with life in this house. Just for a change and even if is only for a few weeks.' He drummed on the cover of the detective novel. 'You grudge me that?'

Egbert Ramsaran started to read. 'Now you could go,' he said.

Sushila appeared in the yard of the Ramsaran house three days later. She wore a tight-fitting, sleeveless dress emblazoned with green and blue flowers of indeterminate species and a broad-brimmed straw hat pulled low over her forehead so that her eyes were invisible. Her slightly plump arms were reddened by the sun. Behind her, Farouk staggered under the weight of two brown suitcases that had seen much travel. A handkerchief was tied around his neck. Egbert Ramsaran watched the procession from the bedroom window.

'Stop!' His piping, querulous tones echoed across the hot yard.

Sushila slowed to slatternly pace and swivelled lazily in the direction of the window, pushing the brim of her hat upwards with the tip of her index finger.

'I was expecting you to come yesterday,' he said.

'I didn't say when I was going to come,' she replied. 'I had some preparations to make. You lucky to see me so soon in fact.'

'Who may I ask is that person you bring with you?'

'That person is Farouk. A good friend of mine. You couldn't expect me to tote them suitcases by myself.' The battle, she suspected, had begun. So much the better. She had come determined not to yield an inch of her sovereignty to this man.

'I don't like strangers walking about in my yard.'

'Well in that case I better go straight back where I come from this morning. I is no less a stranger than Farouk.' Sushila started walking briskly towards the gate.

Farouk, puzzled, shuffled indecisively after her.

'Wait! What you think you doing? Come round to the back and let we talk it over.' Egbert Ramsaran's head disappeared behind the curtains.

Sushila laughed. She retraced her steps.

Farouk cursed. 'You better make up your mind one way or the other. These suitcases don't have feathers inside them, you know.'

They trooped down the yard to the back of the house.

Egbert Ramsaran was there to meet them. Farouk rested the suitcases on the bottom step.

'What you have in there?' Egbert Ramsaran looked disapprovingly at the two suitcases.

'How you mean what I have in there? What you expect? Clothes! I can't walk about the place naked, you know.'

Farouk smiled.

'Let your friend bring the suitcases inside for you. Then he could leave.'

'Not so fast, Mr Ramsaran. I would like to clear up a point with you. I mentioned it when I was here but like you didn't take any notice.' Sushila, removing her hat, shook out her hair. She twirled the hat on her fingers.

'We discuss already all it have to discuss,' he said, his eyes fixed on the twirling hat as if he were mesmerized by its motion. 'Let your friend take the cases inside and leave.'

Farouk lifted the suitcases.

Sushila rested a restraining arm on his shoulder. 'Wait.'

'I said to let him take the cases inside. If it have anything to discuss, we could discuss it later.' Egbert Ramsaran's voice whistled.

'I'm not entering this house until I clear up that little point I was talking about,' Sushila said. The hat twirled; a blur on the tips of her fingers. 'I come here as a free person or a prisoner?'

'What nonsense is all this?'

'Is not nonsense to me, Mr Ramsaran. If I didn't pay attention to such nonsense as you call it, I would have been a prisoner a hundred times over before now. If I hadn't paid attention to such nonsense I would have been tied hand and foot. You have no idea how many people try to pull a fast one on me – try to bundle me up and lock me away in a cupboard. Is better to clear these things up right at the start. I come here as a free person or as a prisoner?'

'Of course you come here as a free person.' His greying, neatly trimmed moustache worked agitatedly. 'Nobody ever suggest otherwise.'

'Free to come and go?'

98

'Free to come and go.'

'As I please?'

'As you please.'

'Free to choose my own friends?'

'What nonsense . . .'

'Free to choose my own friends?'

'Yes. Yes.'

Sushila smiled. 'Good. That is all I wanted to know. And we have a witness.' She patted Farouk. Replacing the hat on her head and resting her hands on her hips, she said, 'You could take the cases inside now, Farouk.'

'All the same,' Egbert Ramsaran added, stepping aside to let Farouk pass, 'this is my house and not yours. You should remember that I have some rights too.' Egbert Ramsaran stared sourly at her and returned to his bedroom.

'You was very hard on the old boy,' Farouk said when he was out of earshot.

Sushila giggled. 'I sure nobody ever speak to him like that before. I thought he was going to blow up.'

'You shouldn't push him too far. He still have teeth to bite with.'

'I'll sweeten him up a little. Don't worry.'

Farouk shook his head worriedly. 'Take care, Sushila. You might be letting yourself in for more than you bargain.'

'If he's Samson, then I'm Delilah. Don't let it worry you. I know how to take care of myself – and him.' Sushila swung her body indolently and laughed full-throatedly.

Sushila took over Rani's bedroom. It had not been lived in since her death and everything had remained more or less as she had left it.

'I never see so much junk in my born days,' Sushila exclaimed to Wilbert. 'Where you mother pick up all this from?'

'She always had it.'

'Is unbelievable the things some people like.' Her attention was caught by the faded photograph of the snowy Swiss mountain with skiers hurtling down its slopes. 'What is this?' She went up close to the photograph and peered at it. 'Why!

Is just a picture cut out from any old magazine. What was so special about this one, I wonder?' She shook with laughter. 'You mind if I remove it?'

'Go ahead,' Wilbert said. 'Is no use keeping it now.'

With a sudden sweep of her hand, Sushila ripped the photograph off the wall and, rolling it into a crumpled ball, tossed it on the floor. 'That's much better,' she said. 'A real improvement.' Where the photograph had been, there was now only a gaping rectangle – like a lost tooth – of lighter coloured paint. Having taken the plunge, she flitted rapidly around the room and, within a few minutes, that bizarre assortment of mementoes was gathered into an untidy heap on the floor. Sushila laughed even louder when she discovered the three stamp albums on the top of the wardrobe. 'I thought only children used to keep stamp albums but I see I was wrong.' She leafed through the albums, her hilarity growing by the second. 'Is unbelievable. Almost all the stamps she have here is Trinidad one-cent stamps. What did she want to do with all this rubbish? Is really unbelievable. I never see the like in my born days.'

'She used to say that one day she might come across something really valuable. Something worth hundreds of dollars.'

'What would she have do with the money? Buy more stamps?'

'I don't know what she would have do with the money,' Wilbert said. 'The only thing I ever see her buy was a pair of gold glasses.'

'I heard about those,' Sushila replied. 'Poor woman!' She gazed at him, more serious now, her eyes clouding. 'Sorry. Is wrong of me to be making fun of she like this. After all, she was your mother. Is very wicked – especially when the woman is hardly cold in she grave. But I can't help it. It just don't make sense to me.' She held out the albums to him. 'Maybe you would like to keep them as something to remember her by. I suppose they might have what people does call sentimental value. I myself don't believe in that kind of thing, but I know for some people it mean a lot.'

Wilbert drew away, suddenly not wishing to touch them.

Sushila shrugged and tossed the albums on the heap. 'If you have no use for them, much less me,' she said. 'They will only clutter up the place and I have my own stuff to find room for.'

Like his mother's death, this act gave Wilbert a sense of release. He would have liked to have seen every shred of evidence relating to her existence destroyed; and this for no reason he could properly fathom except that it pained him unbearably to be reminded of her.

'And what is this?' Going up to the gold-framed photograph and standing on tiptoe, Sushila examined the pallid, sunless face. 'That is she on she wedding-day, not so? You could have frame a nicer picture than this.' She shuddered. 'I couldn't sleep with that in here, to tell you the truth. It would give me nightmares. Whose idea was it to do this?'

'Pa.'

'Funny man, your father.' She unhooked it. 'If it should be anywhere at all it should be in your father bedroom – or yours. Either would be more suitable since this room going to be mine in the future.'

'Since this room going to be mine in the future.' The phrase jarred. Sushila giggled.

'Well, you know what I mean. Not forever – but for the time being at any rate.'

There succeeded an awkward pause.

'How long you going to stay with us?' Wilbert asked.

'I don't know. That depends.'

'On what?'

'You is very inquisitive. Ask no questions and you'll be told no lies.' She laughed, wagging a finger at him. 'How you expect me to know? It depend on a lot of things.'

'Like?'

'Like how I get on with your father for a start.' Sushila studied his face. It was not as fine-featured as his father's. 'You think he going to like me?' she queried lightly.

Wilbert considered. His face broadened into a smile. 'It depends,' he said.

They both laughed.

Chapter Four

1

Important as it was, the chief public building of the Settlement was not the notorious Palace of Heavenly Delights. It was the grocery with the solid red doors owned and operated by Vishnu Bholai. Like Farouk's establishment, Vishnu Bholai's grocery was the only one of its kind within reasonable walking distance. His was a captive market and he prospered as a result. The Settlement had its grievances against him – as was inevitable: Vishnu Bholai was universally disliked because he refused to extend credit to any of his customers. This, however, was not the full story. The Bholais were generally regarded as moving on a superior plane. They were in transit, so to speak, through the Settlement and their children were not encouraged to associate with those of the village. This was acknowledged to be largely the doing not of Mr Bholai himself but of his wife. She it was who kept her husband's more democratic instincts well in check. Mr Bholai had married a little above his station: his wife was reputed to have family with extensive business connections in San Fernando. 'She does give old Vishnu hell,' it was confidently asserted, and heads would nod in bleak satisfaction. 'That go teach him to be high and mighty with we.'

For some reason, the Bholais had decided to call their youngest child Julian: they had given unambiguous Indian names to their three daughters. At the back of Vishnu Bholai's mind might have lurked the example of his childhood friend Ashok. He must have thought it would ease his son's passage through the world as once it had eased his friend's. From the day he was born, the Settlement had been made to understand that Julian Bholai had a great future ahead of him. His father had broadcast the fact to all and sundry. Julian was destined to be a doctor – or a dentist. 'He could choose any of the two,' Mr Bholai said magnanimously. 'Both have a lot of money in it these days. One jab with the needle worth ten dollars nowadays. You pull out one small teeth – twenty dollars and no questions asked.' His froggish eyes bulged contentedly. 'So, you see, it don't matter to Moon and me which of the two he choose to be. The boy will decide that for himself when the time come.'

Nearly all the profits he made in the grocery were being set aside for Julian's education in England. The girls were expected to find themselves suitably rich husbands. 'But with a boy is different,' Mr Bholai enlarged. 'He will have a wife and children to support one day. Now you will understand why it is that I don't give anyone credit. A man in my position can't afford to take risks like that. Is not that I saying' (he was careful to add) 'that any of you will cheat me. But the fact is I never see money come out of credit yet. So how you expect me to take the chance and risk the future of my boy? Eh? If no money does come out of credit, as you yourself would be the first to agree,' (they had agreed to nothing of the sort) 'and I start giving credit left, right and centre, is like throwing good money down the drain. Julian would never become a doctor or a dentist at that rate.' He behaved as if Julian's career was of as vital import to them as it was to him.

Attitudes to Julian in the Settlement varied according to mood. On the one hand, people respected him because he was going to be a doctor – or a dentist. On the other hand, they disliked him because he was, ostensibly, the cause of their not being granted credit. Opinion seesawed from day to day and from hour to hour; but, on the whole, he was more respected than hated. After all, Egbert Ramsaran apart, the Settlement could not boast of any illustrious native sons and few doubted Julian Bholai's future would be as glorious as predicted by his father. Also, Mr Bholai had promised that Julian would not charge more than was strictly necessary for his services – unlike 'other doctors'. 'He will give all of you discounts when the time come. What I don't give you now, he will give you later. You have to learn to think far ahead –

like me.' It was an ingenious argument, calculated to appeal to their forbearance. Mr Bholai was secretly terrified that someone, in a fit of pique, might try to burn down the grocery: he did not relish the idea of wasting money on insurance. Since he seemed sincere enough, the Settlement, despite its better judgement, gave him the benefit of the doubt and no fires were started. To further tip the scales to his advantage, Julian Bholai was a handsome boy; and, as an additional mark of distinction, his hair developed a reddish tint when exposed to the sun. This his father – and the Settlement – interpreted as a sign of manifest destiny.

It was one of Mr Bholai's fondest dreams that his son and Wilbert Ramsaran would become the closest of friends and bring to fruition in a later generation what the earlier generation had failed to achieve. To promote this, he had put himself to extra expense, sending Julian unnecessary miles to school every day. He was prompted partly by sentiment; and partly by the hope that some of what he conceived of as the Ramsaran magic might rub off inadvertently on his son and thus on himself. But, so far, he had reaped few rewards either tangible or intangible; and Mr Bholai was beginning to think his policy a failure.

'Did you see Wilbert today?' he would ask his son on his return from school.

'No,' Julian replied.

'But how come? The school not that big.'

'All the same I didn't see him.' These sessions irritated Julian.

'You don't have to bite my head off for just asking you a simple question,' Mr Bholai said mournfully. 'Still, I expect the two of you is good friends?'

Julian was evasive. 'He in a different class from me, you know.'

'That shouldn't stop you from being good friends.'

'He older than me,' Julian said.

'What difference that make? It doesn't stop you from being friends.'

'It make a lot of difference,' Julian said.

Mr Bholai threw up his hands and sighed. 'I don't understand you boys at all. At your age I was the best of friends with his father. The best of friends the two of we was. Why don't you invite Wilbert to come and spend some time here? That way you will get to know him better. Ask him the next time you see him.' It was just possible that where he had failed Julian might succeed.

Julian promised he would ask but he never did so. Mr Bholai's exasperation deepened. Meanwhile, he intensified his own efforts and, on his occasional unhappy visits to the house in Victoria, continued to plague Egbert Ramsaran with his requests for Wilbert to come and spend some time with them in the Settlement. And, as before, Egbert Ramsaran had continued to refuse his permission. 'Let Julian come here,' he said, 'if you so anxious for the two of them to be friends.' Mr Bholai would have been willing to compromise. Unfortunately, his wife was constructed of sterner stuff and she vetoed the suggestion in no uncertain manner. 'If Egbert Ramsaran too proud and great to send his son to we,' she said, 'I see no reason on earth why I shouldn't be twice as proud and great as he – considering who my family is – and not send my son to he. He have a lot of cheek, if you ask me. Who he think he is? Is not as if Julian is a beggar. He have his cousins to spend time with in San Fernando and they just as rich as Wilbert Ramsaran – and better brought up too. You should have more self-respect, Bholai, and not send your child all over the place as if he is a beggar.' She glared at him. 'You quite right, Moon,' Mr Bholai admitted. 'You quite right.'

Buffeted by these gales of disapproval, Mr Bholai was sorely tempted to give up his quest and let matters take their assigned course. But then Rani's death had intervened and the changes it had wrought in Egbert Ramsaran were not lost on him. Like the clients, like Basdai, he seized on the opportunities it presented and renewed his overtures.

'I know what you after,' Egbert Ramsaran said affably.

'Eh?' Mr Bholai laughed: it was the most positive reaction he had ever been able to arouse. 'I not after anything. All I saying is that it would be nice for Julian and Wilbert to keep each other company.'

'Is not Wilbert and Julian keeping each other company I worried about. Before I know what happening you going to be having Wilbert married off to one of your girls ...' Mr Bholai protested.

'I not going to allow that, Bholai. You was always more of a schemer and trickster than anything else. Is why you never get very far. You just don't do anything in a straightforward way.'

'You not being fair to me, Egbert. The girls hardly old enough to think about such a thing.'

'Maybe,' Egbert Ramsaran said, still affable.

'Is good for Wilbert to associate with children of his own age. Let him come – for a week.'

I'll think about it,' Egbert Ramsaran said. 'Come and see me next week.'

Mr Bholai was heartened. He returned the following week.

'If Wilbert want to go, I have no objection. Is up to him though.'

Wilbert had no alternative but to agree. There was Mr Bholai, standing a few feet away from him, rubbing his hands and beaming delightedly.

'It would be so good for Julian having you there. You could never tell what mischief those boys in the Settlement will lead him into. The people there jealous of him real bad.'

For Mr Bholai, it was a signal triumph.

No one was more provoked or made more indignant by Sushila's audacity in going to live in Victoria than Mrs Bholai. She regarded it as a personal injury and insult. She remembered that last flaunting procession with Sita along the main road when she had had to tug Julian back from the verandah railings. The news of Sushila's success spread gleefully through the village by Basdai – and less gleefully by Phulo – had incited her to such a pitch of violent fury that it ended by reducing her to a state of near collapse. Her children were forbidden from mentioning the names of mother and daughter – for, in

Mrs Bholai's mind, Sita shared to the full her mother's evil intentions. 'If I hear you mention the name of that woman or she daughter,' Mrs Bholai threatened her children, 'I going to break every hand and foot in your body.' She exempted herself from the ban. 'Here I is,' she stormed, 'breaking my back to bring up my son and daughters in a decent way and then to have this shameless whore Sushila and she equally shameless daughter shaking they backside for all the world to see. What kind of example that is to young children like mine?' She went so far as to propose that Sushila might be forcibly restrained from returning to pollute the air of the Settlement. 'I don't want she coming back here,' she said. 'And as for Miss Sita – they should send she away to a orphanage. She even more dangerous than she mother. You see all them book she does be pretending to read? Soon she going to start thinking she is as good – if not better – than my daughters. Who is to say what kind of dangerous ideas she going to plant in they head if she get the opportunity?'

'Is a free country, Moon,' her husband explained mournfully time and time again. 'I don't like the idea of Sushila coming back here any more than you but is nothing you can do about it. Is a free country and it have no law in the books to say that Sushila can't come and go as she please.'

Mrs Bholai did not believe him. 'You just making that up,' she accused him.

'Go ahead then,' he said. '*You* throw the both of them out.'

She switched the argument. Mrs Bholai had a great variety of weapons in her arsenal. 'Is that man Farouk to blame. Is he who give Sushila the child in the first place. Is he they should hang. If it wasn't for he Sita would never have been born to trouble me. I would have been a happy woman today.' More than almost anyone in the Settlement, Mrs Bholai had been affected by Sushila's pregnancy and subsequent outrageous behaviour. The anathema it inspired in her was not easy to explain. She had no reason to be especially offended; but especially offended she had been. It was as if she had convinced herself that Sushila had become pregnant for no other reason than to provoke *her*, and her frantic denunciations had been as much the occasion for comment as Sushila herself was. To Mrs Bholai, mother and daughter were a pestilential pair for whom the fires of hell could never burn brightly or fiercely enough. But the present tempest that raged in Mrs Bholai did not have as its only cause Sushila's joining the Ramsaran household. As if to compound her troubles, she had been told just two days previously that Julian and Sita had been having secret meetings during the monthly visits of the Library Van to the Settlement. The ubiquitous Basdai had been the agent of this shattering piece of rumour. 'I thought it best to tell you myself,' Basdai had confided, her face wrinkled with sorrow at the self-appointed task it was her melancholy duty to perform. 'It can't be true,' Mrs Bholai had replied. 'Julian would never do a thing like that. He wouldn't go behind his own mother's back.' 'Why don't you ask him?' Basdai had challenged. But Mrs Bholai, forthright as her rejection of Basdai's rumour-mongering had been, did not have the courage to ask her son. She did not even have the courage to speak of her fears to her husband: to do so would have given them a status she did not wish them to have. 'If Sita had never been born,' she repeated, 'I would have been the happiest woman in the world today. That child was born to torment me.'

'That is only because you does let she trouble you, Moon. People would think is Lucifer you talking about and not a young girl, the way you does be carrying on.'

Mrs Bholai switched her argument again. 'And then to invite Wilbert to come and stay with we! I won't have him in this house! You hear that? Not while Mistress Sushila living under the same roof as he.'

'Yes, Moon.'

'I don't know why you want Wilbert and Jules to be friends,' she raged uselessly. 'What could be the result of bringing him here but more trouble for me? I glad to see Jules have enough sense not to mix with people like that. But that didn't satisfy you. Oh no! You had to invite him here.'

'You being unreasonable, Moon. Is not Wilbert fault that Sushila working for his father.'

'I don't call it working. I call it addling his brain.'

'Yes, Moon.'

'You should send Jules to another school.'

'You didn't have anything against him going there before.'

'Well I have now.' Mrs Bholai folded her arms resolutely across her bosom.

Mr Bholai sighed and shook his head. 'If that is what you really want I could do it tomorrow. You just have to say the word.'

'Me? Why me?' She belied her resolution.

'You want me to cancel the invitation to Wilbert?' He was gentler.

'Me? Why you asking me? Is you who invited him. Is too late to do that. What's done is done. But if anything wrong I will know where to put the blame. You could depend on that.'

'I think I better cancel the invitation,' Mr Bholai said. 'I could tell him is not convenient after all.'

Mrs Bholai gazed at him scathingly. 'Sometimes I think you is really stupid man, you know, Bholai. How you suppose that will look? After all the years you spend begging his father and when you finally get him to agree to turn round and say . . .' She laughed. 'Use your common sense, man.'

Mr Bholai shook his head perplexedly. 'You is a funny person, Moon. I just never know where I is with you from one minute to the next. First you don't want him to come and then . . . what's the use?'

It was a heartfelt criticism. Mr Bholai was anxious to please and do whatever his wife thought was right. Unfortunately, it was not an easy task to discover her true opinions. She placed the burden of decision-making on him and, at the crucial moments of a project, would cut the ground from under his feet. The crux of the problem was that Mrs Bholai was driven by a host of contradictory desires and notions which she had not learned how to control and subordinate to one another. Taken singly, they might have been plausible and legitimate; but taken together (as was her habit) they were implausible and illegitimate. At any one time, all these contradictory desires and notions dangled alluringly before her like fruit waiting to be picked. Mrs Bholai felt she had simply to reach forward and pluck whichever her fancy chose. She wanted everything simultaneously and, that not being possible, she was therefore an unhappy woman. Reason – as epitomized by Mr Bholai – served merely to increase her frustrations and her husband's strictures reinforced her fury against its thwarting constraints.

Her life in San Fernando before marriage to Vishnu Bholai, she depicted to her children in the most glorious hues; while, in contrast, the Settlement and all who lived in it were depicted in the most sombre tones. Yet, when Mrs Bholai returned to San Fernando to stay with her relatives, she could not resist the temptation to boast of the Settlement where she was undisputed queen, enumerating the manifold virtues and compensations of country as opposed to city life. She talked then of the noise and the traffic and the wearying bustle. It was not dissimulation. She spoke truthfully at both times, for truth was not absolute with her. It arose from the circumstances and needs of the particular hour and thus, as the hours changed, could accommodate quite flagrant inconsistencies. This chain of self-contradictory truths lay looped in her mind.

Her family did indeed have extensive business connections but, to Mrs Bholai's mortification, her own branch of it had none. Poverty had put her into the invidious and humiliating position of having to accept the first respectable suitor who came along; a catastrophe for someone who was by nature choosy. Vishnu Bholai – his ambitions to be a lawyer still intact – was that man and she had to be grateful to him for rescuing her. Nevertheless, her gratitude could not be unmixed. Marriage to her had, undoubtedly, elevated him a rung or two and she demanded to be paid due homage. She floundered, trapped between gratitude for the man who had rescued her; and condescension for the man she had elevated. Over the years, condescension seemed, gradually, to have gained the upper hand, for her husband had not lived up to expectations: the budding lawyer had become the proprietor of the Settlement's only grocery.

It was a tragedy for Mrs Bholai. She worshipped wealth and her husband was a poor man who ran a grocery. When she visited her relatives in San Fernando, their superciliousness forced her into singing the praises of virtuous, hardworking poverty so as not to be unfaithful to the man for whom gratitude was still uppermost on such occasions. Reinstalled in the Settlement, she bemoaned her lucklessness and cursed her husband.

Mrs Bholai believed there was only a limited quantity of success to be had in the world and the smallest symptom of ambition in other people – for example, Sita's reading – filled her with dread. The fragility of her position communicated itself strongly to her: one slip and she would tumble she did not know where. Everyone and everything, not excluding her husband, was a potential threat to the future she had staked out for her children and herself. Naturally, she wished to reserve the maximum amount of success for her own personal use. If one man had a voracious appetite, then there would be that much less available to her. Thus, she could not forgive Egbert Ramsaran, holding him vaguely responsible for her husband's lack of progress. Success and failure were, in her scheme of things, connected together like the two ends of a seesaw. She admired Egbert Ramsaran for what he had done – but she could not forgive him. Comparison with her husband heightened her contempt for the latter. 'Bosom pals indeed,' she would snort. 'Being bosom pals with him didn't get you very far, Bholai! Instead of boasting about it, you should be hiding yourself in a corner!' Mrs Bholai regarded it as her sacred duty, on behalf of her children, to redress the balance of the seesaw.

The ambiguous mixture of scorn and respect she bore towards Egbert Ramsaran flowered in its full bloom when she came to consider his son. The battles of the older generation had been fought and lost. Nothing could be done about it now. Those between the younger generation were still to be fought. It was impossible for Mrs Bholai not to conceive of Wilbert and Julian as natural enemies, locked in a preordained and mortal combat for supremacy. It was a struggle

111

between light (Julian) and darkness (Wilbert) and light was bound to prevail. The Ramsarans were a bad breed, degenerate to a man. Poker! Chinese! Egbert himself! There were many strange stories told about that family. The irrefutable taint of Singh's blood could not be forgotten. And now, there was the affair with Sushila. It was unlikely that Wilbert should have escaped unscathed. Like Sita, he was burdened with an incubus of original sin. Who was to know what lethal germs he might implant in Julian under the guise of friendship? Yet, her opposition to her son attending the same school as Wilbert and going out of his way to do so had been weak. To her family in San Fernando she said: 'Jules and Wilbert Ramsaran does go to the same school. He and Jules thick thick. Mind you, is Wilbert who does search out Jules. Not the other way round. He does keep inviting Jules to stay with him but I don't care for the idea too much. Jules a million times brighter than he.' 'Who is this Wilbert Ramsaran you always talking about?' the ignorant might enquire. Their ignorance astounded Mrs Bholai. 'Like you never hear of the Ramsaran Transport Company? Where you does live? All them red and black trucks you does see going up and down ...' 'You mean ...' 'That's exactly what I mean. The son of Egbert Ramsaran himself. He and Jules thick thick. You can't separate them.'

Though she had not dared admit it even to herself – and here was the essence of the contradiction – Wilbert inspired certain hopes in her. Mrs Bholai would have denied it strenuously, but the fact was that the Ramsaran fortune featured much in her thoughts when her gaze shifted from Julian to her three daughters. Seen in this light, Wilbert was transfigured beyond recognition. It would be appropriate and just if one of the three were to be united with his fortune. This put her in a typical quandary. Wilbert was simultaneously both threat and promise: a two-headed creature with aspect infinitely monstrous or infinitely pleasing, depending on the view one adopted. Mrs Bholai had adopted both points of view. So the fulminations against him and the visit that had been arranged, real as the motives guiding them were, stumbled against another set of motives equally real. Therefore, her fulminations petered out into nothing specific.

On the day Wilbert was supposed to arrive, Mrs Bholai reverted to Farouk, the enemy most convenient to attack.

'Basdai tell me he have murder on he conscience,' she said, 'and I believe she.'

Mr Bholai wondered where it was leading to. 'Careful, Moon. Don't work yourself up. You does pay too much attention to Basdai. Farouk could have you up in court for defamation of character if he hear you saying that. Is a very serious charge.'

Mrs Bholai swept on, heedless of his opinions. 'Then, as if that wasn't bad enough, he does make people waste they money on rum. All them children you does see running about in rags wouldn't be like that if Farouk didn't make they fathers waste money on rum Is a crying shame. The police should take away his licence and give it to somebody like you.'

Mr Bholai sighed. 'You just say is a crying shame that people does waste they money on rum and then in the next breath you want *me* to get a licence . . .'

'If people stupid enough, why not? At least we would have a good use for the money. But what use Farouk have for it?'

'Very true,' Mr Bholai replied a trifle sadly. The possibility of Farouk losing his licence had often occurred to him. 'You quite right. We would have a use for the money which is more than you could say for a man like Farouk who have neither wife nor family to worry about.'

'The solution is simple,' Mrs Bholai announced after reflecting briefly. 'Don't serve him in the grocery. And if he can't buy food to eat he will have to go from here. You can't eat money.' She laughed.

'If you running a business,' Mr Bholai lectured, 'you have to serve anybody who come to you. The law say so. No discrimination against race or creed. How many times I have to tell you that?'

'Chut, man. You making it up. Anyway, Farouk would never report you to the police. He too frighten.'

Mr Bholai sighed, his froggish eyes bulging wearily. 'Even

if Farouk was to go from here, is not to say the police would give me the licence. If I own both the grocery and the rum-shop that would mean I would have a monopoly of trade in the area. The law don't like that either.'

'According to you the law don't like anything at all.' Mrs Bholai was losing her temper.

'Farouk is a good customer. Don't forget that. A lot of money he does make in the rumshop he does spend here. He like to eat well. Money is money however you look at it. Where it come from or who it come from is none of Vishnu Bholai business. All I concern about is that same money going to make Julian a doctor or dentist one of these days.'

It was a good argument, persuasively put, and Mrs Bholai recognized its force. However, it could not prevent her anger from running its appointed course.

'I think you want Farouk to stay here,' she said. 'Like you want Miss Sita to stay here and torment me. Two pound of butter, half-pound of salt, that is all you good for. You for-getting you is the father of four young children? You want them to grow up cheek by jowl with that drunkard and his devil daughter? What your so-called law have to say about that? Eh? What it have to say?'

'Calm yourself, Moon. What it is you want me to do?'

'If you had any self-respect you would move out of here. We would go and live by my family in San Fernando. I can't live in this place a moment longer cheek by jowl . . .'

'Okay. Say we sell the grocery. Where the money going to come from to make Julian a doctor or dentist? Answer me that one.'

'Two pound of butter, half-pound of salt!'

'That is not an answer.'

'Two pound of butter, half-pound of salt. You want to drive me mad.'

By the time Wilbert arrived, the Bholais had reached a fresh state of crisis which had thrown the entire household into disarray.

It was not the first time the idea of removal had presented itself to Mrs Bholai. Whenever the contradictions that ruled her life became too blatant she sought a scapegoat, blaming the Settlement for her troubles and asserting that she would be the happiest woman in the world if they had been living close to her family in San Fernando. Mr Bholai had humoured her. 'Is only temporary, Moon. The moment we get the children off we hands we going to leave here.' 'Chut, man,' she would reply, 'I tired hear you say that. You don't mean a single word of what you saying.' Her grumblings would reach a climax and then die away, leading a subterranean existence until once again the contradictions became too blatant for comfort, when they would resurface. To Mr Bholai's dismay, they had resurfaced in force.

'I can't stand it another second living cheek by jowl with Farouk,' she moaned.

'What you expect me to do, Moon? Lift up the shop on my back and tote it to San Fernando?'

'Get Farouk out of here then.'

'How, Moon? How? As I was saying to you before, it have no law . . .'

'I tired of you and your blasted law,' she shouted. 'If I hear you use that word again . . . you making it all up, Bholai. I know you. Is shame you want to shame me and my children by making we live cheek by jowl with him.'

'You not living cheek by jowl with him.'

'You want to drive me mad, Bholai. That is what you want to do. You marry me just to drive me mad.' She stared passionately at him.

'Please be sensible, Moon. Nobody trying to shame you or drive you mad or anything. You making Wilbert embarrassed getting on so. Remember he is we guest.'

'I don't care what he is, Bholai. You know I always believe in speaking my mind and I not going to stop now for your or anybody else sake. I not cunning and sly like you, two pound of butter, half-pound of salt. If Wilbert don't like it . . .'

'Moon! Moon!' Mr Bholai drew her to him. 'You don't know what it is you saying. Wilbert is we guest.'

He released her. Mrs Bholai staggered away from him, clutching her head. 'Sorry, Wilbert. Is not you I angry with. Is he who put me in a bad mood making we live cheek by jowl . . . I think I'll go and lie down. I have a headache.'

'That's a very good idea, Moon. You go and lie down.' Mr Bholai escorted her to their bedroom. He returned, rubbing his hands apologetically. 'You must excuse Moon,' he said to Wilbert. 'I don't want you to feel this is how we does always be. Ask the children. We is a happy little family really. Is just that Moon hasn't been sheself these past few days.' He babbled on. 'Is not easy having to worry about the shop and four children and Moon is a born worrier.' Mr Bholai sighed. 'Is just she tired. Nothing to do with you at all. Nothing.' He turned to his son. Why don't you show Wilbert the rest of the house, Jules? You not being a very good host.'

'What's there to see?' Julian asked laconically. 'He wouldn't be very interested.'

Mr Bholai looked from one to the other, rubbing his hands as if he were soaping them thoroughly. 'At least you could show him where he going to sleep.'

The bedrooms opened off a narrow corridor running parallel to the sitting-room. Julian rose from his chair and led the way into the corridor in as laconic a manner as he had spoken to his father. He flung open the second of three doors. 'This is my bedroom.' These were the first words he had addressed to Wilbert since his arrival and they seemed to cost him a great deal of effort. 'You'll be sleeping here.' He pointed to the first door. 'Ma and Pa sleep in there and the girls share the room at the back.'

Wilbert entered the room. It was small but light and airy. There were two beds covered with matching green counterpanes pulled tight as shrouds over the pillows. On one – presumably his – was a neatly folded towel and a bar of soap still in its wrapping. The walls were hung with photographs of Julian: Julian as a babe in arms being bathed by his mother; Julian, guided by his mother, cutting a cake with one candle stuck in the centre; Julian, urged on by his mother, taking his first tentative steps; Julian, his mother in the background, cutting a cake with four candles; Julian, his mother waving to him, setting off for school, a satchel slung across his shoulders; Julian, in fact, his mother's watchful eyes presiding, at virtually every stage of his development. Wilbert stared at the photographs wondering where Mr Bholai had been when they had been taken. His absence could not be accounted for merely by assuming he was the man behind the camera. It was not the simple absence of the cameraman. It was something more: it was a denial of his existence. The photographs presented a vision of a world Wilbert had never known; a vision, however perverse and distorted, of tender sentiment and pride. He had no such photographs to commemorate him and he envied Julian. He stared at them open-mouthed.

'That's Ma's work,' Julian said in embarrassed tones. 'She wouldn't let me take them down.'

Wilbert went to the window and stared out across the low roofs of the Settlement. The sugarcane fields stretched unbroken to the horizon; an undulating, restless sea lapping at the frayed edges of the village. Immediately below was the curving main road along which the cars passed in a steady stream. On a dresser next to the window were set out in splendid array rows of model aeroplanes with labels attached saying what they were.

'You build these yourself?' Wilbert asked.

Julian nodded. 'By myself. It was a hobby of mine at one time. I have nearly every kind of aeroplane there.'

Wilbert picked up one of the models: a transport helicopter. He rotated the blades.

'Careful,' Julian said. 'It's only plastic and glue. They very easy to break.' The model did indeed seem extremely vulnerable in Wilbert's clumsy hands.

Wilbert put it down.

'You have any hobbies yourself?' Julian asked politely.

'No . . . well . . . I used to collect stamps at one time.'

'Stamps! I was never very interested in those. I find them very boring. Give me planes any day.' Julian leaned negligently

117

against the door, swinging it to and fro. 'You had a big collection?'

'Not very . . . I don't have it any more. I destroy it.'

'Why? That was a strange thing to do.' Julian laughed.

Wilbert shrugged. 'I lose interest,' he said.

'You could read any of my books while you here,' Julian said. He indicated a laden bookshelf. 'I've got all the classics there.'

Wilbert scanned the bookshelf without visible interest. 'I don't read much.'

'You don't read at all?' Julian seemed incredulous.

'I don't care for it.'

'That's very strange,' Julian said. 'I couldn't live without books, I think.' It was his favourite word: 'strange'.

'I don't find it so strange,' Wilbert replied sullenly. 'I does live well enough without them.'

'Oh well . . .' Julian said.

There was an awkward silence.

'So,' Julian said, 'Your father finally agree for you to come.'

'Yes.'

'You wanted to come?'

Wilbert, his back to him, did not answer.

'If I was you,' Julian blurted out suddenly, 'I wouldn't have bother to come.'

Wilbert turned to look at him. 'Why?' He was taken aback.

Julian swung the door. He laughed. 'You see for yourself how Ma and Pa like to quarrel. It's not because she "tired" either. That's rubbish. You might as well know the truth. They always at one another's throats. I can't think why they ever got married. It's very strange. Very strange.' Julian brushed his hair from his eyes. 'And you must know why Pa was so anxious for you to come here.' He peered at him. 'You know, don't you?'

Wilbert stared at him.

'The only reason he wanted you to come was so that he could boast about it to everybody . . .'

'Why you telling me all this for?'

'I thought you might as well know . . .'

Mr Bholai's voice boomed behind them. Julian fell silent.

'I hope Julian is making you feel at home, Wilbert.' Mr Bholai entered the room smiling cheerfully. 'I want you to treat this place exactly as if it was home.' He slapped Wilbert on the back. 'You must promise me you would do that. The son of my best friend must be no stranger in this house. We'll all be one happy little family.'

'That's what I been telling him,' Julian said. 'I've been giving him all the lowdown.'

After dinner, when the family was relaxing together, Mr Bholai said to Wilbert: 'It have one thing I could never understand and perhaps you could explain it to me since Julian . . . well' (defying his son's clearly expressed disapproval) ', . . what I wanted to ask you was this. The two of you is good friends at school, not so?' Mr Bholai scraped away at his teeth with a toothpick.

Julian and Wilbert looked at each other. It was the question Wilbert had been dreading.

'The thing is,' Mr Bholai went on quickly, 'whenever I ask Julian . . .' Mr Bholai's smile was tinged with apprehension.

'We not in the same class, Pa. How many times I have to tell you that?'

'That is what he does always say.' Mr Bholai dried the toothpick on the sleeve of his shirt, doggedly addressing his remarks to Wilbert. 'It don't make much sense to me.'

Wilbert took his cue from Julian. 'Being in different classes,' he said, 'we don't get much chance to speak to one another.'

'That is what I keep telling him,' Julian said relievedly.

'And you quite sure that is the only reason? What I mean is . . . the two of you haven't quarrel or anything stupid like that?' Mr Bholai stared at Wilbert hopefully.

'Don't be ridiculous, Pa. What reason the two of us will have to quarrel?'

'That is all I wanted to know. You don't have to bite my head off. It would be hurtful to think that my son and the son of my best friend . . .'

'Oh God!' Julian said. 'Why can't you leave us alone, Pa?'

Mr Bholai picked up the newspaper. 'Not another word,' he promised.

The mention of her husband's 'best friend' appeared to revive Mrs Bholai who, up until then, had been subdued.

'How is your father these days?' she asked.

'He well,' Wilbert replied.

'I suppose it must make a big difference having another person in the house.' It was an apparently casual remark, thrown out randomly to stimulate the flagging conversation. Wilbert took it in this spirit; but Mr Bholai, who had begun his nightly exercise of going through the court cases in the Trinidad *Chronicle,* looked up anxiously from his newspaper.

'Yes,' Wilbert said. 'It make a big difference.'

'For better or worse you would say?' Mrs Bholai smiled sweetly at him.

'Now, Moon,' Mr Bholai butted in cautiously, 'that is no kind of question to ask Wilbert.'

'I wasn't talking to you, Bholai. You feel is only you who could ask question? If Wilbert don't want to answer he don't have to answer. Mind your own business.'

Mr Bholai returned to his newspaper.

Mrs Bholai did not press the point, however. She asked another question. 'I hear that Sushila daughter might be coming to live with you as well. It have any truth in that rumour?'

'I haven't heard anything about that,' Wilbert said.

'Somebody was telling me – your grandmother I think it was – that your father was thinking of it. He haven't told you?'

'I haven't heard anything about that,' Wilbert said.

'Now, Moon, all that is none of your business.'

'Keep out of this, Bholai.' Mrs Bholai glared at her husband. She turned again to Wilbert. 'You would like Sushila daughter to come and live with you?'

Wilbert did not answer. He gazed at the vases of flowers arranged with artistic pretensions sprinkled about the room.

'They say Sita is a very intelligent girl.' Mrs Bholai giggled.

'She does read a lot of book – from the Library Van.' Remembering Basdai's tattle about what happened on its monthly visits, her eyes clouded. 'She could count herself a lucky girl if she come to live with you and your father.' Sita living in daily contact with the Ramsaran fortune! Her imagination spawned grotesque images of the benefits that might accrue to her. 'My girls had to do with a lot less. For instance, Mynah teacher tell me she never meet anybody so bright yet. I would have pawned my soul to give my daughters a really high-class education. But all the money we ever earn we put aside for Julian to be a doctor one day.' She was sitting directly beneath the electric light and her oval face was extraordinarily pale in its yellow glow.

Mr Bholai could not concentrate on the court cases. He folded the newspaper and rested it on his lap. 'You have nothing to reproach yourself with, Moon. We doing the best we can.'

Mr Bholai could not concentrate on the court cases. He at the floor, 'a grocery is only a grocery after all. And the Settlement is only the Settlement. You can't expect miracles.' She breathed in deeply. 'Even so, I glad to see it have somebody from the Settlement making they way up in the world.'

'That is the best way to look at it,' Mr Bholai said peaceably.

'Is exactly what I thought you would say, Bholai. No self-respect – that's your trouble. Two pound of butter, half-pound of salt! If you had more self-respect we wouldn't be living here today. My girls would have been going to school in San Fernando, getting a proper education. Instead you have we living cheek by jowl with that drunkard Farouk.'

'Now, now, Moon,' Mr Bholai implored. 'I thought we had finished with that nonsense. You working yourself up again for no reason.'

Mrs Bholai brushed his objections aside. 'You know what it is Sita want to be when she grow up?' It was a rhetorical question aimed at the room in general. She turned fiercely on Wilbert. 'You know what it is Sita want to be?'

The girls giggled.

'Sita want to be a B.A. Languages,' Mynah drawled. 'Everybody know that.'

Mrs Bholai snorted. 'A B.A. Languages! I hope you hear that, Bholai. Miss Sita want to be a B.A. Languages. A child of Sushila want to be a B.A. Languages. But what about your own daughters, eh? What they going to be?'

'Moon, Moon . . .'

'Why shouldn't Sita be a B.A. Languages? What's so strange about that?' Julian, sprawled on the floor, flipping through the pages of a book, looked up lazily at his mother.

Mrs Bholai studied her son sorrowfully. 'I don't know how you could say things like that, Jules.'

Julian clasped his hands behind his head. 'All I'm saying . . .'

'Don't put your hands behind your head like that, son. Is not nice.' It was a superstition of Mrs Bholai that to clasp one's hands behind the head indicated a wish for somebody to die. Naturally, when Julian did this, she interpreted it as a wish for her own death.

Julian laughed and closed the book. 'It's not fair to attack a person behind her back. Why shouldn't Sita want to be a B.A. Languages?'

Mrs Bholai twirled and twisted her bracelets. 'You should be defending your own sisters instead of she – a total stranger.' She stared intently at him. 'She is a total stranger to you, not so?'

Julian skirted round the question. 'The only reason I'm defending her is because she has nobody else to do it for her. Shanty and Mynah and Gita have you. Mind you,' he added, 'I'm sure if she had the chance she could defend herself very well.'

'How you know that?' Mrs Bholai asked sharply. 'Like you been speaking to she or something?'

Julian was adroit. 'You yourself said just now she was intelligent.'

Shanty and Mynah giggled. 'Oh! Oh! Oh!'

Gita, the eldest, remained austerely serious. 'Julian right,' she said. 'Is not fair to attack a person behind their back.'

Julian grinned maliciously at his distraught mother. 'She's very good-looking too. Have you notice? She resemble her mother.'

'Oh! Oh! Oh!'

'Julian!' Mrs Bholai gazed horror-stricken at her son.

'There's a very interesting case in the paper today . . .'

'Shut up, Bholai!' Mrs Bholai twirled and twisted the bracelets on her wrists, enmeshed in the coils of an acute distress. 'Is all your fault, Bholai. All your fault. None of this would have happen if you wasn't so stubborn. You hear how Julian talking about she? Soon Miss Sita will be thinking she is more than the equal of my children. B.A. Languages! What any child of Sushila have to do with booklearning? Is all pretence. I was speaking to Phulo in the shop only yesterday and she say that she sure as she name is Phulo that Miss Sita does only be pretending to read all them book she does tote home from the Library Van.'

'Phulo can't tell "a" from a "b",' Julian said goadingly. 'So how come she know when people reading or not reading?'

'Jules! It does break my heart to hear you say such things.' Mrs Bholai began to cry. 'Miss Sita should be learning how to cook and wash and sew. That is all any child of Sushila should ever want to learn how to do. Is all she will have any use for.'

'Rubbish.'

Mrs Bholai lost control of herself. 'What that wretch ever do for you, eh? What? I will wring she neck. You want to kill me that is what you want to do. Take your hands from behind your neck.'

Julian laughed. 'You being silly.'

'You want me to die . . . to die.' Mrs Bholai sobbed. 'My own son want me to die.'

'I can't take this any more.' Julian got up from the floor, dusting the seat of his trousers. 'You see what I mean, Ramsaran? It's a madhouse you come to.'

'Where you going, Jules? How you could be so cruel to me?' Mrs Bholai tried to grab at her son as he went past but he dodged her and slipped into the corridor. 'Jules . . .'

The door to his bedroom closed.

'Is all your fault, Bholai. All your fault.' Mrs Bholai swayed on her chair.

'I don't see how is my fault,' Mr Bholai said softly. 'Nobody would ever dream we have a guest in this house.' He stared belligerently at the vases of flowers. 'Julian better learn to control that temper of his. Is a little too quick for my liking. He not a doctor as yet.'

The cars went by on the road below, their tyres screeching on the curve. Mrs Bholai, slumped in her chair, paid no attention to her husband. She was more vulnerable to Julian's indifference than he was. Her sensibilities being rawer and more various, they had a correspondingly greater liability to outrage. Having invested so much of her passion and devotion in him, she reacted violently to any diminution in the return she had led herself to expect. Julian recognized this and made full use of it. His 'defence' of Sita was not motivated purely by gallantry: he was fully aware it would enrage his mother; as he was fully aware what the effect of clasping his hands behind his head would be.

He exploited her credulity to its limits. 'I think I'll be a lawyer after all,' he would speculate loudly in her presence. 'They might make me into a judge.' Mrs Bholai swallowed the bait instantly. 'Jules! You not being serious with me. What you want with being a stupid lawyer?' 'I'm being very serious, Ma. You wouldn't catch me dead as a doctor or dentist. I don't like the sight of blood.' Mrs Bholai, as was her habit, vented her frustration on her husband. 'This is all your doing, Bholai. You won't get away by hiding your head behind that damn newspaper of yours. I see your hand in what Julian saying plain as day.' 'I didn't say a word to the boy, Moon. Cross my heart.' 'I don't believe anything you say, Bholai. Liar is your middle name. I always know you didn't want him to be a doctor. You does sneak behind my back and put ideas in his head.' She would start to weep. 'I didn't put any ideas in his head,' he protested. 'You could see the boy only joking with you.' 'I'm not joking,' Julian intervened with all the appearance of absolute seriousness. 'I'm going to be a lawyer like Pa was going to be before he open up the grocery.' Mrs Bholai was beside herself by this time. 'That is proof is all your doing, Bholai. Two pound of butter, half-pound of salt!' And, turning to her son, 'Say is only joke you joking, Jules, and put my mind at rest. You mustn't let him lead you astray. Say you don't want to be a stupid lawyer.'

Julian would give up when he grew bored and tired of the game; or when his mother was dangerously close to hysteria. He taunted her mercilessly; teasingly withholding his favours. Mrs Bholai never learnt to ignore him. Where her husband was concerned her scepticism seemed to have no limits and her powers of forgiveness were nonexistent. However, where Julian was concerned, the contrary was the case. Then it was her credulity which seemed to have no limits while her powers of forgiveness were extravagantly abundant. She treated his absurdities at their face value and refused to rest until she had extorted from him, through bribes and tears and cajolery, exactly what she wished to hear.

A frivolous word from Julian could plunge her into darkest distress; while another equally frivolous word lifted her into lightest ecstasy. Sometimes Julian would persist in his obstinacy for days on end, driving her to distraction, and it was Mr Bholai and the girls who would have to pay for his inconstancy and pettishness. These performances were masterpieces of their kind; so convincing and plausible that he himself appeared to be taken in by them and was angry if anyone should suggest they were a feint. 'This is the end of me,' Mrs Bholai would whimper. 'I not going to forgive him this time even if he come crawling back to me on his hands and knees. It would take more than that – much more than that – to make up for even a tiny part of the suffering his thoughtlessness causing me.' Julian did not need to crawl. His charm never failed to save him and Mrs Bholai was too grateful to remember her vows. 'I knew all along it was only joke he was joking with me. I was a little worried but never really frightened. Boys must have they fun.'

Julian could conjure up feelings and emotions at will. He had inherited much of his mother's chameleon nature; except that with him it served no higher purpose than self-indulgence. With this ability went the capacity to turn off his emotions and feelings at will. Each day, he could invent a new and tantalizing Julian Bholai, quite distinct from the Julian Bholai one had talked to the day before. He would have made a marvellous actor; and, indeed, he tended to treat the world as a scenario written especially for him and the people he encountered as characters to be manipulated. His versatility and elusiveness gave him a startling power over his mother. She, with an inveterate blindness, refused to understand its real nature and, as a result, she suffered terribly.

Shanty followed Julian out of the room. Mynah, taking a file from the pocket of her dress, filed abstractedly at her nails, humming a popular tune. Mr Bholai watched her.

'Stop filing your nails in front of me, child. You should have more respect and manners.'

Mynah stopped her filing, holding the file lightly between her fingers. She continued to hum.

Mr Bholai sighed. 'I wonder where Shanty and Julian get themselves to,' he muttered irritably. 'Shanty! Julian!'

There was no reply.

Mynah jerked her head in the direction of Julian's bedroom. 'They lock themselves up inside of there telling each other secrets.' The light slid sharply off the nail-file, dazzling her father.

'Since when Shanty and Julian have secrets to keep from me?'

Mynah laughed. 'What you mean "since when"? They always had their secrets. Just like everybody else.'

'You have your secrets too?'

'Of course!'

He looked at Gita. 'What about you?'

Gita blushed and stared down into her lap.

Mynah giggled vindictively. 'You should know better than to ask Gita a question like that, Pa. She want to be a nun. Always praying to God.'

'To be a nun you have to be a Catholic,' Gita said.

'Why don't you tell Pa how hard they always trying to convert you in school?'

'Convert you? Who trying to convert you?' Mr Bholai smiled perplexedly at Gita.

'Nobody trying to convert me,' Gita replied morosely. 'Mynah playing the fool. But,' she concluded defiantly, 'I don't see anything wrong in praying to God.'

'Nothing wrong at all in praying to God,' Mr Bholai replied soothingly. 'I does pray myself – sometimes. But it depend on what you does pray for. Tell me what you does pray for.'

Gita frowned and was silent.

'You see, Pa,' Mynah chirped happily, 'even a saint like Gita have secrets from you.'

'You shouldn't make a mockery of God,' Gita said sternly.

'Now, now, children. What kind of behaviour is this? We have a guest staying with we. You should have some consideration for him. Wilbert must be getting a very bad impression of we.' He smiled apologetically at Wilbert. 'Don't let all this fool you. We is a happy little family when you get down to it. But even in the happiest of families you must have your little misunderstandings from time to time. Things can't run silken smooth all the time.'

Mrs Bholai, who seemed to have fallen asleep, opened her eyes at this. 'Huh! Sometimes I really like to hear you talk, Bholai. Things would be running silken smooth if we was living in San Fernando. Two pounds of butter, half-pound of salt!' Having fired her parting shot, she too got up and left the room and went into the kitchen.

'Come, come,' Mr Bholai appealed. 'Let's forget all this nonsense about God and San Fernando.' He summoned up a cheerful smile from the recesses of his despair. 'Did I ever tell you, Wilbert, about the time when Mynah wanted to learn the violin and . . .'

'Pa!' Mynah interrupted without a trace of friendliness. 'I must have hear you tell that story at least a dozen times. And is not very funny either.'

Mr Bholai's feigned enthusiasm was checked. 'But Wilbert never hear it.'

Mynah rose from her chair. 'I'm going to go if . . .'

'Ah! These children!' Mr Bholai looked at Wilbert. 'They have no patience at all with they old father. I don't understand it. Sit down, Mynah.'

'Not if you're going to tell that story.'

'I won't say another word. Not another word. Promise.' Mr Bholai, crossing his heart, shook his head sadly and relapsed into silence.

It had been Mr Bholai's misfortune to be drawn into close association with people more energetic, more ambitious and more ruthless than himself. His was an inert temperament which, left to its own devices, would have followed the paths of least resistance and been content with its meagre lot. Fate had not been so kind to him: it had seduced him from his natural bent and forced him into a series of roles for which he was ill equipped. There had been, to start with, his unlikely association with Egbert Ramsaran; and then, there had been his no less unlikely marriage. He was now busy reaping the fruit of his fatal perversity.

Mr Bholai was a lonely man. He could confide neither in his wife nor in his children. Instead, he seized on his guest and to him uttered traitorous thoughts such as he would never dare to utter in front of his wife and children. 'You is an outsider,' he told him. 'The son of my best friend. To you I can talk like I can't talk to the rest of them. They have no use for me any more.' The froggish eyes dimmed. 'Is one of the reasons I wanted you to come and stay with we. A man must have somebody to talk to otherwise he might go mad and have to be put away somewhere.'

It was not that Mr Bholai did not love his wife and children. He was absolutely devoted to them. His devotion to his wife – or a portion of it – sprang from the fear that he was not worthy of her; that he had won her under false pretences. 'Moon could have marry any of a hundred different men,' he said to Wilbert. 'They was lining up. But it was me – Vishnu Bholai – she choose out of all of them.' He exaggerated the extent of the competition but exaggeration was essential to

128

him in that, at one and the same time, it comforted him to believe he had triumphed over so many rival suitors; and, also, it emphasized Moon's innate superiority.

'Of course,' he elaborated, 'I was a lot handsomer in those days. I didn't have my pot belly then. I remember I used to take she chocolates – the kind with pretty pictures on the box.' He laughed. 'I never discover till long after I marry she that she didn't like chocolates at all.' He became serious. 'I had tell she I was going to be a lawyer and she had believe me. I wasn't lying. I had set my heart on that since I was a boy. You could ask your father. I used to dream about the Inns of Court. Funny kind of name, eh? The Inns of Court. The problem is that you have to have money to study law and where was I to get the money from? I didn't know any Latin either – you need that for the Roman Law. So nothing ever come of it.' He chuckled. 'That was how I end up in the grocery business – not wearing a gown and wig but an apron. Two pound of butter, half-pound of salt. I wanted Julian to be a lawyer but Moon wouldn't' hear of it. "Look where being a lawyer get *you*," she say. You can't really blame she for thinking like that.' He derived a vicarious pleasure from reading – preferably aloud – the cases reported in the Trinidad *Chronicle*. Even this Moon frowned upon.

Tutored by their mother, his children had reached the stage where they tolerated rather than respected their father. He had been effectively cast out from their lives and they treated him with an indifference verging on contempt. It was Julian who, in a moment of inspiration, had coined the phrase 'two pound of butter, half-pound of salt' which was forever afterwards to pursue Mr Bholai. He accepted it all with an outward show of calm and forbearance, only the slight twitch around the edges of the mouth betraying him. Constant repetition brought him perilously close to believing that the name (for Mrs Bholai had pounced on it with relish and made it his name) was no more than his just due. Julian inspired in him the same mixture of fear and devotion as did his wife. If he felt himself to be unworthy of the one, he felt himself to be no less unworthy of the other. He had long ago succumbed to the notion that Julian was the exclusive property of his mother. Sufficient for him was the glory – and undeserved privilege – of having fathered such a prodigy.

Mr Bholai's rebellions against his wife's propaganda were ineffectual and lacking in conviction. None could deny, not even he, Julian's cleverness, handsomeness and goodness except on grounds of jealousy. To do so would have been tantamount to sacrilege. The intermittent accusations he levelled against Julian augmented the already substantial burden of guilt he carried around with him and were generally followed by vigorous disclaimers to the contrary. He would allow no one else to criticize Julian and he could be as zealous in his defence as his wife. 'I don't want you to get the wrong impression,' he warned Wilbert. 'Julian is a good son to me. He is a boy with brains and you can't expect him to be patient with his foolish old father all the time. You have to make allowances for that. If I does complain a little now and then is just because I is a selfish old man. Nothing more. No father could be more thankful and grateful than me for being blessed with a child like him.'

Yet he could not control the note of bitterness which crept into his lamentations. His children had no use for him beyond the satisfaction of elementary necessities: food and shelter and clothing. 'Yet, it have nothing surprising in the way they turn out,' he confessed to Wilbert. 'Is how we wanted them to be after all – to be different from us. To be better. Is why we sacrifice to give them a education. Is like doing another man work – like being a builder. You spend all your time and energy planning and building a great big house for somebody else to live in while you yourself can't do better than a little rundown shack.'

Mr Bholai, seeing the inevitable approaching, had employed delaying tactics. He had tried to prolong their childhood, perpetually reviving – to their considerable annoyance – memories of their earliest years. 'You wouldn't believe how well we used to get on together when they was small. Daddy-father they used to call me. I bet you would never guess that from the way they does behave to me now, eh? It used to be

Daddy-father this and Daddy-father that. Is amazing how things does change.' The sense of rejection, of superfluity, gave rise to harsher moods in which his concealed bitterness found its full expression. 'What happen? What does make people change and become so? Is it something they was born with inside of them? What is it?' He had witnessed so many mutations; while he had remained essentially the same, trying to keep pace but always left behind. Ashok to Egbert. The girl he had married to the woman who despised him. Daddy-father to lonely old man. Where was the key to these transformations? 'Maybe if I had beaten they backsides raw, it wouldn't be like this today. Having secrets from me! I'll teach them how to have secrets. A lot of the blame must rest with Moon. She digging she own grave without knowing it. Playing with fire.' It was a monologue of grief, bitterness and despair to which Wilbert listened.

There was justice in these charges. Mrs Bholai regarded it as her prime duty to protect her children from the evils surrounding them in the Settlement. She had attempted to erect what could only be described as a sanitary screen behind the shelter of which she hoped they would be safe from the noxious influences beleagureing them. If they ventured beyond its protection they were immediately hauled back to safety. The enemy to be repulsed was within as well as without. Mrs Bholai sought to preserve her children from the insidious influences emanating from their father and to monopolize their affections. They were forbidden to serve or even appear in the grocery. 'Leave that to your father,' she advised them. 'He is the two pound of butter, half-pound of salt man.' At every opportunity she spirited them away to stay with their cousins in San Fernando and imbibe a healthier nourishment. 'I does hardly have a chance to talk to them,' he objected. To which Moon had replied: 'What *you* have to talk to them about, shopkeeper?' They had been snatched away from him in order to be bred for a mysterious but higher purpose. In this task, he had no part to play.

'You asleep, Ramsaran?'

'No.'

'I don't blame you. I can't sleep either.' Julian coughed. 'Who could sleep after what happen – except my father?'

They could hear Mr Bholai snoring in the front bedroom. A clock ticked loudly on the dresser, its luminescent dial as if suspended in empty space. There were no cars on the road so late at night.

'You intend to go and see your grandmother?'

'I don't know,' Wilbert said.

'It would be very strange if you didn't go to see her. She might be offended.'

'That's true,' Wilbert said. 'I suppose I had better.'

'It would also give you a chance to meet Sita – the cause of all the trouble. You must be curious.'

Julian's laughter floated across the darkness from the other side of the room. Wilbert turned to face him but could see little apart from the formless shape under the blanket.

'I not curious,' he said. His voice was muffled and sullen.

'But she might be coming to live with you and your father.'

'I don't know nothing about that. Is only a rumour. It have no truth in it.'

'How you so sure?'

'Because I would have been among the first to know. My father would have tell me.'

'He didn't tell you Sushila was coming though.'

'Who say that?'

'Basdai. She was saying how he bawl you up the day she bring Sushila to see him.' He laughed. 'Your grandmother have a very big mouth.'

Wilbert listened to the clock ticking, Mr Bholai's snores blending in with it. He was curious about Sita after all that he had heard; a curiosity intensified by the suggestion that she might be coming to join her mother. However, it was not mere curiosity which was uppermost in his mind. It was resentment. He resented having to be told this by other people; he resented that the suggestion (with all its unsavoury implications) could actually be made. His pride as the son of Egbert Ramsaran had been hurt in a tender spot. What was worse was the appalling suspicion that these rumours were not without foundation. Wilbert realized with something approaching horror that he had lost faith in his father. The man of iron will was being exposed as a sham. It was a betrayal. He recalled what his father had once said to him about weakness. 'For once you take away the whip and start being softhearted, once they feel you have water instead of blood in your veins, they going to be crawling all over you like ants over sugar.' He was right. The ants were crawling over the man of iron will. They were eating him up; sucking him dry. Wilbert was profoundly sickened.

'When you go to visit your grandmother,' Julian said, 'you think you could do me a small favour?'

'What?'

'I want you to give Sita a book for me. I promise to lend it to her but I'm not going to see her until the Library Van come again.'

'I suppose so,' Wilbert agreed reluctantly.

For another hour, he listened to the ticking of the clock, watching the progress of the minute hand around the face of the luminous dial.

Basdai's hut was set well back from the main road. Wilbert walked slowly down the track leading to it, carrying the book Julian had given him. The sun burned down fiercely on his head and the earth was cracked and white. Phulo, who was stringing out washing on a line, was the first to see him. Drying her hands on the front of her dress, she came forward to meet him. She was barefooted and her untidy hair was bundled under a fluttering scarf.

'Ma!' she shouted. 'We have a visitor.'

'What visitor?' Basdai shouted querulously from somewhere inside the hut. 'I have no time for visitors.'

'You will have time for this one. Come and see for yourself.'

Basdai appeared in the doorway of the hut, shielding her eyes from the glare. Her wizened face creased into a smile when she recognized Wilbert. In one hand she held a basinful of rice which she had been 'picking'.

'I was wondering when you was going to come and visit your grandmother.' She kissed him on either cheek. 'Come inside and sit down. You will get sunstroke in this heat.'

There were three huts altogether forming a rough semi-circle: Basdai's and those of her two sons and their families. Basdai's hut occupied the central position in the semi-circle and was of the traditional variety: it was built of plastered mud and had a thatched roof. The other two had pretensions to modernity in that they had galvanized iron roofs. A screen of banana trees fringed the rear of the semi-circle. There were children everywhere, bare-bottomed, dusty and ragged, playing among the chickens which wandered freely in and out of the huts. A kid goat was tethered to a nearby plum tree.

Wilbert was bundled into Basdai's verandah and made to sit down on the hammock. Sharma, Basdai's other and less voluble daughter-in-law, arrived to contribute her quota of welcoming remarks. She was a fat, good-natured woman who smiled at everything that was said. The children crowded round the hammock and stared wide-eyed at Wilbert. He rocked on the hammock not knowing what to do or say.

'If you had come earlier you would have meet your uncles,' Basdai said. 'But they out working in the fields. You want me to send one of the children to call them? They wouldn't like to miss you.'

'I'll see them another time. I here for a few more days yet.'

'Very true,' Basdai admitted. 'Is no hurry.'

'You enjoying yourself with the Bholais?' Phulo asked.

Wilbert nodded.

'They is nice people,' Basdai said. 'If only Bholai would give credit I would have no complaints.' She smiled. 'How you leave your father?'

'Very well.' He spoke in a mumble.

'I glad to hear that. And . . . and Sushila. She settling in okay?'

Wilbert nodded.

Basdai shooed away a clucking hen. 'A man need a woman about the place. I was very glad I could find somebody to ... that remind me. Where Sita get sheself to? Sita!' She turned again to Wilbert. 'Sita is Sushila daughter.'

Wilbert swayed on the hammock.

'There she is! Where you had get yourself to, girl? Like you didn't hear Wilbert Ramsaran come to visit we?'

'She don't hear nothing she don't want to hear,' Phulo said.

'I was having a bath.' Sita approached them from the bathhouse which was discreetly hidden behind the fringe of banana trees, a towel draped over her shoulders. She had combed her wet hair severely back from her temples and tied it in a bun. Wilbert stared at her. She was tall and thin and angular. High cheekbones gave her face a somewhat rigid, austere cast but her lips which were full and well-formed – like her mother's – softened the austerity. She wore a pleated skirt which reached to her knees and a long-sleeved blouse buttoned up to the neck, and she was the only person present – apart from Wilbert – wearing shoes. The fingers grasping the end of the towel were bony and tapering and the skin was stretched tight over the protruding knuckles.

'Say hello to Wilbert,' Basdai said.

Sita inclined her head.

'She dumb,' Phulo said to Wilbert.

Sita stood erect, paying no attention to Phulo. The children, having lost interest, had melted away and resumed their games in the yard.

'Julian Bholai give me this to give you.' Wilbert held out the book for her.

Sita seemed startled by this direct address and stared at the book as if she did not understand what it was and was consequently afraid to touch it.

'Take it,' Wilbert said. 'He give it to me to give you.'

At last Sita took the book. 'Thanks for bringing it.' She paused. 'And thank him for me when you see him.'

'You does read a lot?' Wilbert asked. He thought he ought to say something, but could think of nothing else.

'Huh!' Phulo said. 'Instead of doing she fair share of work like the rest of we . . .'

Sita glanced scathingly at her. 'You finished?' She turned to Wilbert. 'I like to read. It stops me from being bored and having to think about the people I'm living with.' She smiled.

'What she mean,' Phulo said, 'is that she like meeting Julian Bholai by the Library Van.'

'That is none of your business,' Sita retorted with sudden warmth.

'Sorry,' Phulo said. 'Sorry to open my mouth in front of your Royal Majesty. I was forgetting my proper place.'

Sharma laughed her good-natured laugh. 'The two of them always at each other's throat – just like if they was lovers.'

'You must stay and eat something with me,' Basdai said. 'I nearly finish picking the rice.'

Wilbert declined the invitation. 'That would be too much trouble for you.'

'Is no trouble at all.'

But Wilbert was not to be persuaded. This place depressed him. 'Another time,' he promised. He got up from the hammock.

'It was nice meeting you.' Sita smiled awkwardly.

Wilbert went out into the sunlit compound. The chickens scurried before him.

'Don't forget to thank Julian for me.'

Wilbert waved at Sita. 'I won't forget.'

When he got to the road, he looked back. She was still watching him. Then she waved and disappeared into the pitch black of the hut.

Julian was waiting for him on the front steps. 'That didn't take you long, Ramsaran.'

'I didn't mean it to take long,' Wilbert replied.

'You give Sita the book?'

Wilbert held his empty hands aloft. 'What else you think I do with it?'

'Why you in such a bad mood? What happen?' Julian scanned his face.

136

'Nothing happen and I not in a bad mood.'

Julian laughed, brushing back his hair from his forehead. 'Sita say anything?'

'She send to say thanks.' Wilbert moved on past him.

Julian hurried after him up the steps. 'That's all? Nothing more?'

'Nothing more,' Wilbert said.

Julian seemed disappointed. 'That's very strange.'

'It had a lot of people there.'

'You mean you didn't give it to her when she was alone? You give it to her in front of Basdai and everybody?'

Wilbert nodded.

Julian was shocked and upset. 'No wonder she didn't say much. No wonder! That was a really stupid thing to do. Everybody will hear about it now.'

Wilbert stopped. 'Look here. I only do it for you as a favour. Get that into your head. I not your messenger boy. You hear that?' The peasant roughnesses of his face were accentuated. His jaw muscles twitched. 'And another thing. Make sure that is the last time you call me stupid.'

'Don't be so touchy, Ramsaran.' Julian was conciliatory. 'It didn't matter. Let's forget about it.'

But Wilbert was not inclined to forget about it. He stored it up for future reference.

4

In the rush of attention lavished on their brother, the Bholai girls inevitably took second place. Not, however, that they were neglected or forgotten. But the fact was that love and concern in their case were tempered with a healthy dash of realism. Julian was a child of the gods. He had to please no one but himself. No obstacle could block for long his progression through the world: confronted with his manifold perfections, they would be automatically dispersed. His was to be a protracted and triumphal march through life. Unfortunately, it was not quite the same with the girls. Their success would depend on their ability to please others; or, at least, on their ability to please one other person, since they were expected to discover for themselves suitable husbands. Therefore, Mrs Bholai was more alive to their shortcomings.

She did not hesitate to 'speak her mind' on the subject whenever they did anything to displease her. Mentally, she had paired Wilbert (this was the Wilbert whose aspect was infinitely pleasing) and Shanty and was not averse to dropping heavy hints which embarrassed everyone. When Shanty pouted and grew sullen, she pulled her up sharply. 'If you going to make somebody a good wife one of these days, you will have to learn to behave yourself better than that. No man would want a woman who does keep she face long long. You not sucking limes, you know. If you don't believe me, ask Wilbert if he would stand for that kind of behaviour from his wife.' She smiled genially at Wilbert. 'You wouldn't stand for that, would you, Wilbert?'

Normally, however, she gave more general advice. 'Marriage is no joke business,' she lectured frequently. 'Is a very serious business indeed. You have to be very careful and keep your eyes wide open. The three of you should try and learn from what happen to me. Don't take as the gospel truth everything you hear a man say because that could land you up in a lot of trouble. I thought I was marrying a man who was going to be a lawyer ... but you see what I end up with – two pound of butter, half-pound of salt. You have to keep a steady head on your shoulders for once you make the decision it have no turning back. I not saying you shouldn't have some love for your husband. But love, like everything else, have it proper time and place.'

Shanty, Mynah and Gita formed a spectrum whose sole unifying trait was their common ancestry. As children, their separate individualities had been submerged by the chorus of giggles which was their chief identifying characteristic. They were thought of and referred to simply as 'the Bholai girls'. As such, they were interchangeable with each other. Now that they were almost 'grown up', closer acquaintance showed how misleading the original impression of uniformity was.

Shanty, the youngest, was the most immediately striking.

She had a rectangular, padded-out appearance which smothered – perhaps 'blurred' is the more appropriate word – the natural curves of her body. Her face was round and full, with a pair of narrowing, Chinese-style eyes, a knob of a nose and firm, pouting lips. She was a heavy, earth-bound person. A reddish complexion had given her a rather inflamed look. Shanty occupied one end of the spectrum.

Mynah's was the middling position. She was cleaner complexioned than Shanty. Her skin did not possess the latter's inflamed opacity; but then, neither did it possess the smooth brown flawlessness of Gita's. Mynah was distinctly taller than Shanty: her build was not so compressed and was free of that blurred, padded-out appearance. Yet, though her general outline had greater boldness and assurance she lacked, as was implied by her middling status, Gita's ascetic fineness of feature. Mynah's nose was just that tiny bit too flat; her lips just that tiny bit too fleshy. Gita was tall and drooping and pale; a 'bag of skin and bones', as her mother said. They were types which had failed either by overstatement or uneasy compromise to come to full fruition. Looking at them, one experienced a nagging dissatisfaction such as might be felt on seeing stray bits of paper littering an otherwise clean and tidy room. You have the urge to straighten and adjust. And so it was with the three Bholai girls. You were tempted to go up to them and start tampering with their lips and eyes and noses. 'There! That's how it should be. That's much better!'

They differed as well in outlook and temper. Gita did not belie her ascetic appearance. She was of a serious and melancholy disposition; the 'saint' of the family. What was worse, she seemed to revel in the martyrdom it entailed. This distressed her mother who assisted her martyrdom by making her the victim of a relentless persecution because of her religious proclivities. Like love, God too clearly had His time and place. He reduced her chances of acquiring a husband. 'I don't know how you ever expect to find a man,' Mrs Bholai railed at her. 'Who you think would want a woman who always praying to God and looking as if the world just about to come to an end?' Gita bore it all with maddening patience.

'You always fretting, Ma,' she replied with a stock resignation. 'I can't change the way I am. You have to take me as I am. Not all of us was born the same.'

Mrs Bholai could not bring herself to accept this as she could not bring herself to accept so many other things. It was a most distasteful philosophy. 'Come now, Moon,' her husband pleaded, 'it have no point in threatening the child like that. Give she a chance. What you expect she to do? Run out on the road and grab the first man she see passing?' 'Keep out of this, Bholai. If I follow you, I would never get any of them off my hands. But let me tell you this straight, Mr Shopkeeper, I not having any old maid living in this house with me. You will have to take Gita with you and go and live somewhere else. I not having any of that nonsense here.'

Living in this atmosphere of threat and recrimination, Gita responded by emphasizing her religiosity and pursuing her studies with a dedication which none could rival. The fruits of the first were too intangible to assess; but if the fruits of the second were anything to go by, it was obvious – to her mother at any rate – that Gita was a malingerer on both counts. Admittedly, she had evolved a beautiful and ornate handwriting but, that apart, her school reports bore no relation to the hours she spent crouched over her text-books. Even in Bible Studies her marks were mediocre. This stoked Mrs Bholai's fury. 'Pretending! That is all you doing. Pretending! Just like Miss Sita who does spend all she time pretending to read book. Except that you does pretend to pray as well. But it seem to me that God don't hear your so-called prayers. I feel like taking that big Bible you have and knocking your head with it.' And once, when Gita's school report was particularly disappointing, she did something which left even her mother speechless with horror. Gita went secretly and bought half a bottle of rum from the Palace of Heavenly Delights and drank most of it. She was found several hours later sprawled in a drunken stupor under her bed.

Where Gita failed so conspicuously to please, Mynah succeeded. She was her mother's favourite daughter; her prize exhibit, second only to Julian in her affections. 'By far the

140

prettiest and best-behaved of the three,' she would say. 'Is a pity that Gita and Shanty not like she. Even as a baby Mynah was different from them. I remember when I was having Mynah, it didn't have a day when I was sick. But it was another story altogether with Gita and Shanty. Gita especially. I could hardly raise my head off the pillow without vomiting all over the place. Ask anybody if it wasn't so.' Mr Bholai would object mildly. 'I don't remember it being like that, Moon. It was more or less the same with all of them.' 'You!' Mrs Bholai spluttered. 'Who ask you anything? You who can't see what in front of your own nose contradicting me. Well I never! Soon you going to be saying is you who carry them in your belly and not me.'

Thus Gita's and Shanty's sins chased them to the womb. Mrs Bholai could not sing Mynah's praises loudly enough. 'The man who finally marry she should thank his lucky stars. It could only have a handful of men in the whole of Trinidad who deserve she – if it have any at all, that is.' Indeed, as time went on, it became increasingly apparent to her that there were *no* such men in Trinidad; and she came to the conclusion that Mynah would have to find herself an Englishman. It was Mynah who sprinkled vases of artistically arranged flowers about the Bholai sitting-room; and, as extra accomplishments, did watercolour drawings and played the violin in fits and starts.

Between Mynah and Shanty there was an unconcealed rivalry, aided and abetted by their mother's open partiality. Gita, unfitted for such a struggle, acted in vain the part of peacemaker; and Mr Bholai, reduced to the level of an impotent spectator, could do nothing but watch the battles of the warring factions from a distance. Shanty, who had no artistic pretensions, poured scorn on Mynah's efforts. Sometimes their battles were more than verbal and they fought with each other, Mynah usually getting the worst of it; though they both emerged with scratches and bruises. 'These children,' Mr Bholai complained, 'they going to send me to my grave well before my time. And Moon don't help matters. She does behave exactly like one of them.'

141

It was only Julian who commanded anything akin to authority. None of the girls willingly courted his displeasure. Mynah might have tried but that would have meant forfeiting her mother's support. Julian alone could restrain his mother's extremist tendencies by coming manfully to Shanty's defence. They were fellow conspirators against their mother. It was hard for Mrs Bholai to understand how Julian could be so blind to his sister's manifest faults. In temper, he and Shanty resembled one another: they shared the same perverse and obstinate streak. But what was pardonable – and even charming – in Julian, was unforgivable in his wayward sister.

The sanitary screen had not worked effectively with Shanty. She was not unwilling to expose herself to the profane scrutiny of the Settlement, unafraid of showing herself in the grocery, serving and talking to the customers, male and female alike, with no sign of embarrassment or any undue maidenly modesty. She was unaffected when the men sitting outside the Palace of Heavenly Delights whistled at her and doffed their hats. 'If you go on playing the woman with me,' Mrs Bholai warned, 'I going to throw you out of this house. You as shameless as Sushila and Miss Sita. Mynah wouldn't dream of doing the things that you does do. She wouldn't embarrass me like that. But your father have to share some of the blame too for making we live in a place like this.' Nevertheless, Shanty persisted in her errors, supported by her brother who, to Mrs Bholai's dismay, undermined her every effort to direct her daughter on to the paths of sanitation and righteousness. Still, while Wilbert was there, Mrs Bholai did her best to tone down the virulence of her criticisms (though she could not eliminate them entirely) so as to present her daughter in a more flattering light and not sabotage her unspoken hopes; and, to promote them, she left the two young people alone as often as was seemly.

'It looks,' Shanty said, 'as if Ma has plans for us.'

They were in the sitting-room. The family had – allegedly – gone to bed. 'But don't let that worry you,' Mrs Bholai had said. 'The two of you could stay up as long as you like.'

Wilbert laughed. 'What kind of plans?'

'Work it out for yourself. Why you suppose she leave us here?' Shanty giggled. 'Your father really have millions stashed away under his bed as Ma keeps saying?'

'I don't know about that,' Wilbert replied. 'The only thing he have under his bed is books – as far as I know.'

Shanty, drawing her knees close together, pouted irritably at him. 'I don't mean literally. I mean in the bank or somewhere like that.'

'He never tell me about it. But is not millions.'

'That's a relief.' She laughed.

'Why?'

'Because if it was millions I would have to marry you. That's why. As it is, I could take you or leave you.' She threw her arms up in the air.

'Who say I would want to marry you?'

'You would have no say in the matter,' she replied calmly. She narrowed her Chinese eyes and, resting her hands on her knees, swung them easily to and fro.

'Oh?'

Shanty leaned back casually in her chair, clasping her palms together. 'Ma would point a gun at your head. You wouldn't have a chance.' Drawing her legs up under her, Shanty folded herself into a convivial heap, twisting her head to one side. The skin over her knees was stretched with such a taut smoothness, it was easy to imagine her legs were truncated at that point. For Shanty, the situation breathed promise. Wilbert's coming to stay with them had opened up the possibility of an illicit sexual adventure: she had resolved on it even before she had set eyes on him. It was an experiment and virtually anyone would have sufficed. To that extent, her plans had coincided with her mother's. But she did not know how to set about it and, to disguise her latent unease, had adopted an aggressive and bantering tone in all their encounters. It had puzzled Wilbert. Of the three girls he was most drawn to her: her liveliness attracted him. But though she was more friendly to him than either of the other two (Mynah was aloof and Gita was wrapped up in her peculiar affairs), her friendliness had been oblique and inconsistent. Her approachability fluctuated from hour to hour and he was at a loss to know what regulated it. Tonight was the nearest they had come to anything like a straightforward conversation.

'What kind of woman you would like to marry?' she asked.

'I never think about it.' Wilbert smiled. 'What kind of man you would like to marry?'

'I would like to marry someone like Julian,' she replied unhesitatingly. 'He has nearly all the qualities I admire in a man. Intelligence. Good looks. A sense of humour. Lots of other things.' She gazed up at the ceiling. 'But there can't be many like that about.'

Wilbert frowned and said nothing.

Shanty peered at him. 'You jealous?'

'Not at all.'

'You don't like Julian, do you?'

'I never said so.'

'You don't have to say anything. I could tell – I not that foolish, you know.' She squinted at him. 'The two of you don't get on. Anybody could see that from a mile off. Why is that? And don't say it's because the two of you not in the same class. Pa might swallow that but not me.'

'We is different people,' Wilbert said. 'He like reading books. He going to be a doctor. As for me ... well, I have to look after my father business when he die.'

'There must be more than that to it ...'

Shanty laughed. 'Okay. Anything you say. What you want to talk about?'

Wilbert shrugged. 'Anything – but not Julian.'

Shanty curled herself into the depths of the chair. 'You ever kiss a girl?'

Wilbert started. 'No,' he said after a short pause.

'Never?'

'Never.'

Shanty's head sagged. She played with one of the buttons on her blouse.

'What about you?'

Shanty raised her head and looked at him narrowly. 'Once,'

she admitted, 'with one of my cousins in San Fernando.' She laughed mutedly. 'That was fun. Everybody was sleeping at the time – like now as a matter of fact. He was very experienced.' She folded herself even more compactly and shivered a little, as if she were cold. 'Well?' she prompted with a hint of annoyance. 'You can't expect me to do all the work. We may as well make use of the opportunity Ma give us.' She stared boldly at him: she had rehearsed this scene. 'Don't tell me you frighten.'

'I not frighten,' he said. However, he remained as he was.

'Prove it then.'

With an effort, Wilbert got up and took the few steps across to where she sat and stared down at her inflamed, upturned, pouting face.

'Well? Is not a telephone conversation we having, you know.' She spoke carelessly.

Wilbert brought his face closer to hers.

She retreated. 'Switch off the light.' It was a command.

Wilbert switched off the light. In the darkness he bent low over her and Shanty closed her eyes, the lids squeezed tight and puckering. Their lips brushed lightly. A car went by on the road below, its tyres screeching on the curve. He would have been glad of release but there was no likelihood of that: he had committed himself. Shanty's mouth smelled of toothpaste and his expiring pleasure melted away finally in its raw, clinical freshness. He was detached, giving in to Shanty's gratuitous, grappling violence. They groped and fumbled in an awkward, interminable embrace, teeth chattering in their tangled mouths, breathing in rushed gasps. At last Shanty drew away from him, disengaging herself, and sank back into the chair, opening her eyes. She rearranged her tousled hair and straightened her crumpled blouse.

'You enjoyed that? Is never so good the first time. You have to have practice.' She giggled. 'Practice makes perfect.'

'Everything is an art.' Wilbert smiled. 'Yes,' he said, 'I enjoyed it.' In retrospect, it did seem to him that he had enjoyed it and now that it was over, the anticipatory pleasure revived. Maybe Shanty was right. Maybe it would be better the second time. He bent low over her again, but Shanty pushed him away, laughing softly.

'No, no. That was enough for tonight. Is not good to overdo it. You mustn't be too greedy.' She stood up, yawning and stretching. 'Tomorrow night,' she said.

'Here?'

'No. Not here. In the garden. Is safer there.' She vanished behind the partition.

The garden was a collection of strange black shapes. There was no wind and it was warm and close. The slim crescent of the moon was hidden by cloud. Wilbert wandered along the line of the fence which sagged and bellied its way around the garden, plucking at the leaves of the rose bushes and the fruit trees. The frogs croaked deafeningly. Once he turned to look at the house. The windows in the back bedroom were open and he could see a light burning dimly behind the motionless curtains. Then he returned up the steps.

Shanty avoided him the next day; as provocative and contrary as she had ever been. Wilbert sought her out and managed, eventually, to corner her in the kitchen where she was doing the washing-up.

'I can't think why you been following me around all day for.' She was piling dirty cups and glasses in the sink.

'Why you didn't come last night?'

'Last night?' She was casual and offhand. 'Where was I supposed to go last night?' She held one of the glasses under the running tap and scrubbed concentratedly.

'You know well enough. The garden.'

'Oh! That you talking about.' She giggled. 'It wasn't convenient.'

Wilbert grasped her arm. 'You lying.'

She laughed, putting down the glass to drain. 'Let go my arm. You hurting me.'

'Not until you answer my question.' He tightened his grip.

She lost her temper. 'But what the hell you think it is? You think you own me or something?' She tugged resolutely but

146

to no avail. 'Don't get any fancy ideas in your head. I not married to you and I not intending to get married to you. The night before was fun. That was all. Now let me go before somebody come in and find you behaving like a fool.'

'It was Julian who put you up to it, not so? You and he plan it together . . .' Depression crept over him. Depression and rage.

'If you don't let me go this instant I'll scream.' She opened her mouth wide, ready to carry out her threat. 'If I had known you was going to be like this . . .'

Wilbert dropped her arm. He was walking away when Julian entered the kitchen.

'I hope I'm not interrupting anything.' Julian was jovial. 'Just say the word and I'll disappear.'

'You not interrupting anything,' Shanty said.

Julian swaggered around the kitchen, his hands in his trouser pockets. 'I just finished reading a really great book. It's a pity you don't like reading, Ramsaran. You don't know what you're missing.' He slapped his sister on the bottom. 'What the two of you been talking about, eh? Or is it a secret?' He winked at her.

'It's no secret,' Shanty said. 'We were talking about the garden.'

'The garden!' Julian exclaimed. 'That's a strange thing to be talking about.'

Shanty giggled and resumed the washing-up.

'What's Shanty been saying to you about the garden, Ramsaran?'

Wilbert was standing in the doorway. 'Ask her,' he said. He went out and Shanty's laughter billowed behind him. The taste of raw toothpaste still seemed to linger at the back of his throat and he swallowed hard to get rid of it. But it would not go. It had lodged there like a constricting bone.

5

Mrs Bholai was not far from right when she saw Wilbert and Julian as natural enemies. In this respect she was more perceptive than her husband. The barriers to friendship were mutual. It was an elemental antagonism which neither could control. Wilbert was profoundly jealous of Julian. He envied his good looks and the universal admiration he excited. It was impossible for him to compete with Julian's charm and wit. He was slower, more thoughtful and deliberative. Ideally, Julian would have liked to use Wilbert as he used everybody else: as target practice for his exercises in vanity. Wilbert, recognizing the danger, did all he could to resist this: he could feel the temptation to slip under his domination. That morning, with Shanty's laughter billowing about him, his resentment came to a head. He scowled at the photographs decorating the walls of the bedroom; he scowled at the book-laden shelves; he scowled at the rows of model aeroplanes on the dresser. All these objects were like so many physical expressions of his hatred. The room was suffused with an alien, hostile presence. He heard Julian calling out to him.

'Ramsaran! Ramsaran!'

Wilbert did not answer. To be called 'Ramsaran' was suddenly hateful to him; as hateful as 'young master'.

'Ah! There you are, Ramsaran. I was wondering where you had got yourself to. Why you hiding in here? Was it Shanty who vex you?' Julian came into the room and sat down on his bed. 'You shouldn't let Shanty vex you. Tell me what it's all about.'

'I'm sure I don't have to tell you that.' Wilbert stared at the model aeroplanes.

Julian was mystified. 'How you mean, Ramsaran? I don't understand. What's it all about?' He smiled. 'Is it something to do with the garden?'

'Don't play innocent with me, Julian. You put her up to it.'

'To what, Ramsaran? You're talking in riddles. I haven't got the slightest idea what it is you're blaming me for.' He knitted his brows. 'Don't tell me you're still holding that business about the book and Sita against me. Is not that, is it?'

'That too,' Wilbert said.

'If it's a fight you want to pick, Ramsaran, you better go and find somebody else. I don't want to pick no fight with you. I don't believe in fighting.' Julian watched him anxiously.

Wilbert picked up one of the planes: the transport helicopter. He rotated the blades.

'It easy to break, Ramsaran. Be careful.'

'And suppose I break it?' Wilbert faced him for the first time since he had come into the room. 'What would you do if I break it?' He held the plane above his head.

'That's a stupid question. Why would you want to break it?' Julian laughed nervously, brushing, with a characteristic flick of the wrist, straying strands of hair away from his face.

'But supposing I did break it? Suppose I let it fall from my hand and smash on the floor. What would you do then?' It was as if Wilbert were listening to another person talk: a dispassionate witness of a stranger's fury.

'Then I would ask you to replace it.'

'And if I refuse?'

'Don't be childish, Ramsaran. Put down the plane and tell me why you so upset.'

Wilbert's fingers spreadeagled. The plane clattered on the floor, tiny wheels spinning across it. The blades fell off. Julian looked at Wilbert and laughed again. He bent down and picked up the twisted blades. 'What you think you doing, Ramsaran?'

For reply, Wilbert lunged forward and swept the front line of models off the dresser. Injured planes slid in every direction. There were broken wings and runaway wheels and dented fuselages. The laughter had gone from Julian's face.

'You taking it beyond a joke, Ramsaran.' Julian kneeled among the shattered models. 'Why you want to be doing a thing like this for?' There was genuine bewilderment and anguish in his voice.

An odd pity surged in Wilbert but he kicked at the planes again, grinding them under his heels so that the various bits were mauled beyond recognition.

'A savage! That's what you are. A savage like your father.' Julian leapt on him.

In a moment they were rolling on the floor and Wilbert was astride him, digging his shoes into Julian's ribs and pummelling him. 'Yes,' he said, 'I'm a savage and I'll show you what a savage can do. I'll show you.' His fingers gripped Julian's tautened neck. Julian flailed his arms frantically and Wilbert sensed the weakness of the body writhing and squirming under him.

'Surrender. Surrender.' The choked appeals for mercy were barely audible. Julian's eyes – so black! – flooded with fear. His hands pounded the floor. 'Surrender . . . I surrender, Ramsaran.' Tears trickled from the corner of his eyes. 'For God's sake, Ramsaran . . . for God's sake . . .'

Mrs Bholai came running into the room. She screamed when she saw them, flinging herself at Wilbert and attempting to draw his hands off her son's neck. Wilbert was only aware of her as an irritant and pushed her away.

'Oh God! Help us! It going to have murder here today. Bholai! Like you deaf? I tell you it going to have murder in this house today.'

The Bholai girls crowded into the room. Shanty joined with her mother to free Julian from Wilbert's grasp. Mr Bholai's voice boomed in the distance. Wilbert relaxed his grip. Julian closed his eyes and groaned. His neck was red.

'He dead. My Julian dead. Jules! Open your eyes and speak to me. Speak to your mother. I had tell you it was going to be murder in this house if you invite Wilbert to stay with we, Bholai. But you was deaf and now it too late. My Jules dead. Dead.'

Mr Bholai stooped down beside them. 'He not dead. You could see he still breathing.'

Julian opened his puffed eyes and gazed sheepishly at his mother who was weeping copious tears. She crouched over him and taking a handkerchief from her bosom mopped his face.

'Thank the Lord you still alive. Is a miracle how you survive. I really thought he had murder you.' She cradled him. 'And you,' she said, turning on Wilbert, 'you, a guest in this house, was going to murder my one and only son. For what?

150

Tell me.' She stared at the grey wreckage of the planes. 'Look at that! It take Julian years to collect them and in a moment you mash it all up. Then you have the boldface to stand there grinning at me. Grinning!'

Wilbert did not realize he had been smiling.

'This is no grinning matter though. You haven't hear the end of this yet. No sir!' Mrs Bholai mopped Julian's face with the handkerchief. 'I going to make sure your father hear about this. Somebody will have to pay for the damage you cause.'

'Now, now, Moon,' Mr Bholai murmured soothingly. 'You have no reason to turn on Wilbert like that. How you know is his fault alone? I sure they was only playing with one another. Boys like to fight and play rough.' He scrupulously avoided looking at the wrecked planes and Julian's neck where the red marks of Wilbert's fingers still showed plainly.

'That wasn't playing, Bholai. Don't think I was born yesterday. He was going to murder him. Look at Julian face. You see how swell-up it is? You don't get that from playing.' She lifted Julian's head for inspection.

'Boys will be boys,' Mr Bholai said vaguely.

'Boys will not be boys,' Mrs Bholai answered hotly, 'when it come to killing and murdering each other.'

Mr Bholai was silent. He was hoping Julian would come to the rescue; and Wilbert too was hoping for something of the sort. The noble gesture would have been in keeping with his character. However, for reasons best known to himself, Julian remained quiet, submitting passively to the caresses of his mother.

'I think you exaggerating the whole thing, Moon.' He sighed and rested a flour-coated palm on Wilbert's shoulder. 'Still, you boys shouldn't fight so rough. You might really hurt each other bad one of these days, and then it will be too late to be sorry.'

'Huh! He nearly murder your son and that is all you have to say?'

Mr Bholai would commit himself no sterner rebuke. Dusting his flour-stained palms, he walked slowly out of the room and returned downstairs to the grocery.

Mrs Bholai assisted Julian to his feet. She directed a wrinkled finger at Wilbert. He thought of his mother's fingers with nails like pink, seaside shells. Mrs Bholai's did not resemble hers. They were harder; colder. Julian, his back to them, was looking out of the window. The cars went by steadily on the road below. 'You listening to me, young man? My husband too frighten to tell you what I now going to tell you . . .'

Wilbert was not listening to her. The cars went by: cars going to Port-of-Spain and San Fernando; San Fernando and Port-of-Spain.

'. . . I don't care who your father is. He could be Governor of Trinidad or king of the whole world for all I care. That don't make the slightest difference to me . . .'

Port-of-Spain and San Fernando; San Fernando and Port-of-Spain. Julian looked out of the window.

'. . . but the next time you try and harm my son, it will be a different story. Make no mistake about that. Come, Julian. A cup of tea is what you need.'

Mother and son left the room. The girls trailed after them.

For some minutes Wilbert stood among the wreckage. He collected the bits in a heap on the top of the dresser. Overwhelmed with guilt and shame for the petty and senseless destruction he had wreaked, it occurred to him he should try and put them together again. He set to work, sitting cross-legged on the floor; but the task was a patently absurd one.

'I wouldn't bother.' Julian leaned against the edge of the door watching him. His eyes were still puffed but his face was not as red and swollen as it had been.

Wilbert dropped the pieces of mangled plastic he was holding. 'I'll pay you for them.'

'You don't have to do that, Ramsaran. Building them was the real fun. I'm not going to start all over again.'

'But I want to pay you for them.' He spoke roughly. 'I break them so I must pay for them.'

'I don't want your money,' Julian said.

'There must be something else . . .'

'For the moment I can't think of anything. But if you insist . . .'

'I do.'

'I'll let you know when I think of something.'

They looked not at each other but at the wrecked planes.

Chapter Five

1

Sushila redecorated Rani's room according to her peculiar taste, the junk she had scornfully discarded being replaced with junk of her own. She, no less than Rani, had her favourite photographs. However, they were not of snowy Swiss mountains. Instead, she had glossy photographs of famous Hollywood stars. These she obtained from a 'friend' who managed a cinema. Women, though, were excluded from her picture gallery. Egbert Ramsaran remarked on this.

'You notice that, eh? Is a funny thing with me and my own sex. I don't like them at all.'

Egbert Ramsaran raised his eyebrows. 'What about your daughter? You don't like she?'

'Is different with your own child. Though I wouldn't mind telling you when Sita was born and I find it was a girl and not a boy that I had, I nearly dash she to the ground right there and then. For days I couldn't bear to look at she.'

'Is that so?'

'I never make friends with a woman yet,' Sushila boasted. 'The worst kind of woman is those who have scrawny legs and breasts. They think is refined to be like that.' She laughed. 'But I know what men really like.'

'What?'

Sushila roared with laughter.

At any one time Sushila would have at least a dozen photographs pinned in a wavering line along the walls of her room. They were a good barometer of her inconstancy. By some mysterious process, the stars rose and fell in her estimation. Occasionally, the fallen might be reinstated (Errol Flynn had that distinction) but, usually, they disappeared without trace. Thus over a period of weeks, one set of faces might be completely supplanted in her affections by another. Egbert Ramsaran remarked on this too.

'I just didn't care for him any more,' she would say.

'How come?' he persisted. 'Last week . . .'

'Last week was last week,' she pontificated. 'You should never think about what happen last week. What good that ever do? The important thing is the thing that happening right this very minute – like me talking to you. Nothing else concern me. Neither the past nor the future. About the one I can't do nothing and about the other I just don't know. The only sensible way to behave is to take life as it come and not ask too many questions.' She smiled jauntily. 'Worries does make you old. The only sensible way to behave is to take life as it come. I does never ask myself why I do this and why I do that. I does let other people do my worrying for me.'

Sushila was infatuated to the point of obsession with adornment. It was as essential to her nature as regret and worry were inessential. Her metabolism seemed to crave it. To adorn was not merely to improve and make more palatable. It was to make real. Everything, including herself, had to be embellished; heightened; and touched up. She used the heaviest, most scented powders and perfumes. Her lipsticks were brilliant and gaudy. She had developed unconventional ideas of value. For example, her jewellery, though for the most part cheap and tawdry stuff, was appreciated and treasured the more for being inlaid with coloured stones, immediately striking to the eye and of a bewildering variety of shapes and sizes. The fact that they were valueless meant nothing at all to her. Her fondness for frills and laces was inordinate. She had a child's delight in objects that glittered, flashed and sparkled. Surface; appearance: these were the beginning and the end; the limits of her world. She cared for nothing else. Responsive only to the promptings of the fleeting urge, Sushila was neglectful, contemptuous and a little afraid of what might be lying beyond. She spoke truly when she said she let other people do her worrying for her.

Yet, after the unrelieved aridity of Rani's life, Sushila could not but come as a revelation. Her laughter rang through the

Ramsaran house and dominated it. While she worked, she wore short, tight bodices, tied into a knot at the front, which left much of her stomach exposed; and her arms, burnt a reddish-brown by the sun, how firm and fleshy they were! It was necessary that someone be aware of her existence – even if that someone was herself. On several occasions Egbert Ramsaran caught Sushila unawares, riveted by the sight of her own breasts in the mirror; or lifting up her skirts and examining her thighs. Discovery did not embarrass her. She laughed full-throatedly when she saw him.

All men elicited the same response in her. She demanded, if not to be admired, at least to be noticed; and, to achieve her ends, Sushila would flaunt herself shamelessly. A male presence transformed and enlivened her. It was a kind of sport with her; a challenge to her prowess. No man was too old, too young, too ugly, too inaccessible (possession of a wife simply enhanced his attraction) for her to bring her talents into play. It was a pursuit dictated by her own needs and convenience and there was neither tenderness nor regard for her prey. She aroused desire to no purpose beyond desire itself. It was a callous, cynical and selfish deployment of her powers.

Egbert Ramsaran wilted under her provocations. Indeed, provocation is too weak a description of what was taking place between them. It was more like assault. Sushila pursued him ruthlessly and he seemed to have no defences against her. He did try to avoid too close a contact with her; too prolonged an exposure. But Sushila harried him, forcing a recognition of her presence on him. She would not allow him to forget she was there. Her laughter dogged him, penetrating the locked door of his bedroom and invading his dreams. A voluptuous ease was tempting him, clouding his concentration. It was wearing him down as inexorably as water wears down the toughest stone.

Overnight (for so it appeared to him) his will had deteriorated and become flabby. It was unable to resist the new demands upon it. His balance had gone askew – like the almanac on his wall. Sometimes, in the midst of restless sleep, a whirlpool of bewitching urges formed in Egbert Ramsaran's brain and, prisoned in its grip, he was spun round and round and dragged down to some point of explosive dissolution deep within himself. To break free, he had to mobilize every available resource of his faltering will in order to prise his eyes open and regain possession of his fragmented faculties. He would awake, bathed in sweat and afraid to surrender to the anarchy of sleep again. The temptation to let go was irresistible. What a relief it would be if he could abandon himself to these invisible tides washing round him and allow them to carry him wherever they chose. He was soon to realize how far down the path of dissolution he had already travelled.

Singh continued to come to the house occasionally, bringing bags of fruit from the estate, which he would dump on the kitchen floor. But here was no Rani to whom he could give Trinidad one-cent stamps and talk after his own fashion. He was more incommunicable and silent than ever. Having failed to extract even a grudging admiration from him, Sushila began to hector and bully him. She dubbed him 'Mr Gorilla'. She would circle about him trailing the scents of her rich powders and perfumes. 'What big, hairy paws you have, Mr Gorilla!' She touched his hand lightly and jumped back. 'I hope you don't put your big, hairy paws on me, Mr Gorilla.' She danced and flitted about him, her squeals of merriment filling the house. 'What nasty pointed teeth you have, Mr Gorilla. I hope you don't bite me with your nasty pointed teeth. Mr Gorilla getting really angry with me. Grr ... grr ...' She went on in this vein for as long as his visits lasted.

The blood flooded Singh's dark face and he bit hard on his lower lip. 'You just wait,' he muttered. 'I know the kind of woman you is. You just wait.'

Singh turned up at the house unexpectedly one evening. It was obvious that he had been drinking. He shuffled into the kitchen and propped himself up against the big window.

'You should be in the zoo this time of night, Mr Gorilla,' Sushila said. 'You liable to frighten people to death roaming about in the dark.'

'I is not a gorilla.'

157

'You look like one though. And you does behave like one.'

'I tell you I is not a gorilla.'

Sushila laughed. 'What you is then?'

'I is a man! A man! Can't you see?'

'What get into you all of a sudden, Mr Gorilla?' Sushila stared at him inquisitively. She was not quite so assured now.

'I tell you I is not a gorilla,' Singh yelled, 'I is a man!'

Sushila watched him warily.

Singh heaved himself up from the windowsill. 'Don't mock me. I don't like people mocking me.' He lumbered towards her; menacing and begging.

'If you know what's good for you, Mr Gorilla, you wouldn't make any trouble here.' Sushila retreated towards the door. 'You drunk.'

Singh grinned, showing his uneven, yellowing teeth. 'That's right. I drunk. What you running away from me for? Don't tell me you frighten of me.'

Sushila halted. 'You only going to make trouble for yourself tonight, Singh. I warning you.'

'So I have a name after all.'

'Keep away from me, Singh.'

'Try and stop me.' He lumbered towards her. 'What you could do to stop me?' He leered.

Sushila resumed her retreat. 'Is not what I could do. Is what *he* could do to you.'

Singh stopped dead. 'Is that how it is?'

'Yes.' Observing the effect her words had had, she was brazen again.

'You lying.'

'Try and see.'

'You lying!' He leapt at her.

Sushila sidestepped him nimbly, sticking a foot out. Singh, moving clumsily and unsteadily in his boots, tripped and fell on the tiles. He lay sprawled there, ridiculous and enraged. Sushila, her feet planted widely apart, her hands resting on her hips, stood over him laughing like a conqueror.

'What's all this noise and shouting?' Egbert Ramsaran

ran quickly into the kitchen. He stared in astonishment at Singh. 'Singh! What is the meaning of this? What you doing there?'

'He drunk,' Sushila said.

'Lying bitch,' Singh muttered.

'That's enough, Singh. Get up at once.' Egbert Ramsaran's voice whistled. 'I want an explanation.'

Singh, grinning malevolently, hauled himself up painfully and dusted the seat of his trousers.

'She was mocking me,' Singh said. 'And I don't like people mocking me.' He gazed fixedly at the spot where he had recently been sprawled so ignominiously.

Egbert Ramsaran looked at Sushila. He turned again to Singh as if afraid to look at her too long. 'How she been mocking you?'

'She does mock me every time I come here. But I is not a gorilla. I is a man. Anybody could see I is a man. I have the same two arms and two legs and a head. Why she have to mock me for?'

'It still don't give you the right to come in here drunk.'

'I is a man. Like other men. And I not going to let anybody mock me.' He raised his head. 'I know the kind of woman she is. You shouldn't have a woman like she in your house. You should . . .'

'Enough!'

'You shouldn't have she in this house. All she want from you is . . .'

'Enough!' Egbert Ramsaran advanced on him.

'All she want from you is . . .'

'Get the hell out of here, Singh! Get out! Get out!' Egbert Ramsaran stalked the length of the kitchen. 'Don't set foot here again until I tell you. You understand me? I not going to have you coming in here drunk and . . .' He piped a stream of imprecations at him.

'So that's how it is.' Singh nodded as though the truth had just dawned on him. 'That's how it is.'

'Get out!'

Still nodding to himself, Singh walked out of the kitchen and went slowly down the back steps and out into the yard.

'Thank God for that,' Sushila said.

Egbert Ramsaran eyed her gloomily.

That he should have quarrelled with Singh and actually expelled him from the house was unbelievable. It marked a definite break with the past. The whole tenor of his life was shattering and he, Egbert Ramsaran, was assisting at the process. It was a macabre spectacle. His clarity had not deserted him. But what good was it to him now? It only added to his mortification because he could not act in conformity with its dictates. No enemy, had he heartily wished it, could have contrived his destruction so skilfully; could have reduced him to such a predicament.

Egbert Ramsaran was choked with an impotent rage against this woman who had descended from nowhere to haunt him. 'It would be so easy,' he told himself over and over again, 'to send her away. So easy.' He snapped his fingers. 'I just have to say the word and she would be out of here. God is my witness that if I could send Singh away, I could pack she back to where she come from too. I iust have to say the word.' The word was on the tip of his tongue but the word was never said, dying before it could pass his lips. 'I will bide my time. Give her enough rope and she bound to hang herself.'

The opportunity slipped away. It became remote. And, finally, it slipped away altogether. Getting rid of Sushila would have solved nothing. Uncontrollable forces had been unleashed in him. Sushila had set in motion age-old desires and he was powerless in their grasp.

Sushila sensed the imminence of victory. To have secured the expulsion of Singh was a signal triumph. She who had sacrificed nothing stood to gain all. These last nights, ever since the quarrel with Singh, she had lain awake tense with expectancy. Another trophy was about to be added to her collection. Without having to exert herself unduly, she had watched Egbert Ramsaran crumble day by day before her eyes. It had been so easy. The chief threat had been the possibility of her dismissal but that hurdle was safely behind her. It was now out of the question. He had virtually offered himself up to her. Sushila laughed. She was too excited to sleep. Tossing the blanket to one side, she sat up and clasped her arms about her knees.

There passed in review all those hostile faces in the Settlement and particularly that of Mrs Bholai sheltering behind her newspaper and whipping her son away from the verandah rail as if the mere sight of her, Sushila, would cause him to drop dead on the spot. Revenge would be sweet. If she could bring Sita to live here, that would add a new edge to the sweetness. Sushila and Sita living in the house of Egbert Ramsaran! Sushila giggled.

But after that consummation, what? Sushila did not know. Events would take their course and she would act accordingly. For the moment, she was comfortable, settled and extremely pleased with herself. Life had always been kind to her. Extraordinarily kind. Things had never failed to turn out to her advantage. Pleasure, happiness and freedom had fallen into her lap. She had been an amazingly lucky woman. She congratulated herself, putting a complacent trust in the protection of her guardian angel. She had never stayed long enough in one place to witness the price exacted for her amazing good fortune. Sushila, allergic to pain – her own and other people's – had invariably departed in good time, fleeing before suffering like a leaf chased by the wind. She lived on a mounting accumulation of credit. But, so far, her method had worked and Sushila could see no reason why it should not continue to do so in the future. The world was sufficiently vast to accommodate the depredations of someone like her. There would always be somewhere to hide; somewhere to run to. Thus, her arms clasped about her knees, she sat there surrounded by her ephemeral gallery of photographs and waited for events to take their predestined course.

Wilbert listened to the hollow thud of his father's footsteps across the creaking floorboards. They stopped outside his door. Was he coming to see him at this hour of the night? To explain the rupture with Singh perhaps? No. That was unlikely. It might be that an acute attack of indigestion was keeping him awake. His indigestion had been geting worse: he hardly ever stopped complaining about how bad it was. None of these explanations convinced Wilbert and he quelled the temptation to call out. Straining his ears, he listened. The silence seemed to deepen. Then the footsteps moved off, retracing their path towards the front of the house, the floorboards creaking.

He heard his father open the door to his bedroom but he did not hear it click shut. Then, with abrupt decision, the footsteps returned, padding hollowly. This time they did not pause but faded rapidly towards the back of the house. Sushila must have been expecting him for the door to her room opened and closed; and, without a word or whisper being exchanged, his father's footsteps were swallowed up within. After that all was quiet and Wilbert ceased to listen.

2

Sita rocked on the hammock watching the cars go by on the road. A book was open on her lap and her legs dangled over the sides. Her shoes scraped the pounded earth floor. The air was warm and aromatic with the smell of dust and dry grass. Phulo sat on the steps of her hut combing through the hair of one of her children and searching for lice. The heat of early afternoon had smothered activity and when there was a lull in the traffic the only sounds would come from the clucking hens and the monotonous whirr of Sharma's sewing-machine. Basdai was asleep. Beyond the dilapidated fringe of houses hugging the curves of the main road were the green and dismal rectangles of sugarcane. Staring at that burning, offensive green, Sita's eyes acquired a remoteness of depth and a brooding melancholy. She swayed back and forth on the hammock.

A taxi stopped with a screech of brakes. Sita gazed at it idly but her expression changed to one of interest when she saw her mother step out and come quickly down the path. Sita got up from the hammock. Sushila smiled broadly at her as she entered the compound.

'Go and pack your clothes, Sita.'

'Why?' Sita asked. 'Where we going?' As if she did not know too well.

Phulo looked up.

'I come to take you away. Today self you going from here.'

Phulo thrust her child to one side. 'Well, well,' she said. 'It didn't take you long to bamboozle him.'

Sushila glanced at her, not deigning to answer. 'Go on, Sita. Go and pack your clothes. We don't have time to waste.'

'Ma!' Phulo yelled. 'Wake up! Come and hear the big news! Wake up!'

Sharma's machine stopped its whirring. 'What big news?' She poked her good-natured face through the window.

'Sushila taking Sita to live with she.'

Basdai groaned inside the hut. 'What's all that racket out there? I trying to get some rest.'

'Big news,' Phulo yelled hoarsely. 'Sushila come to take Sita with she.'

The children, galvanized into life, poured into the compound and joined in the chant. 'Sushila come to take Sita with she . . . Sushila come to take Sita with she . . .'

Basdai, rubbing her eyes, came outside. 'Eh? What's that you telling me?' She was bemused.

'I say Sushila come to take Sita with she,' Phulo yelled. 'At last.'

'For truth?' Basdai asked, comprehension slowly dawning. 'For truth?'

Sushila nodded. 'Today self.'

'It didn't take she long to bamboozle him,' Phulo said.

'And not only that,' Sushila said. She surveyed them proudly. 'He going to pay for she education too.'

Sita stared at her mother.

'You joking with me,' Basdai murmured.

Sushila shook her head. 'He going to pay for she education and, what is more, he going to send she to a Port-of-Spain school.'

'Well I never!' Basdai exclaimed. 'Even I never thought ...' She was too overcome to go on.

Phulo's mouth hung open. Sita continued to stare at her mother with a robot-like rigidity.

Basdai conquered her astonishment. She cackled joyously. 'I had tell you it would work out but you didn't believe me.' She turned to Sita. 'Is me you have to thank for this. I hope you know that.'

'Why she have to thank you?' Sushila asked.

'How you mean?' Basdai's ardour cooled. 'Is I who arrange for you to go there in the first place.'

Sushila shrugged. 'So what? Is nothing compared to what I had to do.'

'Ungrateful wretch. After all I do for you ...'

Sushila laughed. 'If he was to throw me out, you wouldn't waste any tears on me,' she said. 'Is I who running all the risk.'

'Ungrateful wretch! It gone to your head. But remember what so easy to go up easy to fall down too.'

'I not going to fall anywhere.'

'I will expose you.' Basdai was on the verge of tears.

Sushila protruded her lips. 'That won't do you any good. But feel free to try.'

Phulo's mouth curled bitterly. 'He will see through your tricks.'

'Jealousy!'

'Me! Jealous of you!' Phulo wrung her hands. 'At least I is a decent and respectable woman and don't have to use trickery to get what I want. I have a husband I could call my own.'

Sushila sneered. 'I wouldn't let any man do to me what I does see him doing to you.'

'My children don't have to run and hide they face when somebody say father.'

'A fat lot of good that doing you – and them.' She looked at Sita. 'You going to be better than the rest of them put together. You going to be somebody from now on and they all wishing they was in your shoes. That is the long and short of

164

it. Now go and pack your clothes. We don't have time to waste here.'

Sita went inside.

Egbert Ramsaran had been pacing the verandah restlessly all afternoon, looking at his watch and muttering. 'She should have been back by now,' he said to Wilbert. 'What you think keeping she?' He had asked the identical question a dozen times. 'All she had to do was go and pick up she daughter. That shouldn't take so long. What she could be doing? Is nearly four hours since she left and she say it wouldn't take more than two.' He walked down the path to the front gate and looked up and down the road. 'What could be keeping she so long? What?' He returned up the path and resumed his pacing. 'It getting dark already.' He sat down on a rocking chair; got up; and sat down again. The first stars glimmered. Egbert Ramsaran glanced at his watch. The cows were on their way home from pasture, marching in stately single file. The leader, a bit of rope trailing from its neck, meandered towards the gate which Egbert Ramsaran had not closed. 'Sonofabitch!' He rushed at the animal. It stood its ground. Egbert Ramsaran picked up a stone and aimed it at the animal's head.

'What's all this?' Sushila grinned at him from the road. 'Why you want to kill the poor thing?' She clapped her hands and grimaced at the cow. 'Shush! Shush!'

The cow backed away from the gate.

'You see,' she said. 'That's all you have to do. Simple!'

Egbert Ramsaran dropped the stone. 'What keep you so long? I been waiting for you all afternoon.'

'That was a stupid thing to do. I tell you it would take a little time. Sita had to say goodbye to everybody.' She giggled. 'It had a lot of kissing and hugging going on.'

'You was kissing and hugging for nearly five hours?'

Sushila frowned. 'I didn't know I had a timetable and that you was my timekeeper.'

They climbed the steps to the verandah. 'Never mind,' Egbert Ramsaran said. 'I was just a little nervous. The dark and

all that.' He was placatory. 'So! This is the Sita I've been hearing so much about.' He smiled at her. 'Welcome to your new
home, Sita. Your mother tell me so much about you I feel like
I known you for years.' His unreasonable agitation was being
replaced by an equally unreasonable exhilaration now that
Sushila had come back. He folded his arms round Sita in a
clumsy, muscular embrace, kissing her on either cheek. 'You
nearly as tall as me.'

Sita, despite these overtures, carried herself stiffly and her eyes
did not relinquish their stern, unsmiling seriousness. She submitted to his caresses with an aloof and dignified resignation.

Sushila, detached and ironical, observed the performance
from a distance.

'From now on you must treat me exactly as if I was your
father,' Egbert Ramsaran said. 'And Wilbert as your brother.'
Egbert Ramsaran pointed at his son. 'Let me introduce you
properly to one another. The two of you must get to know
each other and become friends.'

Sita smiled at Wilbert and inclined her head with that same
slight movement with which she had greeted him before. 'We
met already,' she said.

'Oh? When was that?'

Sita looked at Wilbert as if to suggest it was his turn to
speak.

'When I was staying with the Bholais,' Wilbert explained
reluctantly.

'So much the better! So much the better! It make me happy
to know the two of you is not perfect strangers.' Egbert
Ramsaran spoke eagerly. He wished to ingratiate himself with
this girl, to win her favour and approval. 'Your mother was
telling me that you is a bright child. That you want to be a
B.A. Languages – whatever that is.'

Sita twisted her body and stared at her mother. She seemed
annoyed. 'That is something I could never hope to be,' she
said.

'You never know,' Egbert Ramsaran replied cheerfully.
'Didn't your mother tell you I going to send you to one of
them big schools in Port-of-Spain?'

166

Sita averted her head. 'Yes,' she said in the merest whisper. 'It's very . . . it's very kind of you.'

Egbert Ramsaran laughed. 'Well then, that's the first step, not so?'

'You could look a little more pleased than that,' Sushila said, casting a lowering glance at her daughter.

'Is only shyness,' Egbert Ramsaran said. 'Don't bother she. But here we is talking about B.A. Languages and what not and I don't even know what it is.' He could not stop talking. A curious impulsion drove him on. He was aware of it but he could do nothing.

Sita unbent a little. She smiled pallidly at him. 'It stands for Bachelor of Arts,' she said.

'I thought only men could be bachelors.' It was not often Egbert Ramsaran tried to joke.

'It doesn't make any difference whether you're a man or woman.' She looked at Wilbert as if seeking confirmation for what she had said.

He stared at her blankly.

'That's enough for now,' Sushila said. 'Let's go inside.' She yawned. 'It's been a very tiring day.'

The conference broke up.

Within a month, Sita had left her country school and was enrolled as a student at a Port-of-Spain convent. Her reserve, however, did not break down. It was never easy to discover what she was thinking or feeling. She betrayed no particular pleasure at Egbert Ramsaran's paying for her to attend a 'good' school; but neither did she seem displeased by his generosity. Her behaviour towards him was, at all times, formal and correct. He had insisted that she call him 'Pa' (or failing that, 'Uncle') but Sita, while not explicitly refusing to do his bidding, clearly executed his wish only under duress; and then it was not 'Pa' but 'Uncle' which she preferred. She lived like a stranger in the house, setting off for school early in the morning with her books and pink plastic lunch-box and dressed in her neat pleated uniform. When she returned in the evening she helped her mother in the kitchen;

167

and, after dinner, she retired to her room at the first opportunity and worked until she went to bed.

'You enjoying your new school?' Egbert Ramsaran would
enquire.

'Yes.'

'And you does get on well with your teachers?'

'Yes. They're all very nice to me.'

'You have a lot of friends?'

'A few. Not too many. I don't like having too many friends.'

'That's sensible,' Egbert Ramsaran said approvingly. 'The
few friends you have – they want to be B.A. Languages too?'

'Not all of them.'

'You is the brightest girl in your class?'

Sita fidgeted. 'I wouldn't say so.'

'Who brighter than you?'

'Nearly everybody.'

'I sure that is not true.'

Sita laughed deprecatingly.

'You must invite your friends to come and see you here
if you lonely. You mustn't be bashful.'

'I'm not lonely.'

'Still, you must invite them.'

'Yes,' Sita said.

But she never did. Her reserve remained impenetrable and,
in spite of his efforts, Egbert Ramsaran could coax nothing
more out of her. She was just as guarded with Wilbert. What
was happening between her mother and Egbert Ramsaran
could not be ignored. It fell like a poisonous shadow between
them, blocking the development of friendship. If anything,
her embarrassment with regard to him was greater than it was
with his father. Sita could not confront Wilbert without that
poisonous shadow obtruding itself; and neither could he confront her. As if by mutual agreement, they avoided each other's
company. When they did meet there was confusion and hesi-
tation on both sides.

Sushila was deeply irritated by her daughter's behaviour.

'You don't like living here?' she asked.

'I don't mind,' Sita said.

'That is all you have to say? You have no gratitude for the man who paying for your education?'

'I'm very grateful for everything he's doing for me. But you must see it's not easy for me.'

'How? You should be happy as the day is long.'

'It's not so easy,' Sita repeated. 'Put yourself in my position. If you do that you might realize . . .'

'I realize,' Sushila sneered. 'Is all that false pride you have.'

'It's not false pride.' Sita was adamant. 'If you can't see . . .'

Sushila lost her temper. 'I could see well enough,' she shouted at her. 'Like you prefer living in the Settlement with Basdai and Phulo and Sharma? If that is what you want I could arrange to send you back there straight away. They would be only too glad.'

Sita was silent under this onslaught. There were many things she could have said but she had no idea how to begin saying them. In any case, Sita knew her mother would not understand. She would not even be interested.

3

The disparity of character and the lack of understanding that existed between them was more obvious and disquieting to both only because this was the longest period they had lived together as mother and daughter. It had always been so. Prolonged association had simply brought it out into the open. During Sushila's brief, whirlwind descents on the Settlement the truth had been disguised, to some extent, by the fleeting violence of her publicly displayed affection. Yet even that could not entirely obscure the residual uneasiness lurking not far below the surface and becoming more apparent as Sita grew older. The uneasiness was hard and unyielding and permanent. There had been an overly frenzied aspect to those orgiastic sessions; as if Sushila had to flay herself into the conviction that she loved her daughter and was not an unnatural mother. The times they spent together seemed to permit no stillnesses. Silence would descend with unpremeditated sud-

169

denness, revealing gaps of deadening incomprehension which Sushila – never Sita – endeavoured to bridge with a rush of extravagant nonsense; promising her more books, more dresses, more toys.

To Sita, Sushila had been an exotic manifestation, a shifting, impermanent combination of scent and sound and colour. When she was younger, Sita puzzled for hours over this curious creature people called her mother and whose irregular manifestations threw the Settlement into such a frenzy of disapproval and outrage. She had tried to love her but it was not possible to love a shifting combination of scent and sound and colour which was there one minute and gone the next. Her love had nothing to which it could attach itself. All around her she saw people drawn together and welded into comprehensible wholes by relationships denied her: the elementary ties of husband and wife; brother and sister. Excluded from membership of any of these, Sita belonged to no one.

'I too have a mother like everybody else,' she reassured herself over and over again. 'A mother ... a mother ... a mother.' She repeated the word in an endless hypnotic chant, twisting and rolling it on her tongue this way and that. But repetition enhanced its alien qualities and converted it into something unreal. It fractured and broke on her tongue, resolving itself into a jumble of meaningless syllables, devoid of rhyme and reason. 'Mo-ther ... mot-her ... moth-er.' She tried 'Ma' and 'Mummy' – she had once heard the Bholai girls calling their mother 'Mummy' – but they did not work either. Their intimacy was too fabulous.

Then she recalled that somewhere in the world there had to be a man who was her father. So, she experimented with that. 'Fa-ther ... fat-her ... fath-er.' It was no good. Neither did 'Pa' and 'Daddy' improve the situation. She quailed when it occurred to her that Farouk might be the man those fragmenting syllables sought to identify. Sita could not desist from examining herself closely in mirrors and, when she saw him, surreptitiously comparing her salient features with Farouk's. She dismissed the possibility. However, she shuddered inwardly and blushed whenever she went past the Palace of Heavenly Delights and Farouk twirled his beautiful moustache and winked at her with sly good humour. It was he – more than Phulo, more than Basdai, more than Mrs Bholai – who made her life in the Settlement a torment.

Sita developed the habit of talking to herself. 'My name is Sita ... Seetah ... See-tah ...' When even her own name seemed in danger of dissolving into gibberish, the discovery was both exhilarating and terrifying. She applied the same technique indiscriminately to people and things; and, under the influence of her subtle and secret magic, they too became remote and eventually disintegrated. At whim she could create, destroy and reconstruct the world around her. It was how she learned to cope with the abuse and taunting scorn which was inescapably the lot of 'a child of Sushila'. When Basdai screamed at her, 'You is a worthless girl – just like your no good mother was,' Sita would immediately go and stand before the mirror and repeat the phrase until it had worn itself out and lost all its meaning. The trick rarely failed.

Sita was an enigma to those with whom she lived. Recognizing that she was different (it was drummed into her by Phulo and Basdai), she had consciously set herself apart from them. She developed a fierce and distinctive self-regard which expressed itself in a belief in her own singular destiny arising from her unique position. Every act she performed, no matter how trivial, was invested with a ritual significance and solemnity; part, it seemed, of a grand design which she refused to communicate to anyone; a preparation for a world infinitely superior to the one in which, through no fault of her own, she had found herself.

It was this intense self-regard which kept her aloof and separate from those around her, showing itself in the slow and measured style of her speech; in the fanatical care she took of her personal property; and the pains she devoted to the details of her dress. There was the question of shoes, for instance. It was common practice for the children in the Settlement – the young Bholais excepted – to go without. But Sita would never permit herself to appear barefooted in the yard: she was always to be seen in a pair of lovingly whitened canvas shoes. She flew into a rage if anyone dared to use *her* towels, *her* soap, *her* hairbrush – all gifts of her mother. 'It's not hygienic to use what belong to somebody else,' she would explain when she had calmed down.

It was this aura of being set apart which, as much as anything else, brought down the wrath of Phulo and Basdai on her head and encouraged the taunts of the Settlement as a whole. Sita was not blameless. She fostered that hostility and appeared to draw strength from the isolation which it imposed. It was a necessary element of her self-esteem that she should be disliked: it served to reinforce her sense of a singular destiny.

Many of her ideas were derived from the books she read. Sita was a voracious reader and one of her big excitements was the monthly visit of the van sent by the Trinidad Public Library on tours of the country districts. Her reading, an extension of the fervent privacy she cultivated, was sacrosanct. She was unwilling to divulge even the title of the books she read. That she 'pretended' to read was an opinion not restricted to Phulo and Mrs Bholai but shared by most of the Settlement.

Youth and beauty could not survive long in the Settlement. Decay was at the very core of its existence and the women, more vulnerable to its ravages than the men, were the first to succumb. For the young girls, the decline into womanhood was swift, startling and irreversible. It was as if, after a certain stage had been reached, the processes of life were artificially speeded up. From day to day – so Sita felt – it was possible to chart the changes in the faces she knew. When the transformation was complete, their familiar features could hardly be recognized in the women they had become. Their children, doomed to the cycle, grew up with the fated sameness of animals born and bred to a particular role in life. The Settlement taught Sita the horrors of poverty and ignorance. But it was more than pity which it aroused in her. There was fear and repugnance as well.

Her first memories of Phulo were of a slim and pretty girl with unusual greyish-coloured eyes. She must have been no more than eighteen when she married Basdai's younger son and was flirtatiously shy and reticent in front of her husband. Her shortcomings as a wife were commented on indulgently even by Basdai who had bestowed on her the affectionate title of Doolahin. As for her husband, he seemed dangerously fond of her. He regularly brought her little trinkets from San Fernando and encouraged and fomented her wifely incapacities. She was the great favourite of the family, eclipsing Sharma, the wife of Basdai's elder son. But the birth of Phulo's first child effectively marked the end of the honeymoon. Attitudes changed rapidly. Her shortcomings ceased to be charming and the quarrels began.

The sad fact was that Phulo herself had changed by that time. She had sunk into the landscape, growing fatter and less picturesque. Not having been warned of the inevitable betrayal lying ahead of her, Phulo had let herself go. She had taken too much for granted and when she awakened from her sleep it was too late. Without her being aware of it, she had increasingly approximated to the run of women in the Settlement. Phulo became indistinguishable from those who walked with buckets balanced on their heads to fetch water from the standpipe. Her grey eyes counted for nothing now: their novelty had worn off. Doolahin wept but weeping got her nowhere. It hastened the disenchantment. Therefore, the crying stopped.

Phulo mourned her loss of beauty and special favour by adopting a style of dress in keeping with her new status. Discarding her modish blouses and skirts, she wore instead unflattering, hastily assembled dresses which hung loosely from her shoulders and brushed her ankles. Child followed monotonously on child and a generalized coarseness set in. Her voice lost its lilt and lightness and was strident and vulgar; thriving on the daily exchange of abuse with her mother-in-law and husband. The Phulo Sita was familiar with was the Phulo with puffed-out cheeks; with eyes that had lost their sparkle and liveliness and become dull and brutal; with sagging breasts milked dry; the Phulo pursued by a brood of bare-footed, bare-bottomed children who clung to her dusty skirts and at whom she shrieked obscenities. She talked and behaved as though her youth had never happened; as though it belonged to an order of things impossibly remote and far-fetched. Sita was always shocked to remember how young she really was.

Living in close proximity to her mother-in-law had proved a fruitful source of misunderstanding and discord. Rivalries and feuds flourished in the hothouse atmosphere of the family compound. Basdai considered it her duty to supervise her daughters-in-law and see to it that they remained 'up to mark'. Sharma, good-natured and pliable, was no problem in that respect. Phulo, however, was not led easily. Basdai disapproved on principle of everything she did: the way she dressed; the way she brought up her children; the way she kept her house. 'Ungrateful wretch,' she screeched at her. 'I don't know why I ever allow my son to marry a bloodsucker like you. All you deserve is blows and more blows.' 'Why don't you come and try?' Phulo would challenge her. 'I dying for a chance to break every bone in your body into little pieces.' These quarrels would arise out of nothing, coaxed magically out of the hot day.

But what irked Basdai most of all was Phulo's determination to have a proper home of her own. The compound had started – ostensibly – as a purely temporary arrangement while her sons searched for homes for their families. Years passed and nothing happened. A series of renovations, extensions and other minor alterations gave the lie to their intentions and temporariness had merged into all the indications of permanency. For Phulo to want to leave behind the delights of the compound was an unforgivable presumption. Unhappily for her, it never went beyond presumption. It was an open secret that her husband, indifferent to those unusual grey eyes, maintained a mistress in San Fernando. When he was not squandering his wages on her, he was squandering what remained of them in the Palace of Heavenly Delights. Phulo, fighting a battle already lost, saved what she could. He did not hesitate to beat her when she refused to tell him where her paltry hoard was hidden. 'Serve she right,' Basdai declared. 'A home of she own! What next I ask you?'

Nevertheless, when they grew weary of their slanging matches, they could unite on one subject; or rather, on two subjects: Sushila and Sita. Sushila was as much anathema to Phulo as she was to Mrs Bholai, but their reasons were not the same. Phulo could not resist comparing her pitiful condition to Sushila's. In the latter she saw everything she might have been. Worse still, Sushila's good fortune had sprung from her disobedience; while she (and had she not been as beautiful? as coveted by men?) who had obeyed the command to marry and bear children had been the one to suffer. It was unfair; unjust that she should be the one trapped. Injustice had cramped and stifled her spirit; warped it. Phulo wished on Sita the punishment which ought to have been meted out to her mother. And not only on Sita; but on everyone like her who aspired to break their chains.

Sharma had been luckier than Phulo but not because she was any better treated or any wiser. She was luckier in that she possessed a mild and placid disposition in which neither rebellion nor dissatisfaction could have a place. Like Phulo, she had once been slim and pretty; like Phulo, she had once been the household favourite; like Phulo, she had borne her husband a string of children; like Phulo, she was occasionally beaten. Yet, none of these things had embittered her or warped her spirit. She incorporated them without fuss or disturbance, bowing to the universal cycle of rise and decline and never questioning it. Pleasure and pain were modulations in an underlying rhythm which had regulated the lives of those who had gone before her and would regulate the lives of those who were to come after her. What had happened to her was, quite simply, what she had expected to happen – just as she expected to see the sun rise every morning in the east and see it sink every evening in the west. She would have been unpleasantly surprised had she not got fat. She had accepted her displacement as the household favourite by the grey-eyed Phulo without murmur and even joined in the praise of the newcomer. Her brood of children did not weigh on her as they did on Phulo.

Sharma was seamstress to the Settlement, churning out several dresses a week in identical style. 'Can't you sew something different?' Phulo asked exasperatedly. 'Is what the people want,' Sharma answered equably. 'But just for your own sake it might be nice to do something a little different each time,' Phulo said. Sharma seemed not to understand. 'Is what the people want,' she said. She it was who kept the goat which provided a dribble of milk. Phulo, when she had nothing else to attack, would attack the goat for sprinkling its droppings about the compound. 'One day,' Phulo said, 'I going to curry that goat.' Sharma laughed. She bore no grudges. If her husband were to beat her over some trifling misdemeanour or merely because he was in a bad mood, Sharma cried a little but was bright and cheerful again before long.

She took no part in the recriminations against either Sushila or Sita, though Phulo did her best to convince her of their iniquity. 'Everybody have they own life to lead,' was Sharma's verdict, 'including Sushila. If Sushila happy doing what she doing and not interfering with what I doing, why I should bother?' 'What Sushila doing is wrong,' Phulo said, 'is very wrong. She shouldn't be allowed to do what she doing and get away scot free with it.' Sharma was unperturbed. 'It may not be your way and is certainly not my way. But so long as she don't interfere with me...' 'What about Sita then?' Phulo asked, 'why she must be pretending to read all them book for?' 'If the girl like reading, let she read is what I say.' Phulo's patience cracked. 'And what I say is that you just plain stupid.' Sharma laughed. 'If that is the way I is,' she said, 'then that is the way I is.'

At night, Sita would lie awake listening to Basdai's wracked struggles to breathe freely. Her thoughts wandered to Phulo and Sharma and the events of the past day: Sharma sewing her identical dresses; the children playing in the dusty compound; Phulo bent over the washtub shouting at them and in the intervals trading abuse with Basdai. The pattern never altered. Thinking of Phulo she experienced a chilling thrill

176

compounded of fear and repugnance and pity. Could she ever become like her? Could she ever be reduced to such a state of coarse brutishness? Degradation crept up stealthily in the Settlement and by the time you realized what had happened it was too late. It was Phulo who absorbed the bulk of her attention; with whom, despite the overt hostility, she felt chilling reverberations of sympathy. On the other hand, no possible link could exist with someone like Sharma; no point of contact. Nothing was to be learned from Sharma. Indeed, hers was a lesson that could not be learned. It was a dispensation you received – or did not receive. Sharma was neutral and passive; the eternal spectator. Her support – if so vague a benignity could be called support – was of no value; as meaningless as the wind in the canefields. Her placidity was death itself to Sita. Lying there awake at night, listening to Basdai's groans and wombed in the desolate darkness, Sita fell victim to a morbid hypochondria. She was surrounded – but as yet untouched – by a disease whose symptoms she knew all too well. Sita maintained an anxious watch on herself for the signs of infection.

It was on one of the visits of the Library Van to the Settlement that Sita had spoken to Julian Bholai for the first time. He had gone up to her.

'What you looking for?' He was polite and smiling.

Sita did not answer.

'Why don't you tell me? I might have it back home. I have a lot of books.'

'If you have so many books why you bother to come here for?' she replied.

'I wanted to meet you.'

'You shouldn't be wanting to meet me,' she said coolly. 'If you mother should find out . . .'

Julian, covering his discomfort well, grinned. 'You shouldn't let what my mother say bother you.'

'I never said it bothered me.' Sita's eyes combed the van's shelves.

'You looking for anything special?'

177

'No. But tell me why you wanted to meet me.'

'I thought maybe the two of us could become friends.'
Julian stroked the spine of a book. 'I know you read a lot and
as I like reading too I thought . . .' He petered out lamely.

'Is that the only reason?'

'What other reason I could have?'

'Maybe you think . . .'

'I'm not like that at all.'

'Like what?' Sita raised her eyebrows. 'How do you know
what I was going to say?'

Julian laughed. 'What were you going to say then?'

'Perhaps you think you're doing me a favour talking to me.
Your mother can't stand the sight of me. She don't allow any
of her children to talk to me. And then all of a sudden you
decide you want to be my friend. Why?'

'Do you have to know? Can't you just accept that I want to
be your friend?'

Sita shook her head. 'Why would the future Dr Julian Bholai want to be friends with *me*? Does the future Dr Julian
Bholai expect me to be grateful? What does the future Dr
Julian Bholai take me for? I bet it never occurred to you that I
mightn't want to be friends with you. You just took it for
granted that I would jump up and down with joy. Didn't
you?'

Her vehemence astonished him. 'It wasn't like that at all.
You not being fair to me.'

'What was it like then? "Poor little girl," you said to yourself. "Poor little girl. Nobody talks to her. I will take pity on
her. I, the future Dr Julian Bholai, will go and talk to her.
That's bound to make her feel nice." Wasn't that how it was?'

'Not at all.' She had come perilously close to the truth; one
side of it.

'Why don't you tell me how it was then?'

'You not giving me a chance.'

Sita was silent.

'All the people around here . . . they don't even know what
a book is half of them. Even my sisters don't read much so
you can't discuss things with them. It's nice having somebody

you could talk to – even if it's only once a month.' That was the other side of the truth.

Sita was flattered. However, she was determined not to show it. 'I don't believe you,' she said harshly. 'I don't believe a word you say.' She climbed down the steps of the van and walked briskly away from him.

Sita was overcome by remorse. Why had she rejected his offer of friendship? The reasons he had given might have been genuine: she had no evidence to the contrary. After all, he had come out of his way to meet her, defying his mother's wishes. She could not deny it would be nice to have a friend with whom she could 'discuss things': a flesh and blood friend, that is, instead of the phantoms whom she had spun out of her longings. And Julian was the ideal companion. She strove desperately to persuade herself that the accusations she had levelled against him were right and fair. Books apart, they had nothing in common. 'He's going to be a doctor,' she said. 'And I . . . what am I going to be?' Their paths would diverge radically in the not too distant future. It was the height of foolishness to embark on a friendship which was doomed; in which she would be the one to suffer. A friendship had to be permanent and the disparity between what he was to be and what she was to be was too great to allow that. The argument bounced back and forth and she could reach no satisfactory conclusion. She did not want to reach a conclusion. Would Julian be at the Library Van the next time it came? Sita hoped that he would – and that he would not. 'If he's there,' she reasoned, 'that's OK. It would mean he's serious and I'll be nice to him. If he's not there, that's OK too because that would mean he wasn't serious in the first place.'

She waited suspensefully for the van's next scheduled visit. It was like waiting to see how a penny would fall: heads or tails. The days dragged on one after the other. She frowned at the Chinese calendar as if it were responsible for the delay. The appointed day did finally arrive, however. Sita took extra care with her dress that morning though she told herself that it was no more than the care she normally took to ensure she was presentable. To demonstrate there was nothing special

179

about this particular visit (beyond that of seeing how the penny would fall) Sita did not go to the van immediately it was ready for business; as was usual with her. She dawdled some minutes over invented tasks.

'What happen?' Phulo asked. 'Is ten minutes the van there now. Like you tired pretending to read all them book?'

'I have more than enough time,' she said nonchalantly. 'It's not going to fly away.'

Sita let fifteen minutes elapse before setting off for the van which was parked on the outskirts of the village. She walked slowly, not daring to raise her eyes from the road because then she could see at a glance if he were there or not there. Sita chose to prolong the suspense. At last, when she could no longer resist the temptation, Sita raised her eyes quickly and furtively. There was no sign of Julian. 'That's OK,' she murmured. 'I was right to treat him as I did. He wasn't serious after all.' She quickened her pace.

Sita climbed the steps of the van and deposited the books which were due back on the librarian's tiny desk.

'You late today, Miss.' He smiled. 'I thought you wasn't coming. Without you is hardly worth my while stopping here.' He stamped her yellow card and handed it back to her.

'I had some things to do.' She stared at him in confusion.

'Better late than never.'

Sita's gaze swept with an air of businesslike efficiency along the shelves. Book after book she leafed through and returned to its niche. She could find nothing that appealed to her. They were all uniformly dull and insipid. She grew bad-tempered.

'You very hard to please this morning,' the librarian said.

'You have *A Tale of Two Cities*?'

'It not on the shelves?'

'No.'

'Then we don't have it, Miss. Whatever you don't find on the shelves we don't have. Sorry.'

'I have it though.' A voice spoke close to her ear. 'I have nearly everything Charles Dickens write.'

Sita jumped and spun round. Her face was already lit by a smile which she could not bring under instant control. She was suddenly happier. Much happier. She tried to dampen this access of spontaneous gaiety.

'Oh!' she exclaimed. 'It's you. I wasn't expecting ... you shouldn't have done that. You scared me.'

Julian saw how pleased she was. 'I could lend you *A Tale of Two Cities*,' he said. 'I could go home right now and get it for you.'

'You don't have to do that.'

'It won't take a minute. Wait here for me.' Julian, bypassing the ladder, charged out of the van and jumped on to the road. 'Don't go. It won't take a minute.'

'He could break a leg,' the librarian said.

Sita was still smiling. She chose two books at random. 'I'll take these.'

The librarian smiled. 'I didn't know you was interested in this sort of thing, Miss.'

'What?'

He held up one of the books *The Boy's Book of Motor Cars*. 'You want to change your mind?' he asked kindly.

'Of course I don't want to change my mind ... I'm very interested in motor cars.'

The librarian made a note of the books and stamped her card again. 'Here you are then, Miss. If the van ever break down I'll know who to come to.' He pointed behind her. 'Look. Your boy-friend come back.'

'He's not my ...'

Julian was beside her, panting. 'Here it is,' he announced triumphantly, flourishing the book in front of her face. 'I read it some time ago. It was first-rate stuff.' He paused to regain his breath. 'The last bit especially was very moving. "It's a far, far better thing ..." '

The librarian watched. '"I do than I have ever done,"' he chimed in, '"a far, far better rest ..."'

'Let's go outside,' Julian said. 'It's easier to talk out there.'

They climbed out of the van. 'No offence meant,' the librarian said.

Sita climbed down the ladder. Julian jumped. They strolled round the van out of sight of the houses.

'We mustn't go too far.'

'Just over there,' Julian said, indicating a spot where the land dipped to form a crater-like bowl. 'The Hollow' it was called in the Settlement. It was a popular lovers' haunt at night.

Sita squirmed. 'Do we have to go there?'

Julian laughed. 'Don't worry. Don't worry. There's nowhere else we could go. And, unless we very unlucky nobody will see us.'

They scrambled down the grassy banks of the hollow – that grass with reddish-brown blades. Two tall, spreading mango trees grew side by side in the centre of the hollow, providing the only shade from the scorching sun. Julian slumped on the ground and squinted up at her.

'Why don't you sit down? It's much more comfortable.' Julian rested his head on one of the trunks.

'I prefer to stand.'

'Sitting down doesn't mean . . . you should relax.'

Sita hesitated. Then she too sat down, though her back remained stiff and erect. She picked up a stone, scraping the earth off it with her fingernails. 'I'm sorry about what happened last time.'

Julian was gallant. 'What happened last time? Oh that! I've forgotten about it already.'

'Please.' She was vexed by his gallantry. 'You don't have to play the gentleman with me.'

'I'm not playing the gentleman,' he said, affronted. 'I really have forgotten about it.'

'Please let me finish what I was going to say.' She was severe. 'I didn't mean to be so rude to you that day,' she continued, lowering her voice. 'It was just that . . .' She looked at him, scraping the stone. '. . . it was just that I don't like people doing me favours just because they suddenly start to feel sorry for me.'

'It wasn't at all like that with me.'

'There's no reason to feel sorry for me. None at all.'

'I never said I was feeling sorry for you. It was you who said so. Not me.'

182

'That's OK then. I just wanted to clear that up.'

Julian plucked a blade of grass and chewed on it. His hair, tinted red by the sun, flopped untidily over his forehead. He was very handsome. Sita leaned back against the rough bark, smoothing her skirt. She stared at the shifting patterns of light and shadow on the ground. The heat was dry and soporific. It was suffused with the smell of the canes. The wind rustled through the grass and through the cooler green leafage above their heads. On the road, invisible from where they were, the cars went by, their steady drone broken by the screech of their tyres on the curve near the grocery. There was an indistinct rattle of farm machinery in the distance.

'Do you ever dream of going away?' Julian asked.

'I don't allow myself to dream of such things.'

'You wouldn't like to go away? See other places? See snow?'

'That's a different question. But what I would like to do isn't possible. At any rate not for me. That's why I don't allow myself to dream of such things.'

'Don't you ever dream at all?'

Sita did not answer.

Julian laughed. 'You don't mind feeling sorry for yourself, I see.'

'That's not feeling sorry for myself. That's facing the facts.'

Julian nodded. He let himself slip farther down the trunk of the tree so that only his neck and head were upright. 'What would you like to do? Or is that a secret?'

'I'm not sure.' She laughed. 'I would like to roll cheese down a mountainside. I'm not like you. You know you want to be a doctor.'

'I want to be more than a doctor. Making money is not everything.'

Sita raised her eyebrows.

'I would like to write.'

'What would you write?'

'I don't know as yet. Poetry, I think. Yes. I would like to write poetry. Do you read poetry?'

'Not much.' Sita smiled. 'Who's your favourite poet?'

'Shelley,' he said. 'I like Shelley very much. Shelley and Keats.'

'Not Wordsworth?'

'I could take him or leave him,' Julian said.

'I suppose you have everything – or nearly everything – Shelley and Keats ever wrote?' She glanced at him pertly.

'You making fun of me.'

'I'm sorry.'

Julian spat out the blade of grass he had been chewing. He clasped his hands behind his head. 'My mother believes that when I put my hands behind my head like this I want her to die.'

Sita laughed. 'That can't be true.'

'It is. I swear to you. She's a very stupid woman. My father is even more stupid though.'

'I like your father.' Sita was serious. 'What's stupid about him?'

Julian plucked another blade of grass. 'Do you know he wanted to be a lawyer at one time?'

'No.'

'Well he did.' Julian giggled. 'Could you ever imagine *him* being a lawyer?'

'Why not?'

'I can't. And that's because he's stupid. Running a grocery is the only thing he's fit for.'

'You're very conceited,' she said angrily. 'Conceited and cruel. You'll never make a poet.'

Julian was surprised. 'What you have to be getting so angry for? It's nothing to do with you.'

'It's a lot to do with me. Soon you'll be turning down your nose at everybody who is not a doctor or a poet. Including me.'

'I thought you liked facing facts,' he said calmly.

'What's that got to do with the facts?'

'There are two kinds of people in the world. The intelligent and the rest – which is the vast majority – who are stupid. It's the intelligent people who have to run the world.'

'I suppose you regard yourself as being one of the intelligent?'

'Yes. And you too.'

'Thanks for the compliment. But I don't believe that people are born stupid. It's the other things over which they have no control that make them stupid. Things like the place where they were born. Whether their parents were rich or poor. Whether they had a good or bad education. Hundreds of things!' Sita waved her arms violently. 'That's what causes one man to be stupid and another man to be not stupid.'

'What about genes? You ever hear of those? I was reading about genes the other day and . . .'

Sita got up. 'I won't listen to another word you have to say. You could talk all you want but I won't listen.' She blocked her ears.

Julian laughed. 'What books you borrow today? Show me.'

'I'm not showing you.' The Library Van came to her rescue. They could hear the splutter of its engine. 'I don't have time to show you,' she said relievedly. 'The van will be going soon.' She walked away.

Julian ran after her. 'What about next time?'

'I have to see,' Sita said. She clambered up the slope of the hollow and disappeared over the rim.

These meetings became a regular affair: an hour's get-together once a month. Their 'discussions' centred mainly on books – those they had read during the previous month and those they wished to read. A competition developed between them as to who had read the greater number of books in the interval. The enforced secrecy of their meetings – though both would have denied it – helped to increase their pleasure, and Sita looked forward more than ever to the visits of the Library Van. She did not care to probe too deeply into the implications of these encounters, dismissing any speculation as to where or to what they might lead. She allowed herself to drift aimlessly on the currents of their odd friendship. But while books formed the chief topic of their conversations, it was not the only one. Now and again, with a studied recklessness, they drifted further afield and talked – in speculative terms – of love and marriage.

'You believe people should only marry for love?' Sita asked.

'Of course,' Julian answered readily. 'Why would you marry if not for love?'

'Your father and mother marry for love?'

'They are the older generation. Is different with us.' He spoke confidently.

Sita was thoughtful. 'What you call love is not real love,' she said.

Julian was offended. 'You trying to say I'm lying?'

'Not at all,' Sita replied hastily. 'You mustn't jump to conclusions.'

'I don't see what you getting at then.' The sun was burning his hair red.

'What I'm getting at is this. You wouldn't marry someone who was ugly and poor . . .'

'Of course I would – if I loved the person.'

Sita's lips parted in a sceptical smile. 'But the chances of your falling in love with such a person are very very small. You must admit that.'

'Well?' He brushed his hair back from his forehead irritatedly.

'The person you fall in love with would have to be pretty and she would have to be educated. Her skin might have to be as fair or fairer than yours. She would have to be shorter than you because men don't like to have wives taller than them. She might have to have a straight nose and not a crooked one. She might even have to have grey eyes. She would have to be all kinds of things before you could love her. You admit that?'

'Well?' Julian plucked a blade of grass from the earth and started to chew it. 'You can't expect me to fall in love with Frankenstein.'

'I would say your love wasn't real love in that case. Not pure love. In pure love it wouldn't matter a bit that the person was any of those things I just mentioned. In pure love it wouldn't matter in the slightest that someone was Frankenstein.

Pure love doesn't depend on anything. It will last forever – even after the two of you die. If people married for pure love they would never get tired of each other. They would never be unhappy because they suddenly decide that they prefer green instead of grey eyes. They would always be happy.'

Julian scowled. 'So you will only get married for this so-called pure love of yours?'

Sita's eyes darkened. 'I will never get married,' she said.

'You only saying so now. But you can't tell what might happen in the future. One day some rich man with green eyes will sweep you off your feet.' He was bantering.

Sita shook her head.

Julian was amused. 'Who will support you if you don't get married? You intend to spend the rest of your life here being an old maid?'

'Nothing wrong at all with being an old maid,' she answered abstractedly, scrutinizing a strand of her hair and sucking on the end of it.

'Suppose you meet somebody you really love?'

'He mightn't love me.' She brooded.

'But suppose he love you and you love him. What will you do then?' Julian laughed. 'Run away and hide in a corner and say you prefer to be an old maid?'

'I will never meet anybody like that.' She spoke with stubborn assurance.

'Let us make a bet.' Julian extended a finger.

'No,' she replied, drawing away from him. 'What would be the point of that?'

'You see!' He slapped his thighs gleefully. 'That prove that you yourself don't really believe what you saying.'

'It don't prove anything.' Sita fell silent, averting her face from his. This was a favourite ploy of hers: to descend into abrupt silence for no reason he could fathom in the middle of a quite normal flow of conversation. She had retreated into a sphere where he could no longer follow her.

'If you not going to talk to me any more I may as well go home,' he said.

Sita did not answer, staring at the restless interchange of light and shadow on the ground.

Their meetings never ended happily. They always parted on a note of discord and neither could be sure that the other would be there at the next visit of the Library Van. It was Sita, not Julian, who was the main offender. She seemed to court what – for her – would have been a disaster. Their meetings in the hollow were as much a joy as a misery to her. She could not banish the thought that the hour must come to an end and that she must return to Basdai and Phulo and Sharma. It was unendurable. All that she held most dear and precious were saved up and compressed into this hour. Outside of it there was nothing: nothing but the rectangles of bright green sugarcane; the blank metallic bowl of the sky; the strident tones of Phulo; and the wracking cough of Basdai keeping her awake at night. Her silences were a protection; a refuge to hide her misery from him. These hours in the hollow – as she repeatedly reminded herself – could never be to him a millionth of the joy and misery they were to her. For him, the hour he spent with her was merely one way of 'killing' time. It could be no more important (and perhaps a great deal less) than the myriad hours he spent away from her. His real life existed beyond it. Her real life existed within it. It was a rotten bargain and she loathed it. But what was she to do? One incident had summed it up for her. 'Oh, by the way,' he had declared casually as they were plodding back up the slope of the hollow. 'I nearly forgot to tell you – I won't be able to come next time. I'm going to see my cousins in San Fernando.' He peered at her. 'I hope you're not too disappointed.' She was devastated by his casualness. 'Not in the slightest,' she had replied. 'Why should I be disappointed? I hope you have a good time.' He laughed. 'I always have a good time wherever I am,' he said. 'There're very few people I don't get on with.' 'You're very fortunate,' she had answered.

That walk through the Settlement during which Sushila had announced to her that she was soon to take her away came as a timely rejoinder to Julian's casualness. The prospect of release muted the pain the memory of it called forth. And not only that. It muted also the pain of the scornful glances they had received and Farouk's unwelcome cordiality. Even Mrs Bholai's pulling her son sharply away from the verandah rail paled into insignificance. She was going to be leaving all that behind her. The walls of her prison were on the verge of being shattered; smashed to rubble. Her sentence had been commuted and she was to be freed. The windings and twistings of the narrow main road unrolled themselves like a magic carpet before her. She could sit in the hammock and gaze upon the cars traversing its length without longing and allow herself to dream of the day when it would spirit her away forever from this place; just as once, a long time ago, it had spirited away her mother.

Sita had been disappointed when Sushila had said she would be taking her neither to Port-of-Spain nor to San Fernando. However, she had reconciled herself. Compared to the Settlement almost anywhere would be paradise. Her optimism was short-lived. The news of Sushila's instalment in the Ramsaran household deadened Sita. 'Soon you going to be leaving we,' Basdai chuckled. 'Is more than you deserve.' Sita looked at her dumbly. Egbert Ramsaran! She repeated the name to herself several times but the trick did not work. The detested sound revolved recalcitrantly on her tongue. She could refuse to go: they could not compel her. Sita swayed back and forth on the hammock, staring at the cars on the main road. The magic carpet had been pulled from under her feet. This road led only to the house in Victoria where Rani had been condemned to eke out her sad, ghostly existence.

Her last meeting with Julian had been the unhappiest one of all. Sita arrived in a sullen mood. He greeted her smilingly.

'I have some news for you,' he said.

'If it's anything to do with my mother going to live . . . I'm sick and tired of that.'

'It's not about your mother – though it's connected up in a kind of way. Guess who is coming to stay with us?'

'Jesus Christ.'

Julian giggled. 'I see you're in one of your moods.'

'Who's coming to stay with you?' Sita asked mechanically.

'Wilbert Ramsaran. After years and years of licking his father's boots Pa finally succeeded. Ma can't control herself. She . . .'

Sita stared at him dully. 'That should be nice for you.'

'It's not nice for me at all. We don't get on.'

'I thought you got on with everybody.'

'Not with him I don't. He's a . . .'

Sita scowled. 'Don't bother to explain. What about that book you said you were going to lend me?'

Julian pounded his head with his fists. 'It completely slip my mind in all the excitement about Wilbert. I'll bring it for you next time.'

'There mightn't be any next time.'

'The rumour is true then.' His face fell. 'You going to live with your mother.'

'It's possible. Any day now she might come for me.'

'What you want to go and live there for? You must be crazy.'

Sita studied the shifting patterns of light and shadow. 'What would you have me do instead?' She curled her lips.

'Almost anything but that.'

'Anything like what?' she asked drily.

Julian swept his hair back from his forehead. 'You will hate living there. Take my word for it. You'll have nobody to talk to.'

'What about Wilbert?'

'Wilbert!' Julian roared with incredulous laughter. 'Wilbert is worse than nobody. He never read a book in his whole life. He's ignorant – born to be a businessman like his father.'

'So you would have me stay here just because Wilbert never read a book in his life. To judge from you, it's probably a good thing. You really feel you're the only person worth talking to in the whole world, don't you? Well, let me tell you, you're not. Do you seriously suppose I'm going to drop down dead without you? Maybe your cousins in San Fernando might. But not me.' His arrogance, his easy self-assurance, his very handsomeness were loathsome to her; more loathsome than they had ever been. They were oblivious to her troubles. She wanted to hurt him; to make him share her pain. 'You know you'll be leaving this place one day to go away and become Dr Julian Bholai. You're not going to care about me then. Oh no! I would just be some stupid little country girl you used to know.'

'I'm not to blame if I'm going to be a doctor. Do you expect me not to be one just to please you?'

'I don't expect you to do anything just to please me. You will always be free to do exactly as *you* please. That is the difference between the two of us. I have to take my chances where I find them. I can't pick and choose.' Her eyes glowed with anger. 'If I stayed here, do you think I will get another chance to leave? Who's going to give me that chance? You? Your mother? No. I'll end up like Phulo – if I'm lucky. You have no right – no right at all – to tell me what to do.'

'I'm not telling you what to do. Do whatever you want.' He shrugged.

'I shall.'

'Listen, Sita . . .'

'I've listened to you enough.' She turned her face from him.

'I'm going home. Take out your temper on the mango tree. Not on me.' Julian got up and walked a few steps. 'I'll get that book to you somehow. Maybe I'll send it by Wilbert Ramsaran. That will give you the opportunity to . . .'

'I don't want your damn book. Now go and leave me alone. I can't bear to look at you.'

He left her. When he got to the rim of the crater he looked back. Sita was still sitting under the mango tree, her eyes fixed on the ground. He shrugged and walked on.

Her mind was made up. To miss her chance – such as it was – because of some silly squeamishness would be to condemn herself to servitude. If she could withstand the Settlement, she could probably learn to withstand anything the Ramsaran house had to offer. She would be able to take care of herself regardless of her surroundings. These reflections strengthened her resolution. Julian was not indispensable. She was not going to be deflected by the dubious gratification of a dubious relationship.

Chapter Six

1

There was one fact around which Wilbert Ramsaran's life revolved and beside which nothing else mattered: the Ramsaran Transport Company. It was to provide him with his role and function in life. Of that, there could never be any serious doubt or question. From the earliest days it had been drummed into his head that nothing else was expected of him. 'I don't want you to come with any doctor stupidness to me,' Egbert Ramsaran had said. 'Leave that to Bholai. I not going to tolerate any nonsense from you. I sending you to school so that you could learn to read and write and add and subtract – especially add and subtract because that is what your life will be about. Nothing else! That was all I needed in my day so I don't see why it should be any different with you.'

Accordingly, operating on the instructions he had received, Wilbert neglected the frills of education and concentrated his efforts on mastering the arts of addition and subtraction; and learning to read and write tolerably well. These accomplishments successfully achieved, the education of Wilbert Ramsaran came to an effective end. School, as such, held no further interest for him. Wilbert did not seek the companionship of boys of his own age. He had nothing in common with most of them: their ambitions and general outlook were not his. His fate had already been decided and their competitive cleverness and passion for the frills of education irritated him. Nevertheless, he was acutely sensitive to their jibes and was quick to take offence at insults – real and imaginary. He was proud of his natural physical strength and was always ready to call on it to settle arguments.

Having fulfilled his father's commands, he seized every opportunity to absent himself from the irksome confinement of the classroom and to roam haphazardly around the seedier streets of Port-of-Spain to which he was irresistibly drawn. His teachers complained to Egbert Ramsaran. 'Your son does hardly ever be in school,' they said. 'At the rate he seem to be going he won't learn anything.' Egbert Ramsaran's response was disappointing. 'You try beating him?' 'We tried beat him,' they replied, 'but it don't seem to have any effect on him at all.' Egbert Ramsaran laughed. 'He could read and write?' 'Just about,' they said. 'And he could add and subtract?' 'Yes,' they said, 'he very bright in arithmetic.' 'Well then, I don't see what all the fuss is about. That is all I send him to school to learn in the first place. I don't care about nothing else. I wouldn't be surprised if he have more to learn from outside school than inside it.' 'If that is your attitude,' they said, 'we can't do nothing.'

The teachers gave up on Wilbert and he was permitted to come and go virtually as he pleased. The arrangement suited him.

Wilbert was a regular visitor to the hovel occupied by Chinese Cha-Cha and his mistress. He had retained a soft spot for his feckless uncle and enjoyed being in his company. Chinese welcomed Wilbert warmly. With Chinese it was possible to forget about things and – to use a favourite phrase of his – 'take things easy'. In fact, he seemed to do nothing else but take things easy. Wilbert did not have to answer any awkward questions (such as why he was spending his time with him and not at school) since Chinese treated him as a fully adult person, offering him glasses of rum and cigarettes and speaking to him on a variety of subjects with frank openness.

Chinese had given up even the pretence of working, putting the blame on his diabetic condition. 'Sometimes I doesn't even have the strength to lift a glass,' he moaned pathetically. 'You could ask she.' Chinese baulked from referring to his mistress by name. She was an unprepossessing woman. Her hair was matted and greasy and her moonshaped face was heavy and sickly yellow. 'I never see you get so weak yet,' she said. 'If it was as bad as you like to say you would have been dead by now. You could lift a barrel if it had rum inside it.' She smiled at him pastily: it was an affectionate rejoinder. Chinese waved her remarks away. 'Sometimes it does get so,' he added, 'a feather could knock me down.' She shook her head at him. It was her labours which maintained them: she worked on a night-shift in a nearby laundry. Exactly what attracted her to Chinese – and kept her attracted to him – was a mystery. She possessed both those qualities which were anathema to him: application and a hard-headed realism. They were squandered on Chinese but she did not complain. Her affection for him and her patience never seemed to waver. 'She's a good woman,' Chinese would say, nodding appreciatively in her direction. 'A damn good woman. Ugly as sin, mind you. But a damn good woman all the same, eh!'

They lived on George Street near the main Port-of-Spain market. Chinese had drifted here after the break-up of his marriage. He had found the area entirely to his taste and so he had stayed; an intimate of every dingy bar, restaurant and café. 'I wouldn't move from this place if you was to pay me a million dollars,' he said to Wilbert. 'I could never be happy anywhere else. And what use I would have for a million dollars? Eh? I wouldn't know what to do with it. Here it have everything a man could ever need in life. Take food. She' (pointing at his mistress) 'does go across to the market when business finish for the day and take she pick of what get leave behind. We does hardly spend a cent on food. Is all for free. No fuss. No bother.' Chinese sipped delicately at the glass of rum he was holding and gurgled contentedly. 'All the furniture you see in here – this bed I lying on, the table over there, the chairs – I get all that for free or nearly free. They does just be lying about on the street. You just have to know where to look.' He wiggled his toes. The bed creaked noisily. 'I don't go for all this rushing about here, there and everywhere after money. My constitution could never stand up to that. My philosophy is to take things nice and easy. Money is more trouble than it worth. Money and ambition. That is one thing your father never understand.' Chinese took another sip from his glass and gurgled as he had done before. 'What more I need than this, eh?'

The room he occupied was at street level. It was approached up a dank and insalubrious brick tunnel piled with sacks of charcoal (a charcoal merchant had premises to the rear) and cluttered with wheelbarrows, trolleys and other implements of the trade. The room was dark and poorly furnished. Even on the brightest days it was murky – it had originally been intended as a store-room. Daylight fought an inconclusive passage through a small, solitary window protected by a latticed grille. The panes, not easy to get at, had not been cleaned within living memory and were opaque with the accumulated dust and grime. However, since it was always kept open in order to admit the maximum amount of the stale, stagnant air, it did not matter.

The most conspicuous and impressive item of furniture was – appropriately enough – the bed where Chinese passed most of his time. It was a brass fourposter raised high off the floor. Many of the rods were either missing or bent and it quivered and rattled with every movement. The castors were placed in shallow tins of water to prevent the ants from crawling up the posts. It glimmered mountainously in the gloom. Next to the bed and pushed up against the wall was a small square card table with two chairs. In the centre of the table, on a white lace doily, was a red glass vase with a single faded paper flower – a daffodil. These were the basic furnishings but the room was cluttered with other odds and ends: stools, oil-lamps, a chest, a hat-rack with a cracked mirror; the debris, in short, of a lifetime's scavenging and scrounging on the streets around the market.

At the back was a courtyard paved with flagstones. It was here the charcoal merchant held sway in a lean-to shed equipped with a cash register and weighing scales. All around was the peeling, crumbling façade, fringed by a precariously supported wooden balcony, of the squat, two-storeyed tenement. Apart from the charcoal merchant's customers, there was a constant coming and going to and from the standpipe in the middle of the courtyard – the only source of water it seemed in the district, for it was here several of the market vendors (not to mention ordinary passers-by) came to slake their thirst. At least a dozen families shared the tenement, living in conditions not markedly superior to Chinese's. Their washing straddled a criss-cross of lines strung from the balcony. Throughout the day and late into the night the courtyard was a hive of busy but inscrutable activity.

Chinese was lying prostrate on the bed and smoking, flicking the ash on the floor. At the opposite end of the room his mistress was preparing lunch, energetically fanning a coalpot with a piece of cardboard. The coalpot sat on a chest and was surrounded by a scattering of empty rum bottles and packing cases. A wheelbarrow clattered along the tunnel. 'Tell me,' Chinese said, 'you believe in all this money business like your father?' He did not wait for Wilbert to answer. 'Let me give you some sound advice for which you will thank me in later years. Give it all away, man. Give it all away and live like me!' Chinese gestured expansively.

Wilbert laughed. 'Who you want me to give it to?'

'I don't care who you give it to.' The bed quivered and rattled as Chinese hauled himself upright. 'Give it to me. I will get rid of it for you, eh! In no time at all. Another thing, I wouldn't bother to get married if I was you. Is not necessary. Is a crazy thing to do. All you need to do is find yourself a good woman like I find and settle down with she somewhere. That is my recipe for happiness. What you say, eh?' Chinese nodded emphatically and the bed rattled in unison. He stubbed out the cigarette on the wall above his head and threw the butt on the floor.

'That is no advice to give him,' his mistress said. She was bent low over the coalpot. 'You should be the last one to give anybody advice on how to live.'

'Is the best advice any man could get,' Chinese replied unruffled. He lit another cigarette. 'Look at me and you. We not married and we not rich. But we damn happy, eh?'

'That is me and you,' she said, casting a benign glance at

him. Her face was sweaty and moist from the fire. She dried it with the sleeve of her dress. 'The same won't suit everybody. Not everybody could stand living in a place like this, you know. They would want more comforts.'

'True. Very true.' Chinese stroked his chin placidly. 'But I feel Wilbert is more like me than like his father. Wilbert like to take things easy. He wouldn't let things get him down. You could tell that a mile off.' Chinese yawned complacently, rubbing his stomach.

She gazed dubiously at Wilbert and resumed fanning the coalpot.

The smell of fish permeated the stale, overheated air radiating upwards from the narrow streets and the crowded pavements around the market; blanketing the shifting, haggling swarms of people. Open cardboard boxes, filled with the rotting remains of the day's business, were strewn about the pavements or floated in the black, stagnant gutters. The odour of corruption was everywhere. Men and women, decayed as the fruit and vegetables they were selling – for many it was a front to disarm the police – sat crouched on the sacking where their wares were scattered in disordered heaps, offering their sunbaked stock to the pedestrians with a spasmodic and expiring enthusiasm. It required agility and care to avoid crushing their bony extremities.

The mutilated, the diseased, the starving abounded in this part of the city. They congregated here as if for mutual support, security and solace. It was a gallery of moral and physical degeneracy and Wilbert studied the exhibits with a morbid fascination. There were those missing an arm; there were those missing a leg and hobbling on crutches; there were those with flaking, leprous skin; there were those whose bodies were hollowed out cages of skin and bone; there were those abandoned to alcoholic stupor. In every nook and cranny there was a specimen of derelict humanity, vermin-ridden and covered with festering sores; gargoyles waiting for no one and nothing.

Some appeared to have taken up permanent residence, constructing makeshift habitations in the shelter of which they cooked their food on coalpot fires, while fitfully tending their ragged babies, mewling and crawling in the dust and litter of debris. At night they wedged themselves in a huddle against the unyielding stone walls of the market, their heads covered with newspaper. There were those who slept as well during the day, heedless of the noise and the heat and the flies settling on their inert bodies.

One woman frequently drew his attention. She could have been thirty; she could have been sixty. It was impossible to tell. She had stumps for legs and propelled herself along the pavements with her hands. Her speed and dexterity were astonishing as she scampered among the throng shouting at the top of her voice. 'Make way! I don't want nobody to mash me! Make way!' It was all he ever heard her say. She was constantly on the move – though where to it was not easy to say. Her voice was raucous and penetrating, adapted to its task, and she could be heard from a long way off howling her unvarying refrain. 'Make way! I don't want nobody to mash me! Make way!'

Once, when he was wandering among these phantasmal creatures, the woman's weird cries resounding in his head, the odour of corruption heavy in the stifling air, Wilbert had the odd sensation of suddenly being cut loose from all that was normal, predictable and certain. The street was choked with traffic: motor cars, bicycles, lorries, hand-drawn and horse-drawn carts. It had rained and the asphalt was steaming, wafting upwards into his nostrils the smells of decay: of fish and rotting fruit and vegetables. He stopped near one of the market entrances. From the skylights in the high cantilevered roof a dense grey light filtered down to the rows of concrete stalls. Open drains ran the length of the building and the floor was wet. A fishmonger, his hands coated with pearly scales, was slicing up a fish with his cutlass. Behind him, gutted, bloodstained carcasses were impaled on hooks. The stench intensified. He began to feel giddy and somewhat faint. The external and the internal became confused. It seemed to him that it was he who was steaming and not the asphalt; that the warm, cloying taint of blood came from him and not the gutted carcasses; that it was from within him that all these contaminated scents were rising and percolating to the outside. He was embalmed in the process of putrefaction; drifting off into the vastnesses of an uncharted ocean whose deeps were composed of successive layers of degeneracy, exceeding everything he had yet experienced. World upon world of darkness without beginning or end. His identity was being shattered and pulverized by these ascending vapours. He was a carcass, raw, open and vulnerable; an undulation of that incessantly swelling ocean. Wilbert panicked and started to run, his heart thumping; unable to breathe the lifeless air. 'Make way! I don't want nobody to mash me! Make way!' He only stopped when he could no longer hear that cry. Then he breathed easier.

To clear his head and restore some semblance of balance, he walked westwards out of the city past the docks and the lines of ships in the harbour; past the shuttered houses on the Wrightson Road; out towards Mucurapo and Cocorite and the sea. He walked without thinking. He was angry with Chinese and apprehensive of his siren songs in praise of fruitless ease and indolence. Wilbert felt they were deliberately designed to lead him astray; to entice him from the straight and narrow path of his proper duties and obligations.

At the Carenage he paused to watch the fishermen prepare their nets – he could not escape that sickly, fishy smell! – and looked out at the grey, windless sea and the rocky off-shore islands with their sprinkling of tenacious green vegetation. What was it like beyond them? Was it the same endless sea, flat and grey? Those rocky islands standing sentinel in the water were like the very limits of the world. Perhaps the tales he had heard of foreign lands, of people who fished through holes in the ice, were all lies concocted by wicked people. Trinidad was the world. Trinidad was the universe. And the red and black trucks of the Ramsaran Transport Company, the sun round which it revolved. The rest was the fabrication of deceivers. Nothing else existed. Those were the stern realities he had been reared upon and he could not go beyond them. His head aching from the sun and more dazed than when he had started out, Wilbert took a taxi to the bus station and made his way back to the house in Victoria.

2

The regime of sternness which had for so long dominated the Ramsaran household and all who lived in it was being altered beyond recognition. Egbert Ramsaran, with Sushila as teacher, was discovering there was more to life than hard work, sternness and brutality. Sushila had informed him that life was granted for enjoyment. 'What's the point of you breaking your back any more?' she said to him. 'Wilbert is getting a big man now. He should be taking over from where you leave off. Is only right and fitting. Is high time for you to rest and enjoy yourself before it's too late. You should make proper use of the strength left in your muscles.'

Familiar routines which had borne the stamp of eternal verities began to disappear. His daily routine of exercise was phased out and the elaborate equipment transported to the field next door where it was allowed to rust and fall to pieces side by side with the decaying skeletons already there. He claimed the exercises were a strain on his heart. The audiences with the clients came to an end. Sushila had expressed her disapproval of them. 'Leave that for the office,' she advised him. 'Your home is your home. You shouldn't let all kind of people clutter it up and worry you with they problems. Better still, let Wilbert look after that side of the business for you. You just letting him idle in school and waste money.' Egbert Ramsaran relinquished the responsibility; but he charged Mr Balkissoon, his foreman at the Depot – not Wilbert – with the task of collecting the debts in whatever manner he saw fit.

Petitioners from the Settlement – and particularly Rani's relatives – were discouraged from crowding the verandah on Sunday mornings. Sushila too was responsible for this. 'What you want Basdai coming here for to disturb you? She only out to squeeze whatever she can out of you. Sunday is your day of rest and you need all the rest you could get.' Egbert Ramsaran was quick to acquiesce. He was agreeably surprised and flattered by Sushila's concern for his rest and privacy. 'If they must harass somebody,' Sushila added for good measure, 'let them come and harass me. I do know how to deal with beggars like them.' She was given carte blanche to deal with them as she pleased. Thus they were diverted from the verandah to the kitchen to await Sushila's pleasure. Sushila exacted the full penalty. They were given short shrift by her and sent away empty-handed. 'Just wait,' Basdai threatened. 'I going to expose you.' But she never had the chance: Sushila barred all access to Egbert Ramsaran.

Basdai did not know what to say or do and it reduced her to tears whenever she recalled her hand in the matter. As she never stopped reminding everyone, it was she who had schemed to put the worthless Sushila there; and it was she who had berated Rani's multitudinous shortcomings in repentance for having foisted such a wife on Egbert Ramsaran. Now Rani was very bliss. She was like Heaven itself compared to the ruthless and audacious Sushila who was ordering her, Basdai, about the place as if she were a little 'piss'n'tail' girl. The insult! The injury! How much she had gladly endured in the hope that one day she would be adequately rewarded for her patience and fortitude and willingness to serve. Basdai did not know what to say. Her cunning had not bargained with such depths of treachery. Even the unsteady dribble of money which had flowed from Egbert Ramsaran's pockets into her palm had dried up. She pictured it flowing away from her and gathering in torrents of glowing gold around the undeserving Sushila. Basdai watched Sushila's growing authority and tried, in vain, to woo her. Sushila's mocking laughter was all she received in return for her efforts – and untimely reminders of her former treatment.

The chorus of despair turned to Wilbert for relief and comfort. He was reminded that he owed his life to Basdai's generosity. Her daughters' milk had given him nourishment. Surely she deserved something more than this. 'Sushila up to no good,' Basdai told him. 'She out to rob you and your father of house and home. Tell him to send she away. I know all she trickery.' Wilbert was withdrawn. It was not his job to interfere with his father's arrangements. He had no influence on him; as much a bystander as she was. 'I have nothing to do with it,' he said.

The bull died, and not many weeks afterwards Egbert Ramsaran got rid of his herd of cows – again on Sushila's advice. 'What you want with cows? Think of all the worry you giving yourself in keeping them. Is much cheaper in the end to buy milk from outside.' It was a new and delicious sensation to him to be so assiduously mothered. Sushila was a firm but accommodating guide. Day after day she contrived to impress her usefulness and indispensability on him and Egbert Ramsaran marvelled that he could have done for so long without her.

'It does amaze me,' he said, 'to think how blind I was for all them years.' He patted her shoulders. 'Where you was hiding yourself all that time?'

Sushila laughed her full-throated laugh. His gratitude amused her and she toyed lightly with it. 'I wasn't hiding anywhere,' she replied. 'I was there all the time. But you was a married man. You had a wife to think about then.' She liked to refer to Rani and to observe the effect the mere mention of her name had on him. It was the litmus test of her hold on him.

Egbert Ramsaran frowned. 'Don't use that name in this house. She! She wasn't no wife to me.' He massaged his stomach. 'Haunting me from the grave.' He shied away from calling her by name.

'You being unfair to Rani.' Sushila smiled deprecatingly. 'I'm sure she try she best to please you. Rani couldn't help the way she was.'

'I suppose you right,' he admitted grudgingly. 'But what is that to me? She try to eat me up all the same. To drag me down with she. I had to fight to keep my head above water and not drown. It was you who make me into a new man. I don't know what I would have done without you.'

'Is not me alone you should be praising. You should praise yourself too. Whatever it was make you into a new man was inside of you all along. It didn't come out of the blue. It just needed the right person to bring it out.'

'Not anybody could have do that.' He waved a finger close to her face. 'It had to be you and no one else.'

Sushila did not contradict him. She was aware of the dangers inherent in an excess of self-denigration. It could be carried too far and end in him devaluing her own importance in the process. She had to tread gingerly. It was a tougher battle than she had bargained for. That first time he had come to her room in the middle of the night was not a joyous affair. The surrender had been petulant and ungracious. She understood that in coming to her he had desecrated a vital part of himself and she had to coax and cajole him into acceptance. Her embraces were not sufficient. She had to become guide and teacher and philosopher, revealing inch by inch the vistas of pleasure, passion and luxurious ease which it was her privilege and duty to open up to him.

Sushila had won ultimately. Yet, her ascendancy over him, considerable as it was, was not absolute. Even in moments of his greatest gratitude, she could not afford to throw caution to the winds. Her suzerainty was hedged with reservations. Egbert Ramsaran retained vestiges of his old independence and, perhaps, because he had given up so much, what remained was sacrosanct to him and he was tenacious in its defence. Sushila had to seem submissive and pliable; to appear to be led while leading. He was acutely sensitive of any infringement of his prerogatives. Though he eventually did as she suggested, to salve his pride Egbert Ramsaran either invoked different reasons for his actions or tampered with the details of Sushila's remedies. Thus, he stopped his exercises not because there were better ways to use his strength (as Sushila had said) but because they were a 'strain' on his heart; he got rid of the cows not because they were a nuisance and because milk was cheaper from outside but because the smell of the cow-sheds upset his stomach; he did not hand over collection of the debts to Wilbert as Sushila had instructed but to Mr Balkissoon. Sushila had to pick her way along the narrow and tortuous path between self-effacement and magnification of her role. She had to decipher his moods and decide which was more appropriate. There were occasions when it exhausted her; when her tact and cunning frittered itself away to no obvious purpose or advantage.

There was a region of his mind whose defences she struggled valiantly to weaken but which, most of the time, was impervious to her assaults. Egbert Ramsaran preserved an unwavering hold on his money. Despite all his gratitude and the tremendous store he set on her, it was still he who manipulated the purse strings and sought to curb and keep in check Sushila's irrepressible yearnings for the extravagant.

'All that money you have is no good to you,' she pleaded, 'if you don't use it. Think of all the things you could do with it.'

'Like what?'

'Like this house you living in for instance. You should pull it down and build yourself a new one – like those you does see in Port-of-Spain. A man in your position . . .'

'That's not for me,' Egbert Ramsaran said. 'I didn't make my money to waste it. Anyway,' he added slyly, 'you yourself tell me money is not everything . . .'

'But . . .'

'You yourself say,' Egbert Ramsaran pursued smoothly with a mixture of irony and seriousness, 'that whatever it is that does make a person happy that is the thing he should do – regardless of what other people think. So if other people think a man in my position should be living in a fancy house – why I should let them worry me?'

'But if you have money . . .'

'Living in a big house wouldn't make me any happier. Living with you is sufficient for me. That is my happiness.'

Contrary to Basdai's accusations, Sushila did not want to grab his money for herself. She did not have any plans to rob him of 'house and home'. She would not have been capable of it. Sushila believed money existed in order to be spent and it was madness to her that it should be left lying around doing nothing. Who actually did the spending was unimportant. His alacrity in paying for Sita's education had aroused false hopes in her: it had been on the spur of the moment in an initial rush of headiness. Beyond that, Egbert Ramsaran was reluctant to go: his wealth was the last thing he had that he could call indisputably his own and he clung desperately to it. He even refused her requests for new curtains. 'What wrong with the old ones?' he asked. 'They have holes in them,' she said, 'big, big holes.' 'That don't bother me,' he replied. He tried to reduce the monthly salary he had agreed to pay her. 'Remember I supporting both you and Sita now. You should take that into account.' Sushila would have none of it. 'Nobody ask you to support Sita. So it have nothing to do with my salary.' He continued to grumble about it intermittently.

Nevertheless, his tightfistedness did not deter Sushila and she accepted the setbacks it entailed: they were conceived as part of a grander strategy; strategic retreats in a war she was convinced she would win. Her salary apart, by generously admitting defeat on a succession of trifles, she gradually quietened his fears. Her big ambition was to wheedle him into buying a house on the beach: Sushila loved the sea.

'Is not good for you to be cooped up in Victoria all the time,' she said to him. 'I don't find you looking too well these days. You need fresh air and a change of scene. It will improve your health no end.'

'Nothing the matter with my health,' he replied firmly. 'I never felt better in my life.'

'That is what you think. But I been watching you recently ...'

'You serious?' He gazed worriedly at her. Latterly he had become preoccupied with his health.

'You much paler these days,' she said. 'And nervous.'

He examined his face in the mirror. 'I haven't been sleeping too well to tell you the truth.'

'That's the first sign. You sickening for something.'

'What you suggest?'

'A bit of sea air. If I was you I would rent – or better still, buy – a house somewhere by the sea. Then you could go there whenever you want and relax. Everybody buying beach house these days. Is the thing to do.'

'I is not everybody,' Egbert Ramsaran said. 'Anyway, where you expect the money to come from?'

He refused to talk about it further. Sushila retaliated by sulking restlessly about the house for a week. Egbert Ramsaran pondered. Sushila's restlessness disturbed him: it revived his fears of her departure. Sushila knew this and she exploited it to the full: it was a risk but a calculated one. She declared Victoria was slowly driving her mad and pined volubly for the delights of Port-of-Spain and San Fernando. She did not refer once to the beach house. One afternoon she disappeared unaccountably for several hours and declined to tell him where she had been. 'I'm not a prisoner,' she said. It was a prelude to rebellion and Egbert Ramsaran was suddenly terrified that she was not bluffing.

'Don't take on so,' he begged.

'Take on how?' Sushila protruded her hips. 'I not taking on anyway. As you know, I never liked being tied down in one place too long.'

'If you leave, what about Sita? Who else will pay for she education?'

Sushila looked at him and said nothing.

'Is this beach house, not so?'

Sushila shrugged. 'If you going to let a little money come between you and your health . . .'

'Don't be so hasty. Let's discuss it.'

'It have nothing to discuss if you going to worry about money.'

She pressed home her advantage. 'If you want to drop down dead, I'm not going to prevent you.'

'But somebody have to worry about money. Is I who will have to decide where it going to come from.' He stared at her plaintively.

Sushila reckoned the time had come to adopt a fresh tactic. She sat down beside him and, taking his hand in hers, she squeezed it affectionately. Gratitude and relief coursed through Egbert Ramsaran: he felt as he had done on the day she had gone to fetch Sita from the Settlement.

'Remember is not for myself I asking it. Is for you. For your sake.'

'I realize that,' Egbert Ramsaran said.

'Is not for me to say where the money going to come from,' she said modestly. 'But you ever think about that estate you have?'

'You want me to sell it?'

'I don't *want* you to do anything.' She spoke measuredly; reassuringly. 'But I would like you to tell me what you keeping it for. What good it does do to you just sitting there with Singh on top of it? When was the last time you went down there? It wouldn't make no difference to you not having it.'

The spate of her rhetoric astonished him. He was thrown off balance.

'You see!' Sushila cooed triumphantly. 'You have no answer to that. Look at it this way. A beach house is a good investment and it will do your health no end of good. What you have to lose?' She smiled bravely. 'If after two three years you don't want it, you could sell it. It will have people lining up to buy it.'

'What I going to do with Singh if I sell the estate? I just can't throw him out of there. I bet you haven't considered that.'

Sushila had. 'Simple,' she said. 'You will need somebody to look after the beach house for you. A caretaker. And who better than Singh? At least he'll be doing something useful for a change.'

'He mightn't like that.'

'You going to let Singh tell *you* what to do? If you tell Singh he have to go what he could do? He must do as you say.' Sushila was not to be denied.

The proposition appealed to Egbert Ramsaran. From all points of view it commended itself. It would please Sushila; it might conceivably be beneficial to his health; Singh would be adequately provided for; and he stood, if he were clever enough, to make a substantial profit out of the deal: there was no lack of potential buyers. He would extract the maximum price the estate would command and acquire one of the more inexpensive beach properties. Egbert Ramsaran put the estate up for sale.

The neighbouring landowners, who had importuned in vain so many years ago, competed eagerly with one another and expressed their amazement at his sudden change of heart. After protracted negotiation the estate was sold at a handsome price and a beach house bought in its stead. Singh was duly transferred from the one to the other without consultation. The beach house was in poor condition and crying out for repair and renovation, but Egbert Ramsaran felt he had done his duty and Sushila, disappointed though she was by its shabbiness, did not dare complain. They began going there at weekends.

3

It was not many weeks after he had bought the beach house that Egbert Ramsaran fell ill with a fever. For Sushila it was a most inopportune occurrence since he was inclined to lay the blame on the cool sea breezes. 'I never had a day's sickness in my whole life,' he grumbled to her. 'Then I follow your advice and the next thing I know I fall sick.'

Sushila parried the thrust. 'Your getting sick is nothing to do with the beach house,' she said. 'It would have been a lot worse without it. If you had listened to my advice before it would never have happened.'

'Chut!' he replied. 'Never a day's sickness in my life ...'

'The beach house is not the trouble. The trouble is you too old to be working so hard. That's the real cause of it. I tell you a hundred times to let Wilbert take over some of the responsibility. What he doing in school? Is a waste of his time and your money. Is not as if he studying to be a doctor. You should be enjoying your life more. Then you wouldn't get sick.'

'Maybe you right,' Egbert Ramsaran said. 'Maybe you right. Is time that boy was getting his hands dirty.'

Egbert Ramsaran was glad of the opportunity provided by the fever: it was better than any excuse he could have drummed up. He had continued to manage the Company

209

single-handed, tolerating no advice or interference however well-intentioned. It had been his sole preoccupation and, until Sushila's arrival, retirement had never featured in his calculations. However, circumstances had changed in a way impossible to forecast and there were other things competing for his attention. Even now he had no intention of making his retirement absolute. What he envisaged was a progressive slackening of his duties. The time had clearly come to initiate his son into the mysteries. He summoned Wilbert.

'What you learning in school these days?'

'Nothing. I does hardly be there.'

'What you does do when you not there?' Egbert Ramsaran's brows wrinkled quizzically.

'Nothing much. I does go walking about the place.' Their eyes met.

'So you admit is a waste of your time and a waste of my money?' He was matter-of-fact.

'I suppose so.' Wilbert was equally matter-of-fact.

'Well, I going to put a stop to all that time and money wasting. Is hard work for you from now on, my boy. Man's work! You won't have no time for walking about the place.'

Wilbert stared expressionlessly at the almanac.

'You think you cut out for hard work? If you not, you going to be no good to me. I have no time for people who is no good to me. If you not up to the job, is out you going to go. Out! Son or no son.' Egbert Ramsaran's voice whistled. 'I will judge you as I does judge everybody else who working for me. No favouritism. So don't get any fancy ideas.' He rearranged the pillows more comfortably about him, and extended his arm. 'Come. Let me feel your hands. I want to see if they is hands that could work.'

Egbert Ramsaran kneaded his son's palms. He dropped them. 'Not bad,' he said grudgingly. 'Is a start. But they going to get harder, you understand? They have to get hard like iron and steel put together. And not only hard. But dirty! Black and dirty with oil and grease. You frighten to get your hands black and dirty?' He giggled. 'So dirty that people in Port-of-Spain won't want to shake hands with you?'

'That don't frighten me,' Wilbert said. He stared at his palms and at the short, stubby fingers and imagined them as hard as steel and coated with the grime of oil and grease. It was what he had been born for: the fulfilment of his life. 'That don't frighten me,' he repeated.

'Good. That's the idea. I wouldn't have reached where I was today if I had been frightened to get my hands dirty.' He exhibited his palms. 'I starting you right at the bottom and your hands going to get so dirty and black that you will hardly be able to wash them clean with soap and water when you come home in the evening. And you going to be so tired the only thing you will want is your bed. I going to make you learn by heart about every nut and bolt it have in that place.'

Wilbert relinquished the farce of school and donned a pair of overalls. The days he had spent visiting Chinese Cha-Cha and wandering about the streets near the market receded from him; as did the siren songs of his uncle. He had put the aimlessness of those times behind him. His life's work had begun. Wilbert crawled under the bellies of the trucks of the Ramsaran Transport Company and familiarized himself, as his father had instructed, with every nut and screw. His hands grew hard and calloused and became deeply ingrained with traces of dirt and grease which even soap and water would not completely wash away. Wilbert did not shirk his duties. His dour zeal impressed those with whom he worked and he returned home to eat in exhausted silence and tumble into bed. Egbert Ramsaran had been as good as his word. He bestowed no special favour on his son. Wilbert was treated as the other employees were treated. His colleagues in the repair sheds searched diligently for the merest hint of paternal bias but could find none. They were bewildered.

Sammy, one of his fellow mechanics, taxed him with it.

'How come,' he asked, 'the boss does treat you so funny?'

'He don't treat me funny. I does get the same treatment as the rest of you.'

'That is exactly what I mean,' Sammy said.

'Why should he treat me as if I was special?' Wilbert replied indifferently. 'I have a job of work to do and the only thing that count is how well I do it. Being his son don't count.'

Sammy could not accept that. 'It must count for something. If it was my father . . .'

'Well it isn't your father,' he replied curtly.

Sammy was not to be fobbed off so easily. 'We does only work here because of the money he does pay we. If it wasn't for that I wouldn't be here. But you . . . you going to be the boss one day. That is the difference between you and the rest of we. You would expect . . .'

'I don't expect nothing. My being boss is a long way in the future. I don't think about it.' He prepared to crawl under one of the trucks awaiting repair.

'So you will be happy to go on like you is for ten or maybe twenty years? Your father might live a very long time.'

'I have work to do,' Wilbert said, sliding under the truck. 'That is what we here for – to work not talk.'

Sammy could get no more out of him. Wilbert's stoicism remained an enigma. The mechanics discussed it at length among themselves but arrived at no satisfactory explanation. 'Is not natural,' Sammy said. 'Something must be wrong somewhere and he bottling it all up inside of him. Like a volcano which does remain quiet for years and then all of a sudden . . . bang!' There were other things about Wilbert which puzzled and intrigued them. It was their custom, after they were paid on Friday afternoons, to spend the evening touring the rumshops of Victoria. They invited Wilbert to come along with them and 'have some fun'. Wilbert declined the invitation, saying he was tired and wanted to go to bed early.

'You talking like if you is an old man,' Sammy said. 'What you saving up your energy to do? Is the end of the week. Time to have some fun and forget about work for a while.' He grabbed his arm. 'Come and have a drink with we, man. That won't kill you. In fact a little rum will make you sleep all the better.'

Wilbert laughed and detached himself from Sammy's grip. 'I don't like rum.'

'You don't like rum!' The mechanics guffawed. 'We will

212

teach you how to like rum. But you don't have to drink rum. You could drink beer instead.'

'Some other time,' he promised.

'I think you only fooling we about not liking rum and wanting to go to bed early,' Sammy said. He poked him in the ribs. 'Is some woman you have to see, not so? Own up!'

'I don't have any woman to see,' Wilbert said.

'What's she name?' Again Sammy poked him in the ribs.

'I don't have any woman.'

'What she look like? She pretty?' Sammy wiggled his hips.

'I tell you I don't have any woman.' Wilbert raised his voice. 'Neither a pretty one or a ugly one. I don't care for them.'

'You don't like women either?' The mechanics were nonplussed. 'You don't like rum. You don't like women. What it is you like then?'

'I like people not to harass me with stupid questions.'

'It have so many different kinds of women,' Sammy said. 'It must have some you like. What about that girl who does live with you and your father?'

'What about her?' Wilbert replied, his expression hardening.

'Some people think she is one of the prettiest girls in Victoria.'

'Well? So what? What's that got to do with me?' Wilbert stared at him, wrinkling his brows. 'And it have nothing to do with you either.'

Sammy recognized the danger signal. 'Forget it,' he said. 'If you not interested in women is nothing I can do about that.'

The invitation to join them on their Friday evening excursions was not repeated and the mechanics were altogether more circumspect and wary in their dealings with him.

That same evening, as he went past Sita's bedroom, Wilbert noticed that the door, which was usually closed, had been left slightly ajar. 'Some people think she is one of the prettiest girls in Victoria.' On impulse, Wilbert stopped and glanced in.

Sita was sitting at her table under the window and writing busily, her head twisted to one side. The room was clean and tidy. Her books were arranged in neat piles. Insects orbited the ceiling light. She seemed totally absorbed in what she was doing.

The shadow which had interposed itself between them had not disappeared. But what had initially sprung from an understandable embarrassment had become transformed through neglect into something bordering on an unspoken animosity. Each had waited for the other to make the first move; and neither had obliged. Sita had grown too adept at hiding her feelings for her to bring them out unsolicited into the open. She had temporized, searching for signs of encouragement in Wilbert's behaviour towards her; some gesture of implied good will which might have made it easier for her to do so. Unfortunately, she could detect nothing of the kind. This angered her. If Wilbert was determined to maintain his distance, why should she humiliate herself before him? He might rebuff her advances out of sheer vindictiveness. She would not risk that. There was no reason why she should be feeling guilty. She had done no wrong; had injured no one. She bore no responsibility whatever for her mother's actions. Furthermore, it was Egbert Ramsaran himself who had brought her into the house; it was he who had offered to send her to school in Port-of-Spain. No doubt his reasons for doing these things did not have their origin in any genuine kindly feelings towards *her* (Sita had no illusions on that score), but why should she concern herself with that? It was only natural for her to take advantage of his generosity. Anybody in her position would do the same. If Wilbert detested her for it, there was nothing she could do about that. It was a pity – but there was nothing to be done. She was perfectly willing to be friendly: all she required was a little encouragement which did not seem to be forthcoming.

Yet, Wilbert also had been searching and waiting for some sign of encouragement or gesture of good will, but Sita's aloofness and reticence barred any approach. He too was afraid of being rebuffed. Embarrassment turned to bitterness. Who did Sita think she was? This was his father's house and it would, in due course, be his. She was a guest and the least she could do was show her gratitude by being friendly towards him; not the other way round. It was only right that the burden of proof should be on her. Her inordinate pride – for this was how he interpreted her aloofness and reticence – was offensive; the rock against which his good intentions had been dashed. However, his grievance against her had another, more specific cause.

Wilbert had almost forgotten his fight with Julian Bholai and his promise to recompense him for the wrecked aeroplanes, when Julian suddenly presented himself and reminded him of it. 'I finally think of something you could do if you still want to make up for the planes, Ramsaran.' Julian scratched his head and smiled. 'Could I come one day and . . . and visit Sita?' Wilbert was taken aback. 'I don't consider that making up . . .' 'I would consider it so,' Julian said hastily. 'You see, I could tell Ma it's you I'm coming to visit.' 'She wouldn't believe that,' Wilbert said. 'She will have no choice.' Julian replied. 'She could never disprove it unless . . . what you say? Is that a bargain?' Wilbert did not relish the idea but he had no grounds for refusal. Julian did not confine himself to one visit. He became a regular visitor. He and Sita would sit in a secluded corner of the verandah and talk in whispers. Wilbert was not invited to share in these conversations and, if he appeared unexpectedly, their flow of chatter dried up and they looked distinctly uncomfortable. If Sita liked Julian she could not possibly like him. It was this which aggravated Wilbert's bitterness against her and provided it with an identifiable focus.

Wilbert coughed. Sita's head jerked upwards from the paper. She started in surprise when she saw him.

'What you standing there for? Somebody calling me?' Sita half-rose from the chair. She was not welcoming and covered with her hand the closely written page she had been working on.

'Nobody calling you,' Wilbert said.

Sita sat down again. Wilbert advanced a step into the room,

gazing at the hand which covered the writing; the slim, tapering fingers; the sharply defined knuckles; and the network of bluish veins on the wrist. Sita closed the book. It was a diary.

'What you does write in there?' Wilbert's attention shifted from her hand to the diary.

'Anything I feel like. That's what diaries are for.' She drummed on the cover. 'It helps to pass the time.' She stared out through the open window at the field with its shadowy hulks. 'I write down anything I find interesting.'

'Like what?' His tone was tinged with insolence – and curiosity. He gripped the knob of the door, swinging it to and fro. Like all the doors in the house it creaked on its hinges.

Sita looked round vaguely, waving her arms. 'This and that. Nothing earthshaking.'

'Could I read some of what you write?' He extended his hand towards the diary.

Sita shook her head. 'You're not supposed to read what people write in their diaries. It's private.'

'But if is not important . . .'

'That makes no difference,' Sita said. 'It's still private.'

Wilbert nodded slowly; consideringly. The door creaked on its hinges. 'You does write about Julian Bholai in there? Is that why you don't want to show me?'

Sita looked up at him, colouring slightly. 'A diary is private. I'm not going to tell you who or what I write about in it.'

'I bet,' Wilbert said, coming closer to the desk, 'that is only him you does write about?'

Sita laughed. 'Even if that was true, what concern is it of yours?'

'You know his mother have plans for him to marry a white woman when he go to England? You know that?'

Sita tautened.

'He would never marry you,' Wilbert said. 'His mother wouldn't let him.'

'Why are you telling me all this for? What are you trying to gain by it?' Sita stared at him, drumming on the diary. 'Who Julian gets married to is nothing to do with me.'

216

'But the two of you is boy-friend and girl-friend, not so? Why else he does always be coming here to see you? Why else does the two of you be talking so hush-hush out in the verandah?' Wilbert grinned.

'You jealous?'

'Why should I be jealous of a little sissy like him? Doctor! He only going to be a doctor so he could cheat poor people.' Wilbert giggled. 'He ever tell you about the time I beat him up? I had him on the floor begging for mercy.'

Sita applauded. 'Bravo! Bravo!'

'Is true. I had him on the floor begging for mercy.' He remembered the stark blackness of Julian's eyes pleading with him. 'I suppose he was too ashamed to tell you about that.'

'As a matter of fact he did tell me about it,' Sita replied calmly. 'He wasn't ashamed. If anybody should be ashamed it's you.'

Wilbert lunged forward suddenly and attempted to grab the diary. Sita anticipated him and sent it sliding across the table out of his reach. It slipped over the edge and fell on the floor. Getting down on their knees, they scrambled for it wildly. Wilbert howled, clutching his wrist: Sita had bitten him. She laughed gaily and with the diary secure in her grasp she crawled away from him.

'I told you diaries are private,' she said.

'If you wasn't a girl ...' Nursing his maimed hand, Wilbert went out of the room. Sita closed the door and, reclining on the bed, laughed a long time.

4

Julian's visit to the house in Victoria had put Mrs Bholai in one of her typical dilemmas. It was extremely unlikely she should approve of her son needlessly placing himself in such dangerously close proximity to the infamous pair; and of exposing himself to the debilitating and baleful influence of Wilbert Ramsaran: she had not forgotten the fight. However, her hopes for Shanty would be dashed if some sort of connection were not maintained with the Ramsarans. And Julian was undoubtedly the most appropriate medium of contact. Thus, she could not bring herself to do anything about Julian's visits.

Her disquiet was compounded by Basdai who, leaning conspiratorially across the counter, said to her in the shop one day, 'I hear your son and Miss Sita is real good friends. Is not for me to give you advice but . . .'

'You have it all wrong,' Mrs Bholai replied uneasily. 'Is Wilbert he does go to Victoria to see. The two of them is very close friends.' Compared to Sushila and Sita, her ancient fears of Wilbert were trivial.

'Ah.' Basdai fingered her chin, studying the goods ranged along the shelves. 'I must have get my information wrong then.'

'What information?' Mrs Bholai would have preferred not to know.

'I wouldn't worry if I was you,' Basdai said smoothly. 'Although Miss Sita sly and cunning like she no-good mother, it might still only be gossip-mongering and rumour. You know how some people is. But, as I does always say, where you see smoke it must have fire.'

'What information?'

'That they is boy-friend and girl-friend.' Basdai stretched the corners of her mouth into a melancholy smile. 'But I sure if it had any truth in it Julian would have tell you a long time ago.' Basdai yawned, scanning the laden shelves.

'Quite right,' Mrs Bholai said firmly. 'Jules not in the habit of hiding things from me. Is different with his father. But with me, his own mother . . .'

But her confidence was not self-supporting. She told her son what she had heard.

'You letting that old fool bother you? You should have tell her to go to hell and mind her own damn business.'

'You haven't answer my question,' Mrs Bholai said.

'Well,' Julian replied carelessly, 'what if I talk to Sita?'

'You admit it then! You have the boldface to admit it!'

'You want me to lie instead?'

'Oh my God!' Mrs Bholai clutched her head. 'I never

218

dream I would live to witness a day like this. I won't let you go there any more.'

'How you going to stop me?'

'Jules! Jules! How you could do this to me?' Mrs Bholai sobbed. 'You only saying it to hurt me, not so? It's only a joke you having with me, not so?' She was cringing.

'It's no joke.'

'Why don't you spare a thought for my feelings?' She held his hand.

'If I was to spare a thought for every single one of your so-called feelings, I would never set foot out of this house or look at anybody without asking your permission first.' He was beginning to believe in his cause.

'What about all them trips we does make to your cousins in San Fernando? You call that never setting foot out of this house?'

'I hate my cousins in San Fernando.'

Mrs Bholai dropped his hand. 'So,' she yelled, 'you prefer to be with the daughter of a whore than with your cousins in San Fernando? You love that daughter of a whore more than you love your own mother who carry you for nine months in she belly. What she bamboozling your brain with?' Mrs Bholai trembled.

'Obeah.' Julian laughed.

'I wouldn't be surprised. Is what she mother use to bamboozle old Ramsaran with. Obeah! And Miss Sita doing the same to you.' Mrs Bholai gestured extravagantly. Her nostrils dilated and her hoarse voice resounded through the house and could be heard on the road in the intervals when there was no traffic. Mr Bholai listened anxiously in the shop downstairs. 'Bholai! Bholai! Come here this instant and listen to what your son saying.' She stalked out to the verandah. 'Bholai! Like you deaf?' Her voice travelled across the road, penetrating the screen of houses opposite, and frittered itself away in the hot green of the canefields beyond.

Mr Bholai stumbled, puffing and panting, up the steps. His wife leapt on him and dragged him unceremoniously into the sitting-room.

'I want you to listen to what your son saying. This is all your doing.'

'What he saying?' Mr Bholai stared round helplessly.

'He saying that he love that daughter of a whore more than he love his own mother. That is what he saying. And is all your doing.'

'My doing!' Mr Bholai groaned. He took a handkerchief from his pocket and mopped his forehead. 'I sure he didn't say that.'

'Ask him yourself then, shopkeeper.'

'Calm yourself, Moon.'

'I want you to put your foot down, Bholai, and keep him from going to see that wretch. You is his father, after all.'

'You tell your mother you don't love she?' Mr Bholai looked not at his son but at the vases of flowers Mynah had sprinkled about the room.

Julian did not reply. He scraped at his fingernails.

'You should listen to your mother,' Mr Bholai said after a while.

'That is all you could say?' Mrs Bholai hopped furiously about the room. 'That is what you call being a father? Shop-keeper! Two pound of salt, half-pound of butter! Is all your doing. If we was living in San Fernando none of this would have gone and happen. He would never have set eyes on that daughter of a whore.'

'Yes, Moon.'

'Shopkeeper!'

'Yes, Moon.'

'Two pound of salt, half-pound of butter!'

'Yes, Moon.'

In her despair over her son, Mrs Bholai was prepared to go to any lengths to save him from the machinations of Sita. She cast around for allies. Wilbert, she felt, was the only person who could provide the kind of aid she required. Abandon-ing her scruples, she descended on the grey fortress of the Ramsaran Transport Company. Wilbert received her politely – if unenthusiastically – dressed in his soiled overalls.

'I not going to beat round the bush with you, Wilbert. Is Julian and Sita I want to talk to you about.'

Wilbert had conjectured as much. He took her to a wired-off cubicle which served as a waiting-room. It was furnished with wooden benches.

'I want you to put some sense into that boy head for me.'

Wilbert smiled. 'How do you expect me to do that, Mrs Bholai? If Julian wouldn't listen to you, he would hardly be likely to listen to me.'

'But he must listen to somebody.'

'Maybe. But not to me.'

Mrs Bholai got up from the bench. She stood directly in front of him, her fingers entwined in the mesh of the wire. 'What about Sita then? She must listen to you. Is your father house she living in. Is he' (and here Mrs Bholai nearly choked with outrage) '. . . is he who paying for she to go to a first-rate school in Port-of-Spain. My daughters . . .'

Wilbert frowned. 'It's my father you should go and speak to.'

'At least you could try and put a little sense in she head. You could say that Julian would never marry she. That he only playing around. That when he go away to England . . .'

'If that is the case, why worry?'

Mrs Bholai sat down again. 'Jules have a great future ahead of him. She spoiling his chances to be a doctor. She could only drag him down. If she had any feelings at all . . .' Mrs Bholai twirled her bracelets. 'You can't expect me not to worry. I can't stand to one side and see Jules throwing his chances away. I must try and do something about it. They could still write to one another when he in England.' Mrs Bholai's eyes darkened. 'And, who knows but Sita sheself might go to England.' She got up, shaken by the prospect, 'If your father could pay for she education in a Port-of-Spain convent, it have no reason why he mightn't send she to England to become a B.A. Languages.' She laid a hand on his shoulders as if for support. 'You could have a heart to heart talk with she . . .'

Wilbert scowled. 'Why don't *you* go and have a heart to heart talk with her?'

'How I could do a thing like that? I would only lose my temper straight away. But you ...'

'Listen to me, Mrs Bholai, and listen to me well. The only thing that concern me is the Ramsaran Transport Company. If you wanted bricks or gravel delivered I could help you. But I can't help you about anything else. So please don't try and involve me.'

From where they sat they could survey the length and breadth of the cavern housing the workshops and offices of the Ramsaran Transport Company. To their right were the bays where the red and black trucks not in service were parked in two neat rows facing each other on either side of the main gate. Above the main gate there were a series of green-painted metal cages similar to the ones on the ground floor in which they were talking. In these cramped cages the administrative side of the business was carried on by a small team of minions; the soles of their shoes and their legs visible to all who passed beneath. To the left – and to the rear of the cavern – were the repair sheds. Sounds of hammering echoed off the bare walls, brash and metallically insistent. Mechanics, dressed in soiled overalls like Wilbert's, went ceaselessly to and fro whistling and shouting to one another. Engines coughed and spluttered and revved and the smell of oil and petrol suffused the air. The concrete floor was coated with thick layers of grime and scattered pools of oil shimmered with the colours of the rainbow. Strips of sunlight came through holes in the roof but they were not sufficient to dispel the prevailing dank gloom which appeared to ooze and seep from the building itself. The daylight creeping in from the main gate battled against an invisible barrier and succeeded in penetrating no more than a few hard-won feet into the interior before it was overcome; thickened with the gloom and suffocated by it. The atmosphere was subterranean, and electric lights burned dimly in the metal cages and repair sheds. Julian and Sita and the problems they posed seemed very far away to Wilbert: he had not spoken to Sita since their fray over the diary; and Mrs Bholai, impeccable in her pink dress and with her gold bracelets glinting on her wrists, was a wraith from another world.

'I think is a very true thing what people does say.'

'What is that, Mrs Bholai?'

'They does say that if you born with too much brains is almost like if they does make you stupid. And that is the trouble with Jules. That son of mine have so much brains it making him behave stupid, stupid.'

Wilbert agreed. 'And now, if you will excuse me, Mrs Bholai, I must go back to my work.'

Mrs Bholai was not easily discouraged. Wilbert, she had to admit, had not been helpful. But then, neither had he been actively hostile. He had listened to her patiently. That was an encouraging beginning. Her fertile brain teeming with ideas and proposals, she paid him a second unheralded visit. Wilbert received her with undiminished politeness.

'I have the true solution to the whole problem,' she said. 'Let Julian get she pregnant. Then, as you know, they will have to expel she from that convent and that will stop she from wasting your father money. And don't forget is your money as well.' She tittered gleefully. 'That is one side of the question. The other is this. You know as well as me that nothing could frighten a man more than a girl he not married to making baby for him. Love does stop quick quick once a woman belly start to swell up.' Mrs Bholai wetted her lips. 'So my plan is to let Julian get she pregnant. Let him go right ahead! It will put all that nonsense out of his head straight away.' Mrs Bholai paced the metal cage. 'I know what you going to say now. You going to say that Julian will have to marry she.' She stopped in front of him. 'But tell me who it have could make Julian marry she? If she had a father to call she own that would be a different matter. But without a father who it have to make trouble for Julian? She mother?' Mrs Bholai frowned scornfully. 'Just let Sushila try to cause trouble and I go make even more trouble for she. Basdai give me the full lowdown about she. I think that's the best plan. What you say?'

Wilbert agreed.

Sita, however, showed no signs of pregnancy – to Mrs Bholai's unbounded regret. Then, in conformity to that chameleon nature of hers, she shifted her ground radically, and said to Wilbert without apparent discomfort: 'Sita is not all that bad girl really when you think about it. It don't matter who she mother – or father – is. She good-looking. In fact, I find she very good-looking. On top of all that she getting a really first-rate education.'

Wilbert was too amazed even to agree.

Mrs Bholai steeled herself, painfully aware of the sacrifice she was about to make on her son's behalf. 'One of these days Sita going to make somebody a good wife.' She gazed slyly at Wilbert. 'And the time not far off when you will have to be thinking of finding a wife.'

'Are you trying to marry me off to Sita, Mrs Bholai?' He was amused and angry. 'She's not good enough for Julian but she's good enough for me, is that it?'

'No, no,' Mrs Bholai said. 'I wasn't suggesting that at all.' She seemed shocked that any such motive could be imputed to her. 'All I was saying was that she would make somebody a good wife. And why not you?'

'Why not Julian?'

Mrs Bholai twirled her bracelets.

'If I ever decide to get married,' Wilbert said, 'I'll choose my own wife.'

Mrs Bholai was contrite. The plan had backfired. 'I wasn't meaning it like that, Wilbert. God is my witness. You misunderstand me. I was just trying to ...' Floundering, she gave up the attempt at explanation. 'Look,' she said, 'let we forget the whole thing. Eh? Forget I ever say what I say.' There was, fortunately, one consolation to be drawn: if Wilbert refused to entertain the idea of marriage to Sita, then the way still remained open for Shanty. This cheered her up.

'You know, Wilbert,' she started afresh, 'Shanty is a very sensitive girl. You mustn't let all that shouting and laughing fool you.'

Wilbert looked at her.

Mrs Bholai now toyed with her ear-rings. 'She can't take care of herself like the older ones. I think is because being the youngest we spoil her too much. But how could you help spoiling a pretty little girl like that? You would have to be a really heartless person not to.'

The taste of toothpaste lodged in Wilbert's throat.

Mrs Bholai gazed earnestly at him. 'You would never guess what she tell me the other day. "Ma," she say to me – and this was straight out of the blue, mind you – "Ma", she say, "I wonder why we doesn't see Wilbert Ramsaran any more. He so polite and have such good manners." Those were her exact words. And I say, "Wilbert Ramsaran don't have time to waste. He's a working man now."' Mrs Bholai giggled vacuously. 'Wasn't that a funny thing for she to say out of the blue?'

'Very funny,' Wilbert said.

'She make me promise I would ask you to come and see we.'

'I don't have the time . . .'

'That's what I say. "He's a working man now." But she would be so disappointed. You must come and visit we again.'

'Well . . .'

'Keep it in mind.' Mrs Bholai made ready to leave. 'Shanty would be so disappointed.'

Mrs Bholai hurried away in a fog of good will.

Chapter Seven

1

It was with astonishment that Sushila realized she had been in Victoria for four years. She had never stayed so long in one place before.

'Four years!' she exclaimed to Egbert Ramsaran. 'I been living here with you for four whole years.'

'What of it?' he replied complacently. 'You want to have a celebration?'

It was not an anniversary Sushila cared to celebrate: she was far from being in a celebratory mood. Her fourth anniversary in the Ramsaran household coincided with the appearance of her first grey hairs. They were a death sentence. She could not flee from them. Wherever she went they would accompany her; and do so in increasing numbers. She could pull them out – as she had tried to do – but there would always be another set to fill the breach. They were intimations of a disease from which Sushila believed she had been granted a special licence of immunity and therefore had not troubled to take precautions against. She had exploited the considerable resources of her youth and beauty with a reckless disregard for the future, trusting that the empty spaces she had left behind would be automatically filled in. Something had gone wrong: her guardian angel had let her down.

Her endemic restlessness, which during the previous four years had lain dormant, revived. She had no desire to squander what remained to her of youth and beauty on the omnivorous Egbert Ramsaran whose complacency wounded her. They were wasting assets and Sushila wanted to have a final fling and relive former glories. Perhaps it would invigorate and cure her. She had always thrived on novelty and in her present mode of life there was no room for novelty. The monotony of her life in Victoria had sapped her energies. A 'change of scene' might do the trick. A change of scene! The excitement had gone out of the adventure: she had achieved more or less what she was capable of achieving; what she had set out to achieve. What was there to be gained from staying on? Her revenge on the Settlement was as complete as it was ever likely to be; and her hold on Egbert Ramsaran was as complete as *that* was ever likely to be. There was nothing else she could do here.

Nevertheless, Sushila could not persuade herself to act on her decision. In this dilapidated house was more security and comfort than she had ever had. She was fettered by a harness of invisible threads and it was only now when she tried to move that she became fully aware of them. They were not an insuperable obstacle. Sushila could, had she so desired, have snapped her fetters and set herself at liberty. But she delayed. She had grown accustomed to the security and comforts provided by Egbert Ramsaran and she was reluctant to break the threads and discard them.

The daily routine had acquired an insinuating rhythm of its own and her heart throbbed in unison with it. Her duties were not onerous and she could not honestly assert they were utterly distasteful to her. She was conversant with the ways of Egbert Ramsaran. The areas of mutual suspicion and distrust had been gradually whittled away. They had arrived at a compromise. She knew how far she could go with him; and he knew how far he could go with her. The compromise was respected by both sides and became part of the sluggish, domestic rhythm which had lulled Sushila into somnolence, and from which she had been precipitately roused by the discovery of a grey hair. She had woken to find she was a 'prisoner'.

Sushila neither particularly liked nor disliked Egbert Ramsaran. But, sharing the same bed night after night had established a bond of another order between them; and this had nothing to do with like or dislike; love or hatred. The customs and habits built upon the hunger pangs of desire had usurped the place of affection and made it seem unnecessary. No ties of sentiment bound them together: he was not a sentimental man and she was not a sentimental woman. To that extent they had appeared to be perfectly matched. Sushila shuddered when she recalled the relish with which he had described to her Rani's fruitless journeys through the darkened house ('smelling sweet sweet as if she blood was made out of perfume,' he had said) and the blows he had administered on her upturned face. She had shared his relish and laughed as loud as he had.

What use would such a man have for an ageing woman with grey hairs? She could not depend on his gratitude. He could obtain from a hundred different women what he obtained from her. Admittedly she had tried to impress her indispensability on him but she had reminded him just as often of the temporariness of the arrangement. The contest had worn her out and lowered her resistance. If she was no longer able to give him the pleasure she had promised – and what else could she ever hope to give him? – what was to become of her? Already she could feel the stings of his blows on her cheeks. For it was she who had taught him that the body was all; it was she who had suppressed his arguments by the elementary device of clapping her hand across his mouth; it was she, as guide and teacher, who had led him step by step and showed him how easy it was to still conscience and live for the moment.

Sushila carried the knowledge of her decline like a dark secret and every morning she searched painstakingly through her hair for fresh signs of it. She understood her situation clearly. Go from this place she must – before Egbert Ramsaran noticed. But where could she go? Her old friends and contacts had dropped away. However, Sushila did not wish to see her old friends. They would remember her as she had been and that was intolerable. The allure of liberty regained belonged to the past. When Sushila imagined what it would be like – and she imagined it constantly – she pictured herself as she had been in her prime. She was afraid to commit herself to a new adventure in which, deprived of the energies of her youth, she would have no protection against failure. The uncertainty gnawed at her and undermined her resolution;

and though the invisible threads chafed and bit into her, she did not have the courage to break them.

There was a further obstacle in her path: Sita. What was to be done with her if she went away? Sushila did not wish to be burdened with extra responsibilities. Neither could she leave her here trusting to the tender mercies of Egbert Ramsaran. That was out of the question. He might go berserk and she could not say what he might take it into his head to do. The man was capable of anything. Here was the biggest stumbling block to her plans. Sita's fate had never weighed with her before; but now it did: it was a convenient diversion from her other fears. Sushila directed her frustration on to this most concrete symbol of her oppression.

She had been foolish to bring her here and even more foolish to allow Egbert Ramsaran to pay for her education. It had woven another thread into the web binding her. Sita was the primary cause of all her troubles. If it had not been for Sita the temptation to accede to Basdai's wild schemes would not have been as great. She would have remained a free woman. It was for Sita's sake and Sita's sake alone she had sacrificed herself. And what had she received in return for her sacrifice? The experiment of living with her daughter had not been a resounding success. Sushila had been able to establish no area of contact with her. Not that she had tried very hard. She felt that by bringing her to live under the same roof she had done her mother's duty by her and was not inclined to do more. Sita was an essentially extraneous factor in her life. Thus Sushila had taken scant notice of her.

Unhappily, Sita could no longer be easily dismissed. She was blossoming rapidly into womanhood. Daily, it seemed, her latent physical resemblance to what her mother had been grew more striking. Sita's figure – though by no means as voluptuous as her mother's – had filled out, shedding its bony, awkward angularity. Her features were settling into their final form and her movements were assured and decisive. The habitual, solemn expression of her eyes did not vanish but now and then there were flashes of gaiety and mischief. Mother and daughter were exchanging roles. It was at Sita the men whistled and stared when they went to Victoria Market to do the week's shopping. Sushila was frequently stopped on the street. 'What a lovely girl your daughter turning out to be, Mistress Sushila. She going to have all the men rushing after she, you wait and see. You must be very proud.' To which Sushila replied brusquely and without a trace of pride: 'You really think she good-looking? Better wait a few years. All girls does look nice when they come to Sita age.'

To her mother, Sita had become merely another woman; and, by definition, a rival. Sushila examined herself frenziedly in the mirror. She noted an incipient fatness and studied the lines on her face. The fleshy firmness of her arms was on the wane and her stomach bulged. 'Oh my God! What happening to me all of a sudden? Is living in this house that doing it. A change of scene is all I need. By hook or crook I must get away from here. I must get away.' Any word of praise for Sita was sufficient to give her a 'headache' and put her in a bad mood for the rest of the day. 'Everywhere I go is Sita this and Sita that,' she retorted furiously to one of her daughter's admirers. 'Like all you have nothing else to talk about?' She struggled desperately to shake off this crippling jealousy which solved nothing and could only be self-defeating. But her jealousy would not leave her. Sushila's malady was beyond cure.

'You letting all this praise go to your head,' she accused Sita. 'You better watch out. I thought it was book alone you was interested in.'

'I'm not letting anything go to my head. It doesn't matter to me what people say – not even if they said I was ugly.'

'Oh yes? Why you does let all them men makes eyes at you for then? They wouldn't do it if you didn't encourage them. Don't think you could fool me, child.' To call Sita 'child' was soothing and she dwelt lingeringly on it. 'I been round this world long enough to know what is what.'

'I can't stop people from looking at me,' Sita said mildly. 'You're behaving just like Phulo.'

'You little bitch!' Sushila's face had gone blotchy. 'What I have in common with that slave? I don't have nothing in

230

common with that slave. You little bitch. Don't you ever speak like that to me again, you hear. Don't you ever speak to me like that again or I'll rip that tongue of yours out of your mouth for you.'

Sita winced. She had never seen her mother like this. It was a distressing spectacle. 'I'm sorry,' she said. 'I shouldn't have ...' She gazed hopelessly at her mother. The damage had been done and it could not be reversed.

'You think I would be here if it wasn't for you?' Sushila shouted. 'It was for you I sacrifice myself. Give up all that I had. Friends included. For you and you alone I do that just so that same Phulo wouldn't abuse and laugh at you.' Sushila rubbed a hand along her forehead. 'And what do I get from you in return? Headaches! That is what I get in return. Headaches so bad that I does feel dizzy. They driving me mad. Just to set eyes on you does give me a headache.' Sushila swayed on her heels.

'Why don't you go and lie down for a little? That will make you feel better.'

'Nothing will ever make me feel better so long as I have you around.' Sushila gazed feverishly at her daughter. 'From the day you was born you been nothing but a trouble and burden to me. The first time I set eyes on you I wanted to dash you to the ground. Ask Basdai if you don't believe me. She will tell you.'

'I believe you,' Sita said.

'You believe me, do you?' Sushila laughed bitterly. 'How could a child like you know what it was like? You haven't even started to know. You could take my word for that.' Sushila knew how unjust she was being: how irrational; how self-defeating. But justice, reason and common sense had no meaning for her.

Having, as it were, broken the truce and declared her hand, Sushila gave herself over to the attack, seeking out her daughter.

'Just let me be,' Sita pleaded. 'I didn't ask to be born. What do you want me to do? Kill myself?'

'That would be the biggest favour you could do me. But

is my fault for not dashing you to the ground the day you was born. I should have kill you right there and then.' Sushila squeezed her aching forehead. 'These headaches you giving me going to end by driving me mad.'

'I'm not the cause of your headaches,' Sita said, 'and it's not me who is driving you mad. You know what the real cause is.' Sita could not restrain herself: the bombardment was non-stop.

'What is the real cause, you little bitch?'

Sita did not answer.

'What is the real cause?' Sushila grabbed her daughter and shook her frenziedly.

'Don't force me to say something I don't want to say. Let me go.'

'Say it! Say it!' Sushila dug her fingernails into Sita's shoulders.

'Don't make me . . . please don't make me.'

'Say it!'

'All right,' Sita shouted. 'You asked for it. You're getting old! Worn out! No good to yourself or anybody else. Not even to him! You will end up a million times worse than Phulo. Will you let me go now?'

Sushila staggered back from her. She opened and closed her mouth soundlessly.

Sita rushed to support her.

Sushila shrank from her. 'Keep away from me. Don't touch me.'

'You forced me into saying it. You shouldn't have.'

'Keep away. You want me to take leave of my senses but I won't give you that satisfaction.' She caressed her arms. 'Don't think you is a woman because you have two scrawny legs and breasts. That don't make you a woman.'

'You're making yourself ill.'

Sushila snatched up her skirt. 'Look at these! Feel them!' She stroked her legs. Sushila dropped her skirt. 'Oh my God! Is like the Devil himself pounding inside my head. I could rip it off.' She was crying.

'Let me take you to bed.'

Sushila allowed herself to be led to her bedroom and Sita put her to bed.

'Try and go to sleep.'

'It take more than two scrawny legs and breasts to make a woman. It take a lot more. More than you ever dream of . . .'

'Try and get some rest. You don't want him to find you in this condition.' Sita covered her with a blanket.

'. . . a lot more . . . more than you ever dream of . . .'

'Go to sleep.'

'. . . to be a woman, that is the hardest thing in the world. I should have been born a man . . .' Sushila stared at the glossy photographs pinned to the wall. '. . . a man . . . I should have been born a man. Then I would never have to . . .'

Sushila tossed feverishly. Sita closed the curtains and tiptoed out.

2

Sushila's campaign against Sita was fuelled by the regular visits of Julian Bholai and the whispered conversations in the verandah; and whatever the initial drift of her attack it came inevitably to pivot on him.

'I tired seeing his face here,' she stormed. 'Is as if he don't have a home of his own.'

'He doesn't come here more than once a week,' Sita replied. 'And sometimes not even that.'

'Every time I turn he does be here. It does give me a headache just to look at him.'

'He doesn't get in your way. You don't even have to see him.'

Sushila sneered. 'How I could help seeing him since he always here?' She waved a finger in Sita's face. 'I know all this underhand boy-friend and girl-friend business.'

'He's not my boy-friend,' Sita answered sharply, 'and never will be. There's nothing underhand either. If I was going to be underhand I wouldn't let him come here. I would go somewhere else to be underhand.' She opened the door of her bedroom.

Sushila pursued her. 'What the two of you does have to talk about so? That is what I would like to know.'

'Feel free to come and listen any time you want.' Sita tried to close the door but it wedged against her mother's foot.

'I thought it was studies you was interested in. But it seem to me that is only Dr Julian you really interested in. Ever since you get them two scrawny legs and breasts and start feeling you is a woman . . .'

'Don't start up on that again.' Sita tugged at the door.

Sushila laughed. 'He going to throw you away like a old paper bag when he go to England.'

'Please . . .'

'Like a old paper bag . . .'

'I heard you the first time. Let go the door.'

Sushila removed her foot and Sita closed the door and locked it. She went to the window and breathed in deeply, looking at the rusting hulks. She stared in the opposite direction at the sunlit hills and the clapboard houses teetering on the lower slopes. Then her gaze swept slowly past the rooftops of Victoria. She turned her back on the window and on the sunbleached bones of the Ramsaran Transport Company and stared at the books on her desk. Sitting down at the desk, she picked up her diary and drummed pensively on the cover. She smiled, recalling the struggle with Wilbert.

When he had told her that Julian was destined to marry a white woman, he had told her nothing she did not already know; nothing she had not already told herself many times over. Neither was she in the least troubled or disconcerted by Sushila's taunts about Julian throwing her aside 'like a old paper bag'. She was under no illusions as to the outcome of their friendship. The universal disapproval it aroused – Mrs Bholai, Wilbert, her mother – amused her. They all took it far more seriously than she did. Even Julian took it more seriously than she did. She saw that he revelled in the ferment to which their association had given rise. It fed his sense of drama but he was as much its dupe as his mother was. The play had acquired a semi-independent life. He wrote her foolish, impassioned letters in which he called her Isolde and signed himself Tristan. Sita did not reply to the majority of these letters; and when she did she called him Julian and signed herself Sita. Julian was upset.

She had come a long way from their meetings in the Settlement when everything had seemed to be contained in the hour they spent together in the Hollow. Julian had been placed in proper perspective and she could stand back and view him – and herself – dispassionately. It had not been achieved overnight. She had had to teach and train herself to be dispassionate; she had been compelled into perfecting yet another technique of self-preservation. The diary had been her chief instrument.

By writing down everything that happened between them, she was able to distance herself. Filling in her diary became a soothing and necessary exercise which she performed nightly before going to bed. She wrote down their conversations word for word and read them over to herself. She might have been writing about two people who were strangers to her; on whom she had eavesdropped. The Sita represented in the diary was not the Sita who wrote the diary. To further assist her detachment, she enumerated Julian's 'faults' as she perceived them: his arrogance; his callousness; his irresponsibility. These too she read and reread. The diary was a powerful charm: her guarantee against temptation.

However, it was not purely a defensive operation against Julian. There was her own declared intention of never marrying to be taken into account. This had nothing to do with Julian, predating his appearance at the Library Van. Thus, who Julian eventually chose to marry could never be of much concern to her. It was a problem whose solution she would follow from afar and with a passing curiosity. The equation was precisely balanced. She had removed herself, by fiat almost, well beyond the reach of pain and betrayal.

Blissfully free from false hope, there could be no harm whatsoever in their meetings and she could immerse herself in their friendship without fear of the consequences. It was his very 'faults' which attracted her. Julian possessed a freedom which circumstance and nature had conspired to deny her.

He would always be blown with the prevailing winds of time and place. As if by design, the stark colours in which her character had been painted and its brittle, fatal strengths which permitted her scant room for manoeuvre, contrasted with the softer colours of Julian's character. Herself defiantly visible, she admired his accommodating flexibility and talent for camouflage.

There was only one fact she had not succeeded in taming: Julian's eventual departure from the island. Somehow, it was built differently from the other 'facts' which she had painstakingly enumerated in her diary, refusing to yield to the potent charms she had devised. It was like a raw and tender spot on the skin. Let it be and it might heal itself. Rub it and it might grow inflamed. Sita had elected to ignore it but Julian would not allow her to do so. Detecting the fright lurking behind her reticence on the subject, he wilfully probed and prodded the tender spot.

'When I'm in England,' he had said, 'I shall imagine you sitting by yourself here in the verandah and reading. How will you imagine me when I'm over there?'

'I couldn't say.' She frowned. 'I'll probably imagine you imagining me sitting by myself in the verandah and reading.'

'How will you spend your time when I'm not here?'

'I will lie down and pine to death.'

'There you go! Losing your temper with me again.'

'I wouldn't lose my temper if you didn't keep asking me such stupid questions.'

Julian simulated bafflement. 'I don't understand you at all. All I did was ask a simple question.'

Another time he had said: 'Do you realize how time is flying? Every day that passes is one day less till I leave. Every minute is one minute less.' He glanced at his watch.

'Well?' she replied irritably. 'What of it?'

'I was only stating a simple fact.'

'Simple facts shouldn't need stating,' she said. 'You behave as if you're leaving tomorrow.'

His departure, despite her best efforts, remained an unresolved threat.

3

Sushila's condition worsened rapidly. Sita did her best to keep out of her way but that was impossible: Sushila would not let her.

'Why you always quarrelling with Sita for?' Egbert Ramsaran asked. 'This place is like a madhouse. Not a hour does pass . . .'

'I going to murder she. I going to take one of them guns you have and shoot she down dead. Is only when she dead I'll be happy.'

Egbert Ramsaran was amused. 'If you reach under the bed,' he said, 'you will find the gun. Only don't make too much noise.'

'This is no laughing matter. I really mean it. I going to shoot she down dead.'

'Okay,' he said. 'Just reach under the bed and you will find it.'

'Two scrawny legs and breasts don't make a woman.'

Egbert Ramsaran laughed. 'Like you jealous of she?'

Sushila reacted violently. 'Why should I be jealous of that scrawny little bitch? What she have that I got to be jealous of?'

'If she have nothing for you to be jealous of, why get so worked up about it ?'

'You taking me for granted,' Sushila shouted. 'But take care. You will be sorry.'

Sushila's fears spiralled, feeding on each other until they gained a complete stranglehold over her. She could not depend on her judgement for it told her terrible things. Her need to be reassured that her beauty had been preserved intact and undiminished, that she was not being 'taken for granted', assumed the dimensions of a mania. The void within her had to be filled somehow. And who but Egbert Ramsaran could provide the answers she sought? She fell on him frenziedly. But even his reassurances were not sufficient to quieten her. Away from the sound of his voice and the direct and immediate gaze of his eyes, the slit of doubt and mistrust was deposited anew, smothering the fleeting tranquillity she had gained. She was compelled to return to him and demand a fresh spate of words to wash the silt away. Sushila was a glutton whose voracious appetite for praise could never be sated.

'You think I pretty?'

'Yes,' Egbert Ramsaran replied, not looking up from the detective novel he was reading.

'How you could tell if you have your nose bury inside a book?'

'Because I see you a million times before. Today is not the first time.' Wetting the tip of his index finger, he turned a page and continued reading.

Sushila strolled aimlessly to the window, stuck her head outside and came back to the centre of the room. 'How pretty exactly?'

'You not letting me read my book in peace. I'll discuss it with you later.'

She sat on the edge of the bed. 'Let's discuss it now. I very pretty – or only so-so?' She was whining.

Egbert Ramsaran turned another page.

'You not even looking at me!' She leapt forward and seized the book from him, holding it behind her back. 'Look at me!'

He looked at her, frowning.

'Well? How pretty?'

'Very pretty. Now give me back my book and let me read in peace.'

'You don't really mean it. You only saying so. I know you.'

'The book!' His voice whistled. 'Give me back my book.'

'Here! You could eat your damn book for all I care.' She flung the book at him and left the room, slamming the door.

She accused him of having designs on a succession of women. 'I notice how your eyes does follow them,' she said. 'You tired of me. I not blind. You planning to throw me away as if I was a old paper bag.'

'What is this? You never tired telling me that you is not a prisoner. That you free to come and go as you please. But it seem that you want to make me a prisoner. I can't even use my eyes these days without asking your permission.'

Sushila did not hesitate to include Sita in the list of her potential rivals. 'You making up to she. You planning to throw me out and put she in my place?'

'This is going too far, Sushila. Sita is a young girl. Young enough to be my granddaughter.'

'That don't make no difference. In fact . . .'

'Not another word!'

'Who you think is the prettier?' Sushila persisted. 'Me — or she with she two scrawny . . .'

'Stop all this nonsense. I going to lose my patience with you soon. What's wrong with you?'

Sushila was not short of excuses for her behaviour. She complained that she had too much to do about the house and that this was giving her headaches and causing her to sleep badly; and, there was Sita to cope with. 'That bitch don't lift a finger to help me,' she muttered. 'Always saying she have home lesson to do. Home lesson! What you sending she to school for? What use that going to be to she? You should take she out of that convent . . .'

'All in good time,' Egbert Ramsaran said. 'I'll decide what to do with Sita.' He grinned at her. 'You sure you not having a baby?'

'You could set your mind at rest on that score. Is exhaustion I suffering from and Sita is the cause of it.'

'The sea air is what you need,' Egbert Ramsaran said. 'We could spend two weeks in the beach house. I could do with a holiday myself.'

The proposition did not appeal to Sushila: the charms of the seaside had worn thin recently. 'I tired of the beach house,' she replied. 'I want to go somewhere I never been before. Somewhere new. Is as if I can't breathe properly any more.'

Egbert Ramsaran exploded. 'What you think I buy the beach house for? Who do you think I buy the beach house for? Don't forget it was you who make me buy it and now . . .'

'I didn't make you buy it. You wouldn't have buy it if you didn't want to.' She gazed at him sullenly. 'I want to go abroad for a change.'

'Abroad! You better knock that idea out of your head once and for all. Abroad!' He snorted.

Sushila resorted to veiled threat. 'Well something going to have to happen – and soon. It have other people who wouldn't mind taking me abroad. They would jump at the opportunity.'

'Let them take you then.' Egbert Ramsaran was nonchalant. He was accustomed to Sushila's threats. If she had not gone by now, she would never go. He was confident of that and he had ceased to entertain it even as a possibility.

To lend substance to her threats, Sushila would slip away from the house and not return for many hours. When called to account she was provocatively vague as to the nature and purpose of these escapades. In fact, they were innocent expeditions to Port-of-Spain and San Fernando and amounted to no more than surreptitious window shopping: she did not have the courage to look up old friends. But Sushila implied there was more to it than this. To a certain extent, her strategy succeeded. She had jolted Egbert Ramsaran out of his complacency; and that was a prize too valuable to be surrendered lightly. Sushila revelled in conjuring up the shadows of a nonexistent intrigue.

'Who you been seeing?' Egbert Ramsaran asked. 'Is it a man?' He knitted his brows.

'What difference that make to you? It could be a man. It could be a woman. Or it could be neither. What I does do in my spare time is my affair. I does only work here. Remember?' She propped her hands on her hips.

'Don't give me any fancy backchat.' He grabbed her arm and shook her. 'Is some man you been going to see?'

'What if it is a man?'

'So you admit it! What does this man do for you?' He shook her.

'He don't take me for granted.'

Egbert Ramsaran slapped her. 'Who is the man? Tell me his name.'

'I not going to tell you that,' Sushila laughed. 'Is only one thing I will tell you and that is that he don't take me for granted.'

He slapped her. 'Is that Farouk, not so?'

'I not going to tell you who it is.'

'If is Farouk I'll . . .'

Sushila was alarmed. 'Is not Farouk,' she conceded.

'You lying!'

'To see Farouk I would have to go to the Settlement. And I haven't been there.'

'Where you been?'

'Port-of-Spain, San Fernando . . .'

Egbert Ramsaran let her go. 'Watch your step, Sushila. Don't trifle with me. I not going to stand for any nonsense from you.'

'Look,' Sushila said, 'you like it?'

Egbert Ramsaran examined her morosely. She was showing him a frilly new dress she had bought that day in Port-of-Spain and for which she had paid a great deal. The dress would have been more becoming to a girl of eighteen. It was ludicrous on Sushila. Powder and rouge encased her face like a mask. She tripped in front of him, a macabre sight.

'You like it?' Sushila repeated.

'No,' Egbert Ramsaran said. 'It don't suit you.'

Sushila stared at herself in the mirror. 'You talking stupidness. This dress suit me down to the ground. The man who sell it to me say so.'

'They would say anything to get a sale. Give it to Sita. It will suit her much better.'

'To Sita!' The mask contorted. 'Why should I give it to Sita? Is for myself I buy it.'

'You not as young as you used to be and you should bear that in mind when you waste my money buying clothes. You not going to fool anybody by dressing as if you just step out of the cradle. If you not careful you will make yourself look ridiculous. A real laughing stock. Give it to Sita.' He folded his arms across his chest.

'Even if you don't like it, it have other people . . .'

'Other people must be blind.'

The mask was blank.

Egbert Ramsaran smiled, twirling his moustache. 'You know something? I don't believe it have any man. I believe you making all that up. If you really had another man you wouldn't be hanging around here.' He watched her narrowly.

Sushila's confidence sagged. 'You could believe anything you want.'

'Name him.'

'I not going to name anybody for you.'

'That is because you don't have anybody to name.' He was convinced of it now.

'Farouk!' she called out defiantly, seizing on the first name that came into her head. 'Yes! Farouk! Is him I does go to see.'

Egbert Ramsaran regarded her unperturbedly. 'Okay. You could leave this house today self and go and live with Farouk. I not going to stop you.' He laughed. 'Pack your suitcase and leave.'

The muscles on her powdered jaw twitched.

'What you waiting for?' he asked calmly. 'Mind you, I don't blame you for not taking up the offer. Just to make sure I checked up on Farouk the other day and he say he hadn't ...' Egbert Ramsaran clucked his tongue. 'You should have thought of another name.'

'Lies!'

Egbert Ramsaran shrugged. 'You don't have no other man, Sushila. The only man who would have you now is me. I is all you have left and don't be too sure that I wouldn't ... throw you away like a old paper bag if you continue with this nonsense. If I was to throw you out of here, nobody else would have you. Nobody!'

His savagery stunned her. 'It was you who robbed me of my beauty,' she said softly.

'I didn't rob you of anything.'

'Lies! Lies!' she screamed suddenly. 'I don't want to listen to your lies any more. I'm tired of your lies. Night after night you robbed me of my beauty. I was so beautiful. So pretty. And you robbed me of everything.' The mask whimpered.

'I didn't rob you of anything. I took what you had to give. What *you* offered me. That was all I did. You should have remember the worms was going to catch up with you one day.'

'Lies! Lies! It was you who robbed me. I was so beautiful. So pretty.' She caressed her fleshy arms. 'It didn't have a man who would say otherwise. They all wanted me. They was prepared to leave they wife and children for me.' She began to weep, burying her face in her hands, the cheap scent exhaling from her skin. 'You can't rob a person of their beauty and not pay for it. It was all I had . . . all I had.'

Egbert Ramsaran sneered. 'You think a policeman going to come here and arrest me? You think it's against the law like breaking and entering a house? "What's the charge, Sarge?" And you expect him to say, "You are charged with robbing a certain Sushila of her beauty. A most serious crime."' Egbert Ramsaran guffawed.

'That's right,' Sushila screamed back at him. 'That's exactly how it should be. It should be against the law and they should take you away and afterwards let the dogs eat you up.'

'That is one thing they not going to do,' he said flatly. 'Now go and do your crying somewhere else.'

'I going. Don't worry your head about that. I going all right.' She stripped off the dress and bundled it under her arm. Sushila stood there in her petticoat.

'Take my advice and give it to Sita,' he said.

'You . . . you devil!' The mask was grotesque. Sushila ran headlong out of the room.

Neither Wilbert nor Sita had bothered to bestow a more than passing attention on what was taking place in the front room. In their different ways they had learned to ignore these tableaux; and though its intensity surprised them, they did not allow themselves to be unduly disturbed by this latest enactment. They were misguided. That night Sushila disappeared from the house in Victoria. But she had not embarked on merely another escapade of surreptitious window shopping. This time, Sushila had gone for good.

They found her room in a shambles the next morning. Sushila could not have taken much with her. Most of her belongings had been scattered on the floor and trampled on: an assortment of dresses, skirts, blouses and shoes were heaped together in the middle of the room. The battered brown suitcase – the same which Farouk had carried on his head the day she had first walked so boldly into the yard swinging her hips and twirling a hat on the tips of her fingers – had been flung upside down. She had obviously started to pack it and then changed her mind. All the drawers in her dressing-table had been pulled right out and their contents ransacked and emptied on the bed as if she had been searching for something specific and not found it. Brushes, combs, powder puffs, bottles of scent and other odd pieces of bric-à-brac had been wantonly broken and abandoned. Her jewellery had suffered a similar fate: brooches, necklaces, hair clips, bangles and ear-rings had been thrown any and everywhere in dazzling disarray. The glossy photographs of the Hollywood film stars had been torn from the wall and crumpled into balls. In the midst of it all, crowning the destruction and havoc, was the frilly dress she had bought. It had been ripped into shreds; and nestling in the tattered folds was a pair of scissors. A malevolent spirit might have been at work in the silent hours of the night. Sita surveyed the wreckage in silence with Wilbert standing beside her in the doorway.

'She must have gone with only the clothes on her back,' Wilbert said.

Sita bent down and picked up a powder puff which she played with idly.

'Do you think she'll come back?'

Sita shook her head. 'Not this time.'

'How do you know?'

Sita did not answer.

'Is as if she went mad.' Wilbert walked into the room.

'She didn't have to go mad. She was always mad. In a sense,

this is the sanest thing she ever did in her whole life.' She let the powder puff slip from her fingers. Where it fell the white particles of powder hung in the air.

Wilbert looked at her. Her face was bloodless. He felt sorry for her. Never had she seemed so vulnerable. 'You sound as if you have no feelings at all for her,' he said – but not angrily.

'I do have feelings for her,' she said. 'When I was little girl I used to cry when she would suddenly get up and disappear without a word. But I couldn't cry forever. The time had to come when it made no difference to me whether she was there or not there.' Her bloodless face stared at him. 'Why should I begin crying for her all over again? Why?' Nevertheless, she was crying.

He listened to the sense of her words rather than to the words themselves. He observed the delicate curve of the mouth, the firm moulding of the nose, the protuberant cheekbones and slightly sunken cheeks; and explored the unfamiliar, brooding depths of the eyes. In that brief space of time Sita acquired a fresh clarity.

Sita averted her face from him. 'We must clear this mess up,' she said. Her voice was stifled. 'And – we must break the news to your father somehow.'

Egbert Ramsaran did not take the trouble to inspect the damage. When Wilbert brought the news of the night's events to him he had responded with an apparent lack of concern. 'Stop harassing me. I don't have time for such foolishness. If Sushila want to mash up everything she have that is she affair. She will have to walk about naked for I not going to replace a single button.'

'Sita say she not going to come back this time.'

Egbert Ramsaran's eyes clouded with a momentary uncertainty. 'Nonsense,' he whistled. 'Who it have for she to go to, eh? Who? She bound to come back. If not today then tomorrow.'

He went to work as usual and when he returned in the evening he did not have to be told that Sushila still had not arrived. 'She bound to come back,' he said. 'Who it have for she to go to?' He avoided looking at Sita. The pattern was repeated the next day: and the day after. On the fourth day Egbert Ramsaran maintained a rigid silence: and on the fifth he called Wilbert to him and delivered his instructions. 'Knock on my door when she come back. But don't disturb me for anything else. You hear that? Just knock on my door when she come. She bound to come back to me. Who it have for she to go to, eh? Who?'

Egbert Ramsaran immured himself in his bedroom, refusing food and drink. For hours they listened to him pace and once he groaned aloud. He paced back and forth for most of the night and then, towards morning, there was silence. Wilbert crept up and put his ear against the door, trying to catch the smallest sound within. But there was nothing to be heard. It was an unbroken and absolute stillness. He peeped in at the keyhole and saw his father stretched out motionless on the bed. Egbert Ramsaran was lying flat on his back and staring up at the ceiling. Disobeying the instructions he had been given, Wilbert knocked.

'She come back?' The voice that answered was as dead as the motionless figure he had seen.

'No. But ...'

'I tell you not to disturb me for anything else.'

'You must have something to eat, Pa. You must keep your strength up. Sita preparing food for you ... Pa? ... You hearing me? You must keep your strength up. You must have something to eat.'

There was no response to his entreaties; not a shuffle or a murmur. Egbert Ramsaran did not emerge from his bedroom all that day. It was not until the following afternoon he stirred and, opening the door, called for Sita. She had returned from school a few minutes before and was still wearing her crisp uniform. Wilbert accompanied her.

He was shocked by the sight that greeted him. His father appeared to have shrunk and dried up during his incarceration; to have become smaller and frailer and older. Wilbert shuddered. The image of the desiccated pond which Singh had shown him on the estate a long time ago – such a long time ago it seemed to be an experience remembered from another life – rose up unbidden from the obscure recesses of memory. He saw as vividly as if he were there the caked, creamy-white mud, minutely veined and segmented by a mosaic of tiny cracks. There was Singh prodding at it with a stick. His father too seemed veined and segmented and cracked: a pond from which the life was being slowly sucked out and dissipated in the dry air. Egbert Ramsaran's face had a waxen pallor and the eyes were bright and hard: it was a harsh, surface brightness, cold and lacking in depth. The real eyes might have been removed and marbles inserted in their sockets. His skin was the texture of parchment. Wilbert would not have been surprised if the fragile structure were to fall apart and tumble in a disjointed heap on the floor.

Egbert Ramsaran gave no sign of having noticed his son. The marble eyes were pinned on Sita.

'You should have something to eat,' she said. 'It's no good to be without food for so long.'

'Is not food I want.'

'At least a cup of tea then.'

'Is not tea I want.' He coughed and his whole body was racked. 'Come closer where I could touch you.'

Sita approached the bed timidly.

Egbert Ramsaran pinched and kneaded her arms and cheeks. 'Very soft! Very tender!' He removed his hands abruptly and did not speak for a while. The marble eyes were set and frozen. 'That is a nice uniform you wearing.' he began afresh. 'You still going to school, eh? Learning French and Spanish and Latin. B.A. Languages! You real lucky, not so?'

'I'm very grateful for everything you've done for me.'

'Grateful!' He laughed hoarsely. 'Is not your gratitude I want. What good is your gratitude to me? It won't bring...' He had another bout of coughing. 'You won't have much to be grateful for by the time I done with you. You could take my word for that.'

Sita bowed her head.

Egbert Ramsaran hauled himself upright and dangled his legs over the edge of the bed. 'You won't have any more need for that nice uniform. From today your education finish. Finish! You could forget the convent. You could forget about B.A. Languages.'

Sita lifted her head and looked at him. Since her mother's departure the convent had seemed an irrelevance. Her continued attendance there was like planning for tomorrow knowing the world was to end today. If she had performed the motions – putting on her uniform, collecting her books, catching the bus, answering the roll call – it was done out of sheer habit; and because there was nothing else to do.

Her unruffled acquiescence infuriated Egbert Ramsaran. 'And that is not all,' he yelled at her. 'I want you to take all them expensive books I buy for you and carry them out to the back yard. I'll meet you there.' He slid off the bed.

'To the back yard? Why?'

'Because I'm going to watch you burn them.'

Sita was devastated. Her poise crumbled and she slumped at his feet. 'Don't make me do that. Ask me to do anything but that. But please don't make me burn them.'

Egbert Ramsaran laughed. 'You not going to have any more use for books. So the best thing to do is burn them.'

'Let me give them away instead,' she begged. 'I'll give them away. But don't make me burn them.' All her sorrows had come to centre on the books.

'I don't want you to give them away. I want to see you burn them.' He sidestepped her.

'Why?'

'Go and ask your mother. She will tell you why.'

'You really have to do this to her, Pa?'

Egbert Ramsaran acted as if he had only just then become aware of his son. 'Oh! You here too,' he said.

Sita got up from the floor and dashed past them.

'What good will it do, Pa? It won't bring Sushila back.'

Egbert Ramsaran wrapped a blue dressing-gown around him, drawing the sash in tightly. 'You better keep out of this if you know what's good for you.' He left the room, Wilbert trailing after him.

They met Sita carrying a pile of books out to the yard.

Egbert Ramsaran installed himself at the top of the back steps in one of the wooden chairs from the kitchen: from there he would direct the operation. Sita brought a tin of kerosene from the kitchen and a box of matches. All was ready. Egbert Ramsaran stared at the disused, rotting cowsheds.

Sita tilted the tin of kerosene and poured a thin stream of the fluid over the books, spreading it evenly. Wilbert watched her. She was working with a vengeful determination. A match sparked and she applied the flame to the soaked mound of books. Spirals of thickening black smoke rose from the sodden heap. They gathered strength, spreading like a pall across the yard. The tongues of red and yellow flames licked round the edges. Sita poked and stirred the fire with a stick, pouring more kerosene. The flames rose higher and redder. Charred fragments of paper floated into the field and the covers of the books bent and twisted and folded. Sita emptied the tin of kerosene.

She ran up the step and went to her bedroom, returning with the diary. She threw it on the fire. Opening the cover with the tip of the stick, she peered at the closely written pages. They curled brownly at the edges.

Egbert Ramsaran received the direct blast of the fire's heat. Sitting at the top of the steps with his eyes shut, it seemed as if he were in the very midst of the flames. He smelt the kerosene and inhaled the acrid smoke which burnt his nostrils and suffocated him. Yet, the fierce heat was interspersed with spells when he was cold and shivery; when he wished to draw closer to the heart of the fire and warm himself. The shifts of temperature operated like a drug on him, lulling him into a drowsiness from which he had no desire to be roused. He was rocked gently by the ebb and flow of heat and cold; drifting easefully on these tides of pleasant stupor and forgetfulness which came from nowhere and went to nowhere. The fire crackled and there was a disembodied, nonsensical buzz in his ears. But that was pleasant too. Then the buzzing, formless to begin with, acquired a shape. It was a perfect circle, round and complete in itself. The circle was set in motion, revolving slowly on its centre but ever gaining in momentum until it became a dizzying whirl. He was swept up in its movement: no longer a passive spectator of its gyrations. The circle lost its shape, transformed into what resembled a hat that twirled ceaselessly. He danced on the brim, resisting the force which was pulling him into its scorched and flaming interior. It was all confusion now and he was torn between consent and refusal. He was being consumed by the fire. He must breathe a fresher, purer air cleansed of these acrid fumes. With one supreme effort he would break free and be rid of the descending, wheeling darkness. Egbert Ramsaran cried out despairingly. He collapsed forward on the chair as if he were about to tumble down the steps. The marble eyes were glazed and his head swung limply.

'Your father,' Sita said. She tossed her stick into the fire and ran up the steps to help support him.

The doctor came and the doctor went. There was nothing much he could do. 'When Mrs Ramsaran died I told him he ought to come for a yearly check-up. But what's the use?' He raised his eyebrows wearily and swung his black doctor's bag to and fro. 'Still, any man is free to play the fool with his own health. The statutes say nothing against it.' He camouflaged a yawn.

'He didn't like the doctors,' Wilbert said.

'I know,' the doctor replied sarcastically.

'Will he ever recover?'

'Your father will never walk again. His legs are dead. Quite dead. The nerves are like burnt out electric wires – if you see what I mean.' The choice of phrase gave him considerable satisfaction. 'Yes. The nerves are like burnt out electric wires – except we can replace electric wires. However, there is some hope he may regain his speech.' He talked like a salesman; as though his offer were a bargain at the price.

'And how long . . .'

'I was coming to that. It could happen today, next week or in the next five years. It depends on the strength of the patient's will to survive.' The doctor smiled. 'Knowing the kind of man your father was – sorry, *is* – I expect he has a lot of that.'

'Yes,' Wilbert said. 'I expect so.'

Sita announced to Wilbert her intention of leaving.

'Don't feel you have to leave,' he said.

'There's no point in my staying on here any longer.'

'I need somebody to help me look after Pa.'

Sita pressed her lips together.

'At least stay until I find somebody to look after him.'

'People would talk if I stayed on here. More trouble!'

'Let them talk. What you say?'

'Until you find somebody to look after him.'

'Until I do.'

Every morning and afternoon Egbert Ramsaran, wrapped in his blue dressing-gown, was wheeled out to the verandah by Sita. In the mornings he was provided with a copy of the newspaper and in the afternoons with a detective novel. When, at midday, as the sun was creeping up the front path, Sita came to take him inside, she found the newspaper as she had left it; and when, at dusk, as the shadows lengthened, she returned, she found the detective novel untouched.

Egbert Ramsaran sat in his wheelchair, abstracted and motionless; a graven statue fitted with eyes of shining marble. The cows trailed by in their twilight procession, mooning bulbously at him. When they strayed from their customary path down the middle of the road and poked their noses into the front gate, no stones or bottles or tins were hurled at them in repayment for their insolent boldness. He was oblivious not only of the cows but of the passers-by who paused to lean against the fence and stare impassively at the emaciated, collapsed figure whose head sagged on his chest as if he were unable to support its weight.

Wilbert raged at them. 'What all you looking at him for? You never see a sick man before?' He ran down the path and chased them away. Persistent as the flies on Egbert Ramsaran's dining table, they would return before long to resume their vigil. 'I going to shoot one of you bitches.' He brandished his father's pistols.

'That don't frighten we.'

'He gone mad.'

'That's right,' Wilbert shouted back. 'And I mad enough to shoot all of you if you don't clear away from here and leave the man in peace.'

'Is only bluff he bluffing!'

Nevertheless, they were sufficiently cowed by the sight of the guns to maintain a respectful distance from the fence. Eventually, the novelty wore off and the crowds of spectators thinned to a trickle.

The statue with marble eyes was deemed worthy of no more than a fleeting glance.

Chapter Eight

1

Sita was more relieved than she made out by Wilbert's offer
to stay on and look after his father. Not that the house held
any particular attraction for her. On the contrary; it was the
tomb in which her liveliest hopes had been buried. During the
years she had lived there, she had developed no affection for
it. An infectious blight had overwhelmed each of its inhabitants in turn: Rani, Singh, Sushila and, finally, Egbert Ramsaran himself. Neither had she escaped its crippling influence.
Wilbert was the next in line. Nothing that was either new or
good could spring from that soil for nothing of any value had
ever been created in it. It was sterile ground.

But if the Ramsaran household held no particular attraction for her, neither did the world existing outside of it. What
was there to choose between them? Was it better to live alone
in a room in a Port-of-Spain lodging house? She imagined the
sort of room it would be: the narrow bed covered with a
counterpane; the mirror on the wall; the massive wardrobe
pushed into a corner. In the mornings, her handbag slung
over her shoulders, she would hurry out to join the hordes of
clerical staff going to their offices; and she would return exhausted in the evening to have dinner with her fellow-lodgers.
She could hear the footsteps on the stairs and the hollow
voices of people she did not know. Sita recoiled from the picture. She was paralysed by indecision. That other world was
sterile ground too and its aspect was no less forbidding to her.
She was afraid to act and to leave Victoria would be to commit herself to a definite course of action. Whatever her choice
she was done for. Finished. Washed out.

She had wanted something positive and glorious out of life;
something which would have exalted it and endowed it with

a value out of the ordinary. It had always eluded her though she had had glimpses of it. What she had seen as a child in the Settlement had made no sense to her. Phulo with her tucked-up skirts and her dirty brood of children scrambling after her was not life. Basdai drinking rum in a dark corner of the hut was not life. Sharma's passive acceptance was not life. They were as meaningless and squalid as the burning green rectangles of sugarcane; as the hot, dusty days of the dry season when the sky was a fiery metallic bowl clamped over their heads; as the driving rain and mud and windswept cloud of the wet season; as the play of light and shadow beneath the mango trees. Life had to amount to more than the sum total of its parts. It had passed her by in the Settlement. It had passed her by in Victoria. It would surely pass her by in Port-of-Spain. All it had ever given her was a miserable parody of itself.

She had not been able to discover the formula which would transmute the squalor into glory. Her special brand of realism could not come to her aid. It had been, despite its austerity, a realism rooted in her longings and it was of no use to her now that she had to rid herself of those longings or perish. 'B.A. Languages!' she exclaimed to herself and laughed bitterly. 'Isolde!' She was stranded and there was nothing she could point to and say: 'That is what I wish to be.' Door after door had been closed against her and bolted tight. What she was having to face had been foretold on the day she was born; written in the dust and mire of the Settlement. Her friendship with Julian and her having come to live with her mother in Victoria had merely postponed the evil day. It had been tempting to confuse postponement with cancellation. Unhappily, postponement was not cancellation. Happiness was a chimera.

All those books she had devoured so avidly – what were they to her now? Folly and vanity. She could not bear the sight of a book and so she stopped reading. Her convent uniform mocked her and so she tossed it into the dustbin. Delay undermined her power of decision and apathy descended on her. Everything, herself included, was equally flat and dull and insipid; riddled with futility. No one thing or course of action was superior to another: it would be a delusion to pretend she felt otherwise. The world was a dead and arid place. Sita explored the empty spaces in her head. Morning and afternoon she wheeled Egbert Ramsaran out to the verandah and dutifully provided him with the newspaper and detective novel he never touched. The marble eyes did not thank or recognize her.

Even before she had left the convent, Sita had been seeing less and less of Julian. He was working hard for his final examination. The intervals between his visits to the house in Victoria lengthened. Finally, the visits stopped altogether. Now and again they met on the street – usually after school was finished for the day – but these encounters were accidental and brief. 'Sorry I can't stop to talk,' Julian would say, 'but I have a hell of a lot of work to get through this week.' He tapped the books he was carrying and smiled apologetically. 'Anyway,' he added, 'Ma would kick up a fuss if I was late. Anything for peace in that madhouse!' Sita did not try to detain him. Both the excuses he offered – his work and his mother – were true; but she knew their truth was superficial. The deeper truth was that their friendship had passed its climax and there was nowhere else for it to go. She could not pinpoint the moment of climax or the moment it had started to go into decline. They had been going down a blind alley and they had reached the journey's end. There was no cause for surprise in that.

When she left the convent Julian did not enquire after her. He wrote no letters signing himself Tristan and calling her Isolde. When the examination results were published in the Trinidad *Chronicle*, she scanned the minutely printed columns for his name. He had passed according to plan. She folded the paper neatly and laid it on Egbert Ramsaran's lap. Julian seemed to have forgotten about her. Sita did not mind. It could not be long now before he left the island. Now, however, the thought that this departure must be imminent elicited neither fright nor pain in her. It did not matter. Nothing mattered.

She was wheeling Egbert Ramsaran in from his afternoon session when she heard a rattle at the front gate. Sita looked round and saw Julian standing at the top of the path and grinning at her.

'Can I come in? Is Wilbert . . .?'

'Wilbert's at the Depot.'

'What about him?' Julian indicated Egbert Ramsaran.

'He's not going to prevent you.' She spoke levelly. Her hands still rested on the back of the wheelchair.

Julian ventured cautiously up the path. 'I was hoping to find you alone.' He climbed up the steps.

'You have,' she said.

Julian leaned negligently against the verandah railings endeavouring to disguise his unease. 'So, you're playing nursemaid these days.'

'I suppose you could call it that.'

'I always thought you had the hands of a nurse.' He was bantering but almost immediately recognized he had struck the wrong note. 'What I mean is . . .' He gave up the attempt at explanation.

Sita looked at her hands; at the bony, tapering fingers and protruding knuckles. Then she looked up at him. She said nothing.

'How is the patient?'

'The patient is fine. As fine as can be expected.'

They were silent. Sita did not take her hands off the back of the wheelchair; a figure fleetingly arrested in its motion.

'It's been a long time since I last . . . since we last . . .'

'Yes – it has.' Sita regarded him dully.

'How long would you say?'

'I haven't been counting.'

Julian smiled his apologetic smile. 'I couldn't help it. I wanted to come before. But I . . .'

'You don't have to make excuses.'

Julian shied away from her gaze. It was cold; remote. She

256

might hardly have been seeing him. He dropped his eyes to the shrivelled statue on the wheelchair.

'How much can he understand?' he asked.

Sita shrugged. 'Maybe everything. Maybe nothing. I don't know.'

Julian lowered his voice. 'I heard about everything,' he said. 'Your mother running off all of a sudden – that was a very strange thing to do – and then your leaving the convent . . .'

'Let's not talk about all that. It's over and done with now.'

'Perhaps you're right,' he said solemnly. 'Perhaps it's better not to. What's the use of crying over spilt milk?'

'I see you passed your exam. Congratulations. You must be leaving soon.'

His solemnity vanished: Sita's troubles were instantly dismissed. 'In two weeks. That's why I came to see you today as a matter of fact. I didn't know when I might get another chance and I didn't want to leave without saying good-bye properly.' He showed her a blue plastic folder stuffed with an assortment of papers. 'It's all inside there. Passport – you should see the horrible picture they took of me – cabin number and smallpox vaccination. All I have to do is walk on the boat at this end and walk off the other.' She took the folder from him but did not open it. The plastic was cloying to her moist fingers.

'So,' she said stupidly, 'you leave in two weeks.'

'That's right. In two weeks that boat will blow its whistle and I'll be waving good-bye to Trinidad. I can hardly believe it.' Julian paced the length of the verandah in quick, jaunty strides. 'During the summer vacations I'm going to visit all those places we used to read and talk about so much. Paris. Venice. Rome. I have it all planned.'

The summer vacations. Summer. What was it? The phrase had tripped so lightly and easily off Julian's tongue: as if he had a privileged access to its inner meaning. Summ-er. Summer. Su-mmer. He was receding from her, rising higher and higher. Julian was looking down on her – if he looked at all – from an immeasurable height. She was a tiny speck blundering through the nightmarish tropical interchange of wet and dry seasons. He was talking but she was not listening to him any more. She watched the ragged file of cows going past the gate on their homeward journey. The street lamps came on.

'I'm sorry but I have to go now,' she said, interrupting his flow. 'I must get him ready for bed.'

Julian stopped speaking and glanced at his watch. 'Yes,' he replied. 'It's late. I don't want to keep you from your duties.'

'The best of luck.'

'The same to you.'

They hesitated. Then Julian waved and went down the steps. Sita turned her back on him and wheeled Egbert Ramsaran through the curtains.

2

To mark Julian's departure, Mrs Bholai announced her intention of having a farewell dinner. Wilbert was among those she planned to invite. Julian was not pleased.

'If he's coming I'd rather not have a party.'

'I will invite whoever I care to invite. You have no say in the matter.'

'But why Wilbert? Why you have to invite him for? You still hoping that he will marry Shanty?'

Mrs Bholai evaded the question. 'I inviting him,' she said, 'and that's that.'

Wilbert no less than Julian had grave misgivings.

'I would be out of place, Mrs Bholai. I wouldn't fit in.'

'Don't talk stupidness, boy. Some of my family from San Fernando going to be there and they dying to meet you. And,' she assured him, 'not only I would be disappointed but Shanty, Mynah, Gita and Bholai himself. If all of we want you to come, how you going to be out of place?'

Wilbert was bludgeoned into consent.

Unfortunately, her San Fernando relatives cried off at the last minute, pleading the most transparent excuses. Their refusal stung to the quick and Mrs Bholai permitted herself a few harsh words against them, inveighing against their conceit. 'But never mind,' she said, 'is all the more food for we. Let them play high and mighty. When Jules come back a doctor they going to have to change they tune.'

'Perhaps we better cancel it,' Mr Bholai suggested meekly. 'You can't call it a party with only one guest. It would make we look foolish.'

'You must be crazy. Bholai. After all the work I put in you expect me to cancel it? Not on your life. Even if we had no guests I still wouldn't cancel it. I must give my onc and only son a good send-off.'

Wilbert thereby acquired the dubious distinction of being the sole guest at the farewell party.

'Right at the last minute it turn out that nobody else could make it.' Mrs Bholai giggled embarrassedly, appealing to her family for confirmation and support. 'So is only you. You could ask the rest of them how angry I was.'

No one shared her forced gaiety. Wilbert fidgeted in his chair and stared glumly at the floor. Shanty smirked and giggled until silenced by her mother. Julian, after uttering a few frigid words of welcome, had disappeared into his bedroom. Mynah, prim and disapproving, filed her nails. Gita drooped palely. Mr Bholai, who once or twice had essayed a feeble hilarity and met with no response, was sunk in torpor. Finally, he took refuge in the court cases in the Trinidad *Chronicle*. It had been altogether a most inauspicious start to the night's entertainment. Mrs Bholai, infected by the prevailing gloom, lapsed into taciturnity.

A crisp, white cloth covered the dining table. In the centre, providing a splash of colour, was a vase of Mynah's flowers, an overflowing cascade of red and yellow petals and jungle of green stalks. Serried ranks of knives and forks and plates reflected the electric light. The dinner was brought in by Mrs Bholai: a roasted leg of goat; a large bowl of boiled rice; and smaller dishes of curried vegetables. As a special concession to the 'men' there were bottles of chilled beer brought that day from the Palace of Heavenly Delights. For the 'ladies' there were glasses of fizzing Coca-Cola.

'Take your nose out of that damn newspaper, Bholai. Is time to eat.' Mrs Bholai fretted and bustled about the table. 'Julian! If is starve you want to starve you better say. We not going to wait for you.' Mrs Bholai shoved them into their assigned seats. Julian was to preside at the head of the table. Wilbert was placed next to Shanty along one side; while Mrs Bholai shared the other with her two remaining daughters. Mr Bholai sat at the foot. Julian emerged from his bedroom and sauntered to the table. Scraping back his chair noisily, he slumped into the seat. He blinked blearily and rubbed his eyes, yawning at the company.

'Go and wash your face,' Mrs Bholai said. 'Try and remember this is a special occasion.'

The chair scraped and Julian hauled himself up and went into the bathroom to do as his mother had bid. He returned, his face washed and his hair uncharacteristically smarmed across his forehead. With a wry smile, he scraped his chair for the third time, slumped into his seat and looked around drumming with his fingers. Mrs Bholai, stern and unsmiling, cut slices of the meat and doled them out on the plates held up to her. Knives and forks were picked up and heads lowered in anticipation over plates.

'Wait! Wait! You can't begin just like that. First we must all drink a toast to Julian. That is what the beer is for.' Mr Bholai deftly opened the bottles of beer provided.

'What about us?' Shanty asked. 'We don't have any beer. I never hear of anybody drinking a toast with Coca-Cola before. Come to that, I never hear of anybody drinking a toast with beer either. We should have champagne.' She pronounced it 'sharmpagne'. Her knees rubbed against Wilbert's.

'We don't have any sharmpagne,' Mr Bholai replied, 'so is nothing we could do about that. You could drink a toast with anything as far as I know – a cup of tea even. Stop making a fuss and raise your glasses.'

Glasses were reluctantly raised. Mr Bholai stood up. Holding his bottle of beer aloft, he cleared his throat. 'To Julian, wishing him all the health, good fortune and happiness it have in the world.' He brought the bottle to his lips. 'Honoured ladies and gentlemen, I give you the future Doctor Julian Bholai. Hip, Hip . . .'

No one answered.

'Hooray,' he responded himself. 'Hip, hip . . . hooray! Hip, hip . . . hooray!' The beer gurgled in his throat. He dried his mouth and sat down. 'Now we could start to eat,' he said.

Julian and Wilbert had not touched their beer. Mr Bholai – he was not accustomed to drink and the first sips seemed to have gone straight to his head – clapped Wilbert across the shoulder. 'Drink up, man! Drink up! Don't be bashful. We is all big men around here now. Watch how I do it and follow me.' Mr Bholai raised the bottle to his lips again and poured some more beer down his throat. He belched. 'That's what you must do.'

'You could use the glass I provide for you, Bholai, and stop showing off to Wilbert. You don't have to behave like a animal.' Mrs Bholai pushed one of the glasses over to him.

'I don't find the beer does taste the same when you pour it into a glass. Straight from the bottle! That's the way to drink beer.' Rebellion glimmering faintly from his flushed face, he swallowed from the bottle.

'If you want to drink like that you should go to Farouk,' Mrs Bholai snapped. 'Is a blessing in disguise my family not here tonight to see you make a disgrace of yourself.'

Wilbert poured his beer into a glass.

'Can I have a taste?' Shanty begged him. Their knees rubbed: it was a small table and Wilbert could do nothing.

'Shanty!' Mrs Bholai was appalled. 'Beer is not for ladies. You see Mynah asking for beer?'

Mynah smiled into her plate.

'I'm not a high-class lady like Mynah is – as you well know.' Defying her mother, Shanty borrowed Wilbert's glass and drank from it. 'That's nice,' she said. 'I like beer.'

'Shut your mouth, girl. Don't believe that because Wilbert here I wouldn't hit you two good slaps across that mouth of yours.'

'Peace,' Mr Bholai murmured. 'Peace.'

'You keep your peace to yourself, shopkeeper.' She glared

at him. 'This is your fault, Bholai. I tell you not to buy any beer.'

'Stop pestering me, Moon.' He looked at Julian. 'Come on, son. Drink up like your father.'

'I don't like beer. You have it.' He passed the bottle over and Mr Bholai accepted it with a shrug.

'You shouldn't encourage him to be a drunkard, Jules.'

'It was only going to waste,' Julian said.

They ate in silence for a while.

'How is your father progressing?' Mr Bholai chomped on his food with gusto.

'Much the same,' Wilbert replied.

Mr Bholai clucked his tongue. 'Is a sad thing that. That man was as strong as a horse. What muscles he used to have.' He thought of all those exhibitions of prowess Egbert Ramsaran had inflicted on him and it afforded him a secret pleasure.

Mrs Bholai brightened: the reference to Egbert Ramsaran shifted her attention away from the beer and helped to restore her flagging spirits. The recent events in Victoria had surpassed her expectations. Righteousness had prevailed and God had put himself squarely on her side. She could barely restrain the exultation in her voice as she turned towards Wilbert and said: 'You hear anything about Sushila?'

Wilbert shook his head.

'Not a word?'

Mrs Bholai dislodged a sliver of bone from her teeth and set it on the rim of her plate. 'What Sita planning to do now?' Sita's continuing presence in the Ramsaran house was the one aspect of the situation that worried her.

'I don't know.'

'She can't look after your father forever.'

'No,' Wilbert agreed.

'The thing is what she going to do after he die.'

Wilbert said nothing. Shanty's knee was jammed against his.

'Come now, Moon,' Mr Bholai appealed. 'That is not a nice thing to say to Wilbert. Stop cross-examining him and let him eat.'

262

Mrs Bholai noted Wilbert's uneasy silence. 'Still,' she added placatingly, 'is only right she should be looking after him. It was because of him that she reach as far as she reach – she couldn't really have expect to be a B.A. Languages. Sita have nothing to complain about.' Mrs Bholai felt that her assessment was both just and magnanimous.

She switched her attentions to Julian. 'Have some more to eat, Jules.'

'I'm not hungry.'

'You won't get goat meat in England, you know.' She smiled with sugary sweetness at him. 'Have some more.'

'I don't want any more,' he answered bad-temperedly. 'I don't like goat meat.'

'Since when? You always . . .'

Mynah's fork fell to the floor with a clatter, interrupting her mother's indignation. Her head disappeared from view as she groped and fumbled under the table to retrieve it. Shanty pulled her offending knee away but she was too late. Mynah surfaced twittering.

'I hope you have enough leg room under there, Wilbert.'

Shanty stared at her sullenly.

'You'll be catching a cramp soon,' Mynah twittered.

'What's all this about leg room and catching cramp?' Mrs Bholai asked.

'Shanty will tell you.'

Mrs Bholai looked enquiringly at Shanty.

Mynah squealed with unladylike laughter.

Shanty, her face red and inflamed, leaned over the table and, lifting the vase of flowers, emptied its contents on her sister's lap. Mynah screamed. She leapt from her chair and emptied her glass of Coca-Cola on Shanty. It all happened very quickly. The two girls grappled with each other across the table.

'Oh God! Save us!' Mrs Bholai scraped her fingers across the tablecloth. 'And you,' she shouted at her husband, 'why don't you do something? All you good for is to drink and drink and drink. Shopkeeper! Two pound of butter, half-pound of salt!'

Mr Bholai smiled sleepily at his fighting daughters; while Gita, the peacemaker, tried to separate them.

Julian pushed his plate away and got up. 'I'm going from here. This is a madhouse.'

'Where you going, Jules?' Mrs Bholai gazed distractedly from her struggling daughters to her son.

'He not going anywhere.' Mr Bholai suddenly roused himself. 'He not going anywhere. You will stay right where you is, young man.'

'You can't make me.'

'Oh yes? Is that what you think? What would you do if I was to bring my belt to you and peel your backside raw with it, eh? Would that "make" you?' Mr Bholai stood up and unbuckled his belt. He spoke with unwonted authority.

Julian shuffled irresolutely.

'For too damn long you been having your own way around here. You don't like beer. You don't like goat meat. Tell me what you like?'

'I can't help it if I don't like . . .'

'I don't give a damn about that. It wouldn't have kill you to take a sip of beer with me – or to have another piece of goat meat. Is time you start learning to please other people instead of just pleasing yourself. You is not the only one around here with likes and dislikes – though that is what you seem to believe. I have them too – except that nobody does take account of them. I is two pound of butter, half-pound of salt. I don't *like* people calling me that, but I does put up with it for the sake of peace. None of you does ever stop to think how it does hurt me. Well I fed up to the throat with it. You listening to me? I fed up to the throat! And if tonight you don't do as I say, you going to feel the weight of this strap.' Swishing the belt, Mr Bholai stalked across to Mynah and Shanty. 'You two market women will also do as I say. You even worse than market women. They can't help the way they does behave, but you have education – or say you have. What you do with it? Where you hiding it?' He stared at the broken vase. 'Monsters. That is the only name for all-you. Educated monsters which is the worst kind of monster it have.' He turned to face his wife. 'That is what you teach them to be, Moon. It was you who teach them to hate their father so that today they have no respect for me. But I is not the only one who going to suffer – you going to suffer too. They won't have no respect for you either.'

'Liar! If we was living in San Fernando ...'

'If we was living in San Fernando we would have been even worse off. You family would have kick you about like a football ...'

'You! A drunkard and a shopkeeper! Daring to talk to me like that. My children will always respect me. They will always ...' She rested her head on the table, circling it with her bony arm.

Mr Bholai threw the belt on the floor. 'What's the good?' He sighed and opened another bottle of beer. The froth welled over the sides and dripped on to the tablecloth. 'What's the good?' The remains of the meal – gnawed bones and grains of curry-stained rice – were scattered like debris.

'Can I go now?' Julian asked.

Mr Bholai nodded. 'Do whatever you want to do.' He did not look at him.

Julian disappeared behind the partition. The girls followed after him.

Shaking his head, Mr Bholai swayed unsteadily out to the verandah and Wilbert alone remained with Mrs Bholai. It was time he returned to Victoria; time to forget about the Bholais and plunge back into the certainties of nuts and bolts and palms stained black with grease and oil. Outside, Mr Bholai coughed twice. Wilbert left the table and went out to join him. Mr Bholai was creaking slowly on the rocker and smoking. His face was indistinct, except for the frog's eyes which considered Wilbert in silence. The red point of the cigarette glowed dully.

'It's nice and cool out here,' Mr Bholai said. The rocker creaked; the cigarette glowed and spluttered. 'Around Christmas it does get even cooler though.' He did not seem at all drunk. His voice was level and sober. He tossed the cigarette over the rail. It sailed in a thin, red arc to the road below where it rolled into the gutter and disappeared. 'What Moon doing? She still have she head on the table?' The frog's eyes stared across the rooftops to the invisible canefields.

'Yes . . . I must be getting back home, Mr Bholai.'

'Don't go yet. Stay and talk with me a little.' He offered him a cigarette.

Wilbert refused it. 'I don't smoke.'

'Like your father.' Mr Bholai laughed. 'Is a habit I pick up in my old age.' He paused to light the cigarette, the match sparking with a smell of sulphur. 'I sorry you had to be a witness to all this confusion. What they does call it? Washing your dirty clothes in public? I should have keep my big trap shut. It was the beer that make me behave so. I don't know what you must think of me.'

'You shouldn't let that worry you, Mr Bholai.'

'That kind of thing never happen in this house before. We used to be a really happy little family. Not that we didn't have we quarrels. What family doesn't have they quarrels? Children have to grow up. Is senseless to expect them to be tied to your apron strings forever. I right?'

Wilbert nodded.

Mr Bholai sat forward on the edge of the rocker. He crossed and uncrossed his knees. 'Who I trying to fool?' he asked abruptly. 'I can't fool you and I can't fool myself. The beer had nothing to do with what happen tonight. You know that as well as me. It was building up for a long time inside of me. It had to come out sooner or later.' Smoke billowed through his nose. A car went by on the road below, its tyres screeching on the curve. 'You father's a lucky man to have a son like you.'

Wilbert looked askance at him.

'To have somebody to follow in his footsteps, I mean.'

'But you didn't want Julian to run a grocery,' Wilbert said. 'You wanted him to be a doctor. Whereas from since I was small I always knew I was going to follow my father in the business and so . . .' What else was there to say? That was the long and short of it. 'And so the question of my being something different never arise.'

'Of course I didn't want Julian to run a grocery – that is no

266

kind of ambition for a man to have for his son. But what I getting at is this. A son should still have respect for his father even though he's not the most successful man in the world. And, when you come down to brass tacks, what is the great crime in running a grocery? It have a lot more shameful things I could be doing. You agree with me?'

Wilbert nodded.

The rocker creaked. 'Julian don't think of it like that. None of them does think of it like that. They don't take into consideration what I had to fight against. You know what Julian tell me the other day? He say I waste my life. Imagine telling me a thing like that!' The cigarette described an indignant arc as Mr Bholai flung it down to the road. 'He say that all I does think about is money and it have other things in the world beside money. He ask me if I ever wonder about the true meaning of life. The meaning of life! He say it have people who does kill theyself over that kind of thing. Philosophy he call it.' Mr Bholai waved his arms excitedly. 'If everybody spend they time thinking about the true meaning of life what would happen? You have to have a full belly before you could let that bother you and your belly don't get full by magic. Somebody have to sell salt and butter.' Mr Bholai sank back into the rocker. He softened his voice. 'You is a educated man, Wilbert . . .'

'I hardly have any education at all, Mr Bholai. All I know is how to add and subtract.'

'You have more than me,' Mr Bholai said impatiently. 'It really have people who does kill theyself over the meaning of life?' It was a genuine enquiry and search for assurance. 'Because that is one question I never ask myself. It never occur to me. It ever occur to you?'

'No,' Wilbert replied.

'You mean,' he pursued eagerly, 'that is all a load of nonsense Julian was talking?'

'It must depend on the kind of person you are, Mr Bholai. For some people' (he thought of Sita) 'it might make a lot of sense.'

'But you. It make any sense to *you*?'

267

'No.' Wilbert sounded weary.

The frog's eyes shone with relief. 'You put my mind at rest. You is a man after my own heart.'

Mr Bholai, content with the admission he had extracted, yawned and stretched.

'I had better be going,' Wilbert said. The conversation with Mr Bholai had depressed him, stirring a latent unrest which he could not understand. Mr Bholai yawned again. He shook Wilbert's hand.

'Thanks for putting my mind at rest. Now I must go and see what Moon is doing.' He went inside. Wilbert lingered on the verandah. He heard Mr Bholai pleading with her. The word 'drunkard' floated out and a door closed. Wilbert went down the steps to the road and waited for a taxi.

3

'What is the meaning of life?' Wilbert asked Sita.

'The meaning of life?'

'Yes. Do you know what it is?'

Sita laughed. 'What an odd question to ask all of a sudden. And even odder to ask me of all people.'

'Forget how odd it is.' Wilbert was ruffled. 'Just answer the question.'

'I don't know if I can.'

'Try.'

'I just live,' she said, 'I don't ask why.'

'That is all you do?'

'Yes,' she said. 'I live from day to day.'

'It don't matter how you live?'

She looked at him seriously. 'Most of us don't have a choice in the way we live. We've simply got to make do with what we have.'

'Suppose you not satisfied with what you have?'

'Then that is your bad luck,' she said.

Wilbert had been sincere when he told Sammy and the other mechanics he was prepared to go on indefinitely as he was. For him, it was a test of will. He suspected that his father was waiting for him to weaken and break down; and Wilbert was resolved that nothing of the sort would happen. He would ask no favours and seek no special dispensation: he would do as he was bid. If in so doing he inflicted unnecessary punishment and hardship on himself, he was compensated by the reflection that, in the process, he was denying his father a perverse satisfaction.

After the latter's stroke he frequently talked to Sita of the Company and its affairs, expounding the plans he had hatched for making it more 'streamlined and efficient'. In this role he was assertive, delivering his opinions in a loud, confident voice across the dining table. He was victim of a queer, raging optimism. 'What worked in my father's time won't work now,' he explained, chewing noisily on his food and licking his fingers. 'He was falling far behind the times. The trouble was that in his day he didn't have any serious competition to worry about. But nowadays it's a different story. That place accumulate too much dead wood. We should fire at least a quarter of the people we have working there. To survive in business today you have to modernize. No getting away from it. I'm going to reorganize that place from top to bottom when Pa die. I'm going to make everything more streamlined and efficient.'

Nevertheless, it did sometimes occur to him that it was all highly absurd and that his optimism was baseless. His words sounded hollow and empty even in his own ears. His father might not die for years. Was it worth punishing himself? Why should he not throw in his hand? These moods would come upon him suddenly and then he would be taciturn and morose. He toyed with the idea of leaving Victoria and renouncing his 'inheritance' which seemed like a weight dragging him down. It would be novel to make a genuinely free decision and start again from scratch. He would go to one of those lands of whose existence he wanted convincing proof. But Wilbert did not know what it was to make a genuinely free decision: he was ignorant of the art. The Ramsaran Transport Company was the centre of the universe and to escape from it would require an impetus over which he would be able to exercise no control. It would plunge him into the heart of that other universe whose focus was the market and whose presiding genius was Chinese Cha-Cha. There was no compromise; no middle ground between the two where he could safely land. He had been reared on extremes and was capable of responding only to extremes.

Although he took no part in the discussions of the mechanics, old memories and desires would revive as he listened to their idle prattle. Sammy was the most voluble and articulate and his accounts of his adventures with women gave rise to a great deal of hilarity in the repair sheds. The shrieks, hoots and screeches of the mechanics rang through the cavernous building. One such account had stuck in Wilbert's mind: a description of a visit he had paid the previous night to a Port-of-Spain brothel and the encounter he had had with one of its inmates.

'She was like a dog in heat. Like one of them mangy pot-hounds you does see all over the place smelling each other backside.' Sammy sniffed suggestively and the mechanics roared and clapped. 'She was smelling like a rubbish heap. I never meet such a stinking woman in my whole life. Is as if she was rottening. As if water never touch she skin.' Sammy crinkled his nostrils. 'The moment I walk in the place she come straight up to me and start rubbing up she legs against me and breathing heavy heavy all over me and putting she hand inside my shirt. Like this.' Sammy illustrated and his listeners fell about.

'You lying, Sammy.'

'I not lying. Is exactly what she do. "Buy me a drink, darling," she start whispering. "Buy me a little drink and let we go upstairs and have some fun." "Not on your life," I say, "I not buying you anything." She was the ugliest woman I ever see. Fat and blacker than the Ace of Spades and with a bottom sticking out ten miles behind she. She wouldn't stop rubbing up against me and begging me to buy she a drink and go upstairs to have some fun. Like a dog she was.' Sammy spat and surveyed his audience.

'And what you do then?'

Sammy spun round, startled by the sound of Wilbert's voice.

'What you do then?' Wilbert repeated.

Sammy collected himself. 'I didn't realize you was listening,' he said. 'I thought this sort of thing didn't interest you.'

'I couldn't help overhearing.' Wilbert reverted to his customary aloofness.

Sammy grinned. 'What I do then? I do the only thing I could do. I push she away from me. Then you should hear how that nigger start to curse me to high heaven.'

Wilbert smelled afresh the stench of rotting fish and the cloying odour of the bloodstained carcasses impaled on hooks; the swollen gutters; the asphalt steaming after the rain; and heard the cry of the creature who propelled herself along the crowded pavements on the palms of her hands. 'Make way! Don't mash me. Make way!' He saw Chinese Cha-Cha lying in state on a high bed in the darkest corner of a dark room, a glass clasped loosely within his fingers and talking sonorously; he saw lines of washing strung out across a wet courtyard and heard the trundle of wheelbarrows in a dank brick tunnel. Above all, there were the languorous scents of the stale, heated air both dulling and stimulating the senses; invading the cavernous building and washing over him. 'What you do then?' The question had floated involuntarily from his lips.

His confidence in his ability to persevere was severely shaken. He tried to avoid listening to Sammy but that was impossible. Sammy's honeyed, nasal tones had lodged in his brain. He could not keep attention fixed on what he was doing. It wandered and Wilbert, coming to with a start, would realize he had not missed a single word of Sammy's conversation with the other mechanics.

'Why don't you come with me? You could see for yourself then if I was telling the truth.'

Sammy's honeyed voice buzzed in his ears.

'Why don't you come? There have to be a first time for everything. What you say? It might interest you.'

'Who you talking to? Me?'

'You self. Come with me.'

'When?'

'Tonight. Today is Friday. Payday.'

Sammy was talking and he was replying – involuntarily. The words were automatic. He was standing outside himself, a lucid, dispassionate spectator of his own dreams. It had been like that the day he had wrecked Julian's collection of model aeroplanes.

'We'll go straight after work.'

'Straight after work,' Wilbert replied.

Three hours later he was striding along beside Sammy and Sammy was talking incessantly and laughing; and he too was talking incessantly and laughing. It was easy: all he had to do was read his lines from the already prepared script which unwound itself in a smooth, continuous reel inside his head. Each footstep, once taken, was forgotten beyond recall; as were their unending stream of words and laughter. They stopped outside a lighted doorway.

'This is it,' Sammy said.

They skipped up the flight of red-painted concrete steps. The walls had been painted a garish yellow reflecting the light with a sickly sheen. Two men, with greying hair, were standing at the first landing, chatting in soft, restrained voices. They were respectable in their jackets and well-creased trousers. They glanced indifferently at the newcomers, waving them through to a further flight of steps which led steeply up to what was called the saloon bar. The swing doors to the saloon bar were thrown wide open. They entered and looked round. A jukebox throbbed in one corner and a few couples shuffled lethargically across the floorboards. The whole room was drowned in a green, subaqueous gloom, thick and jelly-like, in which whorls of cigarette smoke had congealed into frozen arabesques. Metal chairs and tables were ranged against the walls.

'It does warm up later,' Sammy said. 'What you want to drink?'

'Anything will do.'

'Beer or rum? They is the cheapest things you could buy here.'

'Beer.'

Dodging the dancing couples, they made their way to the bar at the opposite end of the room. Wilbert's eyes had not yet accustomed themselves to the gloom and he waded blindly after Sammy.

'Two beers,' Sammy said to the barman with practised ease, 'and make sure they cold.'

Sammy sat perched on a stool, swinging his legs and beating time to the music on the counter. A mirror reflected the rows of bottles. Wilbert scanned the labels. The barman brought their beer and Sammy counted out the coins and paid him. They moved away from the bar, drifting aimlessly among the dancers. The jukebox throbbed, the popular numbers recurring to universal acclaim.

'What you think of the talent?' Sammy rehearsed a stylish dance step.

'The talent?'

'The girls, man,' Sammy said pityingly. 'The girls.'

Wilbert could see better now. Ranks of unattached women leaned against the walls or sat on the scattered chairs in a variety of poses and attitudes. Some were eager and alert, darting enquiring glances in every direction; while others betrayed not the slightest interest in what was going on around them. One very young girl – she might have been fifteen – was sprawled on her chair, her mouth wide open and her eyes closed as if she was exhausted beyond endurance. Her feet tapped the floor in mechanical accord with the music. The girl next to her, her hands clasped demurely on her lap, smiled modestly and waited to be approached. Her companion yawned languidly, passing her tongue over her cracked lips and scratching her armpits. Another patrolled the edges of the room, constantly adjusting the strap of her dress which kept slipping off her shoulder, and laughing raucously at every remark addressed to her. There were bored faces, haggard faces, stupefied faces, brutal faces. There was pride, defiance, abasement. And, often, there seemed to be nothing;

273

nothing but the ravaged flesh hung out sacrificially every night to be pecked at by the circling vultures and rendered insensible to pain and pleasure alike.

Sammy had joined the dancers. Wilbert returned to the bar which was a good vantage point. He stared at a woman dressed in blue satin who sat alone in a far corner of the room. She was middle-aged and looked like a countrywoman come up to town for the day. Ignored, she sat absolutely still. Her eyes followed the dancers. They radiated a fatigued, maternal resignation. She seemed bewildered – as though she had come to the wrong place and, rather than ask for directions, preferred to stay where she was until the difficulty, by whatever agency, was resolved. A handbag lay at her feet. Bending down, she took from it a pocket mirror, a comb and a tube of lipstick. As she was straightening up, she turned her head and saw him watching her. Simultaneously, her mouth distended, splitting open into a macabre, welcoming smile which showed her blackened gums and several missing teeth. He gulped more beer into his queasy stomach.

'You haven't found yourself anything as yet?' Sammy capered drunkenly in front of him. 'You can't be too choosy in a place like this, man.' As he spoke, Sammy drew his partner closer to him and kissed her on the lips. They whirled away into the centre of the room and disappeared among the eddying dancers.

Wilbert's attention was attracted by a large, ornately framed photograph hanging in an alcove. It was an even more macabre sight than the middle-aged matron who had leered at him. His gaze was riveted by it.

'Who's that man?'

'Is men you come here to look at?' The barman regarded him laughingly.

'That man. The man in the picture.' Wilbert pointed.

The barman shrugged. 'Nobody know who he is.'

It was a photograph of an austere, clerical-looking individual wearing a high starched collar and a black cravat. A meticulously trimmed moustache, streaked with grey, curled at the corners of his mouth. His sparse hair was combed flat across a smooth, unwrinkled forehead. A watch-chain was looped across a tight-fitting waistcoat. The stern eyes stared with impartial severity into the green, music-ridden gloom, though the severity was tempered by the patina of dust which neglect had allowed to settle on the protecting glass. It belonged to a respectable drawing-room. Generations were meant to meditate upon those stern, unbending features. What had gone amiss? What could have plucked and rooted it up from its proper environment and brought it to this, its final resting place – an alcove in the saloon bar of the Bird of Paradise?

Someone shrieked loudly. It was only then Wilbert noticed there was a girl sitting in the alcove directly beneath the photograph. She was flailing her arms wildly at a customer who was stooping over her and trying to get her to dance. Each time he approached her she jumped back from him and shrieked. The man gave up the attempt. She remained hunched, her arms clasped about her and her neck craned forward.

'As mad as they come,' the barman said. 'I don't know why she does bother to come here to tell you the truth. All she does do is sit there the whole night until everybody gone home. She doesn't even drink! A man don't even have to touch she for she to start screaming the place down. If you just go too near – that is enough for she.'

The girl, muttering continuously under her breath and glancing round furtively, shivered and hugged herself as if she were cold. She was as elusive and insubstantial as the wavering reflection of light on water, altering from moment to moment. For some minutes her muttering was cowed and frightened and her gaze was concentrated on herself; then the fright changed to self-pity and the mutter became a low, howling moan and she rocked from side to side, hugging and comforting herself; then the self-pity changed to hostility and, raising her eyes to the room, she glared combatively at everyone; then she was sly and slinking and calculating; then that too faded and she began to mutter again, cowed and frightened and with her gaze concentrated on herself. The cycle was completed.

275

Another man had approached her. She screamed and jumped back from him like a terrified animal.

'Don't bother with she, mister,' the barman shouted. 'She mad. No good at all. Find somebody else.' He laughed uproariously.

The dancers eddied and gyrated in the quivering green jelly. There were more of them than there had been earlier in the evening. The jukebox thumped and throbbed in its corner. The combined influence of the beer, the dancers and the music was having its effect on Wilbert. It enveloped and cosseted him. What was there to be puzzled over? The mysterious portrait, the mad girl, the middle-aged matron were all elements of an indivisible whole of which he was part. He was being absorbed into the music and the green gloom.

'You want anything?' A short, plump girl with woolly, close-cropped hair had come up to him.

'Let's dance,' Wilbert said.

He did not like dancing, but he forgot this as they surged and pushed forward to the crowded centre of the room. The girl let her head fall on his shoulder. She was being dutifully passionate; doing her job. Her face shone with sweat and her thick solid lips were slightly parted. There was not much space for manoeuvre and they shuffled in a small, tight circle. The jukebox pounded tirelessly and hypnotically.

'That's the way!' Sammy sailed past him and disappeared.

'You want a room?' The girl leaned on him, barely moving.

'How much?'

'Is only five dollars. I been on my feet all night.' She lifted her head off his shoulder. 'If you don't want a room you only wasting my time.' She was abrupt and businesslike.

They went to the bar, the girl moving purposefully ahead.

'Give Terence the money if you want a room,' she said.

Wilbert handed a five-dollar note to the barman and received a key in return.

'Number eight,' Terence said.

'I don't like number eight,' the girl replied pettishly. 'What about three?'

'Full up.'

'Five then.'

'Full up.'

The girl scowled. 'Nothing else?'

'Unless you want to wait,' Terence said. 'Number two might be ready soon. They been in there more than half an hour now.' He looked at his watch.

'I don't feel like waiting,' the girl replied. 'I been on my feet all night and they killing me.' She glanced at Wilbert. 'Follow me.'

They left the saloon bar, going out through a side door designated 'Fire Exit'. The music died behind them. They climbed a steep flight of steps to a long, windowless corridor at the top of the building. Black watermarks stained the bare concrete walls. An unshaded electric bulb burned at the end of a grimy cord suspended from the centre of the ceiling. It was quiet up here and their footsteps resounded on the stone floor. On either side there were numbered doors.

The girl showed him Number Three. 'That is by far the best one,' she said. 'Is a real competition to get it though. All the girls does want to go there.'

Number Three looked no different from the rest, presenting the same blank, inscrutable exterior. A crack of light filtered through the gap under the door.

'What's so special about it?' Wilbert asked.

'It have the nicest view,' the girl said.

They walked on.

'Number Five have a nice view too,' she added. 'But is not so big as Number Three.'

Outside Number Eight she stopped. 'Give the key to me. Is a hard one to unlock.' She struggled with the lock. 'This is the smallest and it have no view at all. And, as if that wasn't bad enough, is right next to the Gents.'

To emphasize what she had said, a lavatory flushed and a man emerged buttoning his flies. He hurried past them and vanished into Number Seven. After much twisting and forcing of the key, the door to Number Eight swung open. The girl had not exaggerated its defects. It was a cramped cubbyhole about ten foot square. The windows stared out at the unrelieved brick wall of the adjacent building. Two narrow beds had been crammed into the available space. A chair was placed between the beds. There was a clogged washbasin with a cake of flaking soap and above it a blemished shaving mirror. Fingerprints and obscene graffiti decorated the whitewashed walls.

Wilbert sat down on the chair. The beer had left an unpleasant aftertaste at the back of his throat and his head ached monotonously. His exhilaration was on the ebb and, try as he might, he could not recapture it. He read the scrawled remarks on the walls. Next door the lavatory flushed. The girl started to take off her clothes, folding each of her garments neatly and arranging them on one of the beds.

'You going to remain with your clothes on?' She came and stood nakedly in front of him, rubbing her protruding belly.

He did not answer her. His exhilaration had ebbed to vanishing point.

'You don't have to be shame,' the girl said. 'Is only me going to see you.' She bent over him, breasts elongated and drooping, undoing the buckle of his trouser belt.

He stayed her hand.

Her thick lips curled scornfully. 'I don't have time to waste, you know.' She sat down on the bed, crossing her legs. 'Like you never been with a girl before?'

'Let's wait a while,' he said.

'Five dollars only entitle you to half an hour. You'll have to pay extra for anything over that.' She patted the bed. 'Stop wasting time and let me give you value for your money. Come and sit by me.'

He obeyed her without thinking. With a premeditated violence, her arms entwined and imprisoned him and she pulled him down on top of her, her hands fumbling with his clothes. Wilbert submitted passively to her assault. Her hot breath gushed and spurted rancidly on his cheeks. Groaning and grunting, she loaded him with the dutiful caresses he had paid for and which she was determined to give him. Value for money. It seemed he had set out from Victoria with Sammy an eternity ago. Again he was a spectator of his own dreams: a lighted doorway and the soft chatter of two respectable old men on a landing; eddying dancers in a gyrating, jellied gloom; the enticing buzz of a honeyed voice; a walk down a concrete corridor flanked by inscrutable, numbered doors; the macabre leer of a middle-aged matron. Did these images belong to one and the same dream? Or were they the flotsam and jetsam of other dreams long dreamt? A pair of stern eyes stared out at him through a patina of dust. He could not withstand their chill disapproval. His gaze shifted to the wild and terrified creature beneath who shivered with cold and hugged herself. She was screaming at him, her hands flailing his face, because he had approached too near. He wished to explain that it was a mistake, that he had no intention of harming her. But he never had the chance because she was all over him, her naked limbs thrashing, pinning his body to hers as if for warmth and tearing at his flesh with her fingernails. Then it was he, angry with her for not listening to what he wished to say, who was screaming and repelling her writhing nakedness.

He was out of the bed and trembling with rage. The girl was crawling away from him.

'You wouldn't listen to me! I wanted to explain. But you wouldn't listen to what I had to say!'

'It can't be me you talking to, mister. It must be somebody else.'

Wilbert groaned aloud and sat down on the chair, smoothing his dishevelled hair. His head sank until it came to rest on his chest. Observing no sign of a fresh eruption, the girl reached cautiously across the bed for her clothes and started to put them on. She became bolder.

'I don't know why people like you does bother to come here. What you take me for? Is my job to give people value for they money . . .'

'Just leave me alone.'

'What you waiting for then? Go!'

Wilbert opened the door and went out. He traversed the corridor quickly, chased by the curses of the girl. He raced unseeingly down the successive flights of steps – past the fire exit, past the throbbing saloon bar, past the two respectable men who were still chatting on the first landing – and out to the empty street. He breathed in deeply in an effort to dispel the noxious vapours of the Bird of Paradise.

'What did you say your name was, child?'

'Sita.'

'Sita. I must try and remember that. Is not such a difficult name. What you doing here, Sita?'

'Looking after you.'

'Ah! I sure you tell me that before.' Egbert Ramsaran nodded and relapsed into silence. The sun was creeping up the front path as it had done every day during the last six months. In the distance, beyond the rusted rooftops of Victoria, the hills were a dense smoky blue and the valleys were drowned in shadow. It was two weeks since he had regained his voice. The questions he asked never varied. 'My muscles not so strong as they used to be. They don't do what I want them to do any more. What happen to them?'

'You had a stroke.'

'Is that why I need somebody to look after me?'

'Yes. And that is why I am here. To look after you.'

'Ah. I don't know how I would make out without you to look after me. My son is still too small for that. He's at school learning how to add and subtract. He can't take care of me. His teachers does always be coming here and complaining to me about him.'

'Your son is not at school and he's not a small boy any more. He's a grown man. You see him yourself every day.'

He stared at her. 'I does keep forgetting that. Yes. He's a grown man now. How time does fly.' His brows knitted. 'But why is you who have to be looking after me? What about his mother? What she doing? What she think I marry she for?' He became agitated. 'Call she to me.'

'She can't come to you.'

'Where she gone gallivanting? To she no-good family?'

'She's dead. She died a long time ago. You should remember.'

He calmed down. 'I remember now. You quite right.' He fell silent again, musing. 'It was my biggest mistake to have married she. You know that?' The sun had crept up to the bottom step. 'She does haunt me from the grave. That's what she does do. Haunt me from the grave.'

'It's time for me to take you inside.'

'I can't go inside. Not yet. I expecting somebody.' Egbert Ramsaran swivelled his head. 'That is the reason why I sitting here. I expecting somebody to come back at any minute. Once she come I'll go inside. Why don't you go down to the road and see if you see she?'

Sita went to the front gate and came back to him.

'You see she?'

Sita shook her head.

'She should have been here long before now. What keeping she so long?' His voice whistled as of old. 'Is not that far and she leave here early this morning to go and collect she daughter. She should have been here long before now. You think is the traffic holding she up?' He gazed at her anxiously.

'Let me take you inside.' The sun was licking at the third step.

'I don't like this waiting at all. It does make me nervous. She might never come back. Might never come back.' He wrung his hands. 'I'm very tired with this waiting, child. Very tired.'

'You should rest. Let me take you inside.'

'I can't rest until she come back. I might miss she.'

'You must rest. I'll make certain that you don't miss her.'

'You must knock on my door the moment she come. You promise to do that?'

'I promise.'

Sita wheeled him inside.

Egbert Ramsaran had a second stroke that night and on the following day he died. The news of his death spread quickly and the people of Victoria arrived in droves and leaned against the fence as they had done in the early days of his illness. They were not allowed to enter the house though many expressed a desire to pay their 'last respects'. Wilbert refused. 'He wouldn't have any use for your last respects,' he told them. He was for having no one at all come to the house. 'A dead body is a dead body,' he said to Sita. 'It have nothing to see.'

However, the Settlement insisted on its rights. If anyone had a claim on the dead man, it had. 'He was my son-in-law,' Basdai wept, 'you can't keep me out.' 'We was friends when we was boys,' another said. The chorus swelled. 'It's more trouble than its worth trying to keep them out,' Sita said. Wilbert reversed his decision.

There was little grief exhibited by those filing past the coffin in solemn, awed procession. The eccentric, capricious tyrant had died. They had gained nothing from him in his lifetime. His death at least afforded them a chance to gloat. They had feared Egbert Ramsaran would never die; that he would live on simply in order to plague them. Thus they had come to see with their own eyes that their fears had been unfounded and that this man who had held court in his wooden chair and hurled abuse and insult at them was actually quite dead; exiled to a region from which he could no longer torment them. One by one they came and went, reticent and unsure of themselves at the start but, as the irrefutable conviction and finality of death took hold of their imaginations, with a rising sense of triumph. Singh put in a brief appearance, behaving as he had done when Rani had died: as though he had come merely to identify the body and ascertain the truth of what he had heard. He spoke to no one and slipped away unnoticed, returning to his own exile at the beach house.

The Bholais were there.

Mr Bholai seemed genuinely affected. 'We grew up together like brothers,' he said. 'Bosom pals me and Ashok was.' He considered he was at liberty now to refer to his friend by the forbidden name.

'Bosom pals indeed!' Mrs Bholai snorted. Fortunately, she did not pursue the subject. Her moderation was not prompted solely by feelings of delicacy: she was preoccupied by a happier train of ideas. It struck her as singularly fitting that her first visit to this house should be on the occasion of Egbert Ramsaran's death. Mrs Bholai interpreted his death as a personal triumph and judged herself to have acted generously in consenting to come to the camp of her defeated enemy. Of late, the fates had been extraordinarily kind to her. She could afford to dispense with some of her scruples. In fact, Mrs Bholai's benignity was so far advanced that, catching sight of Sita standing by herself, she immediately went across the room to condole with her.

'This must be a great blow to you,' she said.

'It was to be expected.'

'Is always best to prepare for the worst,' she commiserated cheerfully. 'That is what I does always say. If you prepare for the worst you will never be disappointed.'

Sita said nothing.

'I suppose you going to be leaving here soon? It can't have much reason for you to stay on now.'

Sita smiled. 'No – there isn't. I intend to leave as soon as I find a job and somewhere to live.'

'You shouldn't find it hard to get a job. Not with the education you have.' The benignity receded momentarily into something harder and less forgiving.

'It should be quite easy,' Sita replied. She regarded her questioner imperturbably. 'Is there anything else you would like to know?'

Mrs Bholai was unabashed. Hailing Wilbert as if he were a fellow guest at a party, she hurried up to him.

'I haven't had a chance to speak to you yet. It must be a great blow losing your father. Still, is the future what matter most and you is the boss now.' Mrs Bholai twinkled genially.

Wilbert agreed.

'You must come and visit we more often. Don't wait for an invitation. Just come any time you feel like it. You mustn't stand on any ceremony with we.' Mrs Bholai beamed at him, brimming with her glad tidings. 'Especially as you won't even have Sita to talk to in a short while.'

Wilbert looked at her with greater interest.

She giggled. 'Like you don't know about it?'

'We haven't had the time to discuss it,' he said.

'The two of we was having a chat about this and that when she happen to mention it.'

Wilbert smiled.

'She say the moment she find a job – and that won't be hard for she – and somewhere to live, she going to leave here.'

Wilbert stared intently at Sita.

'Remember what I tell you. Don't wait for an invitation. Come and visit we any time you feel like it. Any time at all. The door will never be closed against you.'

Wilbert nodded absently; and Mrs Bholai, casting a triumphant glance at the corpse of her defeated enemy, departed in high good spirits.

Two days after his death, Egbert Ramsaran was lowered with due ceremony into the gaping hole dug beside his wife's nettled grave in the Victoria cemetery. The Presbyterian minister uttered invocations to the divine grace of God.

5

Wilbert and Sita walked back together from the cemetery. The purple clouds of sunset had spread like bruises across the sky.

'Mrs Bholai told me you said you were leaving as soon as you found a job and somewhere to live. Is that true?'

Sita nodded.

'Why didn't you tell me?' He looked at her. She was taut and erect in her black dress.

'I thought it was obvious that that was what I would do – though it clearly wasn't so obvious to Mrs Bholai.' She laughed. 'As she herself pointed out, there's no reason for me to stay on.'

Their feet crunched in unison on the loose gravel of the roadway. Ahead of them, the ragged file of cows trundled on their homeward journey.

'Where will you go?'

'To Port-of-Spain. Find a room.'

'How will you live?'

'I saw a job advertised in the paper for a clerk – a female clerk – in the Ministry of Works.' She was almost invisible in the swiftly gathering darkness. 'I have all the qualifications they're asking for. Including being a female.'

'Do you really want to be a clerk in the Ministry of Works?'

'It's better than nothing.' Her eyes were pinned on the meandering line of cows.

'When will you go?'

'Next week.'

'And if you don't get the job?'

'Whatever happens – whether I get the job or not – I'll go next week.'

They were nearing the front gate which had been left open. One of the cows poked its nose inside. Wilbert picked up a stone and rushed at it. 'Get out of there, you stupid animal. Get out! Get out!'

Sita got the job. The day she had set for her departure arrived; but, to her disappointment, there was nothing to distinguish it from all the countless days which had preceded it. Time was an arid and featureless desert. She had finished her packing (it had not taken her long) and sat hunched at her desk by the window, her chin propped on her hands, staring at the field where the sun-bleached bones of the Ramsaran Transport Company were strewn and scattered. The afternoon, like so many other afternoons, was warm and soporific. Unseen and unheard by her, the stream sang its discordant song at the bottom of the field. She heard the shouts and laughter of a group of young boys playing on the banks of the stream; of late they had roamed its length with impunity. It was on a day such as this she had sat under the mango trees with Julian listening to him talk about his love of poetry and watching the play of light and shadow on the ground. She saw him, reclining lazily, his hair tinted red by the sun, chewing on a blade of grass.

– Why did you never write to me? I waited for your letters but you didn't write.

– I'm very busy. But I always think of you even though I don't write.

– You're not fooling me?

– I'm always thinking of you.

The soft, embracing lies enveloped her. She luxuriated in them. Sita was unable to rely on herself any more. That hard core of faith, that conviction of a singular destiny which had always guided her, had been destroyed. She wanted to be taken in hand and led; to find strength in something or someone other than herself. In what or in whom was she to look for it? There was nothing at all beneath her to prevent her from falling. She was prepared to fool herself; to listen to lies. But there was no one even to lie to her. She had to invent her own lies.

– Why did you never write to me? I waited for your letters but you didn't write.

– I'm very busy. But I always think of you even though I don't write.

– You're not fooling me?

– I'm always thinking of you.

There was a knock on the door.

'Come in. It isn't locked.'

Wilbert entered. Sita turned round.

'The reason I'm here is to find out if you have everything you need.' Wilbert was awkwardly formal and stiff.

'I think so.'

'What about money?'

'I have enough to see me through for at least a month or two.'

'You should have more than that.'

'You've been kind enough as it is. I'll manage.'

He strolled to the window and looked out at the field. 'It will be strange living here alone.'

Sita listened to the distant shouts of the young boys.

'Is that all? The one suitcase?'

Sita smiled and nodded. 'That is all,' she said.

'I'll carry it for you.'

'You don't have to. It's not very heavy.'

He lifted the suitcase, testing its weight. 'I'll carry it for you.'

Sita looked round the room. 'In Russian novels people sit down before they set off on a journey.'

'Why?' Wilbert looked at her.

'It brings good luck. Gives you time to collect your thoughts. It's a nice custom, don't you think?' She sat down. The shouts of the boys hung faintly in the air. After a minute, she stood up. 'Time for me to go,' she said.

They walked in silence to the Eastern Main Road.

A taxi stopped.

'Port-of-Spain?' the driver asked.

'Yes,' Sita said.

Wilbert opened the door for her. She climbed in. The driver got out and unlocked the boot. He shoved the suitcase inside and closed it.

'Good luck.' Sita held out her hand to him.

'Good luck.'

The car drove off.

Chapter Nine

1

Egbert Ramsaran was lucky to have died when he did. The half-baked militant who had complained to him about the exploitation of the workers had been silenced by a single shouted obscenity that echoed through the concrete fortress assaulting the ears of the exploited. When another half-baked militant had had the temerity to mention something about a trade union, he had been forcibly expelled from the building. Those were the halcyon days. Egbert Ramsaran congratulated himself on his forthright and effective handling of the matter. 'It just take one good kick up his backside to end all that bullshit,' he had boasted.

The forces of change had retreated only temporarily in order to lick their wounds; and when they returned to resume the battle, their strength and vigour had grown, whilst that of the foe was in decline. The single shouted obscenity was no longer sufficient and neither was the vaunted kick up the backside. It was left to his son and heir to discover this.

Wilbert went blindly ahead with his plans to make the Company more 'streamlined and efficient'. There was no attempt to consult or persuade: he had decided to tread in the autocratic footprints of his father. He was the boss and he would *be* the boss. The senior employees of the firm, particularly Mr Balkissoon, were less than pleased by his highhandedness. After all, Mr Balkissoon had been Egbert Ramsaran's old and trusted foreman and it was he who had been in charge during the latter's illness. He considered it his right to be consulted and persuaded. To be pushed around by Egbert Ramsaran was one thing. To be pushed around by his son, quite another. Mr Balkissoon set great store by his dignity. Old and trusted foreman though he had been, his dignity had received some severe punishment from the 'old boss'. He was determined it would not happen a second time round. Mr Balkissoon expected reparations. It had been a disappointment hard to swallow when he had been passed over in silence in Egbert Ramsaran's will. 'Not even a thank-you,' he grumbled to his fellow workers. They nodded their heads in sympathy. Disappointment jelled into rancour.

As a matter of principle, he opposed every one of Wilbert's proposed reforms. 'Your father wouldn't approve of all that,' he said sourly. 'What you need a secretary and a accountant for? He would have consider it a waste of money and that is exactly what it is.'

'That is exactly what it isn't,' Wilbert replied. 'Having a secretary and accountant will save money in the end. It will make everything more rational and orderly. I want to know where every cent going . . .'

'Your father wouldn't approve. He used to manage very well without a secretary and so-called accountant. Is a waste of money.'

'I'm not interested in what my father used to do, Mr Balkissoon. He's dead now. Six feet under the ground – you was there at the funeral. Anyway, I didn't call you here to ask for your advice. I call you here to tell you what you have to do.' He was sitting in the metal cage formerly occupied by his father directly above the main entrance. From there, the entire building was visible at a glance, spread out obediently below his feet.

'I know more about this business than you,' Mr Balkissoon said. 'I been working here since before you was born.'

'So what?'

'It won't work,' Mr Balkissoon mumbled vindictively. 'Nothing you say going to work.'

The lined, grizzled face confronting him across the desk, warm with injured pride, spoke of an obduracy not to be shifted.

'All right, Mr Balkissoon. I don't intend to waste my time arguing with you. I'm just going to say this. You're part of the dead wood in this place – the dead wood that's been collecting for the last twenty years and more. And ...' (Wilbert raised his voice so that it could be heard throughout the building) '... and I'm not going to let dead wood stand in my way. You understand that? I'm going to clean this place up from top to bottom.'

'You threatening to fire me?' Mr Balkissoon leaned across the desk. 'Don't be afraid to tell me straight to my face.'

'I'm not threatening,' Wilbert said, listening to himself speak. 'I'm firing you. Twenty years is far too long for any man to spend in the same job. You need a rest.'

Mr Balkissoon seemed delighted. 'Fine.' He rubbed his hands. 'I had see it coming a long way off. I had know you and me would never get on together. Twenty years' faithful service and then ...' Mr Balkissoon laughed. 'Don't let it worry you that I have a wife and six children to support.' He waved a finger in Wilbert's face. 'But all the same, nothing you say going to work. It not going to work.'

'Get out of here,' Wilbert shouted in the best Egbert Ramsaran style, rising from his desk. 'Get out of here and never let me see your face in this building again.'

Mr Balkissoon proved himself an assiduous propagandist. Sammy was elected the leader of a deputation of workers appointed to plead his cause.

'He have a wife and six children,' Sammy said. 'If you look through the window you will see them standing outside.'

Wilbert did not look through the window. 'He should have thought of them before refusing to carry out my orders.'

'What sort of work he going to get now?' Sammy asked. 'Who will want to hire an old man like him?'

'He should have thought of that too. My decision is final. Final! Now get back to work.'

Sammy grinned. 'So, you playing the big boss now. But that don't frighten me one bit. What work in your father time won't work for you. Times changing. For too long the workers been treated like dogs in this country. All you rich people feel all you is God but God is only dog spell backwards ...'

'If you not careful,' Wilbert said, 'I'll fire the whole lot of you.'

Sammy smiled insolently. 'If you fire we, you won't get a single person to replace any of we. You may as well close down the place.'

'You don't frighten me either. If you choose to starve that is your affair. But my decision about Mr Balkissoon is final.'

'Man don't live by bread alone,' Sammy said. 'It have other things that just as important.'

So, choosing not to live by bread alone, Sammy led the workers out on strike. Pickets paraded in front of the building with Mr Balkissoon's wife and six children as the chief exhibits. Victoria had witnessed nothing like it before and large crowds gathered daily to boo and jeer and shake their fists at the gaunt fortress which had dominated their lives for so long. Sammy displayed oratorical genius and placards were daubed with the slogan, 'Man don't live by bread alone.' The Trinidad *Chronicle* dispatched a reporter to cover the event.

The strike dragged on for a month – until the night Wilbert was awakened by the police and told that someone had tried to set fire to the Depot. He went with them, dressed in his pyjamas. The Fire Brigade was already assembled. A thin plume of smoke snaked upwards from the rear of the building. The silent crowd made way for him.

'Is lucky the Fire Brigade on the spot so quick,' one of the policemen said. 'Otherwise, if the flames had get to the gasoline...' He rolled his eyes.

As it was, the damage was minimal. A repair shed was slightly charred. That was all. It was the climax of the revolt. Tempers subsided in the aftermath of the abortive fire and the majority of the strikers quietly returned to work. Soon, the red and black trucks were rolling again and the metallic clamour resumed in the cavernous interior – though Victoria had the impression that it was more muted than before. Sammy left the district and no more was heard of him; while Mr Balkissoon's wife and six children faded from the public consciousness. If there had been a loser in the struggle, it was the Company – not the workers. It emerged from the fray with its stature whittled down.

However, it was not only the workers' tempers which had cooled. So had Wilbert's ardour for reform and improvement. That night he had gone to the Depot in his pyjamas and seen the thin plume of smoke and the cluster of fire engines, the Ramsaran Transport Company ceased to be the sun round which the universe revolved. It was then he stopped seeing it with the eyes of childhood. The Depot was no more than a squalid shell of stone and mortar. 'If the flames had get to the gasoline...' The merest chance had prevented the life work of Egbert Ramsaran from being blown skyhigh by the antics of a soapbox orator.

The sacking of Mr Balkissoon had been an accident; an impromptu gesture. But accidents were not any the less real for being accidents. They had their consequences and whether these were enormous or trivial, it was necessary to take account of and adjust to them. The wrecking of Julian's model aeroplanes had been an accident, an impromptu gesture which could not be undone. Such accidents constituted the pattern, the very stuff of his life. They were a measure of his powerlessness. The whole edifice he had been bequeathed – around which his life had been organized – had come crashing down on top of him. In a sense, the catastrophe had liberated him. Unfortunately, his freedom was of no use to him: he had not been trained for it. One burden had been replaced by another. His liberation had come too late for it to matter.

2

'How is Julian getting on?' Basdai asked. 'I waiting for him to come back and cure my cough.' She tapped her bony chest.

'He passing all his exams with flying colours,' Mrs Bholai said. 'Nobody could touch him over there.'

'I glad to hear he doing so well,' Basdai replied with a hint of sadness. Good news bored her. She had developed a craving for tragedy. She reverted to a gloomier topic. 'I does still think of that business with him and Sita.'

'That done and finish with.' Mrs Bholai was brusque. 'In the last letter he write he mention some girl ...'

'Like you hear from him lately then? The last time I was speaking to your husband he was saying how he does scarcely ever write . . .'

'Bholai always complaining about one thing or another. Jules can't spend all his time writing we letters. He have other things to think about. You mustn't pay any attention to what Bholai say.' She evaded Basdai's penetrating and sceptical scrutiny. 'As I was saying, in his last letter he mention some girl he was going out with . . .'

'Talking of Julian and Sita remind me of something I been meaning to ask you,' Basdai interrupted. She squinted slyly. 'I notice Wilbert is a regular visitor to you ever since he had all that trouble about the strike and whatnot.'

Mrs Bholai smiled happily. 'You notice that, have you?'

'Is Shanty he does come to see, not so?'

Mrs Bholai was coy. 'Whoever tell you that?'

'Is what I hear,' Basdai said.

'What you hear?' Mrs Bholai asked delightedly.

'They say he does spend nearly all his time with Shanty when he come here.'

'He like talking to Shanty,' Mrs Bholai conceded discreetly. 'The two of them have a lot in common.'

'I hear is more than that involved.'

'That is not for me to say,' Mrs Bholai replied, her discretion straining at the seams.

Basdai stared at her pensively.

'To be frank with you,' Mrs Bholai said impulsively. Then she checked herself. 'No. Is better not to talk about these things.'

Basdai's mouth watered. 'You could tell me, Mrs Bholai.'

'I not sure that I should. It might bring bad luck.'

'Chut!'

Mrs Bholai hesitated. 'You think you could keep a secret, Basdai?'

Basdai was offended.

Mrs Bholai lowered her voice and Basdai brought her head closer. Their foreheads touched. 'To be frank with you, Basdai, I expecting him to propose to she any day now.'

'You don't say, Mrs Bholai!'

Mrs Bholai opened her eyes wide and nodded emphatically. 'But not a word to anybody. You hear? Not a word!'

'Not a word will pass my lips,' Basdai assured her. 'But you sure you doing the right thing by Shanty?'

'Eh?' Mrs Bholai pulled her head back. It was not the reception she had bargained for.

'I wouldn't trust my daughter to a Ramsaran. That family have a lot of bad blood running in they veins. You yourself used to say so. And now . . .'

Mrs Bholai began to regret having confided in Basdai. 'Wilbert is different from the rest,' she said.

'Like father like son.' Basdai wagged a mournful finger in her face.

'I don't believe in all this bad blood business,' she declared confidently. 'And, when you think about it, Egbert Ramsaran wasn't such a wicked man. What was wicked about him? Is only jealousy that make people spread all those stories about him.'

Basdai cackled. 'You certainly change your tune! I remember . . .'

Mrs Bholai went on the defensive. 'I not saying he was a saint. But he had to work very hard to reach where he get to. That is one thing I had always admire him for and it have nothing wicked in that.'

'He reach where he get to because he was a crook. A smuggler! I remember all the whisky and cigarettes he used to bring home for his mother and father – you wasn't living here then. But I remember. He was a crook and a smuggler and I wouldn't be surprise if he had murder one or two people on the side as well.'

Mrs Bholai took a leaf out of her husband's book. 'That is slander, Basdai. You have no proof. You could get into a lot of trouble with the law for saying things like that. Anyway, even if he was all the things you say he was, what that have to do with Wilbert?'

'Like father like son,' Basdai repeated.

Mrs Bholai lost her patience. 'I don't care what you say,

Basdai. All I know is that Wilbert will make Shanty a very good husband. He not like the rest of his family.'

'What about all them planes he mash up? That show he have the same bad blood in him.' Basdai was relentless.

'They was playing,' Mrs Bholai said. 'It was an accident. Wilbert didn't mean to mash up the planes. Children like to play rough.'

'But at the time you yourself had tell me ...'

Mrs Bholai, having lost her patience, now lost her temper. 'I don't care what I tell you at the time. I sorry I ever tell you anything. I not going to stand here and listen to you say another word against Wilbert. You just jealous like the rest of them.'

'I was only trying to warn you ...'

'Warn yourself!' Mrs Bholai grimaced. 'This will be the last time I ever tell you anything.'

Wilbert had taken up Mrs Bholai's offer for no other reason than that the house in Victoria had become unbearable to him. There were too many dead voices to haunt him. It was an abode suited only for the habitation of ghosts. The ghosts of his mother and father, of Sushila and her daughter, of Singh, of the clients – even his own ghost – flitted there restlessly, dogging his every footstep. They gave him no respite. Immediately he pushed open the front gate and walked up the path, the unholy congregation assembled at the top of the steps to greet him. To avoid them, he contrived a hundred excuses for not having to return to the house in the evening. Mrs Bholai was astonished and overjoyed at the alacrity with which he had acted on her offer to 'drop in' at any time; and Wilbert was aware of the hopes which his frequent visits to the Settlement must inevitably nurture. Nevertheless, despite its disadvantages, the company of the living was infinitely preferable to that of the dead.

At the start, Mrs Bholai's solicitude had been overwhelming. She behaved like someone who, after years of fruitless toil and effort to ensnare some rare and wild bird, had woken up one morning to discover it had strayed into her garden.

She pinched herself – it might be a mirage. But this was no mirage. Wilbert was actually there in the living flesh. Then she feared the bird would fly away and never come back. She felt it her duty to sweeten its captivity by giving it her unremitting and undivided attention.

'You sure you comfortable sitting on that chair, Wilbert?'

'Very comfortable, Mrs Bholai.'

'Have something to eat. Let Shanty show you what a good cook she is.'

'I'm not hungry.'

'Not even a piece of bread and cheese?'

Wilbert shook his head tiredly.

'Something to drink then.'

'I'm not thirsty.'

'Let him alone, Moon,' Mr Bholai said from behind his newspaper. 'He will tell you when he hungry or thirsty.'

Mrs Bholai could not contain herself indefinitely.

'You positive you comfortable on that chair, Wilbert?'

'Positive.'

'Come on, Bholai. Be a gentleman. Give Wilbert your chair. I don't know why you always have to be hogging the softest chair in the house.'

'You want this chair, Wilbert?' Mr Bholai was compelled to ask.

'I'm fine as I am. Fine.'

'Okay, Moon?'

'Wilbert only refuse because you too lazy and selfish to give it up,' Mrs Bholai retorted.

Mr Bholai sighed. 'If you go on like that you will end by driving him away.'

'You said you weren't going to stand on ceremony with me,' Wilbert said, 'and I want you to do just that. Better still, forget I'm here. Treat me as if I was invisible. That's how I would like it to be.'

Mrs Bholai could not do that; but she heeded the danger signal and reduced her solicitude to a more acceptable level. She grew – as did the others – accustomed to his presence. Wilbert was sufficiently familiar for them not to feel it necessary to make conversation' and keep him entertained. He talked very little, content to sit quietly while they carried out the usual routines of family life. These held an inexpressible fascination for him. It was soothing to watch the Bholais absorbed in everyday concerns and trivialities: Mr Bholai reading aloud (though nobody listened to him) the court cases in the Trinidad *Chronicle*; Mrs Bholai fretting and fussing without effect; Mynah bent over the dining table filling her drawing pad with sketches; Shanty, her knees folded under her, reading a magazine; Gita drooping palely and staring at her slippered feet. Even the abuse Mrs Bholai hurled at her husband and the undercurrent of enmity between Mynah and Shanty were reassuring landmarks. Their rituals never bored him. The Bholais seemed blessed with happiness. It became harder and harder for him to tear himself away; and it was a punishing moment when he dragged himself up and stammered his farewells.

Mrs Bholai engineered it so that Wilbert and Shanty were frequently left alone. They were clumsy, obvious manoeuvres which generated a universal discomfort. Yet, gradually, the clumsiness and the obviousness faded; and, eventually, they disappeared. It was not that Mrs Bholai had improved her technique: quite simply, there had ceased to be any need for technique. The family departed by frictionless and mutual consent from the sitting-room, Mynah and Gita yielding pride of place to their sister without a murmur. A new mood, which owed nothing to the crude machinations of Mrs Bholai, had stealthily imposed itself. It was as if they had instinctively recognized that the games of childhood were over and their animosities would have to be transferred to a different plane; that there were certain spheres allocated to each into which the rest must not intrude. And Wilbert belonged to Shanty's sphere.

In staying behind Shanty seemed – to herself and the others – to be behaving in a manner entirely natural and fated. She betrayed no awkwardness or embarrassment. Shanty was not conscious of harbouring any ulterior designs: her staying behind, so far as she was concerned, did not commit Wilbert

– or her – to anything specific. She was merely holding herself in a state of receptive readiness for whatever might transpire. Shanty did not tease Wilbert. Nor did she giggle. She was circumspect but not incommunicative; serious but not dour; polite but not discouraging.

Sitting there alone with her, Wilbert toyed with the idea of marriage to Shanty. What was to prevent him from doing as Mrs Bholai wished? As, perhaps, Shanty herself wished? Admittedly, it would not be a love match: he could detect no embers of passion in either Shanty or himself. The arrangements would be a compromise on both sides. If Shanty agreed to marry him, she would be obeying a practical, commonsensical law. The material benefits he could offer her as his bride would balance and possibly outweigh the deficiency of her passion. Her motives would be comprehensible. But what about his motives? What sort of law would he be obeying if he married her? The answer was less clearcut. He would be doing it because he could do worse; because he despaired of ever finding a love match; and, above all, because he felt he owed it to Shanty and her mother for receiving him into their house. However, these were not reasons: they were admissions of defeat. No! He refused to blunder into such a marriage. It was doomed to disaster. He was being bludgeoned – and blackmailed. He would not allow himself to be blackmailed by a misplaced sense of gratitude to these people. Everything else in his life had been decided for him. He had never been consulted. His marriage, however, was one area where he could – and would – exercise freedom of choice and not submit to external pressures. Time was running out. He would make tonight his last visit. There was no other way to extricate himself from this drift into disaster. Tonight. He must make tonight his last visit.

'What's the time?' he asked.

'I should think it's past eleven o'clock.' Shanty did not lift her head from the magazine she was reading.

'It's late.' His voice laboured out the words. He made no move to rise from the chair. The ghosts were lining up to greet him at the top of the steps.

'Don't bother.' Shanty turned a page and went on reading.

The ghosts were clamouring. 'They're talking of building a new road from Port-of-Spain to San Fernando,' he said, striving to shut out the clamour. 'Bypassing the Settlement.'

'Pa was saying something about that.'

'Cutting straight through the canefields,' he added above the clamour. 'A more direct route. It will take ten miles off the journey.'

'That's interesting.'

'It will mean the end of the Settlement,' he said.

'Good riddance!'

Tonight. This must be his last visit. 'I ought to be going. All this talk about new roads . . . I must be keeping you up.'

'You're not keeping me up. I'll tell you when I want to go to bed.' She turned another page. 'You don't have to go even then if you don't want to.'

'But I must!' The exclamation was a sharp, involuntary spasm of pain.

Shanty looked up at him.

Where was he to flee next to seek refuge from that insistent clamour of dead voices? To the Bird of Paradise and the fevered, funereal embraces waiting to swallow him up behind those inscrutable, numbered doors? A tremor of repugnance and horror constricted his stomach.

'What's the matter?' she asked, laying aside the magazine. 'Don't you feel too well?' She came across to him and stared down at his face. It had a basic peasant roughness: the eyes were narrow and set close together; the broad nose jutted out aggressively; the mouth was truculent; the ears were too big. Shanty catalogued his infirmities. The most unequivocally pleasing features were the eyebrows which curved in a gentle, bushy arc and the sloping forehead across which his stiff, wiry hair curled. They were softening traits. 'What the matter?' she asked again.

'I ought to go home,' he said. The constriction in his stomach tightened.

'Nobody's stopping you. The door is open. You can go any time you feel like it.' She looked at him curiously.

A great weight was pressing him into the chair, counteracting his efforts to rise. 'You don't understand. It's not so easy.' Time was running out; his resolution faltering. 'Have you ever thought ... It's much too late. I must go home.' He battled to rise.

'Have I ever thought what?' Shanty intercepted the phrase in mid-air.

'I must go home,' he said.

'Have I ever thought what?' She was cornering him.

He could not wage two battles. 'Have you ever thought why it is I come here so often ... and never want to leave?'

'Well ... because you are lonely.' It was a tentative questioning assertion.

'That's only part of it.' He smiled grimly. 'Guess again.'

Shanty hesitated. 'If it's not because you're lonely ...'

'I'll tell you since you don't know. I'll tell you!' He spoke with a suppressed fury; as though impatient of her stupidity and slowness. 'It's because I can't stand being in that house alone. Having to live with ghosts is too much for me. I can't stand it! That's why I never want to leave. Do you understand me now? It's more than loneliness.' She had dragged it out of him – but he had lent her his assistance. The confession eased the constriction in his stomach.

Shanty said nothing. His fury puzzled her. What ghosts was he referring to?

'So what's your solution? Tell me how you would solve that little problem.' He stared rigidly at her, observing her vague expectancy. 'Your mother would say I ought to get married. That would be her solution.' His fury was subsiding into despair. Time had almost run out for him. 'What's your solution?' He laughed joylessly.

She did not answer him, gazing down at the floor.

'I don't like suspense,' he said.

'It's what you've been waiting for me to do, isn't it? What is it to be? Is it to be yes? Or is it to be no?' He lowered at her. 'I won't make any demands on you. You'll be free to do as you wish – and have the security of a husband. I'm not exactly a pauper – as you must know.' He laughed. 'I'm no

Julian. You said once he was your ideal type of man. But then you can't have everything.'

'If you want to change your mind I wouldn't take offence,' she said. Shanty's feelings told her nothing. Wilbert might have been asking her to go for a walk with him.

He was stubbornly silent.

'If I marry you it's only because . . .'

'I know.'

'I can't promise you anything.' It was an appeal. And it went beyond an appeal. She was accepting him.

Time had run out.

3

'Come on, mister! I never hear of a thing like this at all. You must take a photograph on your wedding day.' The photographer skipped jovially in front of him. 'No, man. We definitely can't allow a thing like this to happen. Not on your wedding day of all days. What does the beautiful blushing bride have to say about all this?'

Shanty appeared to have nothing to say. She clutched her limp bouquet.

'You must take some photographs,' Mrs Bholai whispered to Wilbert.

Wilbert frowned at her. 'I thought we were going to have none of this fuss and bother.'

'You must take some photographs,' she pleaded. 'It won't kill you to do that.'

'What you have to be so bashful about?' The photographer aimed his camera experimentally.

He had trapped them on the lawn in front of the Registry Office. His vociferous antics attracted several passers-by who stopped to watch the unfolding drama. Wilbert grasped Shanty's hand tightly. The photographer interpreted this as a sign of conjugal bliss.

'That's what I like to see! That's more like it!'

The spectacle drew more people. The camera clicked.

'Look at them!' Wilbert sputtered. 'Gaping at us as though

we're monkeys in the zoo! Laughing at us! Just look at them!'

'You've had everything your own way so far,' Shanty said. 'You could at least do this and not complain. It will be over soon.'

It was the climax of a bad morning. A short while before they had been officially pronounced man and wife in a ceremony which had lasted five minutes. Only the immediate family had been invited. Wilbert had insisted adamantly on that; as he had insisted adamantly on the venue: the Registry Office. The 'Marriage Room' (it was sandwiched between the 'Births Room' and the 'Deaths Room') was decorated with bureaucratic gaiety and the registrar, a freshfaced, clean-shaven man, had pondered Shanty's stomach furtively as he instructed them in what they had to do. 'It's really very simple,' he said cheerfully when he had finished his explanations. 'Registering a death is much more complicated.' It was then the photographer had appeared and tucked himself obtrusively into a corner. Wilbert had objected. 'I'm sorry,' the registrar said, 'but this is a public ceremony and you can't prevent anyone from looking on.' The photographer smiled amiably. He tapped his camera and shrugged, indicating that he was merely doing his job. Idle clerks from other offices assembled around the open doors. The registrar called for silence and the general chatter declined into a hush. Wilbert was handed a card printed with the words he must speak. Mrs Bholai sniffed and dried a tear. He began to read. A strip of sunlight fell at an oblique angle across the leather-topped desk and bounced dazzlingly off a gold ring the registrar wore on the small finger of his right hand. Then it was Shanty's turn. The tonelessness with which she read from the card deepened his irritation. His suit was itchy and uncomfortable against the skin and the heat of the morning seemed to have collected under the collar of the nylon shirt he was wearing. He wanted to tear it off. Now, as a final tribulation, here they were being made fools of by the photographer. The wet shirt seemed to have sunk into his skin.

'That's great!' the photographer was saying. 'That's just

great, folks!' He capered merrily. 'The next thing we must do is form a group with the family of the bride.' The Bholais were shepherded and ranked according to height. When they had been arranged according to his satisfaction, he leapt back. 'That's great! That's just great!' He juggled with the camera. 'Let me see you smile. Give us a big smile, folks.'

Mr Bholai stared gravely into the camera. Mrs Bholai dried a tear and produced a wan, stricken smile. It was the best she could do. The bliss of Wilbert's proposal to Shanty was swiftly followed by disillusion on a scale she had never imagined to be possible. He had shattered her dreams of a magnificent wedding with bridesmaids and pageboys in San Fernando's fashionable Presbyterian church; of the congratulatory, admiring flocks of her relatives crowding about her; and of the lavish reception with 'sharmpagne'. 'No,' he said, 'no, no and no again.' He had vetoed her every suggestion. 'Not even a wedding cake?' she asked meekly. 'Not even that,' he had replied. 'I'm marrying your daughter. Isn't that enough for you?' She had been victim of a gross deception; robbed of the joys of what had augured to be one of the supreme occasions of her life. The ceremony in the Registry Office was as melancholy as a funeral service.

'Now,' the photographer was shouting, 'we must have a picture with the family of the groom. Where's the family of the groom?'

'I've had enough of this,' Wilbert said.

'Where's the family of the groom? We must have a picture with the family of the groom.'

'The groom doesn't have any family,' Wilbert yelled at him.

'No family?' The photographer stared at him in disbelief. 'No family?'

'That's what I said. No family! You deaf?'

'This is something I must tell the boys,' the photographer said aloud. He recovered himself. 'Okay. Just one more picture of you kissing the June bride. That will cap it nicely.'

'To hell with you!' Wilbert broke away suddenly, walking quickly towards the specially hired taxi.

The photographer ran after him. 'Mister! Mister! You

letting the June bride down, man. Have a heart. Just one more picture of you and she kissing.'

'To hell with you and your June bride!'

Hostile gazes trailed his flight. 'But look at that, eh!' a woman in the crowd exclaimed. 'Well I never. And on he wedding day to boot.'

'If that is how he treating she ten minutes after they get married,' another chimed in, 'it going to end in murder before the week out.'

'I wonder how she get sheself into a mess like this,' the first woman added speculatively.

'If you two bitches . . .'

'He turning on we now,' the second woman said.

Wilbert reached the car. The driver opened the door and he climbed in. Wilbert banged the door shut.

Mrs Bholai came running up to the car. 'Like you gone crazy, Wilbert? Wait for Shanty.'

The two women cast further reproachful glances at Wilbert.

'I wonder if they going to have a honeymoon,' the first said.

'I hope for she sake they not,' the other replied. 'I would hate to think of what happen if he get in a really lonely place.'

'Murder. I know of a case where this man take his young wife . . .'

Their conversation was interrupted by Shanty's arrival. They eyed her disconsolately.

'If I was you,' the first said, 'I would make sure I say my prayers every night.'

'I know of a case where the day after this man get married . . .'

'If you two bitches don't stop molesting me, there'll be murder right now.' The suit itched him more than ever. He tore off the jacket and tossed it on the floor.

The driver opened the door with exaggerated courtesy and Shanty got in. She dropped the bouquet on the floor. The engine coughed.

The photographer hovered outside the window. 'How you

could treat your June bride like that, mister? You could make up for everything now if you just let me take one more picture of you and she kissing. Just one . . .'

The car jerked away from the kerb. The photographer, his jacket flying behind him, darted in pursuit. 'Give me your address. How else will I get the pictures to you?'

Wilbert tapped the driver's shoulders. 'Go.'

The car was gathering speed and the photographer sped alongside. 'At least my card,' he said. 'Then you'll know how to get in touch with me if you decide you want them.'

Wilbert reached forward and took the card from his outstretched hand. The photographer dropped behind. Wilbert read the card. 'P. Wilkinson. Freelance photographic artiste. Winner of a Trinidad *Chronicle* Award.' He tossed it out of the window. It floated gently down into the gutter. The photographer shook his fist at him. Wilbert laughed, feeling much better.

4

It was late afternoon when they arrived and, in the fading light, the decrepitude of the beach house was startling. The atmosphere of ruin was reinforced by the neighbouring houses which were clean and spruce and in good repair. Egbert Ramsaran had not cared to waste money on the upkeep of his property. He had let it rot and fall to pieces in the salty air. The other houses were all unoccupied at this time of year. April and August were the popular months: they had come there in June – a dead month. The wind sluicing through the slatted fronds of the coconut palms and the low, monotonous growl of the waves breaking on the beach were the only sounds to disturb the stillness. It was cool with the wind skimming off the sea and Shanty shivered. There was no sign of Singh who should have been there to meet them with the keys. Wilbert cursed: it was darkening rapidly.

Shanty wandered off by herself down towards the beach. She stooped suddenly and took off her shoes, slapping them against her thighs to shake out the dry, loose sand. Barefooted, she continued down the slope, the shoes hanging from her fingertips, a shadow among the curving trunks of the coconut trees. Wilbert watched her, forgetting his annoyance with Singh. She was swinging the shoes. One of them slipped and she swooped to retrieve it from the sand. The water swirled around her legs, ankle-deep. He saw her lift her skirts just above the knees and wade in deeper. When a threatening wave approached she would execute a little leap to escape being wet by it. She brought her head virtually on a level with her knees as if she were searching for something in the water. The foam frothed creamily about her.

He heard footsteps. The dancing beam of a torch was visible among the coconut trees. Wilbert remembered his annoyance.

'Singh! Is that you?'

There was no reply but the beam of light halted its confident advance and dodged nervously across the ground. It was impossible to see who was lurking beyond it.

'Singh! Is that you?'

The light advanced cautiously and stopped again, the beam sweeping the darkness. 'That is the boss voice I hearing?' Singh's heavy tones probed the night suspiciously, bringing with them a whiff of rum.

'Who else you was expecting it to be? Come here where I could see you properly.'

Singh materialized out of the shrouding darkness, all teeth. He was carrying a cutlass as well as the torch. Shanty had returned from her explorations. Singh stared at her, surprised and disconcerted. 'The boss didn't tell me ... I thought he was coming up by himself.'

Shanty looked at Wilbert.

'I told you all you needed to know – to get the house ready. That is your job.'

Singh gurgled sullenly. 'If I had know it had a lady coming ...' He dug the cutlass into the sand, leaning on it. 'Where she going to sleep?'

'With my husband naturally.' Shanty laughed. She linked their arms matrimonially, defiant and provocative. 'I'm the new Mrs Ramsaran.' Just as she had acquired the plumage of courtship naturally, so – now that it had served its purpose – she was discarding it. Shanty was regaining her familiar colours.

Wilbert pushed her from him. 'The keys . . . the keys . . .'

Singh was all teeth again. 'So! Let me shake your hands, Miss. Let me congratulate you. The boss didn't tell me a word about this – but then nobody does ever tell me anything. All he say was for me to get the house ready because he was coming up. But not a word that this was to be his honeymoon.' He shuffled up to Shanty, peering at her face. 'It make me really happy to see the boss find a nice young lady like you to settle down with. Real happy. And so short a time after the old boss die as well!' He shook hands with Shanty. She giggled.

'Very touching,' Wilbert said. 'Now the keys . . . the keys. That's what you here for.'

Singh stared at him. He underwent one of his abrupt alterations of mood and manner, becoming gruff and inhospitable. 'You don't need no keys. I'll show you.' He led them to the back door along a narrow shell-strewn path in which broken bits of glass glinted in the glare of the torch. 'Mind you don't cut your foot.' When they came to the door, he kicked and shoved at it. 'You don't need no keys to open this door with,' he muttered, heaving with his shoulders. 'He would never buy a new lock after the old one get rusty. You know how many times I tell him to buy a new lock? But he would never buy one. Not he!' Singh kicked viciously at the door. He was talking to no one in particular. 'Not that we need a door. Any thief who feel like it could climb through the windows downstairs. Where you think all that glass we see come from? Not a pane of glass left standing in one of them windows.' He gurgled throatily, kicking at the door. It swung open.

The beam of the torch punctured the viscous darkness. A salty, marine dampness oozed from the walls. Sand grated underfoot. Singh shone the torch on a heap of dried coconuts and let it play across the mossy concrete floor: this part of the house had never been used. 'Stick close behind me,' he warned. 'If you miss your footing on these stairs you could

307

break every bone you have in your body.' They climbed a curving flight of wedge-shaped steps to the top floor. Singh lit a hurricane lantern on the landing. The brilliant whiteness of the flare blinded them. They followed him into the kitchen where he lit an oil-lamp and set it on a shelf: there was no electricity. Nothing looked as if it could work – or as if it were meant to work. The kerosene stove, like everything else metallic, was coated with rust. Singh scraped a finger along the burners and held it up for them to see. Tiny cockroaches scurried across the linoleum, vanishing into the cracks and crevices. A trickle of brown water flowed from the tap fed by the tank on the roof. 'Is not me to blame for the state this place in. Is not me . . .'

'Nobody's blaming you for anything,' Wilbert said.

'I is only the caretaker. That is all I is. If only you know how much times . . .'

'Nobody's blaming you, Singh.' Wilbert stared at the bleached ceiling. The sea growled distantly.

'Is not the place I would have choose to spend my honeymoon.' Singh rubbed his rust-stained finger against his trousers.

'If you mention that word once more . . .'

Singh was immediately submissive. 'What word? Honeymoon?'

'If you mention it once more . . .' Wilbert clenched his fists.

'Sorry, boss. I didn't mean to make you angry. I was just thinking . . .'

'I'm not interested in what you're thinking.' Wilbert raised his voice.

'Why shouldn't Singh call it our honeymoon?' Shanty asked. 'That is exactly what it is. Our honeymoon. Remember?'

The glance Wilbert bestowed on her was one of pure hatred.

'Thank you, Miss,' Singh said, celebrating the support he had received. 'Still, if the boss don't like it, the boss don't like it.' He was gloomily triumphant. 'This way,' he said.

Taking the oil-lamp, Singh preceded them into the sittingroom It bore the lustreless stamp of Egbert Ramsaran's handiwork. The furniture was minimal and dilapidated. There were three low-slung 'morris' chairs with hard, flattened cushions and a torn leather sofa. In the centre was a small table spread with an oilcloth. Two spare mattresses were rolled and stacked in a corner. That was all. Crystals of salt sparkled in the grooves of the floorboards. Invigorating draughts of air circulated freely through the open brickwork that ran round the tops of the walls.

'If I was you, boss, I would sleep in the front bedroom. Is the nicest one in the whole house. The breeze always blowing in there. That was where the old boss and ... that was where he used to sleep when he come here.'

'We'll sleep there then,' Wilbert said.

Singh, swinging the oil-lamp, conducted them to the front room. A double bed and a chest of drawers were the sole items of furniture. The mattress was rolled back on the bed. Singh opened a window and thrust his head outside.

'We going to have some rain tonight,' he said. 'I could smell it on the wind.' He pulled his head in and opened the remaining windows. 'Rust everywhere you turn in this place.' Grunting, he unrolled the mattress and laid it flat on the bed.

'That mattress stinks,' Shanty said.

'It need an airing,' Singh replied, sniffing at it. 'You want me to bring one of them other mattresses for you to try, boss?'

Wilbert looked at the mattress. 'It will do.'

Singh watched them. 'Anything else I could do for you, boss?' he enquired after a pause.

Wilbert shook his head. 'You can go now.'

Singh shuffled to the door, his eyes on them both. 'I will come back tomorrow morning to check if you have everything you need.'

Wilbert nodded absently.

Singh hovered uncertainly in the doorway. Then he left.

Singh strode quickly along the meandering track that looped and twisted under the arching trunks of the coconut trees, his torch slicing erratic swathes in the darkness. He swung his cutlass, lopping the undergrowth and muttering ceaselessly under his breath. The sky had clouded over. An energetic wind, moist with the promise of imminent rain, fanned off the sea. He stopped when he reached the wooden bridge spanning the lagoon which backed the village. Propping himself against the rails, he took a bottle of rum from the side pocket of his jacket and drank some. Raising the bottle in salute, he smacked his lips. 'To the happy couple!' He had a second swig. The water below him was black. An unbroken fringe of mangrove pressed against the muddy banks, hugging the contours of the lagoon which wound away from the bridge like a controlled expulsion of breath. Towards the sea, the lagoon broadened between shoulders of brown sand and lost its identity in the melee of conflicting currents. 'To the happy couple!'

Singh lived in the village with Myra and his child. His fellow villagers had long since dismissed him as a madman. He had no one there he could call a friend. When he appeared on the street, the children would give him a wide berth. Sometimes, ganging up together, they jeered and threw stones at him, and Singh, flourishing his cutlass, would rush at them. The move from the estate had scarcely affected the manner of his life: he had remained essentially solitary despite Myra and the child. If anything, he had become increasingly wrapped up in himself. All their attempts at friendship having been rebuffed, the villagers had left him alone. He was generally silent – except when he drank. Then he could be ravening; full of a howling sense of the myriad injustices that had been perpetrated on him. This sense of injustice was all that he had. It was his most constant and faithful companion with whom he communed hourly; as constant and faithful as the roar of the sea.

He had emptied the bottle. Singh tossed it into the water and walked on, swinging the cutlass. The first drops of rain splashed on his face and he broke into a trot. He swore loudly as he stumbled and nearly fell. The track petered out into the main street of the village and he tucked the cutlass under his arm. Myra was standing at the door of their one-room shack, scanning the street. She saw the erratic swathes sliced by the beam of the torch.

'I thought you had drowned yourself,' she shouted. 'I tired worrying about you. You never know what could happen with you out drinking yourself to death.' She looked up at the sky. 'And in all this rain as well.'

Singh, elbowing her aside, ran up the steps. Myra closed the door after him. Indra was lying face downwards on the bed, dressed in a shiny, salmon-coloured petticoat.

Myra shook her. 'Get your father a towel. Make yourself useful. You is not a lady of leisure.'

'I don't want no towel.' Singh put the torch on the table. However, he continued to swing the cutlass.

'Take care with that thing,' Myra said. 'One day you going to chop somebody with it. Is not a toy.'

'I going to chop *he* with it all right.' Singh fingered the blade.

'Mouth,' Myra answered. 'Is only mouth you have. You is too big a coward to do anything like that.'

'I'll show you if is only mouth I have.' Singh fenced with the cutlass, parrying imaginary thrusts at his stomach.

'Put that thing down and tell me what happen,' Myra said. 'You see him? He was there?'

I have news for you. Big news!'

Myra and Indra perked up.

Singh sat down heavily on the bed and rested the cutlass on his knees. 'I had gone there tonight thinking it was only he coming for a little rest and relaxation. All he had to say to me was . . .'

'I know exactly what he say to you,' Myra said. 'What's the big news?'

Singh, his head cocked, listened to the rain pounding the shingled roof of the shack. The windows streamed. 'I wonder how they making out up there . . .' He laughed.

'They?'

'Imagine how surprise I was when I turn up there tonight and find he bring somebody with him.'

'What so strange about that?' Myra asked.

'Nothing – except that the person he bring with him was a woman.'

Myra burst out laughing. 'Why shouldn't he bring a woman with him? He's a grown man.'

'This was no ordinary woman,' Singh said. 'This was he wife.' He got up from the bed, swinging the cutlass with renewed vigour. 'The sonofabitch gone and get married.' He snapped his fingers. 'Just like that the sonofabitch gone and get married.'

'Who is the woman?'

'That is the biggest news of all. She's one of them Bholai girls. I don't know which one. But I know she is one of them.'

'That *is* news,' Myra said. 'I hope she have enough sense to give him hell.'

'You should see them.' Singh gurgled. 'They at each other throat already.' He prowled about the room. 'That sonofabitch rob me of everything. I sure the old man had leave something for me. He wouldn't have forget me. But that thief grab it all for himself and wouldn't give me what is rightfully mine.'

'The old man forget about you on the day you was born,' Myra said. 'I don't know where you get the idea from that he leave something for you. If he had not even Wilbert could keep it from you.'

'He is a robber and thief and I going to chop him.' The rain pounded the roof.

'You talking stupidness,' Myra said. 'Is all that rum you been drinking. You is too big a coward to do anything like that.' She might have been goading him into having the courage of his convictions. But she knew he would never do anything.

Singh leapt at her, brandishing the cutlass. 'Who you calling a coward? I'll show you who is a coward. I'll chop you . . .'

'If you lay a finger on me I'll call the police for you.' Myra grappled with him. 'I not joking this time. I'll call the police.'

She wrestled with him, forcing him back. He collapsed on the bed. She took the cutlass from him.

Singh did not resist. The rum had made him sleepy. He closed his eyes and listened to the wind and rain.

Wilbert too was listening to the wind and rain, unable to sleep. Shanty slept soundly, curled up against the wall, not touching him. The taste of their brief, violent lovemaking – the raw taste of toothpaste – lingered in his mouth.

'Do you have any experience?' she had asked. 'Do you know how it's done?'

'I have a rough idea,' he replied.

'Only a rough idea!' She giggled. 'That surprises me. I thought . . . Never mind. I have some experience.'

'You got your experience from one of your San Fernando cousins, no doubt? The one who kissed you?'

She was shocked. 'Oh no! It wasn't with him. I wouldn't do such a thing with my cousin.'

'You kissed him.'

'A kiss is child's play. But I wouldn't do such a thing with him. Not with my cousin.'

'Who did you do such a thing with then?' He was not angry; he was not even jealous.

'If you must know – it was with a friend of his. We did it more than once.' She laughed. 'Do you want to know how many times?'

'No. That isn't necessary. I'll take your word for it.'

Once he had got out of the bed to shut the windows. The wind lashed at the roof and there was a sound as of canvas flapping. He had got out of bed a second time to see if he could discover the cause but it remained a mystery. On the shore, the waves raged rebelliously. The night was interminable.

He was woken by the sun shining on his face. Bright blue sky showed through the windows. Shanty slept with the blanket pulled over her head. He heaved himself out of bed and opened the windows. The morning was fresh and clear. Innocuous waves planed on to the smooth brown beach which looked as if it had been scoured and swept. The sea, which had fulminated so threateningly during the night, was tame and welcoming, streaked and flecked with gold from the newly risen sun. A pair of pelicans sailed low across the surface of the water. They were fishing. He watched them dip and circle and dive.

Wilbert changed into his swimming trunks and went down to the beach, a towel draped around his neck. It was deserted, a shimmering arc fringed by a green awning of coconut trees. The sand, though packed hard and firm, was springy and tickled the soles of his feet pleasantly. The beach shelved gently into the waves and, where they rolled back, the sand was a watery mirror reflecting the bright blue sky and the wheeling birds. The distant headlands were veiled by a gauze of seaspray. Shanty watched him from the window, yawning and stretching. Wilbert spread the towel like a mat on the sand and dipped his toes in the water, testing the temperature. It was cold. He ventured in further, treading gingerly over the uneven beds of chip-chip which formed dense colonies along the edge of the shore. The sharp, pointed shells bristled up from the sand at a variety of angles. He negotiated them safely and, when he was waist-deep, he plunged in. The cold was bracing and he swam with bold, strenuous strokes until he had warmed himself up. Then he lay on his back and floated, his arms outstretched, lulled by the rocking motion of the water. Seeing only the dome of the sky and the clouds, Wilbert felt as though he were floating far out to sea; a piece of driftwood that had been cast upon the ocean currents to circle the globe endlessly. A purposeless wandering.

'Wake up! Wake up!' Shanty was scooping water into his face.

Wilbert waded out of the water and went and sat down on the towel. He let the sun dry his skin. The pair of pelicans had departed and he stared up and down the shimmering, empty beach. About twenty yards from the house was a dead coconut tree, its crown of leaves decapitated. The pitted trunk rose straight up into the air like a telegraph pole. A corbeau was perched magisterially on the truncated summit, its wings folded over its hunched body, gazing along the line of its rapacious beak at others of its kind hopping across the ground and pecking at whatever scraps of food they could find. A fight broke out and there was a flurry of black feath-

ers. A mangy bitch with distended teats wandered respect-
fully on the fringes of the group of birds, dragging itself list-
lessly from spot to spot, its tail tucked between its legs and its
nose to the ground.

Singh, gaunt and derelict, was approaching through the coconut trees, swinging his cutlass. He slowed his pace when he
caught sight of Wilbert and stopped altogether, squinting and
tapping the cutlass against his knees. Wilbert waved for him
to come forward.

Singh shuffled up to him. 'I hope the boss and madam had
a good night. It was a long time since we had a storm like
that.' He bowed to Shanty who had just come out of the
water.

'No complaints from the madam.' Shanty laughed. 'But I
can't speak for the boss.' She wrapped her towel round her
head like a turban.

Wilbert stared at the bitch with the distended teats.

Singh smiled as though he and Shanty had shared a private
joke.

'I'm going inside to have a rest,' she said. 'The heat is too
much for me.'

'Would the madam like me to pick a coconut for she? Coconut water is very cooling – like the calypso say.'

'It's too much trouble. I'll go inside.'

'Is no trouble at all for me,' Singh said eagerly. 'No trouble
at all if that is what the madam would like.'

Shanty laughed. 'You're a real gentleman, Singh.'

'What about you, boss? You would like a coconut too?'

Wilbert scowled. 'No.'

Singh took off his thick leather belt and looped it round
the trunk of one of the trees, strapping himself in so that his
back was supported at the waist. He grasped the sides of the
belt and wedged his feet securely against the base of the trunk.
Monkey-fashion, he scampered up the tree, hauling himself
up with the belt in swift, jerky movements, his knees hugging
the rough bark. His torso vanished among the crown of
yellow-green leaves.

'How many would you like, madam?'

315

'One will do, Singh.'

'I'll pick two,' he yelled. 'Just in case. Keep well clear then. It wouldn't be nice if one of these was to hit you on your head.'

Shanty withdrew to a safer distance. Wilbert stayed where he was.

Two coconuts thudded one after the other on to the sand. Singh shinned down the tree. 'No trouble at all,' he said. 'I is a real expert at picking coconuts. But, like everything else, you have to learn the art. That is the important thing. The art!' He giggled. 'You agree with me, boss? Everything have a art to it.' Singh fetched his cutlass and, picking up a coconut, laid it on the flat of his palm and trimmed one end. With a dexterous flourish, he sliced off the top and presented it to Shanty. 'Drink. You'll see how cooling it is.'

Shanty drank, tilting her head and holding the coconut with both hands. The water trickled down the corners of her mouth in two thin streams which joined at the base of her chin.

'Is cooling?' Singh asked.

'Very cooling,' Shanty replied.

He took the coconut from her and cut it open with the cutlass. 'I'll make a spoon for you to eat the jelly with.' He carved a spoon out of the fibrous covering of the shell and returned the coconut to her.

When she had eaten the jelly, Shanty thanked him and went inside.

With a sudden beating of wings, the corbeau which had remained on its decapitated perch all morning, rose high into the air and glided overhead. Those on the ground followed suit. The mangy bitch trotted away. Wilbert watched it. It came towards the house and clambered through one of the broken windows. It was obviously a rehearsed routine.

'You can't blame she,' Singh said. 'Is an open invitation with all them broken windows. Is what I was saying . . .'

'We'll see about that.' Wilbert got up and shook the sand out of the towel.

He found the litter after a short search, guided by smell

rather than sight: the pups lay scrambled together in an odiferous heap behind the pile of dried coconuts he had seen the night before. Sacking had been spread for them and a cup of water provided. The pups fought and struggled and pushed in order to get at the niggardly teats of the bitch. Fleas crisscrossed her almost hairless back. She slept, oblivious to the fierce combat being waged over her.

Wilbert looked at Singh. 'Very nice and cosy. Sacking, water . . .'

'I didn't think you would mind. Nobody does ever use this part of the house so they not in your or anybody else way.' Singh's feet grated on the damp concrete.

'You should have taken them home by you since you love them so much.'

'It have no room by me,' Singh replied sullenly. 'It have nowhere else for them to go.'

'That's their – and your – problem. Not mine. I want them out of here.' Wilbert jerked his thumb towards the door.

Singh knelt down and stroked the pups. 'They only a few days old. If I was to move them now they would die.'

Wilbert said nothing.

'They have a right to live,' Singh blurted out. 'It don't matter that they mangy and have fleas. They have as much right to live as you have!'

Wilbert was not angry. He seemed to have lost the capacity for anger. 'Sometimes the right to live is no good at all,' he said flatly. 'It's better not to have it. By giving them food and water the only thing you're doing is prolonging their misery. Punishing them. If you were really going to be kind you should have drowned them on the day they were born. That's what you should have done.' He laughed and pointed at the bitch. 'There's your right to live. Look at it!' He went to the door. 'You can do what you want with them,' he said. 'I don't want you to accuse me of taking away their right to live.'

Wilbert returned the next day with a bowl of milk and looked behind the pile of dried coconuts. The pups had disappeared and the bitch sniffed at the sacking in a lost and stupid way. She stared at him with her rheumy, bloodshot eyes.

'What you looking at me like that for?' he said. 'I didn't do anything to you. Go and ask your friend Singh. He will tell you what he did with them.'

The dog shrank away from him, her tail tucked between her legs. He put the bowl of milk on the sacking but she would not touch it.

Dawn was always cool and fresh and translucent, the best time for bathing. The sun would have barely topped the rim of the horizon and the clouds would still be chased with orange fading to white; and the water too reflected the soft, powdered light which, as the sun rose higher, congealed and solidified into broad bands of gold. When the clouds were white and the water gold, it was wise to retreat – for the day proper was beginning. The heat built up inexorably throughout the morning and the sea changed its texture, acquiring a thicker, more oily sheen. Sluggish waves collapsed in frills of foam along the shore, like a tattered border of discoloured lace. Where they broke, the water was muddy brown with the churned-up sand; further out it had the tarnished green of brass; and where it touched the horizon it was a metallic blue. The wind died and the corbeaux slept perched on the coconut trees and the stray dogs panted in the black, fathomless pools of shadow.

It was at this time, when the tide was out, that the beds of chip-chip were exposed and squadrons of women and children from the village would come down to the beach armed with buckets and basins to gather the harvest of shells. The women wore petticoats but the smaller children would be naked. Separate working parties fanned out along the beach. Squatting on their haunches, they laboured long and assiduously, shovelling and raking over the wet sand with their hands; filling the buckets and basins with the pink and yellow shells which were the size and shape of a long fingernail. Inside each was the sought-after prize: a minuscule kernel of insipid flesh. A full bucket of shells would provide them with a mouthful. But they were not deterred by the disproportion between their labours and their gains. Rather, the very meagreness of their reward seemed to spur them on. Quarrels were frequent, their chief cause being the intrusion of an alien group into the staked-out territory of another. Some of these border conflicts could flare into violence. Tempers sparked easily in the scorching sun. Wilbert would marvel at the dogged application that was displayed and the passions fruitlessly squandered. When they had done their harvesting, they washed themselves in the water and strolled at a leisurely pace back to the village, the women's bodies etched in sharp outline by their sodden petticoats.

The incoming tide inundated the chip-chip beds and brought with it a fresh litter of debris – chains of seaweed and coconut shells and driftwood – and the beach contracted to a narrow, wavering strip. As the sun sank behind the awning of coconut trees, the day cooled and became softer once more. The twilight closed imperceptibly over the water until only the creamy caps of the waves were visible. The mauve and purple clouds of sunset, more imposing than those of the dawn, took possession of the sky. It was night again and the insects fluttered through the open doors and windows and hummed and whirred around the hurricane lamps.

Scores of jellyfish had been washed up, stranded by the tide during the night. Their tentacles, half-buried in the sand, trailed like sinuous inkstains from their transparent, rainbow-tinted spheres. Unthinkingly, Wilbert punctured the swollen spheres with a stick as he walked along, listening to the small, crackling report as of a bubble of chewing-gum bursting. He had gone about a mile from the house. The sand here was overrun by a thick tangle of creeper which bore pretty lilac flowers.

An entire trunk of a tree, interred in the sand, straddled the beach. Stripped of its bark, the bole looked as if it had been worked upon by a master craftsman. It had been endowed with a sensuousness and rhythm which the living object could hardly have rivalled. Death had given it power and grandeur.

Possessed of all the tensions of an arrested fluidity, it was tempting to imagine that, these tensions resolving themselves, it would melt, flow away and be reabsorbed into the earth. The trunk and branches had been bleached bone-white by the sun and salt; and the wood itself worn down – metamorphosed – to the texture of living flesh. It suggested totemic splendour; a sacrificial offering to the gods of fertility and plentiful harvests, divorced from its true time and place and function and condemned to rot slowly on this wind-swept, shimmering beach of swooping vultures, starving dogs, chip-chip gatherers and himself.